THE DREADFUL LIVES OF ENOCH STRANGE

Pete Altieri

Blunt Force Press

For information contact Blunt Force Press, PO Box 554, Heyworth
IL 61745
PeteAltieri.com   EnochStrange.com   BluntForcePress.com

ISBN-13: 978-0692153123 (Pete Altieri)

ISBN-10: 0692153128

Printed in the United States of America

For Alex Renee and Peter Robert;
my light in a sometimes dark world.

THE DREADFUL LIVES OF ENOCH STRANGE

PART ONE
Darkness Visible

A dungeon horrible, on all sides round
As one great furnace flamed, yet from those flames
No light, but rather darkness visible.

John Milton, Paradise Lost

Enoch Strange

An existence spawned at a time unknown to man.
A horrid shell not human, not beast, but a sum of all things.
Both prison and jailer in one horrible entity.

A facade gnarled, twisted, and a terrible
Nightmarish vision to behold.
Empathy within conjures endless misery.

Condemned souls sentenced to reside
Within the putrid thing, fully aware of their plight.
Physically bound in agony, misery, and despair.

Unable to escape their impenetrable cell.
Cloaked in mock and ridicule, a stark contrast
To what the prisoner once was in human form.

Every sentence separate from the rest.
Each life more dreadful than the last
For the despicable Enoch Strange.

Dr. Wilfred Weeks, October 1612

1

March 1927

Sister Mary Concordia was running as fast as she could. The March night was cool, and a blood moon was high, providing an eerie red filter over the path that led deeper into the woods surrounding St. Michael's Academy. The young sister knew she wasn't supposed to be outside the convent at this hour as a novitiate in only her second year. The punishment for such a violation would have resulted in hours of punitive chores, 24 hours of fasting, and at least 30 days of confinement to her room, other than to attend daily mass and use the bathroom. A second offense would mean expulsion from the order and going back to her prior life as Emily Randuski in Palatine, Illinois. Still she ran, her chest barely rising more than at rest.

Her mind wandered as she ran, thinking about how Mother Mistress would be furious to know the convent's cat, Boris, had run away again. After a year being well-cloistered from society, Sister Mary Concordia was finally enjoying socializing with others in the church. The older nuns at the convent had begun to accept her, teaching her their secrets, and Mother Mistress let her take care of Boris, which she enjoyed a great deal. Mother Mistress made it known how much she and the other nuns loved the orange and white tomcat and the inherited responsibility that came with caring for him. Her eyes darted back and forth, hoping to find Boris and get him back inside before anyone noticed his jail break. She slowed down to a stop for moment, listening.

"Boris, Boris!" she whispered, fearing discovery. "Where are you? Boris!"

Only the night sounds in the enveloping darkness replied. There was no sign of Boris. The usual choir of crickets, nocturnal creatures that stirred in the brush, and the call of a distant owl were the only noises the young woman heard. Her mind was focused on the idea that Mother Mistress was likely to come check to see if she was in her room. She felt a chill from a stiff breeze coming from the west, and the leaves flapped above her while she shuddered at the thought.

"Boris!" she called out again. There was no reply from the feisty tomcat.

She decided to go a little further into the woods before turning back. Approaching the crest of a small hill, Sister Mary Concordia heard something she couldn't make out. It sounded like a low rumble. Holding her breath, she strained to hear what now sounded like voices. It seemed like a gathering of people, very low and distant – deeper in the blackness of the forest. Staring up at the blood moon, Sister Mary Concordia questioned whether she should continue. She heard the nuns talking this week about the rare blood moon that would appear on this night, but they acted like they didn't want her to hear what they were saying about it. There were many times when she felt like some of the sisters were guarded about what she was able to hear, so Sister Mary Concordia didn't give it much thought. She had never seen a blood moon before. Staring up at a crimson full moon, it almost seemed unreal.

She feared being discovered, knowing the punishment would be severe. With one more year of study as a novitiate, Sister Mary Concordia would begin five years of work in the convent before taking her final vows. She didn't know if an offense such as this would cause her to be removed from St. Michael's, but the curiosity of the source of the voices in the darkness drew her in. She stopped thinking about Boris and stepped quickly, yet gingerly, down the path toward the unknown. The young novitiate knew if she thought about it for a moment more, she would run back to St. Michael's.

The voices got progressively louder as she moved closer. The timber became almost opaque, and the brush was like a wall of impenetrable thorn and thicket. There was now a glow in the distance from what appeared to be a campfire. The voices were clearer to her, yet still low in tone and measured in timbre. One voice was more prominent than the rest, and as Sister Mary Concordia continued ahead, she could make out the other voices in unison answering the apparent leader. To her, it sounded like a religious ceremony, such as a Catholic mass. She still was not able to make out the words, but as she got closer, she decided to take cover off the main path to avoid discovery. Although she had no idea what was going on one hundred yards in the valley below, her gut reaction was dread. Still, she continued forward, the runaway cat still removed from her thoughts. The blood moon was casting an ominous red blanket across the valley in every direction, like paint poured from a giant bucket.

A few minutes later, Sister Mary Concordia found herself quivering with fear behind a dense cluster of bushes, only twenty feet from the gathering. There was a fire pit and an altar of dark stone, with a man standing behind it. He was dressed in little more than an animal skin that obscured his head and upper body, and he spoke with the command of a seasoned preacher at the pulpit. There was a small congregation of men and women kneeling before him, and they were naked in the crisp evening air. She didn't know what to make of this strange perversion. On the altar was a crucifix, yet it was upside down, and the man in the animal skin was drinking from what looked like a human skull. Then he continued to speak to them in Latin.

"In nomine magni dei nostril Satanas! Introibo ad altare Domini Inferi!" he cried out as the congregation before him repeated the infernal words. She didn't know exactly what he was saying, but she had sat through enough Catholic mass to pick out some words.

Suddenly, a woman in a black robe stepped from the shadows and walked to the altar, carrying something in her arms wrapped in a blanket. Sister Mary Concordia was mesmerized at what she was seeing. The naked men and women then began to fornicate as a group, intertwining themselves in carnal lust, of the likes she had never witnessed before. At only 22 years old, the young novitiate had never seen the naked body of a man, let alone the mass of indecency now only a breath away. Being found out by these evil people was a terrifying thought. She was afraid to run back to the path, knowing they would hear her. The noise of breaking twigs and branches underfoot would surely give her away. All she could do was hide behind the bushes.

Now the woman in the black robe was at the altar and laid down whatever was in the blanket upon it. The man in the animal skin dipped his hand into the skull he was drinking from, his fingers stained with a dark red substance. Sister Mary Concordia assumed it to be blood, as the woman opened up the blanket to reveal a naked infant boy squirming in the cool midnight air! The baby was crying, his arms and legs flailing, as the man rubbed the blood on his forehead, saying something she couldn't make out. He reached down behind the altar, then abruptly stood up, his congregation in the midst of their orgy before him and held up a 10-inch knife. The blade gleamed in the moonlight. Sister Mary Concordia gasped as the man brought the knife down upon the infant's chest, the woman in the robe holding him down as his little voice screamed out in pain. His tiny body convulsed in agony! His screams shrill.

Things began to play out in slow motion to Sister Mary Concordia. The bright-red blood that flowed from the infant was dripping from the stone altar as the man held him up to the sky, speaking once again in Latin. Blood poured down his arms and dripped from his heaving chest. His breath was a frosty mist in the chilled night air. The woman let her black robe fall and pulled the animal skin from his body, and the two locked in a bloody embrace of horrific evil, sharing a deep kiss, rubbing the warm blood onto each other's skin. The young nun-to-be was in utter disbelief at what she had witnessed, the cries of the congregation escalating, and the two at the altar now joining in the fornication. They appeared older than the rest. He bent her over the dark stone, knocking the inverted crucifix over; her writhing body cried out, rubbing the sacrificial blood on herself as the disturbing act continued.

Sister Mary Concordia was speechless, the actions in slow motion before her, and the cries were distant and muffled, as though coming through a cup and string. She could hear the screams of the baby over and over again as she crouched in the darkness praying she would not be found out. Yet as the older man and woman continued their desecration of life, joined in an unholy union, she made eye contact with both of them. To her utter horror, they were both faces she recognized! In that moment, all she had been working toward since entering the sisterhood, and everything she held dear with her God, came crashing down like a high-rise building being demolished. The man was none other than the Abbott of St. Michael's Academy – Father Reilly! She would know that face anywhere, even in the light of the blood moon, in mid-fornication at the altar of evil. It was terrible enough he was participating in this abomination, but the woman's identity shook her to the very core of her being. Sister Mary Concordia questioned her faith for the first time in her life as she gazed at the gasping countenance of the Mother Mistress! She had been the young girl's inspiration and rock through her training, and seeing her through this perverse lens was too much to bear. Sister Mary Concordia's bedrock was crumbling.

Without hesitation, she ran away. She fled from the disgusting ritual toward St. Michael's. It felt surreal, like she was running in a nightmare, as if she was moving in place – unable to escape. Sister Mary Concordia didn't know if the Abbott or Mother Mistress had seen her, but she did make eye contact and couldn't be sure. As she ran faster, the visions she had just seen were already haunting her, and she could only hope her presence was undetected.

When she finally got back into her room and to bed, she closed her eyes tightly in a futile attempt to wish away what she had just seen, but the images of the blood orgy were engraved into her mind, and the cries of that innocent baby reverberated in the stillness of the night.

******

In a private dining room on the third floor of the monastery at St. Michael's Academy was a feast fit for kings. The four priests that sat at the table were not royalty, but the monks waiting on them would have a much different opinion on the matter. The way the four conducted themselves, looking down at the monks who served them, was appalling. A simple, yet magnificent oak table with six ornately carved chairs sat in the middle of the Abbot's private dining room. Before being seated at the table, the four had enjoyed drinks and Cuban cigars in the Abbot's office and spent the past hour talking about the events of the night before. To listen to the four of them, one would have assumed they were fraternity brothers from collegiate days gone by, instead of men of the cloth, who met each other years before in seminary school. These men were not the usual clergy – far from it.

Father Patrick Reilly sat at the head of the table, as he was the Abbot of the institution and had been for the past ten years. He was a fit man in his early 60's with a military-style buzz haircut, chiseled jaw and piercing blue eyes. The Abbot was pleasant enough to those who barely knew him, but to those who worked at St. Michael's, he was despised for his brash demeanor and elitist attitude. It didn't take long to pick up on that quality in him. He was hardly what most would have assumed a priest to be like. He spent his early years growing up in Albany, New York before his calling to enter the priesthood. It was years later, as an instructor at a seminary outside of Richmond, Virginia, where he met the other three priests that he chose to dine with on this Saturday afternoon in March of 1927.

To the Abbot's right was Father Cordero Rosa, who made the trip to McHenry, Illinois by train two days before, from his congregation at Holy Trinity Catholic Church in Cottonwood, Arizona. It was a four-day trip by rail, yet he didn't question the Abbot when he was asked to come to St. Michael's. To the Abbot's left was Father Roger Wilkes, who also had a long train ride to northern Illinois from St. Luke's Catholic Church in Hartford, Connecticut. He was looking forward to catching up with the Abbot, as well as the other priests he kept in touch with since they were young priests-to-be at the seminary. Lastly, at the opposite end of the table from the Abbot, was Father Frank Bartolini. He arrived to St. Michael's by car the day before, since he had the shortest trip of the priests, from his Epiphany Catholic Church in Des Moines, Iowa. All three of the priests were roughly 20 years younger than the Abbot, and they looked up to him as a father figure. In some ways, they even regarded him more dearly than that.

There was a knock at the door.

"Come in," said the Abbot sharply, straightening up in his chair, and adjusting his red habit. He wore it for special occasions such as this.

"Lunch is ready, Abbot," said Brother Francis, the head chef at St. Michael's. His job entailed keeping a sensible menu designed for the high school students who attended the prestigious academy and the staff as well. Yet for the Abbot and his inner circle, the monk was tasked to provide some of the most extravagant meals he could conjure. In the ten years the Abbot had been in charge, Brother Francis showed off the culinary skills he learned as an

6

apprentice for a French chef while living in Europe. He didn't like the Abbot much, but in his subservient role in life, the monk never said a word. He could recall a few rare times when the Abbot disliked a dish he prepared, and he would be punished for it. One time in particular, the monk had diarrhea for two weeks after the Abbot had the monk's food poisoned. The Abbot was known for exacting harsh punishment and for extremely narcissistic behavior. Very few of the staff knew about the culinary decadence that went on in the Abbot's private dining room.

"OK, Brother Francis, then bring it in," the Abbot replied. The other priests could smell the incredible aromas entering the room as two monks assisted the chef in bringing in the delectable spread. The monks worked silently and quickly, wanting to leave the room as soon as possible. They were afraid to be in the same room as the Abbot.

The Abbot insisted his guests try some of the monastery's homemade elderberry wine with their lunch, as well as a very expensive sherry that he kept in a private stash. Despite the rest of the country having to abide by Prohibition, the Abbot acted as if it didn't exist. As the four men sipped their wine and sherry, the table was soon filled with an incredible array of fine foods the other three rarely saw. Since the monks and priests often hunted on the grounds, there was plenty of game to eat. They enjoyed a venison consommé Celestine soup, followed by succulent roast duck over baked rice Milanese, and haricots verts in a rich garlic and butter sauce. There was also fresh-baked french bread and homemade butter and honey. Freshly made pecan pie and apple cobbler, the Abbot's favorite, were kept warm on a small nearby serving table with two large carafes of black coffee. It took the monks nearly fifteen minutes to get everything situated.

"That will be all, Brother Francis. Let the Prior know we do not wish to be disturbed for the remainder of the afternoon. Now go!"

The chef nodded to the Abbot and said something quietly to the monks assisting him before quietly closing the door behind them. The Abbot rose and walked to the door, locking it securely before returning to his seat to begin eating his lunch.

******

The Abbot enjoyed his apple cobbler and black coffee, then looked around the table at his guests.

"I want to thank you all for coming on relatively short notice, but this is important."

Father Bartolini also sipped at his coffee, but he had passed on dessert after eating such a large lunch. "Of course, Abbot. None of us would have missed this. The blood moon is such a rare occurrence, and we hold it in such high regard."

"Yes, that's true. Last night was one of the most wonderful masses I've ever attended since our days in Richmond," Father Rosa added. "I have read that many Christians believe the blood moon has a foreboding quality, a prelude of bad things to follow. You know, the superstitious types." He laughed.

"I thought you would all enjoy that. The sisters from the convent haven't seen much male companionship lately," the Abbot said, smirking from behind his coffee mug, "but from the sound of it, you all gave them something to remember for a long time."

The four priests laughed out loud at his reference to the black mass they all attended the night before. Father Wilkes was correct in the power of the blood moon when it came to occultists like the four men seated around the table. The Abbot had picked the date years ago, long before any of them had any idea of what his plan was.

Father Wilkes said, "If I may say so, Abbot, you looked like you also gave the Mother Mistress a good time across the altar."

"Yes, indeed I did," the Abbot replied, his smirk widening. "She gets horny when the moon is full, and so do I." He laughed aloud, gazing out the window, as if imagining them engaged in the act the night before, savoring every bloody kiss and decadent stroke.

"The ritual last night and the infant sacrifice was necessary for what we are about to embark on," the Abbot continued, "and the true reason I asked you all to come here to St. Michael's will now reveal itself."

Father Bartolini had wondered where the infant came from, but was too afraid to ask the Abbot.

As if on cue, the Abbot said, "The sisters brought that infant from the church. It was found two weeks ago in the vestibule of the convent. No one knows who left the boy, but he was wrapped in blankets and left for the sisters to find. It was like an omen from Lord Satan himself." He smirked at Father Bartolini with a sort of infernal amusement. The priest felt a pit in the bottom of his stomach that nearly forced him to vomit at his seat. As quickly as the feeling came over him, it fled in fear.

The three priests sat in uncomfortable silence as the Abbot explained his true motive for the visit. The only noise that could be heard in the third-floor private dining room, aside from the Abbot's voice, was the wind and rain against the large picture window that faced the east.

"I need each of you to find three nuns from your region of the country, who we can use to participate in a special tour of hospitals, infirmaries, and asylums, to cheer up those less fortunate for Christmas," the Abbot said as they squirmed amidst the tension. He knew they would be confused. He also knew that staring at them like he was would ratchet up the fear. Despite their many years removed from the seminary, the teacher-student roles were difficult to absolve. Though their continued friendship over the years, the younger three definitely respected and revered the dark and mysterious Abbot.

"Surely you didn't ask us to come all the way here for this, Abbot. I'm sure you could do such a thing with the fine nuns here at St. Michael's," said Father Rosa, "or certainly with the large pool of sisters from the many churches in Chicago." He forced a smile, wondering if he was going to be reprimanded for speaking out of line.

The wind continued to howl outside as the sun hid behind the clouds and made the grounds outside darker than before. The temperature in the dining room dropped several degrees as well. Father Rosa noticed, as did the Abbot.

"The nuns I need for this mission are not just any nuns. I need nuns who have experienced pure evil in the world. I need nuns who have come face-to-face with the worst of the worst." He leaned back slightly in his chair, noting the curiosity in each of their faces. The Abbot could see their wheels spinning voraciously before him. It was for their incredible intellect and devotion to the cause that the three priests were picked many years before to assist him with this most precious mission.

The Abbot continued, "I've been working on this project almost my entire life, gentlemen. I have spent countless hours studying and translating texts from various languages around the world, but in secret, for fear that someone would know what I was working on. I have been reading in the shadows and compiling an incredible amount of data. I even kept it from all of you. I hope you know I did it because it was just too important to trust anyone. Even all of you, my closest friends."

Father Wilkes finished the last of his sherry and poured himself another. His hand shook slightly. The Abbot noticed. It was his nature to notice such things. In the warehouse section of his memory, the Abbot kept every morsel of data collected, knowing it would likely become of use to him at some point down the road. He was almost always right.

"I believe that I have discovered a dark secret from the very manuscript of one of the earliest Satanists of the modern age. I bet none of you have even heard of Wilfred Weeks from England. He was a prominent doctor in London in the early 1600's. He was able to cure people of illnesses that no other doctor could. Many said he had made a pact with the Devil in order to marvel London with his medical capabilities. They weren't too far off, actually. Dr. Weeks was a Satanist and held some of the earliest black masses ever documented," said the Abbot, looking around the table at the other priests. They were amazed at what they were hearing. "Even Aleister Crowley was said to have been enamored with Weeks, but he was never able to read what I have read."

The Abbot went on, "He was working on something that no one else knew about. He believed that through a very precise satanic ritual, with lots of moving parts that involved magic he was still discovering, he could cause Satan himself to manifest in human form. Much like God claims to have done in the body of Jesus."

Father Bartolini continued to sip at his coffee. He was staring at the Abbot, focusing on every word he was saying, "Please continue, Abbot." He was still in shock from the odd mannerisms surrounding the Abbot reading his mind. There was no telling what dark secrets and magic the elder priest had mastered during his endless hours of study. His mastery of four languages, including Latin, and his encyclopedic knowledge of nearly any subject of conversation, put everyone else in the room several notches below his abilities. The Abbot knew this and was always the alpha male of the pack.

"A young woman stumbled on Dr. Wilfred Weeks' papers one morning, after he was found in bed ill. She was part of his cleaning staff and removed some documents that detailed his denouncement of God and celebration of Satan. She turned him in to a very politically influential Catholic priest in London, Father Portis Larimer, who had the good doctor arrested by police. Most of the papers were burned to ash, and he was hung by the neck in a public execution, for crimes against the church, only five days later. Only the documents I came across survived, and he hid them well. Dozens of searches of his house were conducted, but the secret documents remained safe. The rest I had to piece together myself, which was incredibly difficult."

"Amazing that you found them," said Father Rosa. "How did you secure such rare documents?"

"Don't ask questions you're not prepared to hear the answer to, Father Rosa." The Abbot was cold in his reply, yet his eyes burned holes right through the priest. Father Rosa's mind was immediately filled with dread as those icy blue eyes dug into the depths of his soul.

Father Rosa shifted uncomfortably in his chair. The other two priests looked down to avoid eye contact.

The Abbot continued, "This ritual would be a way to bring Satan himself into human form to walk the Earth and wreak havoc upon God's children. Only those of us who have accepted his infernal majesty would be immune from his wrath. We would live on Earth for eternity at his side, while the human race would be at our mercy. We would experience pleasures beyond our own imaginations – forever."

The three priests stared into the Abbot's piercing blue eyes, unable to speak or move.

"Each of us must come up with three nuns who have experienced true evil. Each of them will make up this procession of twelve, in a direct perversion of Christ's twelve apostles. It will be the residual evil that each of these nuns possesses which will combine to summon Satan himself into human form. They will be sacrificed as Wilfred Weeks' manuscript explains, in every painstaking detail, and we will have our own dark salvation, my brothers!" the Abbot said in a low whisper, as if to avoid anyone outside the private dining room from hearing what he was saying. The Abbot was nearly short of breath at the excitement of being able to finally explain his life's work. Just hearing his own voice recount the happenings at hand was enough to get his blood to boil with anticipation.

"The sacrificial blood that was spilled last night will give each of us the drive to find these nuns. With the incredible magic of the blood moon, coupled with that spilling of sacred blood, our bodies will soar, and our search will be swift. Search every church in your region of the country. Find three nuns who have had traumatic experiences with the sinners of the world, and together we will have our twelve. We will send them on this pilgrimage, and they will end their tour at a location I have chosen, where the sacrifice will be done." The Abbot stared into every fiber of their collective being as he looked around the table. He knew these men had strong convictions from their time at the seminary, where he introduced them to Satanism. He knew even back then, this day would come, and he would need their help. Now was that time, and he could see each of them, in their own way, preparing themselves to fulfill his grand plan. The Abbot seemed pleased that his hard work had paid off.

"You each have nine months to get me three nuns. On the first Saturday in October, we will meet here again. You will bring those three nuns here with you. We will keep them in the convent, under lock and key, until their tour starts in Chicago. They will make their way down the state to an asylum outside of Peoria, in Bartonville," he continued, "where the last stop will take place. It is there they will die. It is there that Satan will walk the Earth."

Silence came over the room once again. Oddly, the wind and rain no longer made any sound outside against the window. It was as if a giant fishbowl had been placed over the four men who sat at the large oak table, plotting to bring Hell itself upon the Earth.

******

The Abbot sat in his office after the other priests had gone to bed in the guest quarters he provided them for the duration of their stay. They would all be leaving St. Michael's in the morning, to go back to their parishes, and to begin searching for the nuns. He had no doubt they would be successful. The Abbot had already done his own exhaustive search prior to the meeting and found three nuns who would be perfect for the job at hand.

There was one other person he needed to make the tour successful. The Abbot knew that most of the nuns were elderly and would need assistance. He needed someone who could handle the luggage, tend to the train tickets, and keep them together. The Abbot also knew this person would be killed along with the twelve nuns as part of the ancient rite from the secret manuscript of Wilfred Weeks. It was a sacrifice he had to be willing to make in order to see this plan come to fruition before he became too old. He was in his 60's now, and his fear was that if he waited much longer, he might die himself before seeing his life's work through to the end. The Abbot knew now was the time to strike, and nothing would get in his way.

Suddenly, there was a knock at the door.

"Yes, come in," he said from behind his large desk. He was still in the red habit from earlier in the day. It was dark outside now. He had the beloved Boris on his lap, purring loudly as he stroked his dense, orange fur.

Sister Mary Concordia opened the door gingerly. She was obviously afraid, as most were when summoned to the Abbot's office, especially late at night. Many heard stories of improper advances on the younger women. She didn't want to believe such things, but after what she had seen the night before, Sister Mary Concordia was repulsed to be in his presence. She could only see him in the strange costume, arms soaked in blood, driving the long knife into the trembling infant. She asked one of the other sisters to go along with her, but Mother Mistress insisted she go alone to see the Abbot. The Mother Mistress did not let on that she knew what the meeting was about, nor did she give Sister Mary Concordia any indication that she had seen her the night before under the blood moon, while she was being taken upon the stone altar.

The Abbot smiled at the attractive novitiate. "Please sit, Sister."

She immediately noticed Boris purring on his lap. Her heart was rising into her throat as she did her best to control emotions. She had thought Boris was gone for good. She hadn't seen him since he had run outside the night before, when she was throwing garbage away. Now he was purring on the Abbot's lap and she felt sure the priest was doing it for a reason. He had to know she had been there last night.

She felt a chill in his gaze. It was impossible for her not to think about him naked, thrusting himself into the Mother Mistress, their bodies entwined in the sacrificial blood. She was horrified to think that he had seen her in the woods, shaking from behind the bush on the other side of the congregation.

The Abbot set Boris down and stood up, then walked in front of the desk, leaning against it. He put his hand on her shoulder and felt her recoil at his touch.

"Are you afraid, Sister?" His jaw was clenched tight, the grinding of teeth was audible. The Abbot slowed his breath purposefully.

Sister Mary Concordia didn't reply. She was petrified. The Abbot moved off the desk and stood directly next to her, his hand still resting upon her frail shoulder. She felt nauseas, like she could throw up at any moment. Boris was sleeping with his back against one of the many bookcases in the Abbot's office. He was content here, yet she wanted to scream out at the top of her lungs.

The Abbot moved even closer to the young novitiate, his habit brushing up against her left arm. She was disgusted that she could feel that he was obviously erect underneath his red habit and was rubbing himself up against her! She abruptly stood up and moved toward the door, crying.

"Please don't hurt me, Abbot." She was sobbing.

"I suggest you sit down, Sister Mary Concordia. I suggest you sit down right now!" the Abbot said forcefully. He was enraged that she had rejected his subtle advances. None of the novitiates he had ever summoned to his office late at night had done so, and even at his advancing age, the Abbot's libido was alive and well. His hubris was bottomless.

He went back to his chair and sat down, and the sister did too. She was still crying, but she was doing her best to keep it under control. Boris climbed back up in the Abbot's lap. He used his left hand to cradle the tomcat's head as he rubbed his neck. It made Sister Mary Concordia very uncomfortable to see him hold Boris that way. It looked uncomfortable for the cat, and she couldn't take her eyes off the Abbot's hands.

"I called you here to tell you about a special calling I have for you. There will be a Christmas tour of nuns going to hospitals and nursing homes later this year. I'd like you to go with them, Sister. They are elderly and will need assistance. You would be perfect, and what a grand experience for you!" The Abbot smiled, barely.

Sister Mary Concordia continued to watch his hands. His right hand was still stroking the cat's neck, yet she wondered why he was waiting to discuss what happened last night. When Mother Mistress said the Abbot wanted to see her, the sister was sure she had been discovered out after curfew. In addition, there was her presence at the Satanic mass. She figured someone had seen her and turned her in to Mother Mistress.

The Abbot did his best not to raise his voice again, but the fact that she kept her head down began to upset him once again. His left hand began to apply pressure to the top of the cat's head, and Boris squirmed under the strain. The Abbot also tightened his hold on Boris' neck, and together, his hands formed a vice.

"So what do you think? Mother Mistress raves about you, and the two of us think this will be a wonderful experience, Sister," he said. She was staring at his hands in horror, as she could see his grip tightening on Boris. His eyes were bulging with fear, but somehow the Abbot kept the cat still as he continued to squeeze even tighter. She thought she heard the bending of bone to the point of breaking.

She looked up at the Abbot, tears welling up in her eyes. She knew he was killing dear Boris, but she realized there was nothing she could do. Still, the flexing of bone was breaking the silence.

"Yes, Abbot. Thank you for the opportunity." His eyes stared deeply into hers. She could hear the strain on the cat's skull as the grip tightened – now bone was breaking.

The Abbot remained seated, despite his desire to reach out to the pretty, yet plain young novitiate. She looked down at the moment blood began to stream from the cat's eyes, nose, and mouth. It quivered slightly and died in the Abbot's grasp. He let Boris fall to the floor like a swatted fly. She began to sob again. The lifeless body of Boris was bleeding on the original hardwood floor of the office.

He continued to stare at the young woman, then stood. "Very good. Mother Mistress will fill you in on the details as we get closer. That is all."

"Thank you, Abbot," she said, standing up and making eye contact briefly as she wept.

The Abbot stared at the door. He had seen the young woman in the woods the night before. He knew she saw the entire thing, and he was not about to take any chances with her talking to others. Starting immediately, she would be cloistered away in her room for private study. He couldn't have her talking with the rest of the staff, and especially any visitors. Sister Mary Concordia would be the thirteenth nun and accompany the rest on their death march to Bartonville in December. He laughed and poured himself one last glass of bourbon with an ice cube, before turning in himself. The Abbot wanted to get a good night sleep so he could deliver Sunday mass for his congregation the following day.

2

The train ride back to Hartford was not as pleasant as the trip out to Chicago the week before. Father Wilkes was riding a steam train, in a first-class Wallingford parlor car built by the Pullman Company for the New Haven, New York, and Hartford Railroad. It wasn't the opulent grandeur of the Wallingford that was the problem, because, at the time, the most extravagant of society were among the passengers. Father Wilkes was enduring terrible nightmares during the three-day trip back to his parish. They were shrouding him in dread. The church had secured him a private sleeping car for the trip and plenty of sleep medication to help him get rest. Yet he was awake at all hours of the day and night, and the older deacon from St. Luke's that he took along with him often found the priest staring out the window of his private car in cold sweats.

"Father, can I get you anything?" the deacon asked, feeling sorry for the disheveled priest.

Father Wilkes turned around listlessly, a two-day growth on his face. His eyes looked yellow with jaundice, yet mapped extensively in tired red blood vessels.

"No. Thank you, Dominic. I'll be fine once we get to Hartford and I can sleep in my own bed again." He turned back around and looked out the window again as the dense woods of southern Pennsylvania sped by.

The deacon nodded and closed the door to his private quarters. He was concerned about Father Wilkes. When the priest did finally try to sleep again, the deacon could hear the screams from his adjoining quarters. Twice during the night the conductor had come to see him about it. Other passengers were complaining that the screaming had been keeping them awake. They would be back in Hartford tomorrow, and the deacon hoped the nightmares would subside.

******

The early morning sun was nearly blinding when Father Cordero Rosa stepped out of his car at the Holy Family Catholic Church in Cottonwood, Arizona. Even in March, the temperatures in Cottonwood were typically like late spring weather everywhere else. By May, the heat would be stifling to visitors who were not used to it. Father Rosa was born in Miami, but had moved to Sedona, Arizona with his mother, father, and two younger brothers at the turn of the century. His father, Angel, had just gotten his pilot's license and was going into business with two cousins in the area who were looking to start a tourism business and wanted to offer plane rides as part of the experience. After spending all his life in Sedona, young Cordero left the southwest for the picturesque hills of Virginia for seminary school. He promptly returned to Arizona, spending several years at a Catholic church in Flagstaff before coming back to Sedona and being the pastor of his own Holy Family Church in nearby Cottonwood. Father Rosa was adored by many, not only for his charismatic ways, but also because he was a local. The parishioners liked that.

On this early morning, Father Rosa was not thinking about the mass he would be delivering later in the morning. He wasn't thinking about the funerals he had slated to officiate that week, or the big Ramirez wedding on Saturday that had been planned for nearly two years by a local prominent family. The middle-aged priest was running for his very life and hoping he would make it to the church in time. The rectory, where he was provided living quarters, was being demolished and re-built. The church had secured him a bedroom at a local hotel several blocks away. He was given a car to drive back and forth, and on this morning, he frantically parked the car in his designated spot and was walking as fast as he could to the church. It seemed incredibly hypocritical of him to be fumbling with his keys to gain access to the church, when only a few short days ago he was in the woods surrounding St. Michael's Academy in McHenry, covering himself with the blood sacrifice and having sex with multiple nuns in the congregation. Looking over his shoulder, the priest made his way inside. He promptly shut and dead-bolted the door behind him. He let out a sigh of relief, his back to the door, sweat streaming down his troubled face.

Father Rosa made his way down the hallway toward his office. He peered carefully into every room along the way, fearing that whatever was stalking his dreams would manifest itself in real life. He could not help the feeling of incredible dread that had swept over him the entire way to Cottonwood by train, and especially when he returned to his hotel room. At night he was in tremendous fear to fall asleep, because the intensity of his nightmares were like none he had experienced. He would wake up drenched in sweat and panting like he had run a marathon. The priest felt as if his heart would explode and could not shake the feeling of terror that would follow him until morning.

Now he sat behind his desk. His personal bible, which his grandmother had given him the day he was confirmed Catholic, was open as he whispered the words that had at one time comforted him. Even though he recognized the hypocrisy of the act, Father Rosa continued to whisper the words quietly to himself that he had been hearing over and over in the nightmare. "You cannot drink the cup of the Lord and the cup of demons; you cannot partake of the table of the Lord and the table of the demons." It was from Corinthians, and he knew it well. Good and evil were struggling inside of him. The nightmares were evil, a shrouding darkness that followed him no matter where he went. Father Rosa couldn't figure out their meaning, and he almost considered calling the Abbot to ask him about the dreams. But he reconsidered, knowing his good friend had given him the task of finding three nuns for the pilgrimage in December. The last thing the priest wanted to do was weigh down the mind of the Abbot who had such an important task at hand.

Father Rosa's hands shook as he held his rosary with his left hand and his bible with his right. He could see outside his window, the bright morning sun nearly blotted out, as a stifling darkness swept over everything he could see. Whatever was in the darkness was looking at him, and he felt a chill down to his very core. A tear began to trickle down his face as the priest clutched tightly to his rosary, praying that the sun would return.

******

Father Bartolini was mumbling prayers under his breath, trying desperately to ignore the horrible banging on the door that led to his sleeping quarters at the rectory of Epiphany Catholic Church in Des Moines, Iowa. Like the other priests who had met with the Abbot over the weekend, Father Frank Bartolini had been plagued by horrible nightmares since leaving St. Michael's Academy. He hadn't slept more than an hour at a time since his return to Des Moines. He considered calling the Abbot or the other priests to ask if they had experienced the same dreams, but he was concerned they would think he was losing his mind and wouldn't include him in the plan. Father Bartolini knew how the Abbot's mind operated, even more than the other two priests, since he was a few years older and the Abbot confided in him about things. On more than one occasion, the Abbot had told him that if something would ever happen to him, that Father Bartolini would be the next in line.

Since meeting the Abbot (then known as Father Reilly) nearly 20 years ago at the seminary, Father Bartolini had always felt a strong connection with his mentor. When he was approached by the middle-aged priest at the seminary about Satanism, it didn't seem strange at all. He looked up to Father Reilly and never questioned him. He had a way with words, and Father Bartolini was completely captivated at whatever the older priest said. It was in his second year at the seminary in Virginia that a young Father Bartolini took History of the Catholic Church with Father Reilly. That was also the class where he met Father Rosa and Father Wilkes, as all three were striving for their Master of Divinity degrees. Father Bartolini was almost five years older than both of the other priests, and with a more dominating personality, he became the apparent leader of the group. It seemed like a lifetime ago that the three young priests were studying for exams together and eventually meeting with Father

Reilly after hours, learning about Satanism and why it was a purer form of religion.

The priest was shocked back into reality as the pounding on his door was coupled with an obvious drop in temperature inside his quarters. Father Bartolini got up from his knees, where he was praying at his bedside, to look out the window at his church across the street. He was almost knocked down to the floor as the shutters of his windows began to flap back and forth, banging hard against the leaded-glass to the point that they were about to shatter to pieces. He knew this was some sort of sign, but he couldn't figure it out. He reached for the bible that he kept on the nightstand near his bed. It had been a gift from Father Reilly upon his graduation from the seminary. The shutters began to bang even louder! The beating sounds on his door were also more intense, as the heavy wooden door sounded as if it was going to split in half.

Father Bartolini ran into the small study where there were no windows. He shut the door and sat behind his desk, staring at the phone. In the distance he could still hear the maddening banging sounds. The chill in the air was visible with every breath and with the thin layer of frost now on his desk.

"Yes, is the Abbot available, Father McBride? I'm sorry to call so early, but it's urgent," Father Bartolini said, doing his best to hide the trembling in his voice. "It's Father Bartolini from Des Moines."

Father McBride was the Subprior at St. Michael's, and the assistant to the Prior, Father Williams.

"Yes, I believe he's in his office. I'll get him," the young priest replied.

Father Bartolini could still hear the heavy wood shutter banging against the windows and wondered how they had not broken yet. He hoped that the Abbot would not be able to hear the noise on the other end of the phone. He also prayed that whatever was outside his door and windows was not able to get inside. The temperature seemed to drop at least ten more degrees while he waited for the Abbot on the phone.

******

The Abbot was inside his office, drinking bourbon, at 6am. It was a very early morning for him, but then, he hadn't slept well in nearly a week. He didn't normally drink at such an early hour, but with the vivid nightmares he had been having, it was the only way he knew to settle his nerves. Since the three priests had left on Sunday, the nightmares he experienced got progressively worse. Last night had been the most horrible he could imagine. The idea that the dreams would get any scarier was a thought he could not bear to think about. Whatever dark entity had been plaguing his dreams had manifested itself into reality last night, sitting on his chest and holding his arms down with tremendous force. The Abbot couldn't make out any features, only piercing green eyes and a bottomless darkness. The entity made it nearly impossible for him to breathe, and despite closing his eyes to wish it away, the dark figure stayed there most of the night. He hoped that maybe it was really a dream, but the Abbot had his doubts.

Suddenly there was a soft knock on his door. He quickly put the bourbon away in one of his top drawers and did his best to compose himself.

"Yes, come in."

Father McBride slowly opened the door. "Sorry to bother you at this early hour Abbot, but I heard you were up, and there is a Father Bartolini on the phone. He said it was urgent."

"I'll take the call in here," the Abbot replied, waving the back of his hand to signal he wanted the Subprior to leave him alone.

"Father Bartolini. How are you?" The Abbot did his best to hide the terror in his own voice.

A crackle of static was loud in the ear piece of the phone. In the distance the Abbot could hear what sounded like banging.

"Abbot, very sorry to bother you at this hour," Father Bartolini said, his voice difficult to make out with the static and incessant noises in the background.

The Abbot wondered what the noises were, but he suspected that the priest was having his share of whatever was attacking him in his sleep. The last thing he wanted to do was to scare the priest into thinking they were both having problems, for fear he would not live up to his promise to deliver three nuns to St. Michael's as planned. The mission was far too important to let obstacles get in the way. No matter how difficult those obstacles may be.

"How can I help you?" The static persisted.

Father Bartolini sounded petrified, there was no hiding it. "I'm having horrible nightmares. Now I'm hearing horrible banging noises outside my apartment, like something is trying to get in!"

"That is very strange, Father."

"Have you experienced anything like this since our meeting? That seems to be when it started," the priest said, the static growing more intense and louder.

"No. I've actually never slept better," the Abbot said, taking his drink out of the drawer and sipping at it. His hand was shaking slightly. Lying came far too easy for the aging priest.

"Maybe I should call Father Rosa or Father Wilkes and see how they're doing?"

"No, that's not a good idea. We don't need to be scaring them over this. It's probably just a figment of your imagination from not sleeping well. Go see a doctor and have him prescribe you something to help you sleep."

The Abbot could hear the loud banging on the other end, amidst the static that was now almost completely drowning out Father Bartolini's voice. It sounded like the frantic priest said "OK" before hanging up the phone. The static on the other end was abruptly cut off. The Abbot had an idea what might be causing these things, but he wasn't sure. He did know it was imperative that the mission continue and that the twelve nuns, with the assistance of Sister Mary Concordia, leave St. Michael's as planned on December 1st.

The Abbot continued sipping at his bourbon, hoping that he would be able to hold things together until December 1st and that whatever was in his bedroom last night was not going to return again. Looking at his wrists, he could see bruising from where the entity had him held down, and he knew that it was certainly not a dream nor a figment of his imagination. Something was trying to tell him something, but what it was, the Abbot could only venture a guess.

3

"Are you sure he's capable, Father?" the Abbot asked, slightly leaning back in his chair, yet not taking his eyes off Father Penning.

It was rare the Abbot would ask a question without first already knowing the answer. And this was not one of those times. The Abbot already had his people thoroughly check this man out, and they felt that he could carry out the plan. His blue eyes bore holes into the priest sitting next to him in the small conference room at the Peoria State Hospital in Bartonville, Illinois. Although he had known the Abbot for many years, it didn't make him feel any better being put under a microscope by the intense glare of the holy man. Or in the case of Father Reilly, the Abbot of St. Michael's Academy, an unholy man. A very unholy man.

"Yes. He can do it. If the carrot we wave is big enough, he will do just about anything, especially if it means his freedom," Father Penning replied. His soul felt filthy, yet he knew that he couldn't do anything to stop what was going to happen. The Abbot was relentless in his pursuit of dirty laundry, and when it came to Father Penning, one didn't have to look far to find a trail of sordid deeds to make even a sailor blush. The Abbot held his cards on Father Penning and was now calling in the favor. It was one the older priest could not refuse, despite the evil nature of it all. Without realizing it, Father Penning ran his thin fingers through his even thinner gray hair and let out a sigh.

The Abbot smiled. He knew the turmoil going on inside the perverted mind of Father Penning. He recognized all the body language. Years ago, the Abbot had found out about a series of affairs Father Penning had been having with young boys at his parish in Belleville, Illinois. The diocese moved him around to avoid the inevitable, but no matter how strict the warnings got, the priest and his penchant for pre-pubescent boys proved insatiable. The Abbot stepped in, as a man of great influence, and brought Father Penning to the Peoria State Hospital to serve as the chaplain. The hospital was an insane asylum, operated on a large 200-acre campus near Peoria. It was opened just after the turn of the 20th century and was known throughout the country as state-of-the-art when it came to caring for the mentally ill in a way that defied the more barbaric methods previously considered standard. The priest was grateful for another chance, but he knew the Abbot and his powerful connections in and out of the church would want to be paid back for such generosity. The Abbot treated life like a game of chess, and no move was made that didn't score some sort of capital for the Abbot.

A few months ago, Father Penning was summoned to St. Michael's to meet with the Abbot, where he was given a task to fulfill, and the Abbot would not take no for an answer. The Abbot implied that he would ruin the aging priest with news of his perverted ways, at a time when homosexuality was not accepted in any way, especially when it involved minors. The Catholic church had not begun to address issues such as this in the public eye, but, behind-the-scenes, those at the top of the hierarchy did not want word getting out involving sex with minors, and they would make sure priests with this problem were whisked away somewhere low profile and kept under close supervision. It didn't always work as planned, but Father Penning knew that without this favor from the Abbot, he would have been working at a soup kitchen in some mid-sized city in a nondescript part of flyover country. His comfortable life would have been gone, and everyone he knew would have proof he was not only a homosexual, but one that had sex with young boys. The elderly priest knew he would never again be able to look anyone he knew in the eye if that were to happen.

"Bring her in here, Father O'Donnell," the Abbot said to the young priest sitting by the door, who had been assisting Father Penning at the asylum.

The young priest stood up and opened the door. "Please come in ma'am. They'll see you now."

The strong smell of her cheap perfume was present before she entered the conference room. The Abbot smiled wryly, thinking that the person he tasked with finding the woman had done an exemplary job. She was exactly as ordered. She was of above average height, in her early twenties, with bleach-blonde hair and heavy makeup. Her bright red lips and captivating green eyes were striking, despite the cheapness of her impression. As the gaze of the Abbot continued downward, he approved of her large breasts that were barely covered in the red bustier she wore. Her long, slender legs that continued past the high-hemline of her skirt were covered in silky black nylon stockings to just above her knees. Completing the ensemble was a pair of bright red high-heels. He knew that this carrot was large enough for the man to do his bidding, and then some. There was a tinge of regret that the Abbot didn't have the time to sample the prize he had bought and paid for, before the patient that Father Penning selected had his way with the young street walker from the southwest streets of downtown Peoria.

"So what do you think, Father?" he asked, glancing over at Father Penning, who seemed a bit taken back by the young prostitute. Her perfume nearly choked him.

"Well, this is a bit more than expected. I think one of the older lunch ladies in the hospital cafeteria would have sufficed." His palms were sweating as he anticipated the snide remark to surely follow.

The Abbot laughed and said, "I realize she's not your type, Father. But I believe this man you have found will take a great liking to her." Father Penning didn't like the salvo one bit.

The woman stood a bit uncomfortably as the two men talked about her like she was a piece of meat. In a way, of course, she was. That may be what really bothered her. In her profession, compartmentalizing her life was a method of survival that kept her sane. Standing here, she felt like cattle at auction. She had been paid well and promised a hot meal and a place to sleep for the night.

"What is your name?" the Abbot asked, his voice sharp and without a scintilla of respect.

She smacked her gum. "Elise." Her accent was bland and purely Midwestern. She had always liked her name, knowing it was the only good thing her mother ever did for her. The last Elise had heard, she was in a halfway house in Joliet after getting out of state prison.

"Well, isn't that a pretty name?" the Abbot began. "A very pretty name for such a filthy thing." His gaze slowly shifted from her ample breasts to the tops of her silk stockings, where it lingered. He didn't even realize he was salivating.

He looked at Father O'Donnell, who was doing his best to be invisible. He felt very uncomfortable as the Abbot began to demean the young woman and hurl insults at Father Penning. He had not taken his final vows yet. He was spending time helping at the Peoria State Hospital as part of his coursework to becoming an ordained Catholic priest. He also loved to play basketball and enjoyed working with the teenage boys who played at the handful of Catholic high schools in Central Illinois.

"Take her to those VIP quarters we discussed on the third floor. Let her freshen up a bit and we'll send him along after we've met with him," Father Penning said to his young assistant, trying not to look at his firm backside when he turned and left the room with the prostitute. He knew the Abbot would notice that.

The old priest was right. The Abbot put his hand in front of his mouth to stifle a laugh, watching Father Penning fight the urge to stare at the young man as he left the room. As much as the situation humored him, the Abbot was equally as disgusted to see the vulgar display of weakness. In the Abbot's game of chess, this was a sign that victory was at hand. The nape of the smitten priest's neck was exposed.

"Very good, then. Now that business is taken care of, can we bring him in here? And can you open a window? That perfume she had on is making me sick," the Abbot said, coughing slightly into the crook of his arm. His mind still had not fully left the bountiful cleavage of the waif.

"Yes, Abbot. I'll send for William."

******

The Abbot stared at the man as he was brought into the conference room. They had a rather uncomfortable metal folding chair set up in the middle of the room in front of the two priests who would be talking with him. He was just under six feet tall, but the man in the grey, dingy patient uniform was obviously very muscular and physically fit. The Abbot would have guessed him to be in his late twenties, with his military-style buzz haircut and a few gaudy prison-style tattoos on his forearms.

"Good to see you, William," said Father Penning as he smiled and motioned for him to sit down.

The Abbot could see the muscles rippling in his arms and legs. He was pleased that the man appeared so physically capable for being in such a dismal place as the asylum in Bartonville. He loathed the place, but it served a vital purpose to the plan. So the Abbot would look past all the things that spooked him about the place. In nearly 30 years of being open, the asylum had a rich, dark history that some of the staff would rather not discuss.

William Weeks nodded to both men as he sat down, facing them, with a hand on each thigh. He tried to keep from fidgeting, but the priest he did not know was staring at him with the most intense blue eyes he had ever seen. William felt as if the man could read his mind, the way his facial features would react to his thoughts about the meeting. It was extremely unsettling and was an invasion of his mind he didn't welcome. His temples burned, and a searing pain ripped through his head and then passed.

The Abbot began the conversation. "I need to be sure you fully understand what we need you to do Mr. *Weeks*." He put an odd emphasis on his surname. The thin smile on his face was obviously forced, but the Abbot was a complex being. Almost everyone in his presence felt uncomfortable for the duration of the experience.

William said, "Yes, I understand."

Father Penning stared straight ahead, trying not to make eye contact with the Abbot. The Abbot had told him about William Weeks, and had asked him to talk with the patient, despite his status at the hospital. Much of the campus was open, with patients living in cottage-style housing in large plantation-style homes. They were housed by common mental disorders, but William was in the only dormitory-type housing on the grounds, and it was kept locked with guards. The C dorm, as it was called, was run more like a prison than the rest of the 66-building hospital because of the condition of the patients housed there. These were the criminally insane patients who were extremely violent and serious escape risks. The women who were of the same condition were housed in the D dorm.

When Father Penning had been told of the patient's name, and that the Abbot wanted him specifically for such a gruesome job, it seemed strange. It wasn't that William Weeks was not violent enough to carry out such a plan, but the concern of whether he could be controlled once things got started. He was worried that once the blood began to flow, the criminally insane William Weeks would go into a feeding frenzy.

"Our deal is still the same, William. I, of course, would have to deny any involvement in this if you were caught," said Father Penning, "and the Abbot as well, of course." He looked over toward the pompous clergyman briefly, and he replied with a slight nod of agreement.

William looked to both men. "As long as I'm given a chance at breaking out of this joint, I'm willing to do what you need me to do. I've had plenty of blood on these hands," he said, holding his scarred and calloused hands out toward them, "and that doesn't bother me at all."

The Abbot and Father Penning were both well aware of William's crimes and the reason he was a resident in C dorm. He had killed a co-worker and his entire family with an axe, after a drunken disagreement at a party. When the police showed up, he was covered in blood, sitting on his front porch with a can of cheap beer, smoking a Pall Mall. William acted like there was no big deal and seemed almost surprised when the police showed up. It wasn't difficult for the court-appointed psychiatrist to find him psychotic and unable to know right from wrong. So instead of being sent to a traditional state prison, William was sent to the Peoria State Hospital, on the hill in Bartonville.

The Abbot asked, "Are you Catholic, William?" Of course, he already knew the answer.

Father Penning began to reply on the patient's behalf before the Abbot glared his way, abating anything further. *Let him answer himself!* The words were spoken without the Abbot moving his lips. The priest couldn't believe the unholy man was able to speak to him this way. He was definitely a student of the dark arts, and it was almost like being in the company of the Devil himself. Father Penning continued to stare ahead.

"No. I'm nothing. I don't believe in God. He's never done a damn thing for me," William replied coldly.

"Very good, then." The Abbot was pleased.

"What about the other part of our bargain?" William smirked as he asked the question. He hadn't been able to think about anything else for the past two weeks, when he learned about his deal with the Devil.

The Abbot replied, "She's waiting for you on the third floor, William. There were bars placed over the windows, and there will be a 24-hour guard at the door, but you'll have her to yourself until the sun comes up tomorrow."

William could feel himself become erect at the thought of being with a woman. He had been locked up for the past ten years and the only women he saw was the occasional nurse from a distance. He had no visitors. He had been kept in solitary confinement under extreme lock and key. The soft skin of a woman had only been in his dreams, and now that it was actually going to happen, it sent his mind on a rapid-fire display of erotic images. William was ready for this down payment on his services.

Father Penning opened the door of the conference room.

"OK, please take him to the third floor." Two guards entered the room as William Weeks stood up.

The Abbot rose also. "Very good, William. Enjoy your prize. We'll see you again in December for your end of the bargain."

William nodded. "Yes, you will."

******

The guard that pulled the first shift on the third floor sat quietly outside the VIP quarters. He saw the other two escort William Weeks into the apartment. Just seeing the notorious patient made the young guard nervous. He had only been employed at the hospital for a year, and he heard stories about a lot of the patients, and what they did to end up in C dorm. It was the story about William and how he had hacked up that entire family, kids included, with an axe that sent chills up his spine.

He was only in the VIP quarters for five minutes when he heard the young girl scream. The guard was under instructions to not enter the apartment for any reason. He was only there to prevent William Weeks from escaping. The girl was not his responsibility, but he could hear the monster slapping her and calling her degrading names. The screaming went on for hours. It was only interrupted by her sobbing and the grunting and animal noises coming from William. The young guard couldn't imagine what he was doing to the young prostitute. Whatever it was, she screamed all night long.

At dawn, when the same two guards showed back up to pick up William, they got a glimpse inside the VIP quarters. The girl was naked, lying on the bed spread-eagle and covered in blood and bruises. Minutes after William was taken back to his cell, two medics arrived from the hospital and took her out in a stretcher. Custodians were summoned to clean up the room, and it took them nearly four hours to complete their work, so that the apartment looked like nothing had happened.

4

October 1927

It was a brisk day in McHenry, Illinois on the first Saturday of October 1927. The sky was grey and menacing, threatening a downpour at any moment. It was the day the Abbot had told the three priests they would return to St. Michael's Academy, along with the nuns that they had selected for the Christmas pilgrimage. A biting wind was blowing from the west and through the train station, causing a large metal sign that read "McHenry Train Depot" to rattle sharply against the wooden frame of the small shelter for passengers preparing to board. Sister Mary Benedicta could feel a dull ache in her arthritic back and knees, typically a prelude to rain. She was almost 70 now, and her health was beginning to slip away. She had served in only three different churches since taking her final vows to become a nun in her early twenties. All of them were in the New England area. Growing up in Cape Girardeau, Missouri, she knew how the wind blew in the flat corn and bean fields of the Midwest. She clutched her simple wool coat and tilted her head slightly forward to avoid facing the wind.

Her first church was in Burlington, Vermont, then upstate New York near Albany, before settling at St. Stephen's Catholic Church in New Haven, Connecticut. Sister Mary Benedicta loved the beautiful colors and architecture of New Haven, but the winters were getting to be too much for her. Her arthritis was getting worse each year, and nothing seemed to help with the pain. She was hoping to get sent somewhere south for her next parish, figuring it would be her last, before she got too old to work. At least then she could say goodbye to winter for good!

The nasty bite of the wind always reminded her of a day she would rather forget just before Thanksgiving in 1910. She was helping the other sisters rake leaves on a blustery day, and the wind was swirling leaves and twigs all over the courtyard. Suddenly the sisters were approached by a frantic police officer, who asked if there was anyone who felt that they could help talk to a crazed man with a hostage they had surrounded in a deli two blocks away. Worse yet, the man had the female hostage at knifepoint and refused to give himself up.

The four nuns looked at each other. They were all experienced in speaking with people in distress at the worst times of their lives. Sister Mary Benedicta volunteered to go with him, since she was the oldest of the group and had more experience. She was also concerned for the other nuns and did not want to put one of the younger sisters into a potentially deadly situation.

The young policeman was relieved and hurried her along toward the downtown business district. A crowd was already gathering outside Elm Street Meats and Delicatessen and spilling out onto the street. A reporter was there from the New Haven Register, with a photographer, trying to take pictures of the melee. The scene was overwhelming to Sister Mary Benedicta, who spent most of her days with the rest of the sisters in quiet study and work. The young officer was pulling her toward the meat shop, where a more senior officer (a sergeant) was in charge of the hostage situation.

"Thank you, Sister, for coming to help," said Sergeant Randolph. Despite the cool weather, sweat was streaming down his face. The mass of people behind them was growing by the second, and with it, the decibel level.

"Of course." She tried to smile. Her calm amidst the chaos was welcome.

"Lieutenant Halford is in Boston at a funeral. He usually handles anything out of the ordinary."

Sergeant Randolph took the Sister by the hand and led her into the small vestibule outside the meat shop yet away from the madness outside.

"Sister, this is a bad situation. The owner of the place is Edward O'Rourke, and he's got a female customer hostage. Two of my officers came to arrest him today. He is suspected to have killed his wife and two young girls," he said, in a measured tone, looking her in the eyes. He decided to leave out the rest of the disturbing details. The details that would explain how he ground them up into hamburger and sold the meat to his customers for a week until it was all gone. Even Sergeant Randolph had a hard time with it, and he knew the nun would probably be scared to death to talk to him.

"Oh my." She was frozen in place.

Inside the meat shop, she could hear a commotion. It sounded like one of the large metal bowls or cookware had fallen to the cold tile floor. She heard a woman scream and a man yelling curses.

"What are you doing, Randolph? Who is that you have out there? You're a liar. You said it was just going to be me and you," screamed Edward O'Rourke from inside the store. He was not visible from where he was crouched down with his hostage. She was shaking with fear and paralyzed in terror. This mad butcher had his left arm roughly around her neck, and she was firmly in his grasp. The right hand held a long, sharp knife. He held it precariously close to the nape of her pearl white neck.

Sister Mary Benedicta said a silent prayer as she walked into the meat shop. Sergeant Randolph tried to stop her, but he was unable to. Before he had a chance to say anything, the nun walked in. She had all her trust in God to protect her and to give her the strength to save the poor hostage. Looking at Edward O'Rourke's darting eyes, she attempted to size him up. Sister Mary Benedicta knew she had never seen true evil before she saw him there behind the meat counter, crouched down with the hostage. There was a terrible feeling of dread that washed over her, only ten feet away from a depraved killer that was acting like a cornered, wild animal.

"Please, my son. Let her go. She doesn't need to be here with us."

Edward snorted. His eyes were moving back and forth, and his breathing was erratic.

The nun stared at him. Her face was warm and caring, yet Edward was somewhere else at the moment and unable to come back to reality.

Sister Mary Benedicta took a step forward.

"Please. Let her go."

Edward stared back at her. His eyes were ice, yet they burned into her memory forever. With his right hand he brought the knife across the hostage's throat, slicing deep into the soft flesh. Sister Mary Benedicta still had dreams of that day, and the bright red blood that had poured down the front of the woman's blue dress the ceramic tile floor. Yet the thing that haunted her dreams still, even more than the blood, was the evil stare of Edward O'Rourke and the smile on his face.

******

As the nuns made their way from the train depot, they walked in a single-file line toward the two cars that were waiting for them and their luggage. As the metal sign rattled again in the wind, Sister Mary Xavier was reminded of a sound that she would rather forget. She was at her first church in Indian Lake, New York and was working with a group of older nuns who would go to meet with patients at the Essex County Hospital in nearby Port Henry. Sister Mary Xavier was eager to help and volunteered one Saturday to go to the insane asylum on the north end of the hospital. It was a two-story addition that housed the county's most troubled cases. The second floor was where the escape-prone patients were kept in cells like a prison. Sister Mary Xavier and her older counterpart, Sister Mary Elizabeth, made their way from the first floor to the second floor with a hospital security guard.

The noise in the asylum was almost deafening. The guard didn't seem to notice, but it was because he had grown used to the sounds. The patients became restless, and some agitated, when new people came into their world. They would bang the metal cups they were given for drinking water. It was this metal on metal sound that triggered the memory for Sister Mary Xavier when she heard the metal sign clamoring in the harsh October wind in McHenry. It brought her back to that Saturday in 1911 when she met a man she wished she had never laid eyes on.

His name was Paul Rosati, and he had been a patient on the second floor for the past six months while the state of New York psychiatrists decided whether he would go to prison or remain in an asylum like Essex County Hospital. He was arrested in downstate Yonkers, just outside of the Bronx, after it was discovered that he was a serial killer they had been looking for. Several of the neighborhood children on his block were missing, and the police finally got a break in the case from a neighbor in the apartment building that Rosati lived in. She told police that she had seen not one, but two of the boys that were on the missing posters in the neighborhood. She told the police that she saw the boys with Mr. Rosati the same day their parents were frantically searching for them and asking questions.

When the police went to question Paul at his apartment, they noticed a foul odor coming from inside. The apartment appeared to be neat and orderly, but the horrific stench of rotting meat was overwhelming. When the officers asked him about the smell, Paul began to act agitated and tried to move the conversation out in the hallway, so he could close the door. An hour later, the police showed up with a warrant to search his apartment, and the true horror of what Paul Rosati had done was there for all to see.

There were human body parts on his kitchen table, on the counters, and he had something cooking on the stove that smelled dreadful. He was arrested on the spot, and he later confessed to killing his own mother and father almost a year before, eating them slowly over the course of several weeks. He told the police it was something he was fascinated with, and once he got a taste for human flesh, he needed to go out and get more. He found that children in the neighborhood were the easiest targets, and they were also very tender and tasty. The police were absolutely horrified. The New York media was even appalled at the cannibalism, especially in 1911, when the city was coming alive with construction and massive immigration from Europe. Even for a city like New York, Paul Rosati was an abomination. The state decided to move him to upstate New York at the secure hospital in Essex County, removed from New York City.

At the time, Sister Mary Xavier was not aware of the history of Paul Rosati's strange fetish for human flesh, and if she had, she would have never gotten as close as she did to his cell. In an instant, he reached out between the bars and got a hold of her. Sister Xavier cried out, and on the other end of the floor, Sister Mary Elizabeth heard her above the roar of the inmates. Things seemed to happen in slow motion. As Sister Mary Elizabeth ran to the altercation, the inmates began to erupt in a frenzy at the action playing out before them. They cheered on Paul Rosati as he dragged the young nun toward his cell and salivating mouth. She was writhing on the floor and doing her best to fend off his strong grip, but she had no chance as he pulled her closer and closer. Sister Mary Xavier was so small and slender, there was even a concern that he could pull her through the bars and into the cell. The thought of that was unimaginable, even if for only a few minutes.

"Come here, you little bitch!" screamed out Paul Rosati, his Italian accent prominent. He had only been in New York for a year after leaving Italy for the promise of America. But instead of doing good things, he preyed on the weakest among society and became a monster.

The next thing she knew, the young nun was up against the cold metal bars of his cell. She still vividly remembered smelling the rot on his breath. His teeth were terrible, and several were missing. That hideous smirk on his face was still etched in the nun's memory. His eyes were black pools of never-ending rage.

A huge boom sounded, and Sister Mary Xavier didn't remember anything else until she woke up the next day in a hospital bed at the other end of Essex County Hospital. She was told that one of the guards had stepped in and pulled her from Rosati's grasp, and that one of the armed guards who monitored the floor from a perimeter catwalk, shot Rosati once in the head and killed him instantly. Sister Mary Xavier had been knocked out from being pulled into the bars, and she got covered in Rosati's blood. She had been taken away quickly from the scene as the guards began the difficult task of cleaning up the mess and bringing order to the chaotic second floor once again.

Sister Mary Xavier continued walking in the single-file line in the harsh wind, as the metal sign's banging noise faded into the recesses of her mind.

******

The last nun in the line was Sister Teresa Anne Marie. She was the oldest of the group. She had been battling a terrible case of the flu back at her parish in Toms River, New Jersey. When Father Wilkes called from Hartford a month before, the Prioress at her convent told her the good news about being handpicked for this special Christmas pilgrimage in Chicago. The church was very excited for Sister Teresa Anne Marie, since she was in her early 70's and as her health problems were beginning to mount, it was nice to see her recognized for a long life and service to God. They even had a goodbye dinner for her the Friday before she left.

As a train began to move away from the station, there was a loud backfire that made Sister Teresa Anne Marie jump. Instantly, that sound made her remember something terrible from her past. It was nearly 20 years ago, in 1908, when she had a near-death experience that had left her scarred. Many sleepless nights could be attributed to her lying in bed, unable to sleep at all, her mind swimming with images of that warm afternoon in May.

She was visiting her cousin Samantha Jean in a small town outside of Burlington, Vermont. They were only a few weeks apart in age and had been very close growing up before Teresa had decided to become a nun. Once her training had begun, they saw less and less of each other. After taking her final vows, the nun had decided to take a long weekend to Vermont, so they could spend some much-needed time together.

Samantha Jean suggested they bring some extra fruit and vegetables from the family farm to the local grade school, since many of the students were poor, their families suffering from a weak economy in the area. Sister Teresa Anne Marie had been pleased her cousin wanted to do such a charitable thing, so the two loaded up one of the cars and had a farmhand drive them to town to the Brimfield Primary School.

When they arrived, the children had just finished their lunch and were outside playing for a short recess before returning to their lessons. The ladies had the school custodian unload the car with the produce while they enjoyed playing with the children. Sister Teresa Anne Marie was playing baseball while Samantha Jean took the teachers up on the offer for some lunch, and she sat at a picnic table watching the fun. One of the teachers, who was sitting with Samantha Jean, began to clutch her stomach. Then another teacher at the table stood up and collapsed to the ground, grabbing at her stomach and crying out in pain. Samantha Jean looked around the playground, and almost on cue, several of the kids were also doubled over, some throwing up and others already down on the ground. She looked down at the bowl of her half-eaten chicken noodle soup and grilled cheese sandwich. That was when she felt the first sharp pain in her stomach. Within a minute, she was on the ground and dead.

By 12:30 pm that afternoon, 76 students and staff were dead at the school. Most of them were outside, but there was one secretary in the office, the cafeteria workers, several students who had chosen to eat inside, and an older custodian who always looked forward to the days when they made chicken noodle soup. Sister Teresa Anne Marie had run into the building to look for her cousin, not realizing she was outside, and she was horrified at the bodies strewn throughout the building.

She didn't even feel the younger custodian, Horace Hermann, who had unloaded the car for them, grab her and force her into a storage closet. She was terrified! He told her that he had killed his wife with poison the other day when she admitted to having an affair with a neighbor. He also poisoned his three young children, since he didn't want the girls to grow up with the shame of what their mother had done. Horace was a devout Baptist, and the revelation shook him to the core. The guilt of killing his entire family was consuming his thoughts, so he had taken the rest of the poison and used it to taint the chicken noodle soup when the cafeteria staff wasn't paying attention. Sister Teresa Anne Marie was shaking with fear, not knowing what the mentally disturbed man was going to do to her. They sat in the warm storage room for an hour or more, as he told her about his entire life story, one heartbreak after another. His speech was a little slow, but there was no mistaking his violent tendencies and the distant look in his eyes that frightened her.

Suddenly, he pulled a pistol from his work pants. At first Sister Teresa Anne Marie thought he was going to shoot her. He did not. He only closed his eyes, put the gun to his right temple, and pulled the trigger. The loud crack of the pistol in the enclosed room left the young nun with a broken ear drum. Even when the ear drum healed, she could hear that loud noise, and ever since, when she heard a similar sound, she was instantly transported to the Brimfield Primary School on that dreadful day in May of 1908.

Now Sister Teresa Anne Marie did her best to leave the past behind as she handed the driver her small suitcase and entered the car. She smiled at the other two nuns and nodded as they began the short drive to St. Michael's Academy.

******

As the cars approached with the nuns and their luggage, the Abbot stood at the window of his private dining room which overlooked the circular driveway below the main entrance of the school. He smiled, knowing that his plan was finally beginning to take shape. It was his life's work. The Abbot watched as the nuns were taken to the former convent on the east end of the grounds, where he had instructed the nuns to be cloistered until their departure in a few weeks. He didn't want them talking to the staff at St. Michael's. He had crafted a good story to tell the employees at the school and church. Why the nuns were visiting and why they were staying in the old convent building. Earlier in the day, the cars had taken two other groups of nuns into the old convent, but to different floors, so the groups were separate for the time being. As with everything the Abbot did, this plan was very calculated, down to the most intimate details, and he knew exactly how he was going to introduce the nuns to each other.

The Abbot looked down at the young novitiate, Sister Mary Elizabeth, her head moving skillfully as her warm mouth serviced his fully erect penis. She had only been at St. Michael's for two months, but the Abbot had put her talents to good use, helping around the office and satisfying his undying urges. Right now, he closed his eyes, aroused at the thought of the plan that was about to unfold, sending those nuns to their untimely death in Bartonville. At the same time, he had his hand resting on the silky, smooth brunette hair of the novitiate as she moved like a well-oiled piston on her knees in front of him.

5

The third floor of the former convent was extremely quiet, but Sister Mary Aquinas was not able to sleep. Upon arrival, the St. Michael's staff put each of the three nuns in their own rooms, which would sleep two when the convent was in use. The simple room was no different than the many others the nun had seen in her years since taking her final vows back in 1880. Born in Waterbury, Connecticut, Sister Mary Aquinas spent her years in service to God with seven different churches in Connecticut, New York, New Hampshire and Massachusetts. It was at her second church, St. Paul's in Orange, Massachusetts, when she did 30-day rotations with the other nuns at the Greenfield County Hospital for the Criminally Insane. At the time, Greenfield was one of the few hospitals in the country that kept extremely violent patients. Most states kept them in prisons staffed to deal with malevolent, psychotic inmates.

As she sat in the breathtaking stillness, she could feel the scar that ran down the left side of her face. Her fingers felt every bump and burr along the snakelike track it made from her temple to her jaw bone. The sister was brought back to a bitterly cold December afternoon in 1888. Sometimes it felt like it had been ages ago, and other times, like it had happened the day before. In her mind, she was taken far from the sprawling grounds of St. Michael's to the mountainous wilderness that surrounded the desolate hospital in Greenfield County.

It had been a typical Tuesday at Greenfield County Hospital, and Sister Mary Aquinas had been visiting some of the more disturbed patients in the company of Father Sasso. Father Sasso had grown up in Boston and had volunteered to work at this hospital, as difficult as it was, because he felt his talents would be put to the best use. He admitted openly that many of the priests he knew would be scared to work within the confines of an insane asylum, and many would resign within days of assignment. On Tuesdays, he would take the nun who was serving her 30-day rotation into building 2, where the most violent were kept in jail cells that bore not the slightest resemblance to a hospital room. The rooms were dark with only a dim light mounted into the concrete ceiling, and a small table top and metal bed that were lag-bolted to the damp concrete walls. The roar on the first floor of building 2 was usually raucous and deafening, especially to someone not used to the noise. At full capacity, the first floor could house 20 patients kept in prison-style cells. These patients often screamed at all hours of the day and night, made banging noises on the bars, or simply yelled gibberish to hear themselves amongst the cacophony.

The second floor was totally silent. The insulation between the floors and the tight fit of the metal fire doors kept the rest of the world out. It was even darker and creepier than the cells on the first floor. The patients housed in the twelve cells on the second floor were plucked from any sane person's worst nightmare. They were predators of children, cannibals, murderers, rapists, and the most sadistic patients that the hospital dared to house. Most spent their days sitting in silence, in an almost catatonic state, rocking back and forth to an imaginary sound track. Others stared out of the small two by two-foot barred window, longingly watching life go on without them. If anyone walked by these cells, they wouldn't hear anything, yet the blood of most would frost over as the eyes of each patient followed them in the darkness. It might be how a rat feels before being fed to a snake, scared at the inevitable outcome while the snake stares on in quiet contemplation.

As Sister Mary Aquinas took herself back to that day on the second floor of building 2, she could feel her pulse quicken and a cold sweat beginning to reveal itself on her quivering face. That dark hallway and the eyes that followed her along the way had given her an incredible sense of dread. She had felt that something was going to happen.

In the last cell to the right was a former medical doctor, Dr. Rollin Arbuckle, who was convicted of killing more than 30 of his own patients in Boston and selling the bodies to various criminals who would trade them in a seedy underworld black market for fresh dead bodies. Dr. Arbuckle didn't ask questions. He was happy to collect a fee for each corpse and to continue his thriving practice on the west side of Boston. It went on for years while he hobnobbed with rich elitists, drinking only the finest wines and going to the theater regularly. He was also quite the ladies' man and a very eligible bachelor in the eyes of most.

When one of the criminals he was dealing with had gotten arrested on something unrelated, he saved his own skin by giving up the names of everyone he worked with, and the good doctor was promptly arrested. He was not made for prison life and was beaten up and brutally raped daily for months leading up to his trial for the murders. This was when Dr. Arbuckle cracked and entered a very dark and disturbing period of psychosis. It was as if the timid doctor had gone away and replaced with a monster who thought only about inflicting pain and misery on anything it could get its hands on. The guards kept him in the last cell.

Every time she was on this floor, Father Sasso would remind her about Rollin Arbuckle. She would walk by the cell, clutching the priest's arm, filled with terror at what was in the cell. His hair was always askew, and he kept a dingy appearance with a uniform that was always soiled and several sizes too big. It was his eyes that always repulsed her. Rollin would stare at her with his intense hazel eyes, and she would feel her insides churn. She knew he was evil, and he was pleased that she knew it.

"Don't look at him, sister," said Father Sasso, walking a bit quicker than usual.

As she turned to the priest to reply, Sister Mary Aquinas felt something around her neck. It was ice cold and strong, like a vice grip. She tried to cry out, but no sound was possible. Terrified, she also realized she could no longer breathe! A rush of panic swept over her as her grasp on Father Sasso's arm let go. She felt her head hit the damp concrete floor. She didn't realize it at the time, but there was tremendous commotion once the priest and a guard at the other end of the hallway realized what was happening. With lightning speed, Rollin Arbuckle had reached out and grabbed the young nun by her throat, and now he had her on the floor as he pulled her toward the bars of his cell with incredible power. Sister Mary Aquinas was out of consciousness for a few seconds, but she saw the bars of his cell get closer to her face, and she braced for impact as Rollin pulled as hard as he could on the other side, growling like an animal. She was in a haze as Father Sasso did his best to pull her back, away from the cell, but Rollin was too strong. He pulled her face into the coldness of the metal bars repeatedly, until the guards rushed into his cell, knocking him to the floor with their batons.

Sister Mary Aquinas slumped to the floor, blood rushing down her face and down the front of her white habit to the concrete. She remembered looking at all the blood and being overwhelmed with the yelling from inside the cell and from those who rushed in to help her out of the area. Hours later, she woke up in another building on the hospital grounds, in a warm bed with fresh bandages on her head and face.

She looked up at the doctor. Concern and shock held his face tightly.

"How bad is it, doctor?" she asked, not able to look him in the eye.

"Don't concern yourself with that, sister," he replied, holding her hand to get her pulse at the wrist.

"How bad is it, doctor?" she asked again, pulling her hand away and now looking him dead in the eyes.

He exhaled. "Bad. Very bad. 67 stitches. I did my best, but there will be a noticeable scar, sister. Several bones of your face are broken too . . . there will be a lot of swelling . . . " The doctor's voice began to trail off.

Sister Mary Aquinas was coming back to reality now. There was a sound now that replaced the incredible silence from earlier. It was rain on the window panes. The tiny tapping of rain that has begun to freeze. It was raining like that the first night at the hospital after she woke up with 67 stitches in her face. The tapping sound was the same. Now feeling the ridges of her scar, she had a sickening realization. Whenever she had memories of that day, they were typically a harbinger of bad things to come. She had been having these visions strongly for the past week, and this was the clearest one of all. Whatever bad things were to follow, Sister Mary Aquinas knew they had to be very, very bad.

******

In another room down the hallway from Sister Mary Aquinas, another nun was experiencing a flashback into the crevices of her past. Sister Maria Anne Michela was tossing and turning in fitful sleep, mumbling something incoherent as her eyes darted back and forth beneath their lids, hiding the terrible vision from the rest of the world. She was back in 1915, at Stateville Prison in Joliet, Illinois, on the night of a scheduled execution of an extremely violent serial killer, Raymond Dalripple. His capture two years before had made headlines across the country, even though his murders were concentrated to the Midwest, leaving the bodies of young women in seemingly random places. A number of the murders happened in the Chicago area, and since he was captured in Illinois, it was decided that he would be put on trial there and executed at Stateville if convicted.

Raymond Dalripple had been a traveling salesman, specializing in housewares for the suburban housewife. His gift of gab and rugged good looks had made it almost too easy for women to let him in when he came calling, eager to see what the dashing salesman had to show them. One look into those steel blue eyes left most women defenseless, and they would never expect his dark side to rise to the surface and lash out like it did. He carried with him a simple suitcase to show a variety of products to sell, and once the inviting housewife had let down her guard, Raymond would strike. Most of the victims had been under 30 years old and attractive. He would rape most of them and then strangle his victim with a nylon stocking he kept in his suitcase. In total, Raymond Dalripple murdered 18 women in Indiana, Illinois and Iowa before being captured. A paperboy in Lansing, Illinois had seen him enter a house on his paper route and observed the attack through an open window. He rode his bike to the nearby police station, and they promptly arrested Dalripple. Unfortunately for victim number 18, she didn't survive the attack. A jury had deliberated for less than one hour before convicting the killer, and a judge sentenced him to death by electrocution.

Sister Maria Anne Michela had taken her final vows only three years before and was serving her God at the St. Patrick's Catholic Church in Dwight, Illinois at the time of Dalripple's execution. On the day of the execution, she had been assisting a priest from a nearby Catholic church as he was visiting with the condemned inmates at Stateville prison. They had heard that despite his denouncement of religion, in the early morning hours of his execution day, Raymond Dalripple now wanted to see a priest. This was common with the condemned, who often wanted to speak to a priest, minister, or rabbi when they saw death anxiously waiting. Father Jeremy Meister was getting his things together to go to death row when a prison guard told him that Dalripple had changed his mind.

"He doesn't want to see you, Father," said Sergeant Jones, a prison guard who ran the death row cell block.

"Really?" asked Father Meister, as he set his bible down. Sister Maria Anne Michela began to put it back into the priest's bag.

Sergeant Jones looked at the two of them. "He wants to see the sister. Her." He pointed to the young and attractive nun.

"What do you think about that, Sister Maria?" the priest asked her, still surprised, since this was an unusual request.

Before she could utter a word, Sergeant Jones said, "We can't be responsible for her going in that cell, Father. He might look like a movie star, but Dalripple is a cold-blooded murdering scoundrel. Don't forget that."

"I don't mind going in to see him. I represent God and my church, and if one of our flock wants to talk to me, then I will speak with him. That's why I became a nun in the first place." She smiled at both Father Meister as well as Sergeant Jones. Her naiveté was charming, but Sergeant Jones was still very concerned.

After much discussion, Sergeant Jones agreed to let the nun talk with the condemned, but only for ten minutes. He told her that he would stand outside the cell, along with Father Meister, and at the first sign of any trouble, they would get her out and subdue the prisoner. Sister Maria Anne Michela agreed to the terms, and together they made the long walk down death row to what they called the death watch cell.

In his cell, Raymond Dalripple was sitting quietly, reading a book on his bed. He was wearing a blue jumpsuit so staff could recognize him immediately as a death row inmate. The rest of the prison population at Stateville wore black and white striped uniforms, like most prisoners of the day. He was cleanly shaven, and his chestnut brown hair was neatly trimmed and combed. At all times, Raymond Dalripple had kept up his appearance, as if at any moment he would be asked to make a sales call to peddle some laundry soap or the latest vacuum cleaner. He smiled at Sister Maria

Anne Michela as she stood outside his cell, while Sergeant Jones used his keys to unlock the door.

"I'll be right out here, Dalripple. No funny business."

Raymond continued his smile, showing off his nearly perfect teeth. "No funny business, sergeant. After all, I'm going to be dead in less than eight hours." He stood up and motioned for the nun to sit down in the wooden chair across from his bunk.

The heavy metal door clanged shut, cutting the silence of death row. Sergeant Jones and Father Meister stood patiently outside the cell, watching the condemned man closely.

Sister Maria Anne Michela looked at the prisoner, trying to set aside his stunningly good looks for the time being. She knew what he had done and that she was sitting only a few feet from an incredibly evil man. The way he smiled at her took on new meaning, after she considered what the newspapers had said about how he had killed all those young women, choking them to death in their own homes with a nylon stocking around their unsuspecting throats.

"How are you doing, my son? Have you found God in your hour of need?" She sat upright in the chair, looking at him, her legs crossed and her hands in her lap as she held her bible close. It was her strength. It had been a gift from her grandmother when she decided to become a nun. Even though her grandmother had been dead for two years, Sister Maria Anne Michela would often hear her voice comforting and giving her strength when she thought she could not go on. Oddly, in the death watch cell, the nun didn't feel her grandmother by her side. She felt very alone, and it made her uncomfortable. She clutched her bible tighter.

Raymond looked her in the eyes, and in a voice as smooth as silk, said, "I'm doing fine, sister. I haven't found God, though. I wasn't looking for him. Should I?" The spit-polished persona of the salesman began to crack ever so slightly.

"God is always there, Raymond. You need not look very far."

Now he leaned forward slightly. It was not enough to cause Sergeant Jones to react, as he was making small talk with Father Meister in the hallway outside the cell.

"I'd rather look for you, sister. Not some god who doesn't exist," Raymond said, quietly under his breath. He glanced out in the hallway, and neither of the men noticed what he said.

Sister Maria Anne Michela shifted uncomfortably in her chair at his comment, as well as the fact that the killer's eyes moved slowly down from making eye contact with her, to her starched white coif, her black habit, her thick black knee-high stockings, and black walking shoes. After he methodically looked over her entire body, head to toe, he met her eyes once again. She knew this was evil incarnate.

"Five minutes, Dalripple," said Sergeant Jones quickly, then resumed talking Chicago Cubs baseball with the priest.

"You want to know why I wanted to see you instead of that priest?"

She didn't answer. She was afraid to make eye contact with him again, and she recoiled when he reached out his hand to rest on her knee. His thumb began to slowly caress her stocking.

"Don't you play hard to get with me, you fucking prude bitch!" he cried out, standing up in the cell and lunging toward the nun.

Sergeant Jones turned around quickly and began fumbling with his keys. Father Meister stood frozen outside the cell, watching Sister Maria Anne Michela raise up her arms to defend herself from the condemned man.

"Hurry, Sergeant!" the priest exclaimed. The metal-on-metal sound of the keys rang out as other death row inmates now began to watch with amusement.

"Feel this, you bitch!" Dalripple screamed at the nun, forcing her hand to touch his bulging penis. "I'd have you on the floor of this cell if I wanted to, sister. No one could stop me! You'd be begging for more." He howled like a wolf at the top of his lungs.

Sister Maria Anne Michela began to cry, cowering in the chair, hoping desperately that they would get her out of this cell. She did her best not to look at Raymond, and it repulsed her that she was forced to touch him. She had neither seen nor touched an erect penis before, and the thought of doing that now was making her nauseous.

Sergeant Jones finally got the right key and began to twist it. But nothing happened!

"What are you waiting for, sergeant?" Father Meister was frantic with worry and watched helplessly as Raymond Dalripple was screaming at the nun, forcing her to touch him, and now unzipping his prison jumpsuit.

The key turned, but nothing was happening.

"It won't open the fucking cell! I can't open the lock for some reason!"

Now Raymond stood before her with his jumpsuit unzipped, as she curled up on the floor, trying to hide behind the chair. Raymond grabbed the chair and smashed it against the bars, sending splinters of wood flying in all directions. He continued to unzip his blues, and in a fluid motion, he took it off and threw it to the concrete floor of his cell.

"Looks like the Devil doesn't want you in here!" Raymond cried out, laughing manically.

"For the love of God, Sergeant Jones! Do something!" Father Meister cried out, pulling on the bars as if they would magically break in half. He could now see the naked Raymond Dalripple, after smashing the chair to pieces, grab Sister Maria Anne Michela and throw her down to his bed.

"You two are going to get a show. You're both going to watch me fuck this nun. It will be the best she ever had," he said in an almost guttural voice, spit flying from his mouth, his erection at full staff. He began to growl.

Sergeant Jones was doing everything he could to open up the cell, but the key was simply not working. Father Meister and now two other guards were pulling and prying on the bars, doing whatever they could to open the doors.

Raymond was tearing at the young nun's clothes. Her habit was half torn from her body, and she desperately tried to cover herself up with the sheets off his bunk. Raymond threw the sheets to the floor. He grabbed the elastic band of her panties and tore them into pieces, exposing the tuft of her vagina. He ripped one of her stockings completely off. The other one was dangling from her foot, which kicked at him in desperation. The priest and guards were shocked and unable to avoid looking at what was happening before them. Raymond was cackling like a maniac, grunting in animal lust at the sight of her young, naked body, writhing around, desperate to get away from his powerful grasp. It appeared that he liked her struggling against him, like a cat toying with a small field mouse before finishing it off.

Suddenly, as if God was watching the scene unfold Himself, the key engaged the lock, and the cell doors opened. The guards, led by Sergeant Jones, grabbed the naked body of Raymond Dalripple and threw him to the floor. Father Meister covered the shaking and hysterical Sister Maria Anne Michela and pulled her from the cell and into the hallway.

"Just let me fuck her one time!" Raymond screamed out as the guards pummeled his head and body with their Billy clubs. "Just once, you bastards! Just once!"

Sister Maria Anne Michela escaped the ordeal with only a few scratches and bruises. Thankfully, her virginity was still intact. The impact to her psyche would last for years. It was typical for her to have nightmares about that day on death row and how she had narrowly escaped her encounter with pure evil.

Now in the quiet confines on the third floor of the former convent, Sister Maria Anne Michela screamed as she awoke from the nightmare. Covered in sweat and shaking with fear, the nun sat up in bed and hoped daylight would come soon so she could take a hot shower and wash the filth of Raymond Dalripple from her body once again.

******

Across the hallway, Sister Mary Rose heard the screams that awakened Sister Mary Aquinas from her nightmare. Sister Mary Rose was also having difficulty with sleep. She was like this any time she slept in a new bed. Many might have thought the elderly nun would have been used to moving around and sleeping in dozens of beds before settling in at her final assignment – usually in the south where the weather was warmer and kinder to the old brittle bones. While many nuns tend to stay in the same region of the country, Sister Mary Rose moved around quite a bit, from her start in Crawford, Alabama to a string of small town Catholic churches in Indiana, Illinois, and Missouri. She even spent two years in California before coming back to Decatur, Illinois where she served at Holy Trinity High School as a math teacher. Of all the good things she had done, teaching was the one thing that Sister Mary Rose loved the most. She enjoyed children of all ages, but the challenge of high school math was something she embraced, and she did what she could to make the difficult subject simple to understand. Her students loved her as much as she did them.

Sister Mary Rose had been reading in the newspaper about a string of suspicious fires in the area. She had read in the Herald and Review about a factory on the east side of town that burned to the ground due to the flammable materials they kept in storage and shipped throughout the country to wholesalers. There were also residential fires that seemed to happen in groups in some of the older neighborhoods, such as the near north side of downtown. It sounded like the work of a bold arsonist who didn't appear to be concerned about being caught. Those were the kind that worried police and fire officials a great deal.

In addition to her time teaching, Sister Mary Rose volunteered her time to help in the kitchen at The Crawford House, a local school for disabled children. The main building was a former residential property that had become their office and meeting rooms, and the second floor was used for housing students who worked on the grounds. There were two other houses on the property, and later, a large single-story dormitory was added to house the boys and girls that attended the two-story school building. It was privately funded by the Crawfords, an extremely wealthy family who had many locally prominent members of their family, including the mayor, a monsignor with the local Catholic church, professors at Millikin University, and a host of business owners of all kinds in Decatur, Peoria, Bloomington, and Chicago. The children who attended the school and lived there were handicapped in a variety of ways. At the time, there was a push, when private money was available, to try to educate the disabled in ways that had not been tried before. The Crawford House was a wonderful institution, and Sister Mary Rose loved to give back and help in the kitchen when they had evening or weekend events at the school. She also enjoyed the company of the other ladies who volunteered their time.

It was a Friday night in September 1919 when Sister Mary Rose was working in the kitchen for their annual chili supper and dance. The gymnasium was filled to capacity (and then some) for the dance, and most of the students had invited family and friends.

It was 9:00 pm when Sister Mary Rose heard the first scream. "Fire!" The entire dynamic of the night changed immediately. Frantic cries were heard, and men attempted to break the glass of the windows without realizing it would make things worse, providing fresh air to stoke what indeed was a small fire. It wasn't small for long, as it spread very quickly throughout the basement, where it apparently had started in a custodial closet next to the boiler room, and within a few minutes it found itself going up the stairs and writhing on the plaster walls and ceilings. Drapes, paintings, and other décor provided the perfect fuel for the quickly spreading blaze that was underway.

A young priest, Father Richard, came into the kitchen to clear out the basement and assist the women to safety outside the building. The women followed the priest up the ramp that was used to shovel coal into the basement for the boiler. It was narrow and covered in coal dust, but Father Richard got them all out, except for Sister Mary Rose and an elderly volunteer. Sister Mary Rose told him to get the rest to safety so she could assist Agnes Wilson, the elderly volunteer who was struggling in the commotion. The nun managed to get Agnes up the ramp, which helped her immensely, as she took the fresh air in gulps. Suddenly someone grabbed Sister Mary Rose's arm and pushed her toward some bushes. In the chaos of the moment and the intense wave of emotion she had felt trying to get Agnes out of the fire, she had lost track of where she was exactly. The pull from the stranger was strong, and she couldn't resist.

"Don't say a god damn word!" a male voice commanded from the pitch black.

Sister Mary Rose was breathing heavily from her escape and immediately began to worry about Agnes. She had seemed to be doing fine. But she couldn't think about Agnes for long.

"The cops are looking for me. You work here or something? I need to hide," he continued. Now he was holding her firmer than before, and it was obvious he had something to do with this fire. For the first time since being outside, Sister Mary Rose could see that all the other buildings were also on fire! Screams could be heard in all directions, and now finally the first fire truck arrived and was joined by the two maintenance men at the school to get the fires under control.

"I'm just a volunteer," she cried, "and I only work in this building." She pointed to the main administration building she had just fled.

"You better not be lying to me, bitch!" he snarled. As her eyes began to adjust, she was able to see him better, especially with the lights from the fire trucks and the police that were now present.

"I'm not. I'm a nun from Holy Trinity. I teach math. I volunteer here at night. Why are you doing this?" She looked at him and hoped to connect amidst the chaos.

He was menacing. He stood just over 6-feet tall and had a muscular build. His eyes were dark and cold, and the soot on his face gave away the fact that he was the arsonist the police were looking for. It appeared he was using Decatur as a sort of home base, as the local fires had recently escalated. His name was Denny Gutierrez. He had grown up in Pana, Illinois and moved to Decatur after dropping out of high school and turning to a life of crime. At first he was into small petty crimes to keep himself fed and drunk all week, plus the occasional prostitute if he could afford it.

"Denny! We know you're here. We have the grounds surrounded." A loud voice over a police megaphone rang out in the crisp night air.

Denny's face was awash in fear. He knew they had him, but he wasn't about to go out without a fight. Desperation was in his eyes as he grabbed Sister Mary Rose tightly by the arm and pushed her around the back side of the administration building to a door he had propped open with a small stick. She was horrified to think they were going back inside the building she had just escaped from, knowing that the fire would be out of control. Smoke poured from the small opening in the door. This was certain death!

"Please, no!" she cried, but Denny didn't pay any attention.

"Denny. Give it up, son. Turn yourself in. There's no use dying here tonight. We've lost enough lives already!" the police boomed once again. There were multiple sirens blaring. Dismounted police were scouring the grounds, hoping to find the arsonist.

Sister Mary Rose could feel the tremendous heat on her face as they entered the basement from the north side. The smoke was thick, but they crawled toward a storage room, trying to stay below the smoke, but it was still difficult to breathe. Once inside the storage room, Denny found a bag of rags for cleaning and put two of them over his nose and mouth, then handed the older nun a handful.

Suddenly, loud voices were heard just outside the door, as the police must have seen them enter the building. Sister Mary Rose could hear the police breaking down doors, searching for them. Their muffled voices were difficult to hear amidst the chaos, and the incredible heat closed in on her left side. She began to feel light-headed and ready to pass out on the floor of the storage room. Denny was also feeling the effects of the smoke and the intense heat from the fire that was now breaching the wall to their left, which was the wall to the boiler room. Neither of them knew it was the boiler room on fire next to them, nor did they realize there were combustible materials present in there, like the buckets of coal and coal dust that left a black haze in the air at all times. In addition, there were various chemicals that the maintenance men used to clean out the boiler when it was not in use.

The tremendous explosion shook the foundation of the administration building. Everything shifted to the east and then to the west. The roof began to collapse as the flames shot out the top of the structure and completely consumed the inside. Denny Gutierrez was killed instantly when the boiler exploded as shards of metal tore through the plaster walls on each side, cutting him in half in less than a second. Sister Mary Rose survived the blast, although she suffered third degree burns over half her body. The blast left her nearly deaf for months, as her ear drums had shattered under the incredible pressure. The only thing that had saved her from the metal shrapnel was the fact that she had been lying on the floor behind a raised solid concrete base that held a hot water storage tank.

Three of the five police officers who had been searching the basement were also killed in the explosion. The other two barely escaped with their lives, thanks to some help from the fire department. They were also able to retrieve Sister Mary Rose from the storage room. It was a miracle that she was found before being consumed by the raging inferno.

After a month in Decatur Memorial Hospital, Sister Mary Rose spent the remaining months of recovery from her burns in a private Catholic hospital near Chicago. She also needed time to heal from the mental wounds of the ordeal. Eventually she was sent to a small Catholic church in Lexington, Kentucky in an attempt to give her a fresh start away from her experience in Decatur.

As she continued to toss and turn in her sleep, the nightmare ended and thankfully gave her a chance to sleep without terror. The bright pink skin of her burn scars glistened from sweat on her face, neck and upper body, as she finally settled in to sleep quietly in the small hours of the early morning.

6

In the dead silence, William Weeks slept soundly. He was on his back on the crude bunk in his isolation cell of C Dorm at the Peoria State Hospital. He had only been asleep for an hour when the dream began once again. For the past two weeks, William had been experiencing strange dreams that would be nightmares to any normal person, but he was at the hospital for good reason. Hacking up a mother, father, and four small children with a dull axe was a surefire way to end up there.

The Peoria police on the scene were shocked at the crime scene and said it was the worst they had ever witnessed. Several young officers had to step outside and vomit at the sights inside the house, especially the bedroom where he had killed all four of the children. It was a bloodbath beyond compare. Body parts were strewn about, and pools of blood were in nearly every room. The father, William's co-worker at the glass factory, was dead in the kitchen from a single axe wound to the head and face. The force had split his head like a melon. His wife must have put up a ferocious fight for her life, as her blood was on the walls and puddled along her escape route from William. She had his axe buried into the middle of her back, and she was found face down trying to reach the stairs to protect the children. William later told police that he had knelt down on her back and broken her neck to make sure she was really dead. He commented, "I always hated that bitch!" There was no doubt William was a violent and dangerous man, but his mental illness was what kept him from state prison and in the asylum.

Something beyond that was the reason he had been selected for such a strange mission.

It had been a month since he had met with Father Penning and the Abbot that first time. Their good faith down payment for his assignment, an attractive prostitute, was still fresh in his mind. She had served her purpose well, despite the fact she had spent a week in the hospital herself, and was still not able to go back to her line of work with all the ripping and tearing that William had done to her body cavities. The mental damage one night with William Weeks had done to the poor girl would last her a lifetime. She would see his menacing face and piercing steel-grey eyes at times in the dark, glaring at her like a pack of wolves on a fresh carcass.

In his dream on this night, William found himself in a large room with metal walls and ceilings and a concrete floor with a drain in the middle, covered with a round, rusting metal grate. It was like he was looking down on the scene below. He could see himself and the Abbot, along with Father Penning and several nuns in black habits and starched-white coifs. William felt himself being slowly lowered down, and as he got closer, he could hear what was being said. The Abbot was speaking from behind a simple wood podium, and the nuns were all kneeling before him. Some were holding hands, and it appeared most were crying or praying – or both. He could see himself, standing to the left of the Abbot, with a large knife in his hand and a strange smile on his face. It gave him goosebumps to see it. He was strangely aroused at what was taking place. William was conscious that there was a very dark and disturbing person coming from his own body. Even though he knew he was dreaming, it felt real.

Then he could hear the Abbot speaking in Latin, and he couldn't understand what he was saying. The wailing of the nuns set a very evil mood to the room. Suddenly, as though on cue, William saw himself step up to the front of the room while a nun in the front row came forward and fell to her knees before him. He grabbed her harshly by the head and twisted her, so she was now facing away from him. The nun was screaming. Her face was turning from bright red to a blueish-purple color. The rest of the nuns were crying louder, screaming, yet still on their knees and holding hands.

He was then shocked to see the knife come up from behind the nun, and he saw himself rake the long blade across her neck. Instantly, blood poured from the gaping wound and bubbled as she attempted to cry out. The nun slumped to the side, and another nun stood before him, bowing and then falling to her knees. He looked around the room to see Father Penning crying and shielding his face from what was going on. The priest's guilt was enormous, knowing he could have just fallen on the sword and confessed to his actual crimes, but instead he chose to make a pact with the Devil and let these atrocities go on.

The lens through which William could view the grisly scene began to fog up, and spatters of blood filtered the barbarity of it all. As the vision faded, the soundtrack continued to stay with him until he awoke from slumber, sweat-soaked but aroused.

******

On the second floor, getting ready to begin her day, Sister Bethany Christina noted the smell of freshly brewed coffee coming from downstairs and immediately thought about a late spring night in 1921. She had been eating an egg sandwich and drinking black coffee at the Hawkeye Grill in downtown Iowa City, Iowa, like she did most nights at 10:00 pm. She was taking her final vows that coming Sunday and was helping her uncle at his dry-cleaning business late at night for extra money to donate to the church. Sister Bethany Christina loved that she could have St. Paul's in Iowa City, as her first parish, where she had gone to church herself as a young girl. It was where she had felt the "draw to God", as she would explain when family and friends asked why she had decided to become a nun. Her grades in school were nearly perfect, and she could have gone to any university in the country. But she still wanted to join the convent and start the process as soon as possible.

On that night at the diner, before her shift at the dry cleaners, Sister Bethany Christina noticed a man sitting in a booth at the end of the row, facing the wall. It seemed odd that he wasn't facing the rest of the diner instead of staring at the wall, but that's how he sat for a very long time. When she couldn't stand the odd feeling any longer, she decided to go over and see if she could offer any assistance.

"Can I help you, sir?" she asked, standing next to him, and realized the man looked extremely troubled. His hair was greasy and askew, and he had a very heavy coat on for a spring evening. It appeared the man may be homeless.

His body odor was overwhelming as he turned slightly to face her. He didn't say anything, but he smiled and motioned for her to sit down. Sister Bethany Christina accepted the offer and took her coffee to sit across from the troubled man. She thought he was probably in his mid-40's. He had gaunt facial features, blonde hair, and graying facial hair stubble. She thought he could have been anyone's father, brother, uncle or co-worker who had fallen on some very hard times like so many others.

"The name is Lyle Miller, sister," he finally said in a very quiet voice, with a hint of a British accent. His discolored and rotting teeth were probably one of the reasons he didn't say much. He seemed embarrassed about it and looked down a lot, rarely making eye contact, which made him seem that much more disconcerting.

She smiled back, then sipped at her coffee. "Nice to meet you, Lyle. I'm Sister Bethany Christina. I am with St. Paul's Church."

"I haven't been to church in a real long time, sister. Not since I left London." He shifted slightly in his bench seat.

"That's OK. We all falter, Lyle."

"What I've done is a bit more than faltering, sister. A lot more." He stared down at the plate in front of him that was stained with egg yolk and bread crumbs from his toast.

She wasn't sure what to say. Instead, she just decided to listen. She sipped her coffee, noting she had only 30 minutes until she had to be at her uncle's dry cleaners. But she lost all track of time once Lyle started to loosen up and tell his tale. The nun had never heard someone speak with a British accent, and she was mesmerized by it. Living in Iowa, she was sheltered from anything other than Midwestern ways.

"Well, the first time I killed a woman, I didn't have sex with her right away. I cut on her for a few days, then I had sex with the parts," he said in the same monotone, quiet voice. His blank stare showed his incredible apathy and disconnect with reality.

Sister Bethany Christina's mind was swimming with what he was telling her. Four hours later, she had heard countless stories about the women he had killed. The nun convinced Lyle to turn himself in to police. She openly wept for his soul when they took him peacefully away in handcuffs. His distant stare was chilling.

******

Sister Marie Colette was also on the second floor of the former convent. She was making her way downstairs for breakfast. She too had smelled that fresh coffee, but that's not what made her think of the past. It was the clanging sound of the silverware on the dishes. That sound reminded her of a nice Easter dinner back in 1904 at Holy Family Church in Bloomington, Indiana. She could remember it like it was yesterday, especially when she heard that sound of the silverware. The murmur of voices also helped her recall the event. There were almost 20 people at that Easter dinner, sitting around a very large table set up in the church basement. The attendees were mostly the staff and volunteers at the church, with a few children who were orphans who had nowhere to eat their holiday meal.

She remembers Edward Van Note running down the stairs, out of breath, telling everyone there was a prisoner in the county jail who was threatening to kill himself. Sheriff Rogers sent him to the church to see if anyone could come help. The Sheriff was the only one at the jail, being Easter Sunday, so he couldn't handle the troubled man. Sister Marie Colette jumped up and volunteered to go help.

Sheriff Rogers greeted her at the jail entrance.

"Thank you so much, sister. I was hoping someone of faith could save this prisoner from killing himself. Especially being Easter Sunday," he said, shaking her hand.

As they walked, the Sheriff explained the situation, "His name is Dansart. Jack Dansart. He's here in Monroe County waiting for trial. He's a hobo. He's been riding trains all over the country and killing young girls along the way. He showed up drunk in a bar in Bloomington, talking about how he killed six college girls last time he was in town. An off-duty police officer heard what he was saying and arrested him."

Sister Marie Colette heard what the Sheriff was saying, but wanted to walk as quickly as she could to stop the man from hurting himself.

The Sheriff continued, "We were able to keep him for public intoxication, and when we began to check out his story, the details fell into place. Then we found the bodies right where he said they were at Evergreen Park on the west side of town. They were in a shallow grave, just like he said."

By the time they got to his cell at the end of the block, Jack Dansart was naked and standing on his bunk, with a makeshift noose around his neck. He had torn strips from his jail uniform to make it.

"Jack, please get that off your neck. You don't want to do this. God forgives you for whatever you may have done!" Sister Marie Colette cried out, seeing the disheveled man standing on the metal cot. Somehow he had tied the end of the noose to the light fixture on the ceiling.

The Sheriff was fumbling with his keys when, without warning, Jack jumped off the cot. The noose cinched up tight, loudly cracking the vertebrae in his neck. He was dead instantly.

Sister Marie Colette had never witnessed something like that and hoped she never would again. The sound made by the fabric noose as it rubbed against the metal light fixture was the only sound she heard. It was so loud, she covered her ears and closed her eyes tightly.

******

Sister Agnes Ignatious volunteered to help with the breakfast dishes before mass. She was excited when she heard the Abbot himself would be delivering the sermon. She grew up in a large family in Mount Vernon, Illinois and was the third of six daughters, so doing chores was something she was used to. She actually preferred working and doing chores, because it took her mind off things she'd rather forget about. Her mother and grandmother used to say, "idle hands are the Devil's workshop". She believed it.

Both her mother and grandmother were devout Catholics, so when she told them of her decision to become a nun, they were ecstatic. Her father didn't seem to care much at all about that or anything, as he was often drunk when he was around. He was having a problem finding work and drank his troubles away with the little money they had to eat with. Her mother took in extra money by mending clothes for people and doing extra housework. Her father would have been furious if he had found out, but her mother wasn't about to let the children go hungry. He was often gone for days at a time and wouldn't be the wiser. Sometimes, when she looked back, Sister Agnes Ignatious probably wanted to join the convent to get away from it. She loved her bible and everything about her faith, but getting out of Mount Vernon was paramount.

Upon graduating high school, Sister Agnes Ignatious had been sent to the Holy Rosary Church in Rocheport, Missouri to begin her studies at the convent there. It was a beautiful church and convent on a sprawling 150-acre patch of ground, just west of Columbia on route 40 and adjacent to the beautiful Big Muddy Fish and Wildlife Refuge. After her first year at the convent, as some of her privileges loosened up a bit, she would go fishing with some of the older nuns. She would recall many gorgeous spring and summer afternoons she could recall, pulling fish from the Missouri River and enjoying her time with the sisters, who now had become her family. She seldom wrote her family in Illinois, and since they didn't have a phone in the convent, there was no good way to reach them in 1908. There was a phone in the church office that was only used by the nuns in dire emergencies.

Standing at the sink now, washing the breakfast dishes, Sister Agnes Ignatious began to drift away to a time she would rather not think about. The background conversations of the other nuns and staff at the former convent cleaning up and preparing for the day began to quiet down to a whisper. These noises were replaced with the sound of a key fumbling in a lock and a male voice cursing under his breath. Slowly, as things came into focus, Sister Agnes Ignatious was able to ascertain with her remaining senses the environment she found herself in. It was dark and smelled of mildew – very strongly. She could hear dripping somewhere in another part of the large room she was in. Feeling around, Sister Agnes Ignatious knew she was in a closet or some sort of wooden barricade on three sides. The fourth side was a wet brick wall. The floor was dirt, and it, too, was damp. She had a threadbare blanket in the corner and a bucket to use for a bathroom, which stunk horribly. There was some dirt thrown in to help cover the smell, but it was still pungent in the dank, musty air.

She didn't know how long she had been in that closet. Time seemed to stand still while she wondered if she would ever make it out alive. Sister Agnes Ignatious prayed constantly and found tremendous strength to survive. It may have been days, weeks or months she was there. She really had no idea.

Later, she had woken up in a hospital bed, her entire body paralyzed with tremendous pain. Even her head hurt if she moved it, and she was trying to look around and figure out what hospital she was in. She had spent time at all the area hospitals, working with the other nuns on to help the infirmed, and their grieving families.

"Sister, I'm glad you're with us again," said a nurse, sitting at her bedside, smiling.

"Where am I?" Sister Agnes Ignatious asked, her voice cracking slightly. She sipped some water. The nurse helped her.

"Columbia General. You've been here for two days. The doctors didn't think you would make it with all the blood you lost."

When Sister Agnes Ignatious heard the word "blood", she began to have flashbacks of what had put her at Columbia General Hospital. She remembered the closet being lit up with a large flashlight and a firm hand reaching in and pulling her out by her hair. She remembered it being pitch black, aside from the beam of the strong light, and when the light moved around, she got a quick glance at his face. He was very young, some peach fuzz on his chin, yet his eyes were sinister. He looked as if something had snapped inside of him, causing his mind to decay into madness. His eyes were distant, a window into his dark soul. She didn't know it at the time, but he was Billy Thompson, a junior at the University of Missouri. He was registered in an English class, two literature courses, speech, and a music class. Billy was failing all of them, because he hadn't been to class since the first week of the fall semester. Something in his brain had snapped, and he became unhinged. He became obsessed with a girl across the street from his rental house in Columbia. That's when everything fell apart. She became his first victim.

The nurse continued, "you also have several broken bones, sister. The femur will take a while to heal, and I'm sure you'll have some pain to manage with it."

Sister Agnes Ignatious had wanted to reply, but she could see Billy's fists coming down on her head repeatedly. Blood was flying from her mouth. She desperately tried to cover her face and shield the blows. The next thing she knew, he was ripping her habit off and spreading her legs on a large wooden table that appeared to be in the middle of the room. Her vision was hazy, but she could make out a shelf along the wall. On it appeared to be severed heads! She couldn't tell for sure how many, despite the fact her eyes were becoming adjusted to the darkness. There were at least three, and she feared she was going to be next, as he locked manacles around her wrists and ankles, forcing her into a spread-eagle position on the table. Below the heads was a crooked, wooden sign. "Idle hands are the Devil's workshop".

She remembered praying out loud, hoping someone would save her from what she believed the young man was about to do. He was salivating at her young and fit naked body, as it writhed on the wooden table, struggling at the manacles to break free. She could hear him taking his belt off as he began to undress, still fixated on her naked breasts and vagina. His dirty hands groped her as she recoiled.

"Please don't do this," she begged, quietly under her breath. Her eyes were shut tight. "Please don't."

Billy merely laughed. He put his face between her thighs and began licking at her vagina. The sensation made her want to vomit. She didn't understand why he was doing it.

As he thrust himself inside her, Sister Agnes Ignatious began to cry. She didn't know if this would mean her removal from the convent. Obviously, she had vowed to be chaste, but yet she didn't know how the church would look at her being raped. Or worse yet, what if she became pregnant with his tainted seed? It would be an abomination in the eyes of God, and she didn't know if that meant her eternal damnation. Monsignor Pendergast would know, but she was afraid at what he might say. Now she was oblivious to his grunting, thrusting, and sweat raining down on top of her. All she could think about was God and how he was looking at this despicable act.

Now the nurse held her hand, and the other hand touched Sister Agnes Ignatious' stomach.

"We did give you a pregnancy test when you were admitted."

The young nun turned her head away from the nurse. She didn't want to hear.

"You were pregnant. Two months."

"Were?" the sister asked.

"You miscarried yesterday, sister. It's probably better that way." The nurse felt so bad for the battered nun. She looked horrible, covered in welts and bruises, as well as serious internal injuries and broken bones. It was the mental anguish she surely suffered that bothered the nurse the most. Now that she was awake, the healing could finally begin. She knew it would take a lifetime.

"What happened to him? Did they catch him? You know, the man that did this to me," Sister Agnes Ignatious asked, making eye contact again with the nurse. The nun's eyes were a beautiful hazel color.

"Yes. The police shot him upon arrival. A neighbor heard your screaming. Probably saved your life." The nurse was writing something down on a clipboard.

Sister Agnes Ignatious stared out the window for a long time after that discussion. She feared for her soul and what would come of it now. As she snapped back to reality and the year 1927, there still was the question of her soul and how she would be judged. It scared her to think about it even 18 years later.

******

In his private residence at St. Michael's Academy, the Abbot was lying in bed, enjoying what he was seeing on the minds of the various people that were part of the pilgrimage. Some played major roles, while other roles were small. Yet every one of them was important in order to see this to the end. After years and years of intense study and orchestrating the plan over and over in his head, it was now finally coming to fruition. Thanks to his endless hours of research and a refinement of his vast mental talent, the Abbot could read the minds of most everyone if he concentrated hard enough. Sometimes that became a terrible thing, as it was difficult to discern between the things he heard from the background noise. Sometimes the visions came in many at a time, and it was difficult to sort them out. He did enjoy the dreams and visions the nuns were having at the former convent, because he knew the more disturbing the sinners they encountered, had been the more likely his plan was to become reality. There were some parts of the plan he researched that were unclear, and with those areas, the Abbot found himself having to add some of his own flair to the ceremony. Though the journals of Wilfred Weeks contained the most minute details, there were sections that appeared to be strangely vague.

What warmed his ice-cold heart the most was what he saw from William Weeks and his dream about the killing ritual that would take place at the conclusion of the pilgrimage. Most would have recoiled in terror at seeing themselves commit such violent and heinous acts, especially to a room full of nuns. William was aroused at the idea. In fact, upon waking up in his isolation cell at the Peoria State Hospital, William went over to the small toilet in his cell and masturbated. He was so aroused at the idea of killing all those nuns in the bloody and morbid fashion that had been laid out that he found himself without an option other than masturbate to completion. While he stroked himself, William thought of how easy the knife cut their throats and the sensation of their warm blood across the front of his body and crotch. While William stroked himself, the Abbot smiled and felt like he may need to do the same thing. He thought about it, but instead called for the young novitiate, since she had become so adept at performing whatever sex act he could dream of.

As soon as the novitiate was done servicing him, the Abbot rose and reviewed the sermon he was to deliver in an hour. He had a busy day ahead.

7

The staff of St. Michael's Academy were preparing the large dining room on the main floor at the former convent for a dinner. The Abbot had told Father Williams, the prior of St. Michael's, what his plans were for the meal and who would be attending. The list was rather long and surprised the prior, who didn't know what the occasion was. The Abbot frequently had private dinners set up for himself and various guests, but the list for this dinner was nearly 30 people, not including the Abbot himself. On the list was all the staff who had been working at the former convent since the nuns had arrived, various clergy from the church, and of course the nuns themselves.

Father Williams had heard about the visiting nuns who were staying at the convent, since they were arranging meals for the sisters, as well as seeing them at mass each day. He did note that most of the nuns were elderly and kept to themselves, for the most part. They were being sequestered in the former convent, which was on the opposite side of the campus from where most of the staff were found and not connected to any other building, except for the tunnel that connected the building to the hot water and steam mechanical system.

The sequestration was by the design of the Abbot. He wanted to keep them away from the rest of the staff as best he could, and even the four groups of nuns had no idea the others were staying at the former convent building. The Abbot purposefully had the groups arrive at different times of the day and night and had them taken directly to the floor where they would be staying. Even the three other priests, who had accompanied each of the groups, were being kept in the guest rooms at the monastery and at an arm's length from the Abbot. He had his eyes on them all and had several of the monks keeping him informed of what they were doing each day. The entire affair was like a giant chessboard, and the Abbot was staying at least two to three moves ahead, as his diabolical mind purred like a Swiss watch.

Never a man to leave anything to chance, the Abbot was meticulous in his planning. He had the groups of nuns go to a different mass each day, to minimize them seeing each other moving about the campus. He had his reasons, and no one questioned his demands. Fathers Rosa, Bartolini, and Wilkes were given more privileges, but they were low key and spent most of their time in their rooms, at daily mass, or in the company of the Abbot. After the horrible experienced each had endured since their last time at St. Michael's, the priests hoped to enjoy some rest and relaxation. But in the two months they had been at St. Michael's, the nightmares they were having did not relent. The Abbot made sure that the intensity was increased a notch at a time, until the three priests were nearly driven mad by the visions.

Father Williams assisted the Abbot in selecting the menu for the dinner, and he made sure that the head chef, Brother Francis, spared no expense to get the very best ingredients to pull it together. Since it was only a week from Christmas Eve, they had decided to go with a holiday-themed meal featuring both lamb and ham, accompanied by an array of succulent side dishes to satisfy the desires of all in attendance. The prior assumed the Abbot just wanted to thank everyone for working extra hours attending to the nuns at the former convent, and maybe he even had a bit of holiday spirit enter his cold demeanor. The prior enlisted the help of his subprior, Father McBride, to get the dining room ready. He had the staff moving quickly to set up the tables, polish the plates and silverware, and set up burners to keep things warm and ice chests to keep things cool. A large radio in the corner of the room played Duke Ellington and other popular music, as well as holiday songs, while everyone worked together to transform the dining hall into a stunning display. The prior knew his boss was a stickler for details, so he was doing his best to keep everyone on task. He had even hired a small band to play during the dinner, and they were setting up and checking their equipment. In less than four hours the dining room would be full, and only the Abbot knew the real purpose of the whole thing. Whatever it was, then prior knew it would be one to remember!

***** *

In the basement of the former convent, Sister Margaret Mary was getting ready for dinner. All day she had been hearing about the holiday dinner the Abbot had planned, and that he was going to speak to the group after they ate. She had been at the former convent with the other two nuns, whom she had never met before they all arrived on that same day in October. After a little more than two months at St. Michael's, she thought it would be nice to meet some other people and find out what the purpose of this trip was. As a nun, she was taught not to ask questions and to trust that God would lead the way. The other two elderly nuns, who were staying in the basement with Sister Margaret Mary, suffered from typical health problems brought on by old age, and the incoming harsh winter weather was giving them ideas of retiring somewhere warm. The rooms in the basement were especially warm, since they were next to the boiler room.

The incredible smells coming from upstairs, especially the roasted lamb and baked ham, not only made Sister Margaret Mary hungry, but brought her back to eight years before when she was working at St. Peter's church in Killeen, Texas. She was in charge of a group of nuns and two young priests from the various Catholic churches in the area, who were bringing holiday meals to hospitals and nursing homes. It was a cold afternoon, a week before Christmas, and they were spreading holiday cheer at the Darnall Army Medical Hospital on the base at Fort Hood.

The soldiers in the hospital were enjoying the holiday dinners and Christmas music when a nurse came rushing in.

"We need a priest to deliver last rites!" she cried out, looking around the room full of the nuns and two young priests.

Father Driscoll stood up. "I can do it," he said, grabbing his bible and rosary.

"Thank you, Father," the nurse said. "Please hurry!"

"Sister Margaret Mary, why don't you come and help me?"

She stood up, knowing the young priest had probably never had to give last rites before, but since taking her final vows almost 20 years before, she had seen it done many times. She nodded respectfully to Father Driscoll and left the ward, following him and the nurse. The Christmas music and cheer in the ward was now quickly diminishing in the background.

As they walked quickly down the hall, they could hear a commotion in one of the patient rooms in the emergency department, as a flurry of doctors and nurses were working on a patient bleeding profusely on a gurney. The patient was a male in his early 40's, in obvious distress, as bright red blood was dripping to the floor and one of the doctors was pushing down on his chest, doing compressions.

One of the other doctors stepped forward when he saw Father Driscoll.

"He's fading fast, Father. He said he's a Catholic. Please get busy, he's delirious from the blood loss."

Father Driscoll nodded and began to take out his rosary. Sister Margaret Mary reached for the patient's hand. It was soaked in blood and trembling. She held it firmly.

"What happened to this man?" Father Driscoll asked, trying to hide the fact he was nervous giving the last rites for the first time. He was thankful the experienced nun was there with him.

"He was shot by police in Harker Heights. They'd been chasing him for miles. He's been on the run from Austin," said the doctor. "He drives a truck. They said he's the one they've been looking for that's been killing the older ladies and stealing their money."

Sister Margaret Mary had heard of the story in the newspapers. The man was Wayne Roscoe, and they suspected he had killed a dozen women throughout the south. As the doctor said, the police had been looking for him over the past two months. From the sound of it, one of the bullet wounds was in his chest, as the medical staff fought to keep his blood pressure under control. He was also shot in the left shoulder, abdomen, and his lower right leg. Due to the loss of blood, he was dying quickly.

Father Driscoll was doing his best to keep his composure, but he was having a difficult time with all the chaos, beeping, yelling, and screaming. He took a deep breath to shake it off.

"Is there anything you want to confess, son? An act of contrition?" said Sister Margaret Mary, squeezing his hand as bubbles of blood formed on the killer's lips.

The man was trying to say something, but she couldn't make it out.

"I believe in God, the Father Almighty, creator of heaven and earth," began the priest, making the sign of the cross.

Again, the dying man was moving his lips, as if trying to say something. Droplets of blood were spattering.

"What is he trying to say?" asked the priest, sweat pouring down his face.

Amidst the chaos in the emergency department, the dying killer managed to say one last thing with his dying breath, "Go fuck yourself, Father."

Then the man spit blood into the faces of both Father Driscoll and Sister Margaret Mary. The red mist peppered their faces. And with that, he passed on to the land of the dead, leaving the nurses, doctors, and especially Sister Margaret Mary and Father Driscoll, stunned at his final words, blood dripping down their quivering countenances.

******

Sister Mary Johana was in her basement room at the former convent, putting her shoes on, as she prepared to go upstairs for dinner. She had been smelling the food all afternoon, and it was very enticing. The meals they had been given since arriving at St. Michael's were decent, but rather bland. She was feeling the constant sharp pain in her lower back and the ache in her left knee that sometimes kept her up at night in pain. In her mid-70's, Sister Mary Johana was ready to go out to a church in California, where her brother and sister lived. The plan had been that when she got to the point where she was ready to slow down, the church would move her to San Diego, where she had family, and with a climate that would be much kinder to her aging vessel.

The pain in her lower back brought her back to 1915 in Boulder, Colorado when she was at St. James High School. She was teaching history to freshman and sophomore boys and girls. She loved teaching and being around teenagers. There was also a beautiful Catholic church in Boulder, St. Mark's, and she loved attending mass there and helping whenever they asked. They had bingo on Friday and Saturday nights, and Sister Mary Johana was more than happy to volunteer. She was still young enough to enjoy the weather in Boulder, skiing every chance she got. She even took groups of teenagers from the school on regular trips to the slopes. It kept her young, and the kids enjoyed it a great deal.

It was October of 1915, and Sister Mary Johana was walking back to the school after helping at St. Mark's. She had left her lesson plan in her classroom, and she needed to go over it for the following day. The school was closed, but she thought she saw a dim light in one of the basement windows. Thinking it may have been left on by mistake, she entered the basement using her key. Once inside, she heard the screams of a young boy. Alarmed, she ran toward the sound, not knowing what could possibly be the cause of the blood-curdling cries.

As Sister Mary Johana turned the corner, she saw the naked body of a day laborer who had become a fixture around the school, Rasmus Rantoul, sodomizing one of her young freshman students, William Ashby. William was a meek and timid student who kept to himself. Rasmus was 19 years old and was part of a large mountain family that resided in a rural area not far from Boulder. He typically worked for one of the contractors that the State of Colorado hired to clear trees and rock to allow for more roads connecting Boulder to other areas. Rasmus was a strong, gangly boy who grew up working hard for his family to survive.

"What are you doing?" she cried out, picking up a piece of metal angle iron that was on the windowsill. William was whimpering, trying to pull up his pants. Blood was trickling down the back of his leg.

Rasmus glared at her, not even attempting to put on any clothes. Sister Mary Johana tried not to look at his lean body, glistening with sweat in the dim light.

"You wanna be next, sister?" he laughed. He took a step closer, and she could smell the strong body odor emitting from his pores.

William managed to get his pants up and ran for the door.

"Go and get some help!" she called out as he scampered away into the night.

Rasmus laughed. "Just me and you now, sis. You want me to do you like I did that little sissy? Hell, I've had at least ten little Nancy boys around here the same way. Right in the cornhole!" She could smell the whiskey on his breath.

Sister Mary Johana began to pray for him, under her breath quietly, as he took another step closer. She gripped the three-foot piece of angle iron in her right hand. In the shadows, he didn't see that she had picked it up. Rasmus was focused on the nun and smirking with the thought of bending her over the small table, like he had so many before. She wouldn't be able to stop him. He forgot all about William for the time being. Sister Mary Johana looked almost angelic in the soft light of the single bulb overhead.

He was only a step away when she reared back and hit him with all she had on the side of his head with the rusted metal. A loud crack resounded as Rasmus fell to a knee, his head reeling and wracked with a sharp pain.

"You fucking bitch!" he cried out, as his right hand grabbed her habit and spun her around. She fell to the concrete floor as he stood up, his 6-foot frame looming over her. The look in his eyes was like she was peering at Satan himself. The mountain boy who labored day in and day out was merely a host for whatever evil resided within.

"Our Father, who art in Heaven," she began as he kicked her hard in her lower back. Rasmus reached down and pulled her up off the floor. He threw her on the table where he had raped the young boy only moments before, his naked body drenched in sweat, but ready for round two with the dazed nun.

"Stop right there, Rasmus!" screamed out Jasper Rawlings, a farmer who had a place just west of the school. William must have run there, hoping to find help for Sister Mary Johana quickly.

Rasmus reached down and tore her habit nearly in half, as the nun lay on her back, the room spinning before her. Then a blast rang out, as Jasper Rawlings raised his shotgun, knocking Rasmus off his feet and halfway across the room. He was dead, full of buckshot, before he hit the floor. In the coming weeks, the story of Rasmus Rantoul would unfold as dozens of young boys in Boulder and other smaller communities came forward, telling police that he had tormented them as well. He had threatened to kill the boys and their families if they had told what happened, and now that Rasmus was dead, they felt they could come forward.

The sharp pain in her lower back constantly reminded Sister Mary Johana of that terrible night in October with Rasmus Rantoul.

******

The sound of a truck pulling away from the former convent reminded Sister Mary Johana of an incredibly hot day in the desert north of Sedona, Arizona. It was July of 1922, and she had been taking a bus trip with other nuns to see the Grand Canyon. It was nearly a three-hour trip, and in the intense heat of the summer, the bus offered little relief, even with all the windows opened. She had been at Epiphany Catholic Church in Cottonwood for only a month when she heard about the bus trip, and she figured it would be wonderful to see the Grand Canyon for herself. Some of the nuns had taken the trip many times before and told her it would be one she would not want to miss.

They were only ten miles south of Flagstaff when they saw a car on the side of the road, with its hood up, and steam rising into the blue Arizona sky. There appeared to be a man, lying down in the shoulder of the road, next to the broken-down car.

"Driver! Please, let's stop and see if we can help that poor man," cried out one of the sisters on the bus.

The older bus driver, mopping his brow with a handkerchief, looked into the rearview mirror, obviously not enthused about stopping in the incredible heat.

"Please, driver. That man needs help!" said one of the nuns, as an uproar of discontent began to percolate in the back of the bus. Though he objected, the driver could not live with the guilt of passing the distressed motorist and pulled over.

Sister Mary Johana and two other nuns were the first to assess the situation. The man was in painter's whites, probably in his mid-30's, and was lying on the gravel of the shoulder, barely breathing, as sweat poured profusely from his body. Sister Mary Johana took his left hand and squeezed it tightly, hoping he would know they were there. He was unconscious. They wondered if the man would be alive.

"Get us some water from the cooler!" she called out to the nuns standing near the bus.

In a few seconds, she had a cup of water, and with the help of the other two nuns, they propped up the man and tried to give him a drink. His lips were cracked and hot, his body was covered in sweat and he began to shiver as a weak breeze swept across the highway. His eyes fluttered as he tried to say something.

Sister Mary Johana smiled and said, "Don't say anything, my son. Just drink the water. Save your energy."

The man was not coherent. He smiled back at her and then limply fell back to the ground. The nuns checked for a pulse, but there was none. Sister Mary Johana let his hand go and set it on his chest. A tear rolled down her cheek.

The newspapers would explain the story.

PRESCOTT MAN SUSPECTED IN MURDER OF TWO COLLEGE GIRLS

Police report that Arthur Chesterfield, a 34-year-old man from Prescott, was found dead on the side of highway 17, just south of Flagstaff, on Tuesday. A bus carrying a church group to the Grand Canyon found the man unresponsive next to his car, which had apparently broken down. While searching the car, police discovered a distinctive woman's bracelet, which the family of one of the missing University of Arizona students, who went missing in May, claimed she was wearing. Upon searching Chesterfield's rented home, they found both girls buried in shallow graves near a flower garden. Coroner Thomas Kincaid reported that both girls appeared to have been raped and tortured, as they both bore similar burn marks and cuts all over their bodies. He could not discern how long they were kept captive. Chesterfield was a single man with no known children, working as a house painter and traveling around the southwest for the past ten years. He was born and grew up in Little Rock, Arkansas. Police believe he may have killed others, but at this time, there is no evidence of other crimes. Police throughout the southwest are checking for any unsolved murders or missing person reports, to see if Chesterfield could have been responsible for other heinous acts.

******

The twelve nuns were stunned when they stepped into the dining room. On display was a room full of holiday décor, a wonderful spread of food, a band playing "Parade of the Wooden Soldiers" in the corner of the room, and dozens of faces that some of them were familiar with since their time at St. Michael's Academy. The Abbot was at the head of one of the long tables, laughing and conversing with several of the staff who had prepared the dinner. There were three priests sitting at the same table, the very same priests who had accompanied the nuns on their trips across the country. The prior and subprior were present, along with Brother Francis, who was checking to be sure the food was getting out to the guests. Everyone appeared to be very happy, and it may have been since it was only a week until Christmas and holiday cheer was in abundance.

The Abbot stood up and motioned for the band to be quiet for a moment. The guests, who were all now seated at their assigned places, waited to hear from him. They all felt very special being included in such a fancy affair.

"Thank you all for coming to dinner tonight. I would like to thank Brother Francis and his wonderful staff for putting this all together, on relatively short notice," he said, as a resounding applause erupted in the room. Brother Francis nodded, obviously taken aback by the accolades of the usually ice-cold Abbot.

"I would also like to thank all the staff here for taking good care of our special guests at this old convent building. You've all brought the place to life these past two months, and I appreciate it." He smiled broadly, until it almost hurt.

"Please enjoy your food and the wonderful music provided by Clarence Knight and the Lakeshore Orchestra," he added, then sat down. Clarence Knight bowed slightly, and his band resumed as the guests began to eat the tremendous feast before them.

The prior, standing next to the Abbot, leaned down to say something in his ear, "I don't think I've seen you this happy in your time here at St. Michael's."

The Abbot, still smiling, stared straight ahead and said simply, "It's Christmas, Father. Now go on and enjoy your dinner as well."

"I can't wait until Wednesday. My brother and his family are coming for a visit and to stay for Christmas. I haven't seen my nephews in over a year." He sat down next to the Abbot.

The Abbot smiled and replied, "That sounds wonderful. I'm sure you'll have a great time with them." He sipped his red wine and took in the surroundings, pleased with how the night was unfolding so far. The Abbot shifted slightly in his seat, as his erect penis began to dig uncomfortably into the side of his thigh.

******

As the dinner plates were being cleared away by the kitchen staff, the Abbot rose once again, this time to a podium at the front of the dining room.

"Our guests who have been staying here will be leaving us tomorrow. They will embark on a pilgrimage of the state, visiting various hospitals, infirmaries, and asylums to help those who are in dire need. They will be spreading a message of love at Christmastime that we hope will help these lost members of the flock, so they do not feel alone." His feigned sincerity fooled even his sharpest critics in the crowd.

Sister Mary Johana felt tears well up in her eyes, knowing that she would be a part of what the Abbot was describing. Some of the other twelve nuns had the same reaction. They were all sitting at a special table at the front of the room. The Abbot smiled at her, as if he knew what she was thinking, and the nun felt a warm glow sweep over her body.

The Abbot continued, "Our very own Sister Mary Concordia will be escorting the nuns on the trip."

Sister Mary Concordia was also seated at the main table, next to Father Wilkes. She had known about the trip for several months now but didn't realize they were leaving in the morning.

Suddenly the lights went out. The dining room was pitch black.

"There is nothing to worry about," the Abbot said from the podium. We will have this fixed in a moment. Please stay seated, and do not panic."

Suddenly Father Rosa stood up, and with the help of Father Bartolini and Father Wilkes, they led the twelve nuns, along with Sister Mary Concordia, to the rear of the dining room. There they were taken to a staircase and down into the basement. As they left the room, they could hear the chatter increase, as the darkness began to make the guests uneasy. Hearing the movement of some around them, while the Abbot told the guests to stay seated, was concerning some.

"Please hurry, sisters," whispered Father Rosa at the head of the procession to the basement. "We must hurry."

Father Bartolini was the last one in the group, and he placed a small block of wood beneath the door to prevent anyone in the dining room from opening it. He followed the group into the boiler room, where they were taken to the entrance of the steam tunnel. A blast of hot air poured from the tunnel as they stooped slightly to enter, led by Father Rosa, who had gone over this route several times. It was dark and dreary; the hiss of steam could be heard along the humid concrete walkway. Sister Mary Concordia was scared, knowing the diabolical nature of the Abbot. She was aware of what he was capable of. She began to wonder if she would ever see St. Michael's Academy again.

******

Panic began to take hold, as it had been nearly ten minutes since the lights went out in the dining room. The Abbot was outside, having left through the only door that led to the exterior of the building. The December air was chilly, but it felt invigorating to him, knowing things appeared to have gone according to plan.

"Go on and block the door, Brother Michael," he told the young monk standing next to him. "Once you do that, go on and get this started, just like we talked about. Then I want you to meet me outside the monastery, at the north door, so I can explain what happens next."

"Yes, Abbot." The young monk ran off into the cool night air to fulfill the command.

The Abbot briskly walked across the campus to the north door of the monastery, and that was when he smelled the smoke for the first time. Two fires, simultaneously set outside the dining room, would quickly erupt in a ball of fire to be seen for miles against the backdrop of a clear night sky. There were only three doors that led from the dining room, and each of them were securely blocked off to prevent anyone from leaving. His only regret, standing in the shadows, was that he was not able to hear the screams of those trapped inside. The prior, who had looked forward to the visit from his family, scratched and banged on the door that led to the basement until most of the skin was gone from his fingers and hands, but to no avail. Father Bartolini saw to that. Brother Francis, who had been standing outside the kitchen when the lights first went out, was trapped like the rest. He was trampled by the rush of people who thought that the kitchen might offer an escape route. One of the fires set by Brother Michael was inside the exhaust that led from the ovens to the outside air. They quickly discovered that there was no way out through the kitchen, as the fire seemed to rage from all directions, while they beat and clawed at the concrete walls. The fire engulfed them with vigor, as inhuman screams and guttural cries for help went unanswered.

Brother Michael was out of breath when he arrived at the north entrance as instructed. He did not see the Abbot and assumed he got there before him. He didn't understand why he was asked to start the fires, but he knew better than to question the Abbot. Brother Michael felt honored that the priest trusted him with such an important task. He was also grateful that he was not one of the condemned, sentenced to die a miserable and painful death inside the dining room.

"You've done well, my son," the Abbot said, stepping from the shadows, and burying a knife into the young monk's sternum. Brother Michael resisted briefly, then was overcome as the blade sunk deeper inside, twisting and turning through his flesh, like the tender roast of lamb at dinner.

******

The Abbot made his way back to the dining room and was amazed at the destruction the fire had delivered. Two of the four walls were already collapsed, and now the fire was spreading to the remainder of the former convent. He wasn't concerned about the blocked doors, as there would be nothing left of the building by the time the fire department showed up. The Abbot also knew that arson would be the last thing the fire department would suggest. The fire chief and two of his staff were members of the group that met in the woods each month, paying homage to Satan himself. The Abbot had spoken with the chief earlier in the week to remind him of the details, and he was assured they would have a skeleton crew on that evening and would take longer to arrive at the scene than usual. The Abbot's instructions to the chief were to let the former convent burn to the point that demolition of the remaining structure was the only option feasible.

There would be 67 dead from the fire. There were no witnesses left behind to talk about the twelve nuns who had stayed there for the past two months. Brother Michael's body was discovered near the monastery, and it was assumed that he had something to do with the fire, but that he was likely murdered by an accomplice still on the run.

The three priests moved the thirteen nuns through the tunnel to the infirmary building, where they would be safe until morning, when they would leave the grounds for good to begin their journey. The Abbot of course knew it was a death march to Bartonville and the Peoria State Hospital. That was where the final plan would take place and his life's work realized.

The wailing of sirens could be heard in the distance as the Abbot patiently waited and prepared to embody incredible sorrow and pain for the loss of so many lives, especially this close to Christmas. He would tell the reporters who arrived that he was thankful that the rest of the staff at St. Michael's were off on holiday vacations, and so they were not present at the dinner. The local news coverage of the fire would report emphatically that the Abbot was found trying to save people from the dining room, but was unable to successfully do so. Details would include that his face was coated in soot and his hands were cut from the efforts. The Abbot was treated for minor burns at a local hospital that night and released soon after.

He had not slept so peacefully as when he returned to his private quarters.

8

The steam locomotive was screaming down the tracks, making an ungodly screeching sound of metal-on-metal, as the Abbot ran down the aisle of the passenger car. His eyes were wild and full of dread. His hair, usually coiffed and ever-perfect, was soaked in sweat and askew. His mouth was wide open and screaming, but no sound was audible over the hideous sound of the Abraham Lincoln, of the Chicago line, as it careened from side to side through the turns along the route south toward Joliet.

The Abbot saw no one in the seats, though they were filled. The passengers were all dead, eyes staring off longingly to a time when they were not deceased. He was running from car to car, but saw nothing ahead of him. Behind him, he could hear the swishing and sloshing sounds of what he knew was nearly upon him. His heart was thundering inside his chest, as he could hear the incredible beating sounds in cadence to his feet running as fast as they could. No matter how fast he ran, it felt as if he were running in place.

He paused for a brief moment to catch his breath. Like his heart beating wildly, the Abbot could hear the tremendous whooshing sound of the air going in and out of his lungs, despite the insane whine of the locomotive on the metal tracks below. Before he moved forward again, the Abbot looked back. Just as he feared, it was coming fast, and even though he shut the door behind him, the incredible force broke through the metal and tempered glass as if it were made of warm butter. Shards flew in all directions as the Abbot turned to run, pieces of metal and glass tearing through his flesh like shrapnel. The passengers at each side of the aisle began to grab at him as he bounced from seat to seat, in a frenzy, intoxicated with utter dread and madness. The bony fingers dug into his skin, while the Abbot twisted and turned away from them, in his desperate run to make it to the next car.

It made its way down the aisle behind the Abbot. A coppery smell was evident as he began to feel the mist on the back of his neck. Then his feet began to lose traction on the metal floor of the passenger car, now slick with the liquid that was fast overtaking the doomed priest. The passengers at each side of him were standing up as the car was tilting dramatically from one side to the other, the liquid now sloshing at knee level. The Abbot didn't know what to do, yet he kept pushing onward. The undead were tore at the skin on his face and chest as blood cascaded down his body. He fell down to one knee as the river of blood swept over him. The power of the flow knocked him against the door that led to the next car. His body jolted to a stop. He could feel the blood enter his mouth and begin to fill his lungs, slowly drowning him. The undead continued to grab and claw at his skin as he began to lose consciousness. The light began to fade, and the Abbot felt himself drift from the world of the living to an incredible blackness that was never-ending.

******

Father Rosa was also in one of the passenger cars on the Abraham Lincoln. Sitting on either side of him were the frozen bodies of the dead, their vacant eyes burning through him. He also saw the Abbot, running by as a wave of crimson blood washed through the car, taking everything with it, like a spinning cyclone of water down an awaiting drain. Father Rosa cried out to the Abbot as he went by, but the older priest paid no attention. His mouth was fixed in an open position, screaming out, but no sound could be heard. Father Rosa's ears were bleeding from the incredible roar of the locomotive, and when he gazed out the small window to his right at the fleeting landscape, sparks were observed coming up from the tracks as they moved at warp speed into oblivion.

******

Father Wilkes was in another one of the passenger cars. He was cornered by the undead. They tore at his writhing body, like an army of ants moving in slow motion on its prey. He felt no pain, but he knew the end was near. The passengers around him tore at his eyes, and the final thing he saw was the Abbot falling to his knees as a wave of bright red blood engulfed them within moments. Father Wilkes thrashed about in desperation, trying to get free of the dozens of claw-like hands pulling him down to the floor of the passenger car. The blood was thick and hot, almost to the point of boiling, and his final thoughts were of death and why he didn't see a bright light at the end of a tunnel. He saw nothingness and felt incredibly empty as his body was hurled end over end into the solid metal wall of the train car.

******

Father Bartolini was in the last passenger car. He stood paralyzed with fear at the door, his face up against the glass, the horror show playing out before him. He had first watched Father Rosa screaming out as his ears bled in the cacophony of metal screeching sounds. Then the wave of blood had swept over him, taking the priest down with the rest of the undead passengers. Father Wilkes had been next, after being cornered by the rotting corpses that moved ever closer, and overwhelmed him by sheer numbers. He, too, was overtook by the river of blood as it tore through the train cars – one after the other until it splashed up against the door where Father Bartolini stood. He saw the entire scene play out, ending with the Abbot running frantically down the aisle, his eyes intense and sweat pouring down his face as he ran faster and faster, hoping to make it to the next car. Father Bartolini tried desperately to open the door, even if it were only a small crack, to allow the Abbot access to the last passenger car. He was unable to budge the handle that appeared to be frozen shut. Father Bartolini pounded on the glass now, the Abbot was nearly upon him, but he was unable to do anything but watch as his mentor fell to a knee, and then become swept up in the mayhem. The blood was nearly six feet high and nearly taller than the door. Father Bartolini could see nothing.

From behind him, the middle-aged priest heard an unholy rumbling sound. It was as if the metal and glass around him in the passenger car were straining against incredible pressure. His ears began to pop as the strange sensation constricted his breathing. The creaking of metal stressed beyond its breaking point and bolts snapping in two, acquiescing to the pressure, were coming from every direction. The last thing he remembered was being covered in the raging river of blood. The entire passenger car gave way to the force and disintegrated to nothing along the tracks, as if it were never there.

******

The next morning, only hours after the fire that brought the former convent to embers, the three priests sat down for breakfast with the Abbot. They had spent the last few hours sleeping on cots in the infirmary, and they were now in a small conference room where the Abbot had arranged a simple breakfast before the nuns left on their trip. One of the young monks from the kitchen staff had prepared the meal, consisting of eggs, bacon, fried potatoes, and toast, with lots of coffee. The Abbot had refrained from the coffee, saying he already had a cup before the priests arrived and that it was not agreeing with him. The nuns were given hard boiled eggs and fruit with some milk on the other end of the first floor of the infirmary in the cafeteria.

Each of the men sitting around the table looked at one another, not realizing they all had the same horrific nightmare before joining together for breakfast. Even the Abbot, who was typically stoic and beyond emotion, was unnerved at the strange dream of the train car. It seemed so real, and the fact that he could still feel the wetness of the blood, really made him wonder if there was some significance to it. However, he would do his best to keep his mind on task as the plan moved forward. The Abbot refused to accept failure.

Father Wilkes was on his second cup of black coffee when he felt the sharp pain in his stomach. It was intense, and he coughed, then realized there was blood on the back of his hand from covering his mouth. Then Father Bartolini followed, doubled over in agony.

He felt the incredible pangs in his abdomen, followed by vomiting on the tiled floor. His vomit was red with blood. Father Rosa stood up, as if to propose a toast, then grabbed at his own throat, making a gurgling sound before falling face-first into the table, knocking his plate to the floor. Blood trickled from his mouth as he twitched violently then fell to the floor next to the other priests. The three clergymen were thrashing in a bizarre dance as death overcame each of them within two minutes.

The Abbot waited for them to stop moving, calmly stood up, wiped his mouth with the napkin from his lap, and pushed his chair back in before leaving the conference room. He was not surprised to find the body of the young monk outside the room, also doubled over from drinking the coffee. He normally didn't drink coffee, but the Abbot urged him to do so, and he didn't argue. No one ever did. The Abbot made sure the pot of coffee was tainted with nearly a full cup of arsenic, figuring that the excitement of the night before and the bitterness of the strong coffee would mask any trace of the poison to their palettes.

As he left the infirmary building, the Abbot watched the cars being loaded up with the nuns and their luggage. Sister Mary Concordia was sitting in the passenger seat of the first car. She looked afraid, as if she knew something bad was going to happen. Since knowing about the trip, the young sister had feared the real reason for the pilgrimage. She knew the Abbot too well, and after the horrible fire in the former convent, she was terrified of what he had in mind. As if she sensed the Abbot staring at her, she glanced over to him. He stood there on the steps of the infirmary building – grinning. She felt an incredible sense of dread as the car pulled away, the smiling face of the Abbot in the rear-view mirror, as they left the grounds of St. Michael's Academy and made their way to the train depot.

9

Sister Mary Concordia had tossed and turned for nearly an hour before finally falling asleep. The St. James Catholic Church in Dwight, Illinois had put the nuns up for the night in their convent after their train arrived just before dinner on Saturday. The nuns at the convent served them a simple meal of boiled chicken, white rice and carrots, then entertained them with some wonderful singing and fellowship before showing them to their beds for the night. Sister Mary Concordia was concerned the nuns would be going to the women's prison in Dwight, a state-run facility, that the Abbot had scheduled for their trip, as a means to bring some cheer to the female inmates and staff. The first stop was earlier that same day in Joliet, at a privately run shelter for abused women. They had met a handful of the 38 women who were currently living there. Some were too afraid to come out to meet the sisters, which sometimes happened with survivors of violence in the home. Despite being victims, some of the young women who came there felt guilty, as if they had done something wrong. Those with children were kept in the basement where they had sleeping rooms and a common area more conducive to children. If they didn't have room, there were other places they could move the women with young ones.

Sister Mary Concordia knew the elderly nuns were already tired from a full day, and with a week-long pilgrimage scheduled, Sister Mary Concordia had serious concerns that it would be too much for the older nuns. Visiting with the battered women was difficult work, and even the most senior nuns couldn't help but feel empathy at their dark stories. No matter what, a good nun always seemed to take a little bit of the pain with them. Some would say the older nuns bore so much pain from all they had counseled through their years of service that they might not even have the strength to walk through the gates of heaven after meeting St. Peter. Of course, the nuns would scoff at such an accusation. They enjoyed doing whatever they could to make the person they were assisting feel better.

There were three rooms provided to the sisters from St. Michael's Academy. Each room had two bunk beds, a four-drawer dresser with a small mirror, a desk and chair, and a closet. There was a common bathroom for each floor, with a stand-up shower stall. The single room at the end of the hallway was where Sister Mary Concordia could be found, and it had its own bathroom and shower. She felt almost embarrassed to have a private room while the other sisters had to sleep in bunk beds. But no one complained or questioned her authority, since the Abbot had appointed her for good reason.

As she began to drift off into sleep, Sister Mary Concordia saw a huge concrete staircase going straight up into what appeared to be clouds. They were dark and foreboding at the top of the immense stairs. In a single file line before her were each of the twelve nuns on the trip. The young nun was the last one in line and found herself feeling incredibly frightened as they moved slowly up and closer to the menacing clouds. There was a moss coating most of the steps in varying thicknesses, and there was a howling wind coming in from the right side that was stinging Sister Mary Concordia's face. She did her best to hold her scarf and hat in place as they inched closer to the top. The only sound she heard was the intense wind and their footsteps on the concrete. It was more like a slow march, and with each step they took, Sister Mary Concordia felt a blackness sweep over her entire body which she could not shake.

Suddenly, Sister Mary Concordia felt her head enter the dark clouds, and surprisingly, she was able to see the top of the massive staircase. The line of nuns before her were inching closer to the top step, and she wanted to scream out for them to stop. It appeared as if the staircase was ending and there was nothing after it! It was almost like reaching the top of an incredibly steep mountain with a sheer cliff directly on the other side. Despite her attempts to cry out, she made no sound.

The first nun to make it to the top step continued slowly marching right over the side and into nothingness – or so it appeared. Each of the remaining nuns calmly did the very same thing. There was no pause or looking back. There was no scream or sound of any kind. They simply walked off the top step and disappeared! Sister Mary Concordia was overcome with intense fear like she had never felt before. She wanted to stop them from going over the side, but it was no use. The procession continued until she herself was standing on the top step. Despite her terror, Sister Mary Concordia plunged off the staircase, just like the others before her. She hurdled head first into the darkness before her, not knowing what was waiting on the other side. The young nun was in a blackened spiral down.

Suddenly, Sister Mary Concordia felt her body become lighter than air. She was floating, and her vision came horribly into focus. Beneath her was a giant cast iron mechanism, with a mouth the size of a large swimming pool! Inside the mouth were rows and rows of teeth, moving with a slow but perfect rhythm. Inside the mouth were body parts moving amongst the teeth, which as she got closer, revealed themselves as sharp gears. She had the odd sensation of floating above the huge mouth, as the nuns in front of her were torn apart by the massive metal gears. They spared nothing as they churned flesh and bone into a bright red byproduct that flowed like water.

Her body began to float, and she went past the mouth of the mechanism and down its side. There was a huge handle there, of metal and wood, with a giant hand moving it along. Then she heard a hideous, deep laugh, and when she looked directly up, she saw none other than the smiling face of the Abbot, cranking on the handle of the mechanical beast that was tearing the nuns to pieces. The laughing continued even as Sister Mary Concordia landed on something hard at the base of the grinder, shaking everything in sight with incredible power. From where she was now standing, when she glanced up, she could see the underside of the monstrosity, and from it, the mangled remains of the twelve nuns. She was repulsed to see such a gory sight. Even more disturbing was the shape of the bloody discharge of each nun, and how it formed a perfect cross along the conveyor belt. It was moving slowly, as each of the crosses inched closer to the flames of a raging fire pit. The deepness of the flames was captivating, and it seemed that there was no end to their insatiability.

The next thing she knew, Sister Mary Concordia was being picked up by the giant hands of the Abbot. His laughter was still vibrating everything in its path, and now she was being held over the churning gears, still wet with the blood of her fellow sisters.

Sister Mary Concordia sat straight up and screamed as loud as she could, only to find herself in the convent at St. James Catholic Church in Dwight, Illinois. She was in one piece and the Abbot was nowhere to be found, her heart racing wildly. She lay awake until the sun came up, and she heard the rest of the nuns getting up to start the second day of their trip. They were all early risers. She could not help but wonder what the nightmare meant, and if it was any foreshadowing as to what awaited them at the end of this journey. She shuddered to even think about it.

******

The next several days brought much of the same to the nuns from St. Michael's Academy. They spent time at a nursing home in Pontiac, an orphanage in Normal, the burn unit of a Catholic hospital in Bloomington, and a state-run home for the blind in Lincoln. Sister Mary Concordia managed to keep them all accounted for as they got on and off the trains that took them to each stop. The nuns seemed to enjoy the adventure, despite being tired at the end of each day. The Abbot had made all the painstaking arrangements so that their room and board were covered at each stop along the journey. He had spent years planning this, and it showed, as every minute detail seemed accounted for. The more Sister Mary Concordia thought about it, the more it frightened her that something horrific waited for them all at the end of the trip. From what she knew about the Abbot, he was not about to allow a nice and neat ending to this story. She had watched him sacrifice an infant before her very eyes! The way his perverted advances still left her feeling filthy was only a sliver of the tremendous disgust she had for the Abbot. She reviled the man, and it shook her up, causing her to question her faith. She stood strong and felt God knew best the course she should take. Sister Mary Concordia figured the Abbot's final plan would have to be something dreadful, and worrying about it became increasingly consuming to her thoughts.

For now, she slept. They had been on the train for only a half hour, but due to the difficulty she was having with sleep, Sister Mary Concordia managed to catch a nap whenever she could, and on the train it seemed like an easy thing to do. They had left Lincoln, Illinois and were going to be arriving in Bartonville for the final stop of the journey before they would head back to McHenry on the Corn Belt Line. Oddly enough, when she got all the nuns seated on the train, the conductor had no package waiting for them with the tickets for the final leg of their journey. For each of the other stops, that was how the young nun had gotten the tickets for the next train. She could feel her pulse quicken.

"I'm sorry, sister. I don't have any tickets for any of you ladies," he said, checking his coat pockets and the leather, zippered bag where he kept his paperwork for the day. He even turned out the pockets of his trousers, just to illustrate the point. Shrugging, he added, "Nothing."

******

Sister Mary Concordia awoke suddenly to three short knocks on the door of her private sleeping car.

"Sister, we have arrived in Bartonville," said the conductor, who was given instructions before the nuns boarded the train in Lincoln to give the young sister her own private car, so she would be well rested upon their arrival. He also made sure that no one bothered her and that he woke her upon arrival.

"Thank you, Lester." She sat on the edge of the cot, her black stocking feet on the floor, and yawned as she reached her hands into the air to stretch. She quickly put on her leather shoes, straightened her habit, and left her private car to meet up with the rest of the nuns.

******

The nuns were greeted by four orderlies from the hospital to assist them and carry their bags. Sister Mary Concordia stood open-mouthed at the site before her. The nuns were chattering amongst themselves, excited to be on the last day of their trip, and that it was Christmas Eve. She couldn't believe her eyes! At the train depot in Bartonville, awaiting them to the north was a huge concrete staircase, with seemingly hundreds of steps going up the hill that led to the Peoria State Hospital. There was a large metal sign that bore the name of the hospital at the base of the stairs where they would begin their journey to the top.

As Sister Mary Concordia looked up to the top of the large staircase, she didn't see the dark, foreboding clouds that she had seen in her nightmare a week before. Instead she saw a large building made of large blocks of limestone, known as the Bowen Building of the Peoria State Hospital. She had heard stories of the methods of psychiatry the staff implemented here in Bartonville, unique to the rest of the asylums in the country. Their patients were housed in a new cottage-style that was less imposing, and the metal bars were removed from the windows, allowing them to move about the 200-acre campus with little restriction.

As the nuns began their slow ascension of the stairs, Sister Mary Concordia couldn't help but think about the huge meat grinder in her dreams that had churned the nuns into bloody pulp in the shape of crosses and the hideous laughing of the Abbot as he turned the crank that moved the gears. She took the first step and wondered how many more steps she would make in her life before meeting with whatever disturbing end the Abbot had in mind. The fact she was going to die a miserable death at the hands of the Abbot was the only thing Sister Mary Concordia knew for certain as she climbed the concrete stairs.

10

The Abbot was on his second scotch with an ice cube, and he winced as it went down, thanks to a terrible case of heartburn. He hadn't been eating much more than soup with crackers and a steady diet from the assortment in his personal liquor cabinet. In addition to the discontent inside his stomach, the priest had been plagued with nightmares every night since the fire that had claimed so many lives a week before. The usual calm and collected Abbot was not himself, and knowing that fact, he was his own worst enemy.

The phone on his desk rang shrilly. He nearly fell over in his chair.

"Hello," the Abbot said, his heart thumping.

"Merry Christmas, Abbot. I wanted you to know the nuns are here and safe," said Father Penning, sounding a bit like he had also been drinking some holiday cheer.

Despite the pain in the pit of his stomach, the Abbot smiled.

"That's good to hear, Father."

Father Penning continued, "Yes, it is. I have them resting now in some bedrooms in the nursing school. After dinner I will be taking them to the chapel for Mass."

The Abbot nodded, despite being alone. He poured himself another drink.

"Is everything in place like we discussed?" the Abbot asked him, wincing again.

"Yes. Just like we discussed."

The Abbot noticed a slight hesitation in the response from the priest.

"We are still in full agreement what is to be done, Father. Correct?"

Father Penning, his façade beginning to crack, said, "Yes. I just wish we didn't have to do it this way." The cracks now widened, and crumbling would soon begin.

The Abbot immediately made any cloudiness in his head dissipate on command. Hearing the old priest beginning to fall apart at a time when he needed him the most was infuriating. After years of planning this night, to now be concerned with a key component, threw him into a murderous rage.

"Father Penning! Get yourself together right now! Do you hear me?" the Abbot boomed, standing up behind his desk and slamming his fist down with fury.

Father Penning swallowed hard. He knew the Abbot could detect the fear in his voice. He had been having his own share of nightmares, especially in the last week. He was afraid to do what was being asked of him, but he also understood the dreadful Abbot would not hesitate to ruin his career as threatened. It had taken him three drinks to summon the courage to call.

"Yes, sir. I will take care of all you have asked," Father Penning said, as firmly as he could. His insides churned.

The Abbot knew he was cowering on the other end. He had never liked the elderly priest, but with all the Abbot knew of the man's shady past with young boys, he provided the perfect sacrificial lamb. In the eleventh hour, he knew the best thing to do was to encourage the priest to carry out the plan. If Father Penning could fulfill his duties, that was all the Abbot needed of him. Nothing more. He was disposable.

"That's good. Do not test me. I trust that you will take care of this, and that everything will go as we planned." The Abbot's voice was thick with disdain, heavy with authority, and dripping with evil.

"Yes, Abbot." Father Penning could feel two hands gripping his throat as he dropped the phone to the floor. There was no one in the bedroom with him, but the old priest could feel the intense grip of two strong hands squeezing his throat. The room began to spin. He knew it was the Abbot in a show of force. Father Penning didn't know how he did it, but there was no other reasonable explanation.

The phone swayed by the cord next to Father Penning's head, as he lay semi-conscious on the hardwood floor of his bedroom. The room was spinning faster, and all he could hear was the Abbot's maniacal laugh coming through the phone, taunting him cruelly. The priest knew the only option was to carry out his sadistic plan and hope that God would find forgiveness to save his damned soul. Still, the Abbot's laughing continued.

Closing his eyes, Father Penning wished for his death at that instant. He begged that he would take his last breath, his final heartbeat, and cease to live. He would not be so lucky.

******

"Come on, sisters. This way please," said Father Penning as they left the student dining room where the thirteen nuns ate their Christmas Eve meal. The kitchen staff had prepared them a wonderful dinner of baked salmon, fried potatoes, fresh green beans, and plenty of cornbread with homemade butter. They even had apple pie and egg nog for dessert, which the sisters thought was wonderful after a long week's journey.

"Thank you for a wonderful meal, Father Penning," Sister Mary Concordia said to the priest, smiling.

"You're welcome, sister. Now let's get everyone down to the chapel so we can have a wonderful Christmas Eve mass. I think you'll enjoy it." He did his best not to make eye contact with the young nun.

"Is everything OK, Father? You seem very nervous. It's Christmas Eve!" she said, looking forward to the mass. "Praise Jesus!"

Father Penning did his best to smile, then he turned around and lead the nuns to chapel. He silently prayed under his breath as they walked. Tears were in his eyes.

"God, forgive me."

******

Sister Mary Concordia was mesmerized by the incredibly detailed artwork on the walls and ceilings of the small chapel on the far west end of the hospital grounds. Father Penning rushed them along as quickly as possible and asked the nuns to be quiet as he finished preparing for this special Christmas Eve mass they had planned.

The pews had all been removed, and the sisters were asked to kneel in two rows of six each, with the young Sister Mary Concordia centered behind them, also kneeling. The lighting in the chapel was sparse, only lit by the wall sconces and candles at the front of the room surrounding the altar, and in two rows toward the back of the room. She was taken aback at the intricacy of the artwork. On the front wall, behind the altar, was a sorrowful scene of the crucifixion of Jesus Christ, with dark and depressing colors. The details in the face of Christ gave her a chill. It was as if he were there with them on this night.

On the wall to her left was a dark and chilling image of Satan's descent to Hell as he was cast from heaven. Along with Satan were frightening demons with piercing eyes as they swirled around in the art as Satan fell. There almost seemed to be movement in the painting, but in the flickering candlelight, it might have been just an illusion. Sister Mary Concordia tried not to stare too long, because she swore the demons were swirling around the devil and looking directly at her.

On the right wall was a depiction of an epic military battle, in all its bloody and gruesome detail, in a large open field surrounded by dense forest and nefarious things lurking in the shadows. She couldn't make out exactly what battle it was, but there were hundreds of soldiers clashing in brutal hand-to-hand combat. They were mauling each other with swords, crossbows, spears, and a variety of ghastly inventions of misery. Sister Mary Concordia found it nearly impossible not to look at the masterful piece, but upon seeing the anguished faces, she could almost hear them screaming faintly in the distance. It seemed oddly out of place. When she looked away, the sound stopped. Despite this oddity, Sister Mary Concordia was willing to hear the tortured cries from the bloody scene in exchange for being able to gaze upon its sinister beauty. It continued on the back wall, however, the light was too dim to make out details. On the ceiling were dark clouds and a sky at twilight. It appeared the clouds were listlessly moving as a light breeze came through. The entire room was something to behold, yet Sister Mary Concordia would admit it did not seem like any Catholic church she had ever been to. It was much darker and foreboding.

Sister Mary Concordia was not the only nun in the chapel perplexed at what she was seeing around her in every direction. Sister Mary Benedicta was in the front row, nearly center, and very afraid. She could not overcome the intense feeling of dread, but she was instructed by Father Penning to kneel in this place and quietly reflect on the joy of Christmas Eve while he did his final preparations. In the second row, at the far end, Sister Mary Aquinas was staring at the painting of the fall of Satan, and it scared her to the point that she was considering getting up and leaving the chapel. She found the artwork captivating, yet at the same time harmful to her very soul. While there were a few of the older nuns with their heads down in silent prayer and reflection, the rest of the sisters were very observant of their surroundings, and they all in some way found it incredibly disturbing.

******

"You must go, please, go now!" exclaimed Father Penning, as he stared into the eyes of the young Father O'Donnell. His hand lightly touched his shoulder, then he withdrew and shut the door. He locked it with the deadbolt.

"Please, Father," the young priest cried out, pounding on the door from the outside. "Let me help you!"

Father Penning leaned his head against the door and began to cry. All the tremendous efforts made to pull this diabolical plan together was more than the fragile priest could handle. He wanted to say something back, but he knew it would only make it worse. Wiping his tears away, Father Penning tried his best to put on his game face and stand before his captive congregation.

As he walked into the chapel from the back of the room, he could only think about Father O'Donnell and hoped he would not do anything stupid to put himself in jeopardy. He knew the young priest had a lot of promise in the clergy and enjoyed working with the boys' basketball team at a local Catholic high school. Father Penning didn't know how this night would end, but he had a deep down, roots choking at his innards, kind of feeling. It would be very bad. The Abbot was a cold and calculating man, who took everything very seriously. Father Penning hoped he would escape this chapel alive, but he had serious doubts.

******

Very few people knew about the Abbot's private study. It was much better that way, since inside the small room were many rare pieces of literature, artwork, jewelry, coins, and other treasures that would allow most thieves to retire, if they were able to purloin the inventory. The room was only accessible by a sliding door that was very well hidden against the dark mahogany wood paneling in his office. There was a small desk and chair, but no windows. Some walls were adorned with some of the collection he kept, but the rest were covered with bookcases, crammed end to end with a variety of texts he studied. There was even a small fireplace and couch, where he often enjoyed sitting and gazing into the flames. The Abbot found this very relaxing, and he often claimed his visions came at these moments of private reflection.

On this Christmas Eve, he was doing just that. The Abbot was sitting on the small couch and staring into the flames. His eyes were steely and intense. His face resembled chiseled rock in the flickering light. Inside the fire, he could see things far beyond the grounds of St. Michael's Academy. Slowly, the images of a distant chapel came into view, with thirteen nuns kneeling and the elderly Father Penning at the altar. He was making final preparations for the momentous occasion. The Abbot felt an incredible rush, realizing that his hard work and meticulous attention to detail enabled him to have a front seat for what was about to happen to the thirteen nuns. The thought that Satan would arrive soon was overwhelming and invigorating.

The Abbot waited patiently before he would address the congregation. His mental prowess had enabled him to communicate this way, despite being over 150 miles away in the confines of his private study. The flames flickered against the sweat that trickled down his clenched jaw.

******

William Weeks was standing in the shadows at the front of the chapel. He was in awe at the artwork; his eyes were drawn to the drifting clouds and seemingly endless grey sky on the ceiling. It was breathtaking, and William never felt more alive. The powerful scene before him, with the thirteen nuns on their knees in solemnity, produced a live electricity searing deep into his flesh. He donned a hooded black robe that hid the raw power, rage, and strength beneath. To his left was another patient, Tim McCullough, who he had recruited to help with the mission at hand. Tim was an older guy who was one of the smarter people he had met at the hospital. He was also very small and thin in stature, and William thought he might need someone his size to help with the escape promised once his job was complete. He was given an architectural drawing of the chapel so he could plot his escape, and William believed he had a good plan in place. Once they were off the hospital property, William would have to decide how he would handle that loose end. For now, he would keep Tim on a short leash.

Father Penning was making his way toward the altar at the front of the chapel. William had lit the candles that surrounded it, as instructed. Everything had been set in its right place, including the large metal bucket he was told had to be set up in front of the altar and covered until ready for use. William had run through the dozens of steps of the plan every moment he could. He spent many sleepless nights thinking about every possible scenario, since he knew enough about the Abbot and Father Penning to realize things were not what they appeared. He made sure Tim knew that what had to be done was going to be incredibly violent, but payment would be his freedom. William was promised he would be allowed to run away and that he would not be pursued, despite the fact they kept him in a locked cell due to his violent and psychotic nature. He was also given a slight loosening of the restrictions he was under in his isolation cell, and he was able to request anything he felt he needed to carry out the mission.

As Father Penning approached the altar, his pale face was glistening with sweat. His eyes met William's for a brief moment, and the elderly priest looked like he was praying for death. He nodded quickly, then stood behind the altar, looking over some of the papers that he requested be set out for him. Glancing out at the nuns, he was overcome with guilt, knowing the sentence that was going to be imposed on every one of them. He was also impressed with their solidarity, as many of them were holding hands, heads bowed in silent prayer. Father Penning knew that his own cowardice for not owning up to his sins of the flesh was partially the reason the nuns were being sacrificed. He felt nauseas.

The scene was one of dread and pure evil. The artwork on the walls and ceiling was moving slowly in the somber lighting. There was also an extremely deep hum that was omnipresent throughout the chapel. It was a constant sound from somewhere unknown.

Suddenly a booming voice came from every direction! Everyone was looking around at the source. Just then a loud clap of thunder was heard in the sky above, and everyone in the chapel knew the familiar voice. Two of the nuns in the second row wept.

"Bow your heads, sisters! Bow your heads in submission to me! I am the embodiment of Satan himself!"

There was no mistaking the harsh, unforgiving voice of the Abbot.

******

Sister Mary Concordia was shocked to hear that voice. She knew it was the Abbot, but it was uncertain where he was. It sounded like his voice was coming from every possible direction! She noticed several of the nuns were now crying, and it was becoming contagious, as she felt like weeping herself. Yet, she kept telling herself that the only chance she had to survive whatever was about to happen was to keep her wits about her – no matter what.

"*Hail, Lilith the black rose, Goddess of Hell. Full of darkness and lust. Blessed is the fruit of your womb, the demons of the pit and Satan's offspring. Allow Satan himself to manifest into human form and reign supreme on this infernal Earth!*" the booming voice echoed throughout the chapel, as the nuns cried out loudly in distress. They had never heard a Satanic prayer in their lives.

"*We are gathered here in your majestic presence, infernal lord Satan! We have gifts for you, in exchange for your manifestation to human form. We ask that you come to us here, as a man, and show us how beautifully evil our mortal world would be in your control. Please accept our gifts.*"

Sister Teresa Anne Marie tried to get up from her knees but was unable to move her legs at all. It was as if she was stuck to the floor! Something or someone was holding her down! To her left in the front row, Sister Mary Benedicta was experiencing the same thing. One by one, all the nuns began to frantically look around as they realized they were unable to move from their position. Thunder again sounded as the clouds on the ceiling above were moving faster. The sky began to darken, as if it were ready to pour down rain at any moment. The temperature in the chapel dropped at least 20 degrees. They all realized now that something was horribly wrong. Several other nuns silently cried at the realization.

******

The Abbot was staring into the flames in complete concentration as he spoke to the unwilling congregation in the chapel at the Peoria State Hospital. He was able to do this without moving his lips, thanks to endless hours of studying the dark arts of the occult. His discovery of Dr. Wilfred Weeks was a true breakthrough in his knowledge of the earliest form of Satanism. Dr. Weeks was a true pioneer of all things infernal. The Abbot was drawn to his texts when he had the opportunity to get his hands on some of the documents that were thought lost but found hundreds of years later. There were countless favors exchanged, blood spilled, and bodies hidden to get his hands on the papers of Dr. Weeks. It was the final work from the groundbreaking Satanist of the 1600's, in the days before his arrest and eventual execution. Some of the scholars of the subject questioned that the documents had even existed, and thought they were maybe the work of fiction from those who loved the intrigue of the unknown. The Abbot had always disagreed with this view, and in his earliest days as a priest in upstate New York, he continued to work on finding them.

Very few knew the documents were real. Even fewer knew the papers were written on a subject that Dr. Wilfred Weeks called *Darkness Visible*. Dr. Weeks was a fan of English writer John Milton, who published *Paradise Lost* in 1667 and used the phrase *darkness visible* in the iconic poem. It was used to describe the flames of Hell.

> *A dungeon horrible, on all sides 'round*
> *As one great furnace flamed, yet from those flames*
> *No light, but rather darkness visible*

Now the Abbot was looking into the flames in his study, like his own darkness visible, and watched the nuns below panic, once they realized there was no escape from impending doom.

******

Once he heard the words, *please accept our gifts,* William Weeks began to move quickly into action. All those sleepless nights in his cell, going over the steps, prepared him for this. In moments, he was behind Sister Teresa Anne Marie, but she had no idea he was there. William grabbed her firmly by her hair and pulled her head violently back, the nape of her neck exposed in the dim light. Her cries were drowned out in the chaos. Another clap of thunder was heard, this time louder, as the nuns next to her screamed in terror at the site of the large man, clad in a black robe, with a large knife at the sister's throat. Whatever was holding her firmly to the floor had now released its grip.

"We hereby give this gift to you, Satan. Please accept her life blood. Let her blood be a symbol of your mortal life here on Earth with us. Let us see the way, Satan!"

Tim was pulling the tarp from the large metal bucket at the same time that William was dragging Sister Teresa Anne Marie toward him. The knife was directly on her throat, and she was screaming and flailing around, desperately trying to break free. William pushed her down to the metal bucket as the knife dug deeply into her throat, the bright red blood spewing like a fountain. He loved the way it felt when the sharp blade dug into her flesh. Due to the cold temperature of the chapel, steam was rising from the pooling blood.

"As her blood flows, so let your Earthly body come forth, Satan! Let us see your Darkness Visible!"

As on cue, another boom of thunder rang out. The chapel was in total mayhem as Sister Teresa Anne Marie went into her death rattle, while William shook the last drops of blood from her jugular vein. He tossed her aside, and Tim pulled her to the back of the altar. William ran back to the nuns and grabbed the next nun in line, Sister Mary Benedicta, pulling the older woman across the floor as the rest of the sisters reached out to try and save her. The entire scene played out to Father Penning, who was in shock at the brutal display. He thought he was supposed to lead the events, but instead was frozen in place as the massive voice of the Abbot resounded throughout, leaving him impotent. He thought the Abbot was at St. Michael's, nearly 150 miles to the northeast, and had no idea how the demonic priest could be here in Bartonville orchestrating this blood lust. However he was doing it, it was his new reality. Father Penning wasn't surprised the Abbot had this up his diabolical sleeve, and he wondered how many other surprises would spew forth before this night was over. The priest knew he would not leave this chapel alive.

Thunder clapped once again, and the dark skies flickered. A fine mist of rain began to fall from the ceiling. Everyone looked up in utter disbelief and realized in the same terror-filled moment that it was not water – but blood raining down upon the chapel. Frantic eyes darted about the room, all while William Weeks was taking one nun at a time to the large metal pail, slicing their throats, and letting their blood flow. Tim was barely able to keep up as William appeared to be getting faster and faster, slitting the throats of the nuns and tossing them aside. Both men were covered in blood.

With each nun who was sacrificed, the Abbot would repeat the phrase, *"As her blood flows, so let your Earthly body come forth, Satan! Let us see your Darkness Visible!"*

The blood continued to rain down from the ominous sky above as the paintings on the wall appeared to come alive. The demons in the painting on the left wall began to soar among the clouds in their descent, blood pouring from their eyes and down the wall in streams. The battle scene on the right was also awash with blood as the soldiers began to move in a struggle to the death, the blood flowing to the floor like the rest. Swords were slicing into flesh as the warriors screamed in agony, body parts flying through the air along with arrows, sharpened steel, and boulders launched from catapults. The battlefield was riddled with the dead.

After the sixth nun was murdered, the blood was ankle-deep in the chapel, and the blood rain continued to fall, gaining in ferocity.

"My God! Please forgive me," whispered Father Penning, shocked at the extreme carnage. He felt helpless and began to look around for a possible way out before the entire chapel was filled with blood or the building imploded under the tremendous show of force.

He began to move away from the altar and nearly fell as blood poured down from the artwork of the crucifixion on the front wall. Just like the other art pieces, so was the artwork of Jesus on the cross came to life before everyone's eyes. Father Penning saw a small door that he knew led to a narrow hallway and small office that the priests sometimes used to prepare for mass. Just as he put his hand on the door knob, he felt something grab him from the floor, below the blood that was now almost to his knees. He desperately reached for the doorknob, but was unable to open the locked door. Whatever was clawing at the priest was ripping into the flesh of his legs, and it was pulling him straight down until his head went below the blood. The priest fought to regain control and get his head above the blood, but the hands that had a firm grip on his legs were not allowing it. The agony of them tearing at his legs was second only to the sheer terror of the sensation of being pulled under. His vision was hazy, and his hearing was muffled as the force kept pulling him down, then letting him up enough to barely catch a breath, before repeating the process again. The last thought he had was that he wished he had just resigned from his job and not given the Abbot the opportunity to force him into being a part of such a heinous act. *How could he do such a thing?* As he went under the last time, Father Penning thought of Father O'Donnell, hoping the young priest got away. He heard the faint laughing of the Abbot as he acquiesced.

Thunder and lightning were almost non-stop now as blood rained down in buckets upon the frantic scene inside the chapel. William had the last nun over the metal bucket. She barely fought him. Sister Maria Anne Michela seemed to realize that there was no use in resistance, and she spent her final moments praying to God and hoping the pain would be minimal as she was murdered by this cloaked madman. His knife dug into the flesh of her neck, and blood poured into the bucket, which was now nearly filled to the top.

Sister Mary Concordia was also praying. She was the last nun alive and the chapel was now almost waist-high in blood. The bodies of the murdered nuns were now floating in the crimson fluid.

She had no idea what was in store for her, but it did not look like she would survive the night either.

"Lord Satan, we have given you twelve gifts, as you have asked. I beg of you to manifest yourself in human form! Show yourself to us, Satan! We ask that you darken this Earth with your presence!" the Abbot was screaming these words in a controlled burst of pure energy and incredible emotion.

It was then that the ground shook while the chaos of thunder and lightning boomed throughout the chapel, mixed with the cries of those who were still hanging on to the fringes of life. The building moved several feet. Long, winding cracks began to run up and down the plaster walls and ceilings, as large pieces began to crumble and fall. The blood was now waist high and began to swirl in a concentric pattern, slow at first, then gaining with intensity. Dead bodies were moving fast while bobbing up and down in the torrent of blood, and the frothing waves of red were splashing against the failing walls. The unholy site was one to behold as the building slowly began to collapse upon itself, all the while moving in unison down below the ground to an awaiting inferno.

******

The Abbot was wide-eyed and panting as he watched the spectacle of *Darkness Visible* in the flames. His body was convulsed into position, almost frozen in place, as his eyes took in the display. He knew the texts talked about a chaotic end that would give birth to the manifestation of Satan, but beyond that, he was as much in the dark about what would happen next as the few who were still alive in the madness. Something deep inside of the Abbot began to shift, and with it a sense of fear that there could be something amiss in the final plan that was unfolding. He dismissed the thought as negativity creeping in to what was proving to be his magnum opus.

******

William Weeks was hanging on to the third rung of the ladder that led to the bell tower, while trying to hold Sister Mary Concordia. She dangled into the rush of blood pouring into the hallway.

"I think I've got it open!" screamed Tim, from several rungs up, trying to open the hatch that led to the bell tower, and hopefully, their access to freedom.

"OK, I'm coming up with her!" William called out, his voice barely audible in the rush of noise.

"Just leave her, William. We aren't gonna get far with her. She's barely alive as it is," Tim said. His eyes were anxious, hoping that William would come to his senses and let her drown at the bottom of the rung ladder, attached to the concrete wall.

William moved up with the nun.

"She's our ticket out of here. We need to keep moving before this place all gets swallowed up in that hole!" he said, pulling the young nun behind him toward the bell tower.

Now looking outside, William and Tim saw a foreboding sky above as the chapel began to sway from side to side, the evil storm raging inside. It was a blood-red hue with an infinite number of stars in its backdrop. There was a sort of serenity and terror mixed into one as both men stood speechless at the sight. Sister Mary Concordia was coughing, and her eyes began to flutter as she started to come back around. William knew there was not much time left.

William stood her up and forced her head out of the open window of the bell tower. Sister Mary Concordia was horrified at what she saw and immediately was aware of what was going on as he flashed the steel of the knife blade in his right hand.

"Please, don't do this!" she cried, frantically struggling in his firm grasp. A stinging rain was coming down in sheets, and dark clouds were swirling above them.

William plunged the knife into her neck with a savage ferocity, his jaw clenched tight. It took all the strength he had to hang on to the young nun and not fall from the bell tower as it began to sway while the chapel slowly began to implode. Sister Mary Concordia cried out, but no blood flowed. William could not believe it! He drove the knife in once again, forcefully cutting into her supple flesh. Still no blood, and the nun was seemingly unaffected by the action. She was crying, and it was not from pain or injury, but by the sheer terror of being in such a precarious situation.

"Leave her, we need to go!" yelled Tim as he balanced himself in the window opening, the tower now violently swaying as the roof of the chapel below began to split down the middle. Slate shingles were flying in all directions. He could see glimpses of inside the chapel, through the fissures in the roof, and all that Tim could observe was the maddening swirl of the blood. Everything inside was going down into an apparent drain running below the ground.

"My Satan, please present yourself! We beg of you, Lord!" the frantic voice of the Abbot could be heard faintly from inside the chapel as the rain outside came down even harder and the wind picked up in speed.

Sister Mary Concordia felt a tremendous pull from below as William continued to attack her with the knife. Even a direct blow to her heart was useless. She was not bleeding and felt no pain, only incredible pressure from his strong blows.

"I can't hold on any longer!" screamed Tim, as he lost his balance and fell toward the crack in the roof. He landed hard on the main ceiling joist that was now splintering into pieces. Then, with a pause, he glanced up at William with an unbelievable terror in his eyes. He fell backward into the swirling mass below, and in an instant, he was swept down into the abyss.

William didn't know what to do. He was afraid that if he didn't kill the last nun, his deal would be null and void. He was smart enough to know that something had gone terribly wrong and that he would be lucky to be alive when this ordeal was over, let alone a free man. He felt an incredible pull on the nun, who was now slowly being torn from his grasp. He did what he could to hang on, but inch by inch, the sister was being taken away. William would have to find a way to get out of the bell tower and avoid certain death. He could also see the mayhem inside the chapel as the crack in the roof opened even wider. The plaster walls were now completely crumbled, exposing the wood lath behind them. There were no signs of life inside, except the cries of the Abbot, who was pleading with the Devil to reveal himself.

Sister Mary Concordia screamed out as she fell from William's grasp and straight into the torrent below. Like Tim, she fell on the ceiling joist, now barely there, as the roof was crumbling down in large pieces.

"Dear God, please help me!" she cried, hanging on to the large beam, and feeling herself slipping into the concentric swirl of blood below.

Just then an unearthly growl let loose and shook what was left of the chapel. She had never heard such a horrific sound in her life. The chapel began to spin, slowly at first, but soon picking up speed. The building began to fall to pieces and into the pool of blood below. Yet when Sister Mary Concordia looked down, she didn't see the swirling blood, but instead a mouth. It was agape with huge, rotten, razor-sharp teeth, waiting to devour the chapel into its hellish nothingness!

"Please, God, you cannot let this happen!" she cried out, as she fell away from the ceiling joist, the spinning motion of the chapel causing her to lose her balance.

She was hurtling downward, end over end, screaming the entire way into the bestial mouth below. The guttural growl let loose once again, and whatever was left of the chapel was swallowed up like it had never been there in the first place.

William was in midair as the bell tower finally gave way and fell to the putrid, awaiting mouth below. He jumped as far out as he could, his powerful legs hurling him outward and away from the chapel. William fell with a resounding thud on the wet mud, breaking most of the bones in his body. He was unable to move anything but his head as he looked on in horror at the demonic display before him. A giant tongue came out of the huge mouth that had swallowed up the chapel before his very eyes. It grabbed him by the left leg, pulling William closer.

"Fuck you, God! Fuck you!" he screamed out, as rain pelted his face and the blackened tongue dragged him inside, leaving nothing behind.

The storm raged on for the rest of the night, and by morning, the first rays of light showed absolutely no evidence that such an incredible display of evil had ever occurred.

******

A young woman, with blonde hair and intense green eyes, sat up in her bed at St. John's Hospital in Springfield, Illinois. The incredible thunderstorm outside was keeping her up, and the contractions were becoming more frequent. She wished that she had family or a friend there for support.

"Are you doing OK, Elise?" asked Elma, the third shift head nurse in the maternity ward.

She had been with the young woman since she was admitted two days before, with severe abdominal pain. Her baby was not supposed to be born for another two months, but the doctors were concerned that with the recent extreme trauma she had gone through, the baby was in danger.

"The contractions are coming faster," Elise replied.

Outside the hospital, the dark storm clouds were frightening. From the clouds came an ominous entity, swirling and spitting rain with it, and moving toward the hospital roof. It was the culmination of thirteen beings – thirteen horrible things that had committed the most heinous crimes. As the entity moved closer, the thirteen hideous souls that comprised it merged into one even more despicable thing. Yet as quickly as it came, the entity was gone, slipping silently into the hospital building below.

Elise arched her back as a sharp pain suddenly pierced her body. The baby inside began to shift and shudder, as if it had also felt the intense pain.

"Pain again?" asked Elma, looking for her chart to see when she was given pain medicine last.

"Yes, but this was different. It felt like something going into my body. Oh, it hurts!"

"I'll get the doctor, maybe that baby is determined to be born tonight," the nurse said, leaving the room to find the doctor.

Elise felt incredible dread. The baby was moving inside and ready to come out. As a prostitute, Elise really didn't know who the father was. There was only one man who she hoped could not possibly be the father, and that was the last man she had been with, who nearly beat her to death seven months before.

11

The Abbot let out a primal scream and was thrown across the study into one of his bookshelves. It shuddered under the tremendous force, causing several books to fall to the hardwood floor around him. From the fireplace, an invisible hand had grabbed the Abbot and caused him to travel headfirst across the room, defying gravity. The strength of the unknown entity caused the aging priest to feel an instant terror that made his heart race wildly. His breathing was challenged with a seemingly endless pressure upon his chest. As his vision of the chapel collapsing into the ground began to blur out of focus, the Abbot felt a miasma of pure evil seeping from every direction. The horrific pressure made his body hurt, especially his head, as intense pains tore through his brain like powerful electric current. The pain he had felt earlier in his stomach was back, and sharp pangs caused him to double over. He thought he heard a distant boom that seemed to shake the floor and pull the walls and ceiling in slightly under negative pressure. The plaster began to crack slightly and was the last sound the Abbot heard before he screamed a second time.

From inside the flames and beyond came the evil. The Abbot felt the floor shake again as an incredibly loud noise came from two floors below. The Abbot's private dining, office, and secret study were on the third floor of the monastery building and whatever it was that made the sound was repeating it over and over like a heartbeat. He stood up, trying to gain his composure, brushing plaster dust from his hair and robe. The Abbot could feel the shaking in his feet as the thumping sound became louder and louder.

"Patrick! Patrick! Are you there, my boy?" a guttural demonic voice cut the din from one of the floors below.

The pounding continued, getting closer. Two more books fell from the shelves, and several of the important papers on the small desk fluttered to the floor.

For once, the Abbot was at a loss for words. No one called him Patrick but his mother and grandmothers; all had passed away many years before. Who would even think to call him that here at St. Michael's?

Once again the voice resounded, "Where are you, Patrick? I'm coming for you!"

Now the Abbot was moving away from the sliding panel door of the study. Whatever was calling out to him by his birth name was getting closer, as was the insidious thumping sound that began to shake the walls as it approached. More books fell, and the small globe he kept on his desk was now on the floor, bouncing along. He knew that it was useless to hide behind the small desk, because whatever it was that was coming up the stairs for him was going to get him either way.

Whatever was calling for the Abbot was now in his private office. He could hear the heavy breathing and smell a putrid odor that was not readily identifiable permeating beneath the door.

"Open this door, or I'll break it down, Patrick Reilly. Father Patrick Reilly!" the demonic being said in a mocking tone, rattling the door slightly in its metal track. The Abbot was terrorized and didn't know what to do or say.

Suddenly, the door splintered into thousands of pieces as a tall, thin man stood in its absence. The Abbot stared in disbelief at the figure, too dark to make out any details. Whatever evil feeling was surrounding him earlier was now nearly suffocating the Abbot. He knew he was in the presence of someone beyond what mortal man would know as evil. He was truly a darkness visible, like the line from the famous Milton poem.

As the tall man looked up, some of his face was visible beneath the top hat he wore. He had on a black dress coat and pants that looked like they were from another century. The being had a very powerful face with a distinct jaw and muscle tone. The pallor of his skin was greyish, and as it moved another step into the study, it was obvious that this thing was very much dead and the cause of the horrible stench. He was a walking and talking dead body from a time long past.

The Abbot was appalled at the terrible site. His voice quivered, a very rare occurrence for the narcissist priest.

"Who are you?" The study was now completely silent.

"I am Dr. Wilfred Weeks, and I've come to ruin your day, priest."

******

It was the fall of 1669, and Dr. Wilfred Weeks knew his time was short. He could hear the policemen coming to the front door of his home on London's east end, the hoofs of their horses giving them away as they approached down the cobblestone of McNaulty Street. The young medical doctor was a single man, and a very eligible bachelor to most of the female socialites throughout the city. The doctor could have had his pick from any one of the beautiful rich women, but his work was of paramount importance to him. He was a tall, slender man, with striking good looks and fiery red hair, yet a very intense face that was shrouded in a dark ambiance. As the police began to bang on his front door, Dr. Weeks was doing his best to hide the documents he had been working on for nearly ten years. It was his most important work to date, and he called it Darkness Visible. There was no human alive that he could confide in over it, since he was very far ahead of his time. Years from now, students of the occult and Satanic worship would debate the very existence of Darkness Visible, never fully understanding the true depth of the work.

His good friend, author and poet John Milton, had used the phrase in his famous poem *Paradise Lost*, yet very few would ever know that it was from Dr. Wilfred Weeks that the words originated and not the other way around. At the time, very few knew of John Milton, as he wouldn't become nearly as well-known during his life as he would in death. Rumors swirled that Milton lost his sight due to his dabbling in the occult, having to use his own daughter to write down the words he spoke to her from his bed. Most of London knew of Dr. Weeks for his incredibly good looks and sharp intellect that kept him in many of the social circles which were comprised of the wealthiest and most properly educated in London. Despite Dr. Weeks' appearance at social functions, a distance was always kept between him and others, so he could keep focus on his work. No one had any idea how dark and perilous that work really was. Everyone assumed that it was related to medicine.

Now Dr. Weeks could hear the police breaking down his front door. They would be at his office door in moments. He knew why they were here. They wanted him for various crimes, but most of which was that he openly worshipped the Devil. For the past two months, Dr. Weeks had been having a sexual relationship with one of the young girls he hired to keep his house clean, clothes washed, and meals on the table. He seldom left the house, since most of his time was spent locked up in his office reading and experimenting in the occult. The girl, Beatrice Sheldon, was in her early 20's and a virgin when she was deflowered by Dr. Weeks, and she didn't like it that the young doctor had other girlfriends he would take to bed from time to time when he needed a break from his intense studies. Scorned and furious with Dr. Weeks, Beatrice decided to go to the London police with some of his writings that she had discovered when cleaning out his office, while he was asleep on the couch. In the documents she brought to the police, there were many references to Satan and various demonic prayers and invocations that he had been working into what he called a black mass. At the time, there were very few practicing Satanists, and the police were as appalled as Beatrice with the writings of the good doctor, knowing it was a crime against the Church of England to worship the Devil. A warrant was issued for his arrest by the end of the day, and on this morning, the London police were ready to bring in Dr. Weeks. Knowing that the doctor had deep political influence in the city, the police brought plenty of reinforcements and made sure they had things legally correct before arriving on his doorstep on McNaulty Street.

There was a large loose stone covering a void in the fireplace, where he used to cook some of his late-night meals at the south end of his office when his hired help was fast asleep. He stashed as much of Darkness Visible into that hiding spot as he could and put the rest in the fire. He knew his work was not complete, but if it got into the wrong hands, it could be devastating. He didn't trust it would burn up before the police got into the office, so he hid away the most important parts, and burned his notes. Dr. Weeks hoped to have at least one more month before it would be finished, and then he could try out the plan to see if he could summon Satan himself to Earth. He was very close, but he knew now that his dream would never become a reality.

"Open the door, Weeks! Open it up, or we'll break it down!" yelled a middle-aged policeman at the door. A dozen others were behind him, guns and Billy clubs at the ready.

Dr. Weeks was calmly sitting in a chair by the fireplace when the door came crashing in. The police threw him to the floor and handcuffed him before taking him to the nearest precinct and into a jail cell.

Dr. Weeks wasn't in that jail cell more than three days before he was hanged in public, only a few blocks from his home. Thousands of citizens were there to see the once heralded young doctor, now disgraced, lifeless, swinging from a rope. The police did pull the papers from the fire, but they were not able to do much with the notes. They considered the unfortunate matter of Dr. Weeks closed.

******

The Abbot couldn't believe what he heard. *Dr. Wilfred Weeks*! He had been dead for more than 250 years! It was impossible! His grey, rotten skin told the Abbot that the man was indeed dead and coming back from the grave. As the undead doctor moved closer and removed his top hat, the Abbot was able to see more facial features than he cared to. The fiery red hair was wild and disheveled, just as he had read from the journal kept by the doctor's jailors. His eyes were intensely blue. They were the bluest eyes the Abbot had ever seen, and they appeared to stare deeply into his soul. The Abbot was frozen in place.

"Sit down, Patrick," Dr. Weeks said, taking his top hat off and setting it on the desk. He motioned for the Abbot to sit on the small couch.

Without hesitation, the Abbot sat down, his legs quivering in the presence of the very dead Dr. Weeks. The smell of rot was now completely permeating his study, and he held a handkerchief to his nose in an attempt to hide the offensive odor.

"I see you don't like the smell of death, Father. Well, you certainly have caused enough death in your life," he said, leaning forward slightly in his chair, "So, you would think you'd be used to it." His blue eyes never left the aging priest, and his countenance was unwavering with hatred.

The Abbot didn't know what to say. The fireplace roared behind Dr. Weeks. He still felt a tremendous pressure all around him, and the sickening feeling in the pit of his stomach had developed into a searing pain that coursed through him. He had spent most of his adult life reading about Dr. Weeks and his amazing studies into Darkness Visible, yet sitting only a few feet from him now, he felt an incredible sense of shame and inferiority.

"Things went very wrong tonight, Patrick. Did you know that?"

The Abbot swallowed hard. "No, I did not. I followed your plan step-by-step, Doctor."

The books on the shelves shook slightly. "No! No, you did not!" Another book fell to the floor.

Before the Abbot could reply, Dr. Weeks stood up and pounded his fists on the desk, breaking it into four pieces. The fire crackled louder.

"It was unfinished. You could not have followed it step-by-step, because it was not done!" said Dr. Weeks, leaning even closer to the Abbot, who was now petrified.

"You added a thirteenth nun to the ritual. Why did you do this?"

The Abbot was trying not to make eye contact, but it was impossible not to be captivated by those searing blue eyes and crazy red hair of the dead doctor.

"She was only supposed to help them. Sister Mary Concordia was only there to make sure the plan was a success," the Abbot said, fearful to respond at all.

The stench from Dr. Weeks was enough to make the Abbot vomit. The pain in his stomach was even more intense now as he shifted uncomfortably on the couch. He wondered if he should run to the door, but he knew that the Satanist would stop him and things would be worse.

"Each of those twelve nuns was hand-picked because of their interaction with someone of incredible evil. You got that part of it correct. Those diabolical sinners would make up each of the twelve equal parts of Satan on Earth. A deliberate perversion of the twelve apostles," his voice was escalating in volume as the walls shook. "So why did you add a thirteenth nun?" He kicked a piece of the desk across the room.

The Abbot's mind was racing. He didn't know what to say.

"She was young. She didn't have any interaction with a sadistic person like the others. She was pure. She was a virgin!" replied the Abbot, defending his actions to the man who had created the ancient texts.

Now Dr. Weeks was pacing back and forth, anger seething from every part of his body, as he ran both hands through his wild red hair. The Abbot reached for his stomach. The pain intensified with each step the doctor took.

"Yes, she was a virgin. Yes, she was pure. But she did interact with someone with a horrible past. You changed my work by adding her! How dare you!"

The walls continued to shake as books began flying from the shelves to the floor, across the room to the wall surrounding the fireplace, and at the Abbot himself. He shielded his face from them as they struck him with ferocity.

"But who? Who did she know that would have been so terrible?" Tears began to well up in his eyes.

Dr. Weeks stopped pacing and moved to within an inch of the Abbot's shaking face.

"You! You, damn it! You!" said Dr. Weeks, his rotten breath coating the priest's face like a wet blanket.

The Abbot was shocked at the response. "Me?"

"Yes! You! She saw you that night at the black mass. Don't you remember the sacrifice of the infant? You have the blood on your hands of dozens upon dozens, you worthless wretch! You arrogant bastard!" he exclaimed, smacking the Abbot across the face, nearly knocking him off the couch.

The Abbot's mind was flooding with emotion and cluttered with thoughts of what he just heard. *Could it be? Could I have tainted Darkness Visible by not realizing that I myself was a despicable human?* The hubris of the Abbot had made looking at himself in a negative way nearly impossible. He knew that Darkness Visible was not complete, but all he had read and all of his personal study made him believe that he could complete the work that Dr. Weeks had started. He had made several trips to England in his youth, finding the home on McNaulty Street, which had been converted over the years to a post office. He was able to gain access to the former office of Dr. Weeks, sealed off from the rest of the post office with solid plaster walls. He himself had found the texts inside the void of the former fireplace. The Abbot had read the words that Dr. Weeks had written, and he knew them better than anyone.

Suddenly the Abbot felt those same invisible hands throw him down to the floor as Dr. Weeks stood over him, glaring and raving mad.

"All of your arrogance. All of your narcissistic ways have caused a major problem!"

The pain in the Abbot's stomach was at a fever pitch now. He grimaced in agony, holding both hands over it, in a futile attempt to deaden the pain. The remainder of the books were flying off the shelves and swirling around the study. The wood floor began to buckle, and the plaster walls and ceiling reverberated with the incredible force.

"And then you used one of my descendants in your plan. You had the incredible arrogance to think that you could use my own flesh and blood to carry it out! How dare you?" he screamed as chunks of the plaster ceiling began to fall down. The wood floor buckled all around the quivering Abbot, writhing on the floor in pain.

The Abbot knew that William Weeks was a descendant of Dr. Wilfred Weeks. That was why he chose the man. He thought having a blood relative carry out the plan would be a sort of homage to the 17th century Satanist.

"You thought wrong, priest! You thought very wrong!" his demonic voice shook the entire room, as if an earthquake had struck. The Abbot was terrified!

"All of your arrogance! You changed my work without regard for all I did to create it. Now the infernal thing you created is not Satan in human form. It is a very dark and evil entity, but it is not what I intended it to be. For that you must pay, dear Abbot! For your disgusting hubris, Patrick, you will pay!"

Now the Abbot was rolling back and forth, the pain in his stomach beyond compare. The sounds in the study were reaching a maddening level as the room continued to shake. The enraged Dr. Weeks stood in the center, his hands reaching the sky and his head thrown back in a hideous display of anger.

"You will now see what you have done, Patrick Reilly! You will now be born again and see the err of your ways!" said Dr. Weeks, his eyes closed and his mouth wide open, growling with hate.

The Abbot felt something move inside of him. He clutched at his stomach, the pain becoming too intense to endure a moment longer. Suddenly a tearing sound could be heard as he felt something rip. It was his own skin!

Dr. Weeks was still in the center of the room. Books were swirling around. Pieces of the desk that he had broken were also levitating in the air. The room was quivering in his infernal presence. Chunks of plaster and dust began to cloud the air.

"Come forth! Come forth!"

The tearing continued as what appeared to be a small, gnarled hand came through his stomach. The Abbot was horrified at the sight, yet despite the incredible pain, he could not take his eyes off what he was seeing. The hand continued to move from his body, and then another, as something vile pried itself from his stomach and chest cavity. Bones were snapping, and skin was ripping. Blood was flowing from the cavernous opening.

"You lived your life with good looks. You had the gift of intellect, unnatural speaking abilities. You had everything but you chose to abuse it. You chose to disgrace me by changing my life's work and using my own flesh and blood to carry it out!" the doctor said, his arms still stretching to the sky.

The Abbot was delirious with the overwhelming agony of the creature that was now climbing out of him. It was like a nightmare, yet he knew deep down it was not a dream. The pain was exquisite, and the disgusting thing that was crawling from his still warm body was real.

The creature began to stand up, blood and a black ooze was dripping from his frail body. He was not quite five-feet-tall and hunched over. His body was covered in sores and tumors that made movement very painful. His face was hideous, with yellow eyes and terrible deformities that made him look more like a monster than human. The Abbot was horrified to see what had just climbed out of his body, and while he should have been dead, Dr. Weeks was keeping him alive to enjoy the show.

"Now you will become everything you were not. Now you will live for all eternity in this new body. You will forever be trapped in this putrid beast!" said Dr. Weeks, now staring at the Abbot, who was fading fast, but still aware of what was going on.

The hunched over creature was now also staring at the Abbot. He looked closer at the monster and saw his mouth was sewn shut. A crude, crisscross pattern of rough string was used to keep his mouth closed, with enough of a gap between the sutures to allow him to drink through a straw – and no more.

As the Abbot began to bleed out on the floor of his study, the flames from the fireplace began to consume the books that were flying around the room. The study began to ignite as the Abbot felt the intense heat on his skin. Dr. Weeks wanted him to feel the pain of burning, as he was unable to do anything, his new body hunched over and watching the entire infernal spectacle.

"You will now die, priest. Your former body will be consumed with fire and die an agonizing death. Yet your new body will continue on – FOREVER! You will be here at St. Michael's serving the church and the hypocrites who call themselves men of the cloth. You will be treated horribly, just as you treated those who served you," he cried out, his red hair swaying wildly in the chaos.

The Abbot was screaming in indescribable agony as the flames began to consume him and the rest of his private study. Flames licked at the walls, floor, ceiling, and bookshelves, and a thick black smoke began to rise. As he began to fade away from the mortal world, his new body was looking down at him, a disfigured and grotesque face staring on with fascination at his own demise. It was as if the creature understood how he was being transformed from a once-great man into a vile, miserable thing.

As the scene played out, Dr. Weeks stood at the doorway of the study, his hands resting on the hunchback's gnarled shoulders. The Abbot looked up at the both of them, and with his final agonizing breath, he heard the last words he would ever hear as a living thing.

"Meet your new self. Your name is now Enoch Strange."

PART TWO
Low Twelve

Who will be there when I draw my last breath?
Who's eyes will mine be the last to see?
A brief pause as I pass on from this world
Will be my low twelve when darkness comes to call.
Pete Altieri/Low Twelve

PETE ALTIERI

1

Summer 1985 - Wichita, Kansas

Philip Edwards was trying to keep his composure. It seemed lately his temper would flare up at the most inopportune times. This was one of those days. It was Friday night, and he had a long week at the office. It was simply miserable dealing with incompetent co-workers to get the major sales report done for his boss, Andrew. Philip spent several late nights working in his glorified jail cell, also known as a cubicle. Death by cubicle was more like it. While other employees seemed to ingratiate and accept the padded room without a ceiling - Philip did not. The rest of his department adorned their cubicles with pictures of their kids and grandkids, banners from their favorite sports teams, or pictures of vacations in warm places so they had some solace on those dreary winter days. Philip did none of that. The only thing he had hanging up was one family picture with his wife and two kids and a simple sign he bought one day at a yard sale that read "TGIF". Philip loved Friday because it meant he would have two days away from Andrew and his cubicle and time to spend with his family. He loved them beyond compare. Friday was a day filled with anticipation of good things to come.

No one else in the department worked past 5:00 pm, but Philip did, and he hoped that Andrew would realize how hard he was working and give him the promotion. The report was very important to a large corporate meeting where Andrew had to address the board of directors to help explain why sales were lagging. Low sales numbers put everyone on edge, especially Andrew who was constantly catching heat from above. Praise was dealt infrequently and seemed to wane quickly, while the negative kind came up often, and when it did, it lingered. Philip knew he had been overlooked for far too long, and he refused to let this promotion slip by. He would simply will it to happen, or so he thought. Philip knew the promotion would come with headaches, but he was willing to deal with that for a lot more money and a ticket out of the cubicle into a real office. In his own office, Philip could shut the door and keep everyone else's germs to themselves. The cubicle offered none of that, and every cough and sneeze seemed to be amplified. Philip often reached for his hand sanitizer and vitamin C drops to combat the sickness all around him. He did his best to hide his fixation with germs, but you didn't have to work around Philip long to know, that he was bat shit crazy about being clean, orderly, and following procedures at all times.

He was trying not to lose his temper now in the line at the pharmacy, picking up some medicated cream that Tammy needed for a rash on her leg. His wife, Janice, thought it was just prickly heat, but Philip didn't agree and insisted she be taken to the doctor. When she was prescribed the cream, he volunteered to pick it up on his way home from the office. He would likely gloat when he got home about how he was smarter than the average guy for knowing it was something that needed medication. Janice didn't argue with him, because she knew that Philip had a low self-esteem issue. If it made him feel better for a while, then so be it. She had lived with his germ phobia and odd ways for nine years now. Their daughter, Tammy, was 8 years old now and well aware of her father's obsession with cleanliness, germs, and meticulous order. The youngest, Todd, was barely three and didn't know much more than what cartoons he liked and what time food was served. Both kids were his pride and joy, and he enjoyed spending time doing things together. He and Janice liked their Friday movie night the best, and the kids were still young enough to look forward to it with vigor.

Directly in front of Philip in line was a young Hispanic woman with a baby in a stroller and a toddler running around her yelling something repeatedly in Spanish. The toddler was sniffling and sneezing, and with each mucous membrane explosion, Philip felt like he needed to run away to a bathroom and thoroughly wash his hands and face. If he had his choice, he would have bathed in hand sanitizer. Speaking of sanitizer, Philip knew that he left a small bottle in the console of his car. He kept a larger container of it in his trunk so he could keep the smaller bottle full at all times. Right now he was facing a sea of germs with nothing at all to stop it. In the distance he heard a terrible instrumental version of "The Safety Dance" on the pharmacy intercom. *We can dance if we want to, we can leave your friends behind.* He always hated that song. He wished he was somewhere else. The storm around him swirled with ominous clouds and impending rain.

Finally, Philip was second from the counter, in a line that was winding into the vitamin aisle by now, as people stopped by on their way home from work. He noted there was an elderly couple behind him, talking about someone they knew who had the flu in July, and despite having had their shot, had to be hospitalized over it. Behind them was a man in his 30's on a cell phone, and as everyone within earshot knew, he was talking his mother about what lice shampoo to buy for his daughter. Philip felt his skin crawl at the notion. The man on the phone was telling his mother that she had gotten them at camp and that he had to wash all the bedding and upholstery. His mother was yelling back at him, but all anyone could hear was an inaudible static-filled rant. His mother sounded hostile, adding yet another layer of chaos that seemed to engulf Philip on this Friday after work. He was overwhelmed but keeping things under control. Barely.

He hummed along with the chorus of "The Safety Dance" and hated himself for it. *We can dance, we can dance, everybody's takin' the chance.*

"Thanks for your patience. How can I help you today?" said the young cashier, a round band aid covering her bottom lip piercing. Philip couldn't help but wonder how many germs would get into that small hole in her lip.

"Picking up a prescription for Edwards. First name is Tammy." He noticed a bottle of hand sanitizer on the counter and helped himself to a glob to clean his hands while the cashier worked on taking care of his request.

******

Philip was smiling now in the confines of his Honda Accord. It was meticulously clean at all times. He went to the car wash at least twice a week but vacuumed the inside top to bottom every other day. A lint roller was in the glove compartment just in case he needed a quick clean up.

Now he could resume his love for Friday as he took the usual route home, complete with Tammy's prescription, two rental DVDs for them to watch tonight and tomorrow, some assorted snacks, and a bottle of wine for him and Janice to enjoy when the kids went to bed. It was her birthday tomorrow, and he had made reservations at a favorite Italian restaurant of theirs. Then they were going to a new jazz club to watch a local band. Tonight was sort of a pre-game to all that, and Philip hoped that he would get lucky tonight after the movie, the bottle of wine, and the quiet of the kids fast asleep. Even something like sex was a thought-out activity that required a lot of preparation and planning. He always showered after.

Janice was ordering pizza for tonight, but Philip never indulged. He read a story once in a magazine about what young kids do to food in restaurants, and it featured a vile tale about a pizza place that urinated on pizzas if they didn't like the customer. Philip vowed to never eat a pizza again unless he was making it himself. Janice had some frozen pizza for Philip to make for himself and then eat with the family.

He tapped his finger to Cab Calloway's "Everyone Eats in My House" as he pulled on to Lake View Drive, only a few blocks from their house. It was 1212 Lake View Drive, and within a few moments he was pulling into the driveway. He could feel the stress of the week slowly leave his body as he hit the button to raise the garage door. It was a large 18-foot door for the two-car garage, and it took a larger opener to raise it. They had the door company add custom cedar woodwork in a herringbone pattern, which increased the weight of the door a great deal, but they both loved the way it looked. Slowly the door raised up. For some reason, someone had left the overhead lights on. Philip hated to waste electricity, so this was something he didn't want to see coming home on a Friday – or any day for that matter.

Suddenly he saw something that didn't look right in the garage. Philip shut off the engine and stared ahead in disbelief. He even took off his glasses and wiped them with the cloth he kept for that purpose in his glove compartment. The wall where he kept all his wrenches and assorted other tools was in shambles. There were several fist-sized holes in the pegboard over the drywall. Not even half of the tools he kept hung, in meticulous order by size, were where they were supposed to be. The metal hangers that he used were bent, and the rest were missing. His workbench below where the tools were hung was a mess. There were muddy footprints going into the garage from outside, to the work bench, and then into the house. Philip was furious! Then he heard the screaming.

******

Philip's head was swimming with thoughts and all of them were very bad. It felt like he was in a dream as he ran from his car into the garage, ducking his head under the door that was stuck part of the way up. Hanging from the overhead door track was the lifeless and bloody body of their neighbor, Brian Hagarty. Brian would come by and cut the grass, trim hedges and trees, clean the gutters, and do various things for Philip. He was more than happy to pay Brian, a senior in high school, to do those chores, and he enjoyed contributing to his college fund at the same time. The Edwards' home was on a large 4-acre lot with a sprawling yard, two dozen maple and pine trees, and large hedges to help keep the privacy Philip always wanted. The closest neighbor was two football fields away.

Now Brian was hanging from the metal track, handcuffs joining him at the wrists. His half-naked body was full of gashes and deep cuts in what had to have been a slow and miserable death. His face was frozen in terror. His eyes were open wide, telling a story so horrible it would freeze blood to ice. The mouth was agape in a mid-scream posture, while his lips were cracked and swollen. A pool of blood, still warm, was growing in size toward one of the floor drains. His body swung slowly in the summer night breeze.

Sickened at the site, Philip covered his eyes as he brushed by the bloodied corpse and made his way to the house. Outside the doorway, by the light switch, was a bloody handprint on the door frame. It was fresh, and Philip had no idea whose it was, yet the hand seemed large, like a full grown man's. He heard the screaming again, and more agonizing thoughts raged through his skull as he staggered into the kitchen. A strong scent of body odor was prevalent.

125

"Where the fuck is the chainsaw?" a large, booming man said in the dining room, to the left and out of view.

A chilling scream pierced the air. "Please, no! No! My God, no!" It was a female voice, hoarse and ragged with fear. The terror was real.

Philip was panicking now. He realized the voice belonged to Janice, and it settled in his stomach like a rusty metal anchor.

"How should I know? Watch your mouth around these children!" another man sounded out. This voice sounded proper and more educated than the other much gruffer and gravelly tone. He sounded older as well.

Then a third person chimed in. This voice sounded like it had a Southern accent. He was loud and came across like he was in charge.

"Here it is. Now let's get this done!" Janice was screaming incoherently.

The motor of the chainsaw suddenly cut the warm, humid air. Whoever was holding the saw was pulling the trigger to make it whine louder, adding to the terror. Philip's anxiety and fear went to places he'd never imagined as he crept slowly through the kitchen and closer to the dining room. He was petrified of what he was going to see, but his family was inside. He knew there were three men to deal with, and he had no weapon. Slowly he rose up from his crouched position behind the butcher block table in the middle of the room to see if he could grab one of the kitchen knives Janice kept near the toaster. He didn't see them. They were gone! His fear ratcheted up at the thought of unknown people inside his house armed with six sharpened cooking knives.

"Daddy!" sounded from across the kitchen, as Todd came running toward him. There was fear in his little voice. He held up his hands to signal the toddler to stop, but Todd kept running across the ceramic tile floor. His little bare feet made a pitter-patter sound as he sped along toward Philip. He looked petrified!

Suddenly someone stepped out of the dining room and into the kitchen. He was large and clumsy in the dim light. Philip ducked down below an open lower cabinet door. The man turned on the overhead light above the butcher block. Todd stopped mid-step as the bright light forced him to cover his eyes. He was shaking with terror, and instinctively he began to urinate in his pants. Todd held his head down and cried as his urine pooled up at his own tiny bare feet.

"So that's where you went, you little bastard," said the man whose voice he heard asking about the chainsaw. He was a large-framed young man in his early 20's, with several tattoos on his muscular arms and a bald head that gleamed in the bright light. He grabbed Todd before he could get to Philip. The boy squirmed in the man's grasp, crying out and reaching for Philip.

"You're a nasty little bastard. You got piss all over me!"

Philip started running toward the garage when he felt something hit him hard on the back of his head, sending him sprawling across the floor. Then everything went black.

******

Philip awakened to cold liquid splashed across his face. He sputtered and shook his head back and forth quickly. Immediately he realized that his glasses were missing. Everything was blurry at a distance. He could feel a sharp throbbing pain in the back of his head, where something had hit him before he blacked out. He felt a wave of nausea sweep over him, and, realizing he was tied to one of their dining room chairs, Philip leaned his head to the left and vomited up whatever was left in his stomach. It stung his throat and left an awful taste in his mouth. Throwing up made his head hurt even worse. The throbbing was intense.

"It's about time you woke up, sleeping beauty!" said the same bald man Philip had seen in the kitchen moments before. The man backhanded Philip really hard across the face, punctuating the intense pain he now realized was all over his face and upper body.

Philip was out of the daze he was in. He could hear Janice whimpering in the dim light. He couldn't make out anything but shapes at a distance without his glasses. His body was awash in terror at all the unknowns going on around him. Philip was a person who needed to be in control. His well-structured life, filled with schedules and procedures, was now in utter turmoil, and the stress that he was enduring was palpable. His heart was racing wildly, and he found it difficult to control his breathing. Things were slipping quickly out of his control. Thinking about the situation made Philip throw up again. The sting was even worse to his throat.

"Janice? Are you OK?" he said in a quiet voice, realizing they were not alone.

Janice only cried. She was trying to say something, but her words were unintelligible. She cried out as someone slapped her face. Philip pulled hard at his restraints at the sounds coming from his loving wife. Despite his sometimes cold demeanor, Philip did love Janice and the kids more than anything. Hearing her cry and babble hurt him deeply, and he felt the ropes cut into his own flesh as he continued to pull at the restraints.

"Oh she's just fucking dandy, my boy!" said another man in the room that Philip couldn't make out. Then the chainsaw sounded again, and Janice let out a scream. "Just fucking dandy!" A hideous laugh followed, still drowned out by Janice's hoarse screams and the whine of that 35 cubic centimeter chainsaw engine. The smell of gasoline and the exhaust was thick in the stagnant air of the dining room.

Suddenly Philip felt someone extremely strong grab him and the chair he was tied to and move him across the wood floor toward the family room. He could hear Janice whimpering and doing her best to communicate with him in a state of delirium. Her voice was raspy and drenched in misery. Philip wanted to reach out to her, but he was unable to move his arms even an inch the way he was tied down to the chair. He could not make out much in the shadows of the dining room as he was dragged past her. A tear fell down his cheek.

"It will be OK, honey," he said quietly. "I love you." Desperation had his voice in a choke hold.

"Well, wasn't that fucking sweet!" The man laughed again.

Abruptly, Philip was thrown down to the living room floor, his face hitting the polished hardwood with a crunch as his nose was broken to pieces. Blood was streaming from his nose and into his mouth, running down his chin. He spat out two broken front teeth. The pain was intense, but the terror that swept over him was all-consuming and maddening. *Where is Todd? Where is Tammy? Is Janice OK?* The questions ripped into his brain in rapid succession. Panic had fully taken hold. *Who are these guys, and why are they doing this? Was it a robbery?*

"Pick his ass up. He needs to see this shit," said a completely different man than he heard before.

In his jumbled mind, Philip was trying to assess how many people he was dealing with here in his house. Was it six? Maybe seven? He couldn't keep track. Before he could give it another thought, someone roughly picked him up from the floor with the chair and sat him upright. Philip felt someone put his glasses on, the right lens was severely scratched, and the frame was bent, but things slowly came into focus. He took one look and shut his eyes hard to protect himself from such a deplorable vision.

"Open your fucking eyes, fuck boy!" cried out one of the voices he had heard before.

"Daddy!" he heard Todd's tiny voice cry out. He was crying.

The large, bald man was now grabbing Philip by the hair and yelling into his face. Spit was flying as the burly man continued to scream at him.

"You better open those eyes, or I'll rip them out one at a time with a rusty spoon," he said in the Southern voice he heard before.

Philip looked up and saw a nightmarish sight. Both of his children were nailed to the living room wall across from the fireplace, with what appeared to be the tent stakes that Philip kept in the garage with his camping stuff. The stuff he had never used, but wanted on hand just in case. Todd was squirming in pain and crying out, held at a strange angle with one single metal stake sticking out of his collar bone. The toddler was going into shock from the pain. He was losing blood and fading from consciousness. Philip was driven mad at the sight.

"It hurts, Daddy. It hurts really, really bad!" said Todd, barely coherent.

The bald man started laughing again. It was a cavernous, deep, yet dark laugh.

"It hurts, Daddy!" the large man squeaked, mocking Todd's cry for help.

"You son-of-a-bitch!" yelled Philip, tugging at his binds – both arms and legs. The ropes tore at his flesh in the effort.

Now the bald man turned toward him and got into his face yet again. His eyes were open wide and alive with madness. He was clearly off the rails of sanity.

"You better shut the fuck up, Daddy. You hear me?" his Southern drawl seemed stronger as his rage began to tick up a few notches. "You ain't seen nothing yet." He started laughing again. He reached down and picked something up that was out of Philip's sight. Then he held the lifeless body of Tammy in front of Philip. Her face was horribly swollen and black and blue. She looked like she'd been dead a while, as her skin was a light blue color. Her eyes were open, yet vacant and absent of any sign of life. He tore at the ropes once again, as the bindings ripped painfully at his flesh, causing his wrists to bleed profusely.

"You son-of-a-bitch!" cried Philip, tears streaming down his face at the site of his lifeless daughter. The man threw her down like a sack of laundry. Philip had an awful feeling at the heavy thud on the floor.

"I told you to shut up. You don't wanna listen, then?"

"No, please. Don't hurt anyone else. We can work something out. You want money? You want any of the stuff in the house? Take it. Take all of it. Just please let us go." Philip was hysterical, his voice ragged and strangled. His breathing was rapid and out of control, and his heartbeat continued to thunder on.

The bald man looked Philip directly in the eyes and laughed again. This time real slow at first, then building to a maniacal cacophony.

"I'm your nightmare maker!" his voice boomed into the vaulted ceilings of the living room and reverberated back and forth. In one fluid motion, the man grabbed a wood-handled axe that was propped up against the wall and swung it with precision, chopping off Todd's head with a dull crunch and sharp cry.

Philip tried to scream out, but there was no sound. He felt his entire world collapse on all sides. He was thrashing in his chair, desperately pulling at his restraints, but to no avail. The ropes were very tight and expertly tied. They continued to tear at Philip's wrists. He arched his back as much as he could, and again let out a silent scream. Veins were protruding from his neck, his entire face and neck bright red in fierce resistance to what he just witnessed. It was like a nightmare. A nightmare he couldn't wake from. Again the maniac, still wielding the axe, laughed out loud.

This time the laugh was different. The bald man walked toward a dimly lit area of the living room, out of the view of Philip. He heard glass breaking, and then shouting – like two or three adult males arguing.

"Why do you have to do that stuff? I mean, really!" said the man with the proper, educated voice from earlier.

"Why don't you mind your own god damn business?" asked the large bald man in his Southern drawl.

"You two need to cut this out. We need to wrap this up, and then I'm burning this house to the ground. Too much evidence around here to hang us ten times," said a totally different voice Philip had not heard before.

The man with the proper speech replied, "You will do no such thing! Put that thought from your mind. You are not lighting this house on fire and bringing every cop and fireman in the area down the main road we need to take in order to get away from here."

Philip was breathing heavily, trying to do what he could to keep it together despite the fact he had seen his dead daughter thrown around like a rag doll, and then his little son decapitated by a blood-thirsty killer. *What is going on with Janice? Is she still alive? Thank God she didn't have to see that. My God! How can I go on without the kids?* He began to weep uncontrollably.

"OK, Philip. It's show time, my man! Pull it together!" said another man from the dark area of the room. He slowly came walking toward Philip, and it was the same bald man from moments ago! Yet his voice was completely different, and his demeanor was not nearly as aggressive.

He pulled out a hunting knife and cut the binds that held Philip to the chair. It was a welcome feeling as the ropes fell to the floor and blood began to flow into his hands and feet again. His wrists were gouged by the rope, but it was still a good feeling to be out of the bindings. Philip tried to stand, but the man put a firm hand on his shoulder.

"Now, don't go getting cute on me. You don't do a damn thing without me telling you what to do. I'll slit your throat if you even think about trying to run. Plus, your legs will be tingly for a good 30 minutes," he leaned into Philip's face, "so you aren't going anywhere." His eyes were pure evil. Like bottomless pools, all Philip could see was a cold darkness inside.

Philip merely shook his head in the affirmative and stared at the large bald man in disbelief that he was so different from before. Yet this new persona was extremely firm and deliberate. Now the man grabbed Philip by his shirt collar and belt and lead him toward the dining room where he last saw Janice alive. His legs were asleep, and it felt like he wasn't even walking at all. The bald man was so strong and powerful that Philip felt like a marionette in his firm grasp.

"You ready for this shit, Phil?" the man said, laughing in a more high-pitched tone than before, as they crossed the threshold into the dining room. He tightened his grip on Philip's shirt collar, twisting it to almost choking him.

Suddenly the dining room was filled with light, and the true horror of what was waiting for him was in the middle of the room. His wife, Janice, was spread-eagle on their formal dining room table. It was a gift from his grandparents when they got married. Now his beautiful wife was barely dressed, bloodied, battered, and holding on to life by fraying threads.

"Oh my God!" cried Philip, falling to his knees. Tears were streaming down his face. His entire body shook with anger, rage, and helplessness. His nerves were like stretched piano wires, frayed and snapping one at a time.

Janice turned her head slightly and acknowledged her tormented husband. She had been beaten up by the large bald man, savagely raped for hours, and now the metal tent stakes were through each of her hands, keeping them down to the beautiful oak table. Her bare feet were also staked down to the table, but in a spread-eagle position, so she was available to the bald man if he chose to take her again. Janice continued to pray for death to come. Her entire body was sore, and she was in and out of consciousness. Janice was so hoarse from screaming that no sound would come out. Like her husband, she would let out the most primal silent screams until her eyes bulged out with a vengeance. Death could not come to claim her soon enough.

******

As Janice lay on the table, knowing that the end was about to come, she remembered earlier in the day and how everything turned upside down. She was getting the kids ready for day camp. She was cooking breakfast and making lunches, and they were buzzing about what was going on that day in summer camp. Life was good. Then the doorbell rang. She went to answer it, and a well-dressed young man was standing outside with a briefcase. He was bald and broad-shouldered, and obviously strong, yet there was something very charismatic about him. The man told her he was a salesman and sparked her interest talking about a new laundry detergent that was the best to get stains out of clothing. He was a natural, and he won her confidence to invite him inside. Once he gained access and realized there were no other adults in the home, the man erupted into a raving maniac, and the day became an eternity of sheer terror. Tears escaped her bloodied and crusted-over eyes, knowing that it was her bad judgement which had lead to all this. If she had listened to Philip and never allowed the man inside the house, this all would not have happened. The guilt was unbearable. It was a dagger in her dying heart. Still, death would not come to call.

Suddenly the quiet moment was shattered with the roar of the chainsaw. The bald man walked into the room laughing in an unnerving way, waving the chainsaw around, while revving the motor to add to the mayhem. Philip was cowering on the floor as the man walked past him, lowering the saw as he approached the table and Janice. She looked so pitiful, completely defenseless as the maniac had the chainsaw only a few inches away from her crotch. Janice closed her eyes as tightly as she could and began to whisper prayers, as she did her best to blot out her reality. She braced for unimaginable pain and hoped it would be over quickly.

"I'm your nightmare maker, baby!" the bald man screamed out, his Southern twang now back, and his volatile persona back in full gear. His eyes darted about the pathetic victim before him, and he became aroused at the idea of what he was about to do.

He lowered the chainsaw down and blood flew in every direction possible. The bald man let out a booming laugh and continued to push the saw into Janice's flesh and bone. The saw jumped up and down as it met with resistance, and the blood continued to spew, painting the dining room walls and ceiling. Janice's back arched awkwardly, and her mouth was open wide in a final silent scream. Then the pain was over. Still the bald man pushed on until he literally cut the woman in half. The saw idled now, and the man backed up from the table, covered from head to toe in blood, brain, and bone fragments. Philip was still on his knees, completely catatonic from what he had witnessed. He also was covered in her blood – only the whites of his eyes could be seen as he knelt down in defeat. He had nothing left to give after what he had seen on this night.

"I hope you liked the show," the bald man said, turning to Philip. He laughed, in a low guttural way. The man raised one of his powerful arms and wiped the blood from his face. It didn't do much good.

He shut off the chainsaw and tossed it to the floor. He pulled the hunting knife from its sheath and moved with stealth toward the dazed Philip. He didn't say a word as the bald man swiped the large blade across his throat, severing his jugular vein and spouting his own blood now like a fountain. Phillip imagined the picture of his family that he kept in his cubicle at work. He almost laughed at the irony that he was thinking about that cursed cubicle he hated so much, in the fleeting swan song of his life. The last thing he saw before collapsing to the floor was the bald man wiping the blood off on his pants before putting the knife back into its sheath.

******

An hour had passed when the bald man walked away from 1212 Lakeview Drive. It was early morning, and the sun was casting a fresh light upon the landscape. Freshly showered, fed, and a clean set of clothes was just what he needed to move on. A red and white 1973 Ford pick- up truck was parked in the woods off one of the country roads nearby. He had parked it there earlier.

"Let's go," he said in a bland Midwestern tone.

Turning on the engine, the cassette player came on, picking up where he had left off. He smiled when he heard "Back in Black" and turned it up a little. He also pulled out an old spiral notebook from under the seat. He spent a few minutes writing in it and enjoying the music. He felt alive.

Glancing in the rearview mirror, something caught his attention. Looking into his own eyes, he felt like himself now. He felt like the Nolan Weeks that he had been his whole life. Over the past two months, Nolan would start to feel weird right before one of the people inside of him would take over. There would be nothing he could do to stop them, and even worse, he would be a bystander watching from the sidelines while they acted out their horrible fantasies upon the innocent. Nolan lost count at how many there were. The sights he had seen since they invaded his body were dreadful. Just when he thought he knew them all, another would step out of the shadows and take over for a while. Yet now, as he looked at himself, he knew that for the time being, it was only Nolan. Despite that fact, his eyes were still cold. No matter who was taking charge, his eyes couldn't lie. His eyes told the tale. His eyes would present him to anyone who wanted to look, as someone who was the embodiment of pure evil.

He began to question if he was any better than the others. As they moved seamlessly in and out of the control seat, there was almost no way to know who was who. It was those eyes, though, that he saw in the rearview mirror, and he knew they would show his enemy that he meant business. Deadly business.

Then he thought about something his Uncle Donny told him about his time in Vietnam. He remembered him talking about setting up claymore mines around the camp perimeter, so if the enemy attacked, the good guys could set them off. He told Nolan that the side that you pointed toward the enemy actually said right on the mine, *this side toward enemy.* He could still hear Uncle Donny sitting at the kitchen table, chain smoking and drinking black coffee, talking about how the mines were filled with hundreds of small BB's. He seemed to enjoy telling Nolan how the mines could tear a man in half if he got close enough. Nolan thought of that now and how his own hate-filled stare would be like his own claymore mine: ready to explode and eliminate anyone who tried to stop him.

I'm back! Yes, I'm back! Back in black – I'm back in black!

Nolan turned up the stereo before pulling away in search of some hot, black coffee. Thinking about Uncle Donny and his old man made him want some even more, and maybe even a pack of cigarettes. Camels – just like the old man. It sickened Nolan to think of himself acting like his Dad. He knew what his Dad was. He had seen what his Dad did. Some things can't be unseen.

For now, Nolan sang along to the music and knew he had a lot of ground to cover and plenty of hunting to get done. It was only a matter of time before he would be a spectator again and one of the entities inside of him would erupt and need to feed. This side toward enemy.

2

Fall 1994

Nolan stared out the two-foot by two-foot barred window of the holding cell in the prison's main building. He was watching cars drive along 11th Street, on the north side of Huntsville State Prison. The oldest prison in Texas, Huntsville started taking inmates in 1849, and is the home of the only execution chamber in the state for males. It is the busiest in the US, with more than 500 executions since the death penalty was reinstated in Texas in 1982.

"What ya lookin' at Weeks?" said the very large Sergeant Roland "Rollie" Whitlock. His body was rippled with muscle beneath the impeccable uniform, with shoes highly shined, and all his hardware sparkling in the bright fluorescent lights above.

He was getting his prisoner ready to be restrained to the chair inside the holding cell, as other correctional officers were briefing a member of the media and his camera crew, scheduled to interview Nolan Weeks, in another room. Sergeant Whitlock oversaw the correctional officers assigned to the main building, which were typically the most spit-shined and best of the best, to keep up good appearances for any of the top brass that liked to show up with politicians around election time. He was going to be reaching 25 years with the department, and he was hoping to get a transfer to the Department of Parks and Wildlife, where he could spend his days outside rather that cooped up with the most despicable in Huntsville. He did enjoy the work, but the people (both inmates and co-workers) were becoming harder to deal with, and after two bitter marriages that crashed and burned in divorce court, he was ready for a change.

The other officer in the cell was on a knee chaining the prisoner to the chair. Nolan was staring out the window still. Sergeant Whitlock watched the prisoner closely, as the young officer was in a vulnerable position. Nolan Weeks didn't move at all.

"Ain't seen outside a window for a year, Sarge," Nolan replied in his slow drawl, "Shit looks different."

"I bet."

Sergeant Whitlock gave the restraints a good, thorough check, which was partly due to Texas Department of Corrections protocol, and partly because he was working with a new officer for the past two weeks. Officer Bobby Lewis was from nearby Oakhurst, Texas and was a third-generation corrections officer. His grandfather started working at Huntsville right after coming home from World War I in 1918, and his father in 1941 until he retired in 1971. Both were well-respected at the institution by officers and inmates alike. They were of an era where altercations with the inmates were common, and his father was once nearly killed during a cafeteria riot in 1965. He had a huge scar that ran from his left ear and halfway across this throat, from a piece of plastic that was used as a weapon. Huntsville State Prison was in the new officer's blood, but he was young and still learning his way around.

It was due to his correctional officer lineage that he was chosen to work with Sergeant Whitlock on this special detail with Nolan Weeks. Every inmate at Huntsville knew all about Nolan Weeks, and he was a target from day one, which is why they had to house him in protective custody with at least four officers taking him wherever he needed to go. Sergeant Whitlock had overseen his safe-keeping recently.

After his recent stay of execution, Weeks had become a celebrity around the prison, since any victory over the guards, warden or the State of Texas was cause for celebration. The warden despised Weeks for the attention he brought with him, and a constant parade of protestors outside the main gate, and non-stop calls from newspapers, news networks, and more drove him crazy. His secretary would keep a stack of phone messages and give them to him at the end of each day, to which he would respond by throwing them in his office waste basket. Warden Vernon Greene was only a year from retirement and the last thing he needed was an inmate like Nolan Weeks. He already had his retirement home built outside of his home town of El Paso, where he and his wife, Eliza, would settle in and spend more time with their grandchildren. He also planned to do a lot of fishing and anything else that had nothing to do with Huntsville State Prison.

The warden's hatred of Weeks was no secret around the "Walls Unit" (as the inmates called the institution), and for that, he was now their hero. Prior to that, there was one hell of a bounty on his head with a prize of guaranteed exaltation to god-like status among the rest of the prison population. It was Warden Greene who wanted the continued sequestration of Weeks, to not incite the others in his presence. As much as he disliked Weeks, he didn't want a riot at Huntsville that would tarnish his otherwise good standing in the Texas Department of Corrections. If he played his cards right, he might even get a nice consulting job in corrections for a few years, only having to attend an occasional meeting to bring in $100,000-a-year plus benefits. He even considered writing a book about his time at Huntsville, and being the one in charge when Nolan Weeks was executed would make a fine bookend to a long career in corrections. Warden Greene wanted to keep the peace, and when the governor called about the reporter coming to interview Weeks, he reluctantly agreed, in hopes to score more points before retiring.

A buzzer sounded down the hallway, and moments later, Sergeant Whitlock's radio went off.

"I've got the reporter and his crew, and we're heading your way, Sergeant."

"Roger that, Tom. We're here waiting."

Nolan finally broke his stare down of 11th Street and looked straight ahead at the metal door of the cell. There were several deep scratches in the paint from previous inmates who had occupied this cell and banged on the door for hours out of sheer frustration at their predicament. He knew that Officer Lewis was directly behind him, and there was no missing the hulking figure of Sergeant Whitlock to his right as the holding cell door buzzed loudly again, then opened.

Standing outside was another correctional officer and a 45-year-old man in dark civilian dress clothes, with a very thin frame and pensive look about him. Nolan stared directly into the man's eyes. The man met his gaze and felt a deep chill, and his graying hair tingled across his scalp. Behind him were two crew members to run the video camera, lights, and sound equipment. The network tried to get a crew of four plus Brent, but the prison wasn't going for that many people being in a room with Nolan Weeks for that amount of time. It was already a huge risk with the skeleton crew there now.

The man sat down in a chair on the other side of the hard-plastic table from Nolan. Despite his more than 20 years of experience as a reporter, Brent Dowling had never been face-to-face with a serial killer. Even though this was the break he'd been hoping for, Brent had spent several sleepless nights thinking about the horrible things that had been reported about Nolan. Every time he closed his eyes at night, images of the tortured victims haunted him. The grisliest crime scene pictures ever taken were the direct result of the man sitting only two feet from him. Brent thought he looked a little smaller in person. *Maybe it's that shitty prison food?* Thinking about prison food reminded him of several stories he had done as a beat reporter in Los Angeles, on how bad it was at the county jail. Brent zoned out looking at the tattoos on Nolan's forearms. The rest disappeared into his orange jumpsuit. His upper body was powerful and bulging under the uniform.

"Thanks for letting us do this. I'd like you to meet Danny Allen who will be running the video camera with deck lights, since you didn't want us bringing in any other lights," said Brent, as Danny nodded to the officers, then started getting his camera stuff set up.

The officers kept looking at the crew and equipment and didn't say anything.

Brent continued, "and my sound guy is Sal Russo." Sal was getting the minimal sound equipment set up.

"You got any smokes?" Nolan said smirking, with two crooked teeth peering out. His leg chains rattled and reminded Brent why he needed to be restrained. He felt a chill again.

Brent pulled out a pack of Marlboro reds and set it down in front of Nolan. Although Brent quit smoking years ago, he had heard from one of the guards at the sally port that a way to break the ice with inmates was to give them cigarettes. Sergeant Whitlock slammed his hand down and grabbed the Marlboros.

"Do not put anything in front of him, sir! You got me?" he barked at Brent, who jumped back in his chair nearly a foot.

Brent sputtered, "I'm sorry, Sergeant. I know better than that!" His heart was beating wildly. He wondered if the others in the room heard it. He felt stupid, after he just was briefed on things not to do. Number one on the list was to NOT give anything to an inmate. Even a piece of gum was not allowed.

"This man can kill you with a lot less than a pack of smokes. He's chained up for a reason, sir." His stern command was soaked in authority.

Nolan stared at Brent again. Brent shifted in his seat, then looked down.

Sal blurted in, "I need to set up a lapel microphone on the inmate. Is that OK, Sergeant? It's got a thin cord attached to it that I need to plug into my mixer."

Sergeant Whitlock held out his hand and replied, "let me see that thing." He inspected the small microphone, then handed it back. "It's fine."

Nolan was very content watching the crew set up and Sal put the lapel microphone on his jumpsuit and run the cord somewhere that he couldn't see.

Sergeant Whitlock added, "if it was up to me, this wouldn't be going on. The warden is catching heat from the man who sleeps in the governor's mansion. Some political bullshit."

"I understand," said Brent, looking up at Sergeant Whitlock.

"There's talk about another execution date coming up quick. So, we need to get this wrapped up quick. There's no guarantee he'll make it to the end of this," said Sergeant Whitlock. His tone was grim.

Brent nodded.

"The warden said we had to leave you guys in here with him. Are you sure about that? I'd be afraid to leave a pack of wolves alone with this scum bag."

Sal and Danny looked at each other nervously. They were staring at Nolan, and both were having random flashbacks of the news footage they had seen the night before at two of his kill sites. One was in Topeka, Kansas where Nolan butchered a mother, father, grandmother, and four children ranging from twelve to three. It was one of the bloodiest scenes ever recorded, and the bodies were so eviscerated, the detectives had a hard time identifying them visually. The blood-painted walls and ceilings were even more disturbing. In the formal dining room, the walls and ceilings were painted with the blood of the family, and the work was done as if a professional painting crew had been hired. The white drapes in the room, as well as the beautiful wood floors, were completely untouched by the blood found everywhere else.

The other crime scene they observed on video provided to them by the network was in the small town of LaDonna, Missouri. A Sunday school class at the Family Baptist Church never returned home that afternoon. A class of 22 children of elementary school age were slaughtered at the hand of Nolan Weeks. He raped the teacher, Selma Hutchins, who had two of her own children in the class that were forced to watch the maniac savagely attack her. After he was finished using Selma, he used a fishing knife to slit her throat, spraying blood upon the frightened faces of her students. Every exterior door in the church was stuck shut, as many of the kids ran to various exits, only to find they were trapped inside. The details of what the monster did to those 22 children is a sordid tale of beatings with broom sticks, taking a 20-pound-sledge hammer to the skull, burning several alive in a pantry, and others by his own hands. One of the younger children was found on the kitchen counter, her arm partially eaten raw by the killer.

At both crime scenes, and many others across the country, the killer would scrawl messages on the walls in blood. Most of the time he would write out NIGHTMARE MAKER in all capital letters and in prominent places at the scenes. He sometimes would paint an entire room with the blood of the victims, as he did in Topeka, with incredible skill and craftsmanship and seemingly no equipment to do the work. State medical examiners did not believe there was enough blood from the victims at the Topeka scene to paint the room the way it was done. But none of the many blood samples that were taken showed any blood other than from the victims.

Brent glanced at Nolan, who was looking out the window again, but smiling.

"Yes, those were the conditions," Brent said, also looking out the window, trying to figure out what Nolan was smiling about. "We'll be OK here with him."

Officer Lewis stepped out in the hallway. Sergeant Whitlock made his way toward the door as well. He looked sternly at Brent. He handed Brent a book of matches.

"Use these for the smokes, but don't let him near them. Just stomp the smokes out on the concrete floor. We'll get them cleaned up. Can't leave an ashtray, or he'll beat you to death with it if he gets the chance. All that camera equipment and crap you've got – it's on you if he gets a hold of something."

Brent felt a chill. *He'll beat you to death with it if he gets the chance.*

"We'll both be right outside this door. If you start screaming, we'll hear it and get in here right quick. But he can do a lot of damage in the time it takes us to get in. You got two hours. That's it." He tapped firmly on his military-grade watch.

Brent turned toward the large officer and nodded. He glanced at the large wall clock that said it was 10:12 am. His career was on its final dying gasp at CNN, as his nasty divorce had been made public with his ex-wife's accusations about physical and mental abuse, plus every detail of the two separate stints in rehab for alcoholism.

He had gone from being a morning anchor on NBC for fifteen years to the cable channel that had a much smaller audience, in a late-night slot, co-hosting a sleazy celebrity gossip show. Their ratings were terrible, so he hung on to his job with white knuckles and a prayer. He was approached by another cable network about doing a reality show based on his recent visit to rehab, but he declined. Brent knew things were going downhill, but a reality show would be the end of his career in news.

Sergeant Whitlock said something into his hand-held radio. The buzzer sounded again, and the door of the holding cell banged shut. The silence was instant and gripping.

"You wanna light me one of those smokes? Can't reach." Nolan laughed and held up his arms about an inch from the arm of the chair to show Brent he wasn't kidding. He smiled, his two crooked teeth showing.

Brent's hands trembled slightly as he opened the pack. He didn't realize Nolan was watching him and noticed his fear. A true predator notices weakness. Nolan was a human predator, who was being caged at the time, but the slightest thing could trigger him into rage. When he was on trial, he had stayed at a jail in Austin and nearly killed two inmates during a fight that started at a basketball game. One of them tried to pull the ball away from Nolan, and he beat the man nearly to death on the concrete. Then someone jumped on his back to pull Nolan off the twitching body, and he was also promptly beaten up and carried out to the infirmary on a stretcher. Throughout the rest of his trial, the sheriff kept Nolan in a single-man cell and far from the general population. After what he showed the other inmates, Nolan was not as despised as he had been, with all the media attention the case was getting. Every network was leading with the story on their news programs, and the cable news channels were parading around every expert they could find about crime scene investigation, the motives behind the serial killer, and a variety of sensational titles.

"You better hang on to that cellophane," Nolan said.

Brent reached out to put the cigarette in Nolan's lips, then struck the match to light it for him.

"What was that?" Brent asked.

"That cellophane. You better keep it from me," answered Nolan, the lit cigarette hanging expertly from his lips. Then he inhaled deeply, closing his eyes as he let out a cloud of smoke.

"What do you mean?"

"I killed a man or two with less than that." Nolan smirked.

Once again, the silence was overwhelming. Brent looked at the metal door and remembered what the officer said about hearing him scream and wondered if he would survive these two hours with Nolan Weeks.

Sal said, "I'd like to check some levels, Brent."

"OK. This is Brent Dowling and today is Monday, October 10th, 1994. I'm at Huntsville State Prison in Huntsville, Texas. This is an interview with Nolan Weeks," said Brent.

"Go on, Mr. Weeks, say something, please," said Sal, twisting a few knobs on the mixer.

"Saying something. Check 1, 2, 3, 4." Nolan laughed.

Nolan stared at them, slightly amused with the recording devices and steno notebook where Brent was keeping meticulous notes. It reminded Nolan of his own notebook that he had been writing in.

Suddenly Brent looked up from his notebook and set the recorder off to the side of the table and pressed the record button.

Danny added, "We're good to go whenever you are, boss."

Brent took a long, deep breath.

"So where should we begin, Nolan?" asked Brent, feeling slightly more at ease now, knowing the killer in front of him was securely bound. On cue, Nolan jingled his leg chains, just to keep Brent on the edge of his seat. Literally.

Suddenly the video camera shut off, and the deck lights that were providing the limited lighting they could bring, dimmed. The silence in the room was palpable, and Brent looked up uneasily at Nolan. He was smiling in the limited fluorescent lighting above.

"That's strange. I've never seen that before," said Danny, tapping the camera with his palm, but still nothing. He looked around at the power cord to try and track down the issue.

"My gear shut down, too," added Sal, also tracing the various cables down, like any tech savvy sound man would.

Brent kept his eyes fixed on Nolan, who continued smiling.

"Strange," Danny muttered, "It just came back on!" He shook his head and laughed.

Sal, also laughing, said, "Me too. That was strange."

Danny said, "We're good, Brent."

Nolan rattled his leg chains again.

"I guess we should start at the beginning," Nolan said, another lit cigarette hanging from his lips. His eyes were intense.

The bald head was a little stubbly now, since he wasn't given the use of a razor every day. Only once a week since he'd been at The Walls. Nolan did his best to get some exercise to help pass the time and stay strong, but on death row, they only had one hour each day in a caged area for one inmate at a time. His options were limited, but he made the best of it with a fairly rigorous routine of crunches, push-ups, and lots of stretching. As he sat there in the holding cell, his prison jump suit was about one size too big, but his brawn filled it in some. At 30-years-old, Nolan was getting a little slower than he was in his younger years, but he made up for it in experience and a bent for violence few could match.

Brent replied, "That sounds like a good idea. But I really need to ask you a question before we begin this interview, Mr. Weeks."

"Call me Nolan. Mr. Weeks was my daddy. Or the grandpa I never met." Nolan exhaled a huge puff of smoke that filled the small room with a haze.

"I need to ask you, Nolan, why did you choose me to do this interview with you?" Brent asked, his eyes locked in on Nolan's facial expressions. This question had driven him nuts since he heard about the interview request from his boss, Larry Baldwin, who seemed as shocked as Brent was. *No offense, Brent, but why the fuck would he want you? Seriously. You? Fuck! I've got every fucking reporter from the network calling me about it. This could put you right back on the map. Maybe even a ticket out of cable news. Back on the fucking map!*

Nolan squinted his eyes slightly, and it seemed like a dark shadow crossed over him and to the other side of the cell.

"I need you to do something for me when this is all over with, Mr. Dowling," he said, deliberate and serious.

Brent seemed surprised by the response. Of the hundreds of replies he thought that Nolan would come back with, that was not one of them. Not even close.

"Mr. Dowling is my daddy. Call me Brent."

Nolan smiled. "You got a deal, daddy."

Brent stared back at the killer intensely, trying not to take the bait of his witty remarks. "Seriously, though. What can I possibly do for you? I mean . . . you're on death row. Do you want me to find you a lawyer to get you out of here?"

"No. It's nothing like that at all. You gotta do something for me when I ask you to do it. It's not illegal. Just promise me you'll do it. I'll take your word. If you do, then we can talk as much as you want, about whatever you want. I'll make you a superstar." Nolan smiled. "A very rich superstar."

Brent took a sip of water and thought about offering Nolan a drink, but remembered what Sergeant Whitlock said about giving him anything. His mind was swimming with thoughts about what Nolan was asking of him. He wanted Brent to promise to do something, but wouldn't tell him what that something was. It was unsettling, to say the least, to let his mind wander to the infinitely sick options the demented killer might dream up.

Then Brent thought about sitting at home, approaching 50, with no real skills other than reading the news. He knew his show was on the air only because the network had no new shows ready to go. It wouldn't be long before they let him go. His once movie star good looks were fading fast, and a well-known problem with alcohol, pain meds, and marriages would keep the employers at a distance. His options were few. When Brent's agent was contacted by Nolan's attorneys, they both knew his career would ignite with options.

Everyone in the news media wanted an exclusive with Nolan Weeks, but he never spoke. Insiders tried to get to some of the guards at the county jail and then at Huntsville, and the news was the same. "He doesn't talk to anyone." Letters poured into the prison from a variety of thrill-seeking morbid teenagers, lovesick killer groupies, and even everyday people just genuinely curious enough to write a letter. There were amateur and professional psychologists alike who wanted to learn what made him do the ghastly things he did. Nolan had them thrown into the garbage, without opening a single one. He never used the phone to call anyone. No one applied to be on the approved list for visitors, and Nolan didn't add anyone to it himself.

He did enjoy watching TV in the dayroom before he was transferred to death row. Once he was a resident of the row, that came to a stop. Nolan began writing down things on the weekly allotment of paper that he could have. These papers were never shared with others, but he did mail them out monthly. Who he was mailing them to was a rather strange matter. No one wanted to talk about it. Nolan would give the papers to an assistant to the Warden, and where it went from there – no one knew. They were mailed from the prison mailroom to a post office box.

There was one other strange thing about inmate Nolan Weeks. While he had no visitors, incoming mail, or phone calls of any kind, there was a monthly installment of $50 made to his inmate account. No one knew who was sending him the money, but Nolan was happy to use it to buy snacks and other things he needed to make his death row experience bearable. Even the Warden himself didn't know who was sending the stipend. Sometimes outside groups who fought for those who they felt were imprisoned unfairly, raised money to add to the inmate's "books" to make their stay a bit more endurable. The Warden assumed that was the source of the money.

Brent suddenly snapped back from a wandering mind under intense pressure.

"I really don't feel comfortable promising you something I don't know about."

"That's up to you, daddy. I have no idea how many days I got left. They gave me that stay, but the warden is doing his best to get me killed before the end of the month," Nolan said, looking again out the window. "Son-of-a-bitch wants me dead in a bad way."

"You're saying it's not illegal or anything sexual? You know what I mean," Brent asked, awkwardly.

Nolan laughed. "You think if I wanted a piece of ass, I would have called you? I ain't that desperate yet. I'd take a crack at one of those cute reporters on TV. The ones in short skirts, stockings, and heels." His laugh continued, a bit more than Brent felt comfortable with. He wondered what Danny and Sal were thinking behind him.

Brent returned the laugh, lowering the tension a notch. Danny shifted slightly behind him.

Nolan said, "It's not illegal. Just a simple favor when this is all over with. Just think of the ratings. This is the only interview I've done. We all know that. So, let's cut the shit." His mouth turned to the start of a snarl. "Hell, you could write a book, too."

Brent of course knew this was the only interview he had granted. He had made no comments to the media at all upon his arrest or other instances where he was taken out in public. Throughout his trial there were supporters of Nolan Weeks, basically those against the death penalty. There were plenty of those who wanted him to hang from the nearest tree for the horrific killings that he carried out on a cross-country rampage that lasted two years. The FBI established a task force to finally catch him, with nearly 100 field officers looking at every grisly crime scene and following the thousands of leads that poured in.

This interview would be done over a two-week period, with one two-hour session every other day. Brent would spend the off days working with the behind-the-scenes crew, editing down the footage they would be shooting, and recording voice overs as needed. The network sprang for an extra hotel room for the editing, so they all had their own rooms to sleep in. The editing room had the smell of take-out pizza and bad truck stop food hovering most of the time.

"I know. My career has been in the shitter lately," said Brent in a low tone.

"I know. They do let us watch TV in the joint. It's about the only thing you can do. Not on the row though."

Brent maintained eye contact with Nolan. Whenever Nolan would rattle one of his chains, Brent would startle and look down toward the noise. Nolan made a game of it, maintaining his control over the situation. No matter how restrained Nolan was, there were ways that he somehow got the upper hand.

"So, what's it gonna be?" Nolan asked, his neck muscles tightening.

Brent swallowed nervously. He knew that everyone in the room was looking at him. It felt as if he had been hurled into a gigantic vice, and someone was slowly tightening it, turn by painstaking turn. He knew there was only one answer. He hated himself for being in the situation to have to make the decision.

"Yes, I agree. You got one favor from me, Nolan. That's all."

Nolan smiled, the muscles in his neck, face, and jaw began to ease.

"Ok, then. You boys ready? You ready to go to Hell?"

Nolan's laugh was hideous and soaked in evil. Danny, Sal, and Brent all stared down at the floor, wishing they were somewhere else.

3

Brent looked at the clock in the holding cell and saw that the guards were almost 30 minutes late. He was sitting at the table, going over his notes from the first visit two days ago, while Danny and Sal were checking things out with the audio and video for the third time. Two days ago, there were some issues with the electronics, yet they all knew that the problems were not caused by equipment malfunction, but from Nolan – somehow. None of them wanted to admit that fact, so getting new cables and cleaning all the connections with contact cleaner seemed like a more rational reaction. It wasn't hard to convince themselves that electronics can randomly not work the way you wanted.

Just then the buzzer sounded, and the heavy metal door slid open. Sergeant Whitlock and correctional officer Bobby Lewis had Nolan by each arm and walked him into the cell. Sergeant Whitlock's demeanor commanded attention always and without question. He did it, however, with a smile.

"Good morning, gentlemen," said Sergeant Whitlock in his thick south Texas drawl, nodding to them as Nolan shuffled in. "We had a bit of a delay this morning, so I apologize for being late."

Nolan looked tired. There were circles around his eyes, and the smile he had during the first visit was now gone. He looked longingly out the window, oblivious to what was going on in the holding cell.

"We had to take the prisoner to the infirmary. He woke up sick," said officer Lewis.

Sergeant Whitlock chimed in, "We almost pulled the plug on this today, but the warden wasn't having it. He said the show must go on. Or as my Momma used to say, you got that skillet hot, now fry up them taters." He laughed.

Nolan continued to look out the window. Officer Lewis began the process of chaining him to the chair. Nolan didn't say a thing and was obviously not feeling well. The pallor of his skin even looked off.

After a few minutes, Sergeant Whitlock went over the rules again with Brent and his crew, then the buzzer sounded and the cell door slid open. Once outside in the hallway, the buzzer sounded again, and the heavy door closed with a thud and a mechanical locking noise.

"Nolan. I'd like to start from the beginning today," Brent said, staring at the killer in front of him. Today, Nolan seemed less physically imposing as he turned away from the window and engaged Brent. Nolan's eyes seemed dark. Brent was looking down a path leading to something foreboding.

Brent took out a cigarette and put it into the inmate's mouth, then lit it for him. Nolan took a deep drag and stared at the ceiling for a moment. He exhaled.

"OK, then. Let's do this." Smoke clouded his face. He smiled slightly.

******

It was a hot July day in 1985 when Nolan drove out to his parents' house in Heyworth, Illinois. He took the turn off Route 136 on the east end of town and noted how bright the sun was that day. He didn't like going to their house unless he needed to. His father, Tom Weeks, had borrowed a stump grinder to finish off some trees he had cut down. Now several months later, Nolan needed it back for a job he was trying to get done at his trailer in nearby Waynesville. He hoped that his father would be out working whatever odd jobs he could find around town. He had been laid off from the Clinton power plant for more than a year, and he never could get back to what he once was. Only three years from retirement, Tom had turned to drinking heavily once he got the lay-off notice. It started with about six beers in the morning, then by lunch he was drinking whiskey. He would keep on drinking whiskey until he passed out, half the time pissing his pants wherever he collapsed.

Tom Weeks had always been a drinker, but it went into overdrive after he got laid off. He was a miserable drunk, and living with him was nearly impossible to endure. Nolan left because of his dad's erratic behavior and the way he was toward his mother. He was both verbally and physically abusive toward her, and for that, Elaine had also started drinking to self-medicate the depression from living with Tom. She started going to church almost every day, and she began to spend most of her free time buried in a bible and quoting scripture at the strangest times. She began to fill the house with crosses, pictures of Jesus and the Virgin Mary and other gaudy garage sale trinkets that gave the house a sort of carnival-like atmosphere. Elaine also loved to watch the seedy televangelists, and without Tom knowing, she often sent them money. If Tom had found out she was doing it, his rage would have erupted after calculating how much beer and whiskey he could have bought with that money.

The winter months were the hardest to endure, as keeping Tom indoors for periods of time sank him into an endless depressed state. Elaine would not be able to get to church as often as she liked when the roads were bad. With the two of them sinking further into their respective holes, it was strange to say the least. Both were shells of their former selves, and Nolan hated to see it. He knew it was time for him to go, and he bought himself a small mobile home with money he had saved up from his job working for a local roofing contractor. The trailer wasn't much, but it was his, and he was out of their crazy house!

As Nolan drove down the long gravel drive, he saw both his mother's car and his father's old Ford truck parked in the driveway. *Damn it. It just couldn't be easy. Get the grinder and go. No chance.*

Nolan pulled up next to the truck, noting there was a pile of newspapers in front of the steps. There were at least five or six. He also immediately realized that the family dog, Sparky, had not came running out to greet him. Any visitor who approached the old farm house would hear Sparky bark and then be subjected to his wagging tail, slobbering tongue, and excitement at their arrival. He had done that since he was a puppy, and even though he was starting to show his age, the loveable mutt would bark and ignite with enthusiasm when company came calling. So the fact Sparky wasn't to be found made Nolan worry something was wrong. Very wrong.

Nolan looked in the bed of the truck, hoping the stump grinder would be there. It wasn't. He gingerly approached the house, noticing an officious odor – like death hanging heavy in the humid air. As a kid growing up in the country, he was familiar with what death smelled like. The familiar stink of a dead field mouse in the walls or a sick raccoon that had crawled under the house to die was what came to mind. This was worse. Upon opening the screen door that led to the porch, he saw Sparky laying on his side, obviously dead. The smell was rank, and he held his arm up to mask the scent.

"Sparky!" he cried out, kneeling next to the family dog. His ribs were showing, as if he starved to death. His food and water bowls were both empty. Sparky was stiff, and Nolan knew he had been dead for days. In the stifling July heat, flies were already claiming the spoils. It crushed Nolan to see him like this.

"Mom? Dad?" he called out and heard nothing but silence.

Nolan opened the front door of the house. It creaked open. Immediately upon entering, the same smell of death was there to greet him like a brick to the face. This time it was so strong he nearly threw up. He saw a basket of laundry near the door that his mother must have been folding, and he reached for a dish towel to hold up over his nose. The sweet smell of death still found its way past. The heat and humidity inside the house amplified the stench that much more. His parents didn't like air conditioning, so it was unbearable with the horrible rankness.

"Mom? Dad? Anyone home?"

Stepping into the dark living room, Nolan saw piles of beer cans strewn about. Also evident was the abundance of crosses his Mom had on the walls, along with plastic statues of Jesus, Mary, and other saints and religious symbols. With each step, the disgusting smell attempted to overtake him. He reached over to turn on the overhead light, and that's when the horror show took center stage!

"Oh my God!" he cried out. His eyes struggled to focus under the extreme brightness.

There was a dead body of a woman lying on the couch, dressed like a prostitute, posed in a way as if she were watching the television on the other side of the room. Her grey skin and bulging eyes made him cringe as he looked around the room at other bodies that were set up, posed in strange ways, like an old man reading a newspaper, sitting in his father's recliner. Or the two small girls in dresses who were on the floor, playing with dolls, their little bodies stiff with rigor and haunting with distant stares. Nolan didn't know what was going on. He wondered if this was somehow a dream. He vomited behind the recliner, then staggered on toward the kitchen. Sweat was pouring down his face.

"Mom! Dad!" he screamed out. Only silence replied, and the vacant stares of the dead in the living room. The stagnant air hung heavy as he fought back the urge to vomit again.

As Nolan entered the kitchen, he saw the dead body of his mother sitting at the table, her arms at her sides and her head thrown back, in some sort of awkward pose. Her body was bloated and purple, and the only way he knew it was her was the bathrobe she wore. It was the flowered one he had gotten her for Christmas the year before, yet now it was draped over her naked body, wide open, revealing her bare puckered breasts. The chain she wore with a silver cross was around her neck. Nolan felt like he had to throw up again, his head swimming with the horrible imagery before him. There was a very large crucifix on the wall above her head, and a framed picture of Jesus.

"Dad! Where the fuck are you?" he cried out, fighting back the tears at seeing his own mother dead and sitting up like she was. He hadn't seen her in a few months, and the last time he was at the house, they had fought about her drinking. Now he wished he could take back those hurtful things he had said.

Walking into the dining room, the bodies did not stop. There were two bodies at the table, sitting up in chairs, but they were totally naked. They appeared to be a middle-aged man and woman. The bodies were so discolored and bloated that it was difficult to tell much about what they had looked like while alive. The man was missing most of his left arm, and the woman had lost her right leg at the knee. On the dining room table was an assortment of bloody body parts, a meat cleaver, mixed in with empty beer cans and a half empty bottle of Calvert's whiskey. Nolan threw up again, this time on the dining room floor, as he saw a rat scurry away with something in its mouth. He didn't want to know what it was, but he feared it was human.

"Who the fuck are you, and what the fuck are you doing in my house?" a male voice said from behind him. It sounded like a New York accent.

Nolan spun around quickly, seeing his father staggering toward him, with a sledgehammer firmly in his grasp. His eyes were wild, darting about in an obvious state of lunacy.

"Dad! It's me. What the hell is going on here?" asked Nolan, backing up and looking around the room for something to defend himself with. "What happened to Mom?"

Tom Weeks stared at him, the sledgehammer swaying back and forth. "Dad? I ain't no one's Dad!" The heavy accent sounded very strange coming from Tom, who had a slight Southern drawl, raised by parents from Arkansas.

"What? Dad, what the hell is going on here? Who are all these people?" Nolan continued to back up as he was now entering the kitchen again. He did what he could to shield himself from seeing his mother.

"They are my friends. We're having a party, can't you tell?" Tom said, a strange smile on his face. He reached over to the kitchen counter and picked up what looked like a small human hand. Tom took a bite out of it, tearing at the dead flesh with his teeth.

Nolan threw up again. Spitting and spewing up what was left in his stomach, Nolan reached for a knife and held it up in a menacing manner. He glanced to his left and saw his mother in her death pose, appearing to stare up at him and smile.

"Stop right where you are, Dad. Don't take another fucking step."

Tom laughed, dropping the small hand to the linoleum floor with a dull thud. "I told you that I ain't anyone's Dad. My name's Paul. Paul Rosati. I'm from Yonkers." He took a step closer to Nolan, his eyes fixed on the young man.

"Dad, you've lost it. You're talking crazy. Your name isn't Paul. It's Tom. Tom Weeks." Nolan moved backward into the living room now.

Tom stopped and shook his head slightly. Then he looked up at Nolan, something different was in his stare. His voice was different, it was odd.

"Now what is going on here? We all need to remain calm," said Tom, this time in a British accent. He continued to hold the sledgehammer and took a step closer to Nolan. His eyes were engaging.

"Dad?"

"I'm not your father, son. But you are pissing me off, and I'm about to bash your bloody head in!" said Tom, waving the sledgehammer at him. "My name is Lyle, and I'm definitely not your father!"

Tom moved closer, sizing up Nolan as if he was ready to strike at any moment. Nolan stumbled, walking backward, and nearly tripped over one of the two dead girls on the floor. He noticed two more bodies stacked up behind the couch as he grabbed the fireplace mantle to steady himself. Nolan was perplexed at the obvious change in his father as he closed in. Who exactly was he, and what was going on?

"Don't knock eating human flesh unless you try it," Tom said, his eyes still open wide and crazy-looking. He giggled quietly and continued to move closer to Nolan, the sledgehammer swinging slowly. Now he was back talking in that New York accent.

Nolan didn't know if he could get close enough to do any damage with the knife before his dad could hit him with the sledgehammer. He knew the last thing he wanted was to become part of the dead dinner party here in Heyworth. As Tom crept closer, Nolan found himself in an awkward position with the fireplace at his back and no good avenue to get out of the house. He reached down to the coffee table and picked up an empty whiskey bottle. Tom's eyes looked quickly at the bottle as Nolan brought it crashing down on top of his head.

"Son-of-a-bitch!" screamed Tom, dropping the sledgehammer and reaching for the gash that now opened up. Blood was rushing down his arm and to the hardwood floor of the living room.

Nolan moved in for the kill, driving the steak knife into Tom's chest. Tom's eyes rolled back in his head as he began to spin in a tight circle, stumbling over the two dead girls and their dolls. His face was contorting and shifting in a very strange sort of way. Reaching for a shelf, Tom knocked over a dozen small figurines from his mother's extensive collection of cheap, cheesy religious idols. Something was dreadfully wrong with his father, and despite the horrible things he had seen in the house since arriving this morning, Nolan could not help but feel a deep guilt for what he had done. He was obviously in some sort of mental distress with the disturbing display of changing from one personality into another. Tom began to lose his balance as he fell backward toward the fireplace. A sickening crunch was heard as his skull landed hard on the edge of the brick. The force of his fall knocked a large corner piece from the fireplace edge. His body jerked slightly, then was still.

Nolan stood there in the middle of the living room, his chest heaving and his mind racing.

"Dad, what the hell?" he said, kneeling next to his father. He could see his chest rising and falling, but taking shallow breaths.

Tom was trying to say something as his lips moved slightly. A pool of blood was growing beneath his head and spilling out on the floor. The room began to shudder, as if there was a small earthquake happening underfoot. Nolan could feel the earth shifting beneath him. The overhead light of the living room dimmed then intensified for a moment before the light bulb shattered into hundreds of tiny shards. The room was now dim, and under the gaze of the dead, Nolan felt an incredible sense of terror. Dread grabbed him by the throat and was not letting go.

As he looked down at his father, Nolan saw something dark like a shadow slither from his open mouth. The dark figure moved like thick, heavy smoke and made its way to his own mouth. Nolan tried to close his lips, but it was of no use. The miasma of evil gained entrance, no matter what he tried to stop it. Whatever it was moved from Tom's mouth and into his! It took less than five seconds. The moment it was over, Tom's chest ceased to rise again. Oddly, a clock on the wall of the living room suddenly stopped ticking. In the deafening silence of that moment, Nolan let out a guttural scream that shook the walls. Something evil was born.

Nolan was thrown across the room by unseen hands, landing hard on the ceramic floor of the entry way. He staggered to stand, and his head was spinning out of control. Nolan felt dizzy and completely caught up in a whirlwind. He had no idea what had just happened, but he knew that his father was dead. His eyes stared in complete desolation, and a pool of dark red blood circled his body like a chalk outline at a murder scene. Nolan looked around the living room, at the prostitute on the couch, at the man in the recliner, and at the two girls on the floor, now kicked over and no longer playing happily. Tears were streaming down his face when he looked once more at his mother in the kitchen, and then to the dead hand on the floor next to her. It was sheer madness. Nolan screamed again. Louder this time.

He ran to the bathroom to look in the mirror. Staring, he saw nothing but himself, wondering about the dark entity that had left his father and entered him. He opened his mouth and looked inside, but he saw nothing. He did note there was a sort of burnt taste in his mouth, but nothing he could pinpoint. He reached for a bottle of Listerine in the medicine cabinet, took a long pull, then spit it out in the sink. The burnt taste was still there. Nolan noticed two more bodies stacked up in the bathtub, blood spatters on the surround, and a hacksaw on the floor. He screamed once again and ran from the bathroom.

Nolan felt compelled to open the bedroom doors as he made his way down the hallway, half-crazy from what he had witnessed. In his own former bedroom, there was four or five bodies of young women in various forms of undress. One, who appeared to be in her twenties, was spread-eagle on his bed and totally naked. There was an assortment of sex toys on the bed next to her. His mind wandered as to what his father had been doing with the woman, dead or alive, and he felt a sickening urge to vomit again. Then Nolan opened the door of his parents' room and found another three or four bodies on the floor. He was losing count but knew that something had obviously gone horribly wrong. Maybe the terribly hot and humid summer pushed the old man over the edge? Whatever it was, it was horrible.

Nolan was now in the garage, looking for the gas can that his father kept for the lawnmower. He grabbed it and noted it was nearly full. Without delay, Nolan started spreading the gas around on the floor as he ran through the house. The smell of the gas in the stifling humidity, mixed with the dead bodies, was enough to make him throw up again. He made a point to leave a trail of the flammable liquid in every room, and when he reached the back door, he took the lighter from his breast pocket and lit the blaze. Within moments, a river of fire raged down the hallway, splitting off into each bedroom, the bathroom, and then into the kitchen, dining room, and living room. Flames were lapping at the walls, laying claim to the years and years of memories the family had endured. The plaster walls, wood floors, furniture, and dead occupants were engulfed in a roaring inferno. Listening closely, he could hear the tormented cries of the dead who were being released from their prison, now passing on to the next world as a thick, black smoke rose into the hot, cloudless July sky.

An acrid smoke filled the hallway as Nolan left the house, tears streaming down his face. He ran to his truck and backed out of the driveway, heading to Route 136, then westbound to his own house in Waynesville. As he left Heyworth, Nolan could hear the noon siren cry out, immediately followed by the wail of volunteer fire department trucks as they made their way to the burning farmhouse.

******

Nolan was lying in bed, trying to figure out what he was going to do. He wished that the entire morning had been a dream. But he knew it wasn't. The smell of smoke on his clothes reminded him that it was a terrible reality. He also knew that it wouldn't be long before someone would be trying to get a hold of him to let him know about the fire. Had anyone seen his truck out there? Did anyone see him driving away down 136? In a small town like Heyworth, it was very possible. Nolan knew that McLean County cops would be at the scene, since the local two police officers wouldn't have any idea how to investigate a burning house with a couple dozen bodies inside. It was likely they'd bring in the state cops for this one. He knew they could get tire tracks and probably other physical evidence that would possibly tie him to the scene. Not to mention the fact that he had been estranged from his parents since April, and it was very likely they had told others about the falling out. His father loved to drink coffee most mornings at the Chat n' Chew, and it was more than probable he had mentioned it to one of the locals. Elaine saw ladies from the church nearly every day, and it was also likely she would have mentioned it as well. Nolan would be a suspect for sure.

Just then he felt an odd sensation, like being submerged into a warm bath. He stared down at his body, as he lay in bed, and wondered what was going on. Something inside of him had changed. He didn't know what it was, but the more he thought about that strange shadow, the more he dreaded what could possibly be happening. He suddenly felt compelled to get up from bed, which he did, as if he were no longer in control of his own body. Nolan could see himself, through his own eyes, packing clothes, toiletries, and other items into a duffel bag, and leaving his mobile home.

Nolan tossed the duffel bag into the truck and got in, firing up the engine. He was leaving for somewhere, but he didn't know where somewhere was. There was a strong feeling inside of him that was beginning to take over the controls. It felt like being on a bus as a passenger, enjoying the view but not having any say in where they were headed. Nolan couldn't explain it, but he let it happen. There was nothing he could do to stop it. Now, he was perfectly fine to let someone else take over, so he could try and sort out all that had happened.

Just shut the fuck up and drive. We got people to kill and places to see. Let's go!

The Chevy truck roared down the road on that hot July afternoon, with no specific destination in mind. Nolan didn't argue.

4

"So that was the first time you heard the voices?" asked Brent, sitting up a bit straighter as the words of Nolan Weeks began to weave the story of how he ended up at the Huntsville State Prison and firmly planted on death row. At least for now.

A cigarette dangled from Nolan's lips, smoke making its way up his face and toward the metal ceiling. His eyes were bloodshot, and his voice was a bit hoarse.

"Yeah, that was the first time I heard one of them."

Brent was staring at him intently.

"How many of them were there? Didn't your doctor testify at your trial that there were twelve?" Brent asked, still looking at Nolan's eyes. He noted they looked like a road map, with red lines going in every direction. He didn't look good.

Nolan's chains rattled. "At that time I didn't know how many there were. It was just one at first. The dominant one. But there were more. Twelve of 'em." He took another deep drag and closed his eyes as another wave of smoke left his lungs and made its way up toward the ceiling vent.

Brent leaned toward Nolan just a bit. "That must have been frightening."

Nolan smiled, cigarette expertly dangling, "No. It was frightening once they started doing what the hell they wanted to do."

"You didn't have any control over them?"

Nolan laughed, spitting the cigarette to the concrete floor. Brent stomped it out.

"None at all. I was just a passenger watching it all go down. One nightmare after another," Nolan said, staring back at Brent until he uncomfortably made him look away.

Brent didn't respond. He began looking through some notes, but that was only so he didn't have to look at Nolan. Brent knew the killer was staring at him. He could feel it.

"I remember driving for a few hours that first night before we stopped," began Nolan, "and that was the first killing spot. That's where I broke my cherry."

"Your cherry?" Brent knew he wasn't talking about his virginity, but it seemed like the obvious question to ask, though he knew the answer.

Nolan laughed again, his grin revealing two crooked teeth. "Yeah, my killin' cherry."

******

Nolan parked the Chevy in an IGA parking lot in Belleville, Illinois. The bulb had burned out in the light above the parking spot, so it was the darkest place on the lot. He finished smoking his cigarette and crushed it out in the ashtray that was now overflowing. He didn't care, because he knew he wasn't going to be in the truck much longer. For now, his duffel bag was on the passenger's side floorboard, next to the bag rolled around three or four empty McDonald's coffee cups. They were helping him stay awake on the mindless drive south along highway I-55 in Central Illinois. Endless corn and soybean fields lined each side of the highway as he moved further south toward St. Louis.

Nolan took a piss behind his truck, hidden in the shadows. Then he made his way toward a patch of woods, where a narrow path seemed to lead the way. Nolan had no idea where he was going since he left Waynesville. Yet there seemed to be a general calm over the situation, despite the insanity back in Heyworth at his parents' house. No matter what he did, Nolan could neither shake the image of his mother in that strange pose, cold and dead at the kitchen table, nor his father chasing after him with a bloody sledgehammer. They were like still photographs being thrown in his face one at a time. Snapshots of what Hell must look like, with piles of bodies, blood and brain spattered on the tub surround and human parts strewn about the house. Nolan could hear his father rambling on in that strange voice, saying he was someone else. The look in his eyes told Nolan that he had completely disconnected with reality. The smell stayed with him more than twelve hours later, as he smoked cigarette after cigarette to try and hide the sickly-sweet odor from his memory. It was no use.

Nolan noticed that for the two hours he was in the truck, it had felt like someone else was driving. It had felt like the person driving changed at some point. They started out listening to a Black Sabbath cassette tape he had in the stereo, and then they abruptly changed to a country station, old stuff like Johnny Cash and Hank Williams. He also noticed that the person who wanted to listen to the old country music didn't want to smoke and drank a lot of Pepsi. Then he began a chain-smoking marathon until he arrived in Belleville, cranking the old Sabbath tape to the limits of the cheap stereo he had in the truck. The smoker was the one who liked drinking black coffee. It was an odd sensation, but it felt like there were two different people driving the truck, and Nolan was only an observer. He had no voice. For now, that was OK, but Nolan knew that something malevolent was about to unfold. He tried not to think about it, but it was of no use. He could hear the low murmur of several men talking somewhere in the background, but he was unable to figure out the source. Nolan could only catch a stray word here and there, and hearing "kill", "murder", and "whore" was enough to paint a dark and dismal picture.

******

"What was that like? You know, being an observer."

Nolan was looking out the window. His eyes still were bloodshot. He coughed twice.

"Strange, I guess."

Brent shuffled through the papers in front of him, not wanting to make eye contact with Nolan.

"I'm sure. Can you describe it?"

Nolan turned away from the window and looked at Brent. The killer's eyes were bottomless. Something was changing with

Nolan, but Brent couldn't put his finger on it. He was obviously tired, but there was something else. A something that was evil, but hiding in a dark corner somewhere, waiting for the perfect time to strike. Brent only hoped the chains the officers put the killer in each time were strong enough to hold him down. He didn't think Sergeant Whitlock would make it inside the cell fast enough if anything happened. Nolan's arms were powerful, and his chest and shoulders were solid muscle. Even in his sickly state, Nolan was very intimidating, mentally and physically.

"One time I got thinking about the early days of it. Felt like I was on a bus. You know, a school bus," Nolan said, slow and deliberate. He smiled faintly. "A big, old, yellow bus. Driving around the country and packed full of killers. I had to sit in the very back seat while they took turns driving."

"Wow. I'd never heard that before from you."

"That's because I never said it out loud before." Nolan coughed.

Brent continued to look at Nolan, the chains binding his legs to the chair rattled.

"There were twelve on the bus with you?"

"Yeah."

"So, who was the first victim?" Brent asked. "How did that happen?"

Nolan looked back out the window. Brent heard Danny move behind him, and then there was silence in the room as all three of the men stared intensely at condemned inmate. They knew what they were about to hear was something they could not un-hear. It was going to be the stuff of nightmares. Dark and horrible nightmares. The silence was deafening.

"It was that first night. When we stopped in Belleville. I parked my truck in a dark corner of the parking lot of an IGA . . ."

******

Summer 1985

Nora Yates was anxiously waiting for Jimmy Tallis to call her back. Her parents were going to be home any minute from the fish fry at the VFW, and her 10-year-old brother had been asleep for at least two hours. She hoped Jimmy would call once more, so she could talk to him again while she was alone. Staring at the phone on her nightstand wasn't making him call any faster.

"Come on, Jimmy," she muttered, standing at the second-story bedroom window and looking out at the well-lit and manicured lawn on the west side of town.

The house was built 40 years before along one of the many rural roads that connected Belleville to the various small farm communities that surrounded it. There was a corn field on one side of the house and a soybean field on the other. The nearest neighbor was a quarter mile down the road, and that's the way they liked it.

Her walls were adorned with a mix of large posters and smaller full color pictures that she had torn from a pile of teen magazines purchased with the money she made babysitting. Duran Duran, Billy Idol, and John Stamos were in the majority of the clippings. She was listening to the Def Leppard album "Pyromania" and starting to move more into hard rock and heavy metal with her musical tastes, much to her parents' dismay. Jimmy was into heavy metal, and since his hair was a bit long, just in reach of his shoulders, her dad didn't like him at all. He liked to blame her declining taste in music on Jimmy, too. It didn't help that Jimmy drove a Trans-Am and always had his music loud, causing the bolts on the car to rattle when he was sitting idle. Nora had asked him to turn it down when he showed up at her house, but he continued to play his music loud, which cemented the fact that he was despised by her father. Even her mom was starting to not like him. But Nora didn't care, because she loved Jimmy and couldn't wait until they were married with two kids and living somewhere far away from Belleville.

I wanna touch you . . . photograph!

Suddenly, Nora thought she heard glass break from the back of the house. She paused the cassette tape and the entire house was silent. There was no more glass breaking, but she was confident that she had heard it. Then it sounded like someone was walking around inside the house on the first floor. The original hardwood floors were creaking as the intruder made his way room to room. Nora heard it. A shiver made its way up her spine, only to settle like a lead weight in the pit of her stomach. Listening intently, she could hear talking downstairs. *Was there more than one person in the house? Would her parents be safe when they got home any minute? Would she and her brother be safe? Could she make it to grab the shotgun in her parents' bedroom?* Her dad had shown her and her brother how to load and shoot several types of guns at a young age. This was real though, and not make-believe. She even forgot for a few minutes about Jimmy and if he would be calling her.

"Did you really have to break that window? Christ!" said a male voice downstairs. Nora slowly crept toward her bedroom door, listening with her ear pressed up against it. Thankfully, it was already closed.

"Why don't you shut the fuck up?" replied another man. His voice was gruff and had a strange accent she wasn't familiar with. She heard something break, and it was likely one of her mom's glass vases she had in the foyer. That meant they were nearing the stairs leading up to Nora and her brother!

Nora decided not to wait another second. She ran down the hallway toward her parents' bedroom where she knew her dad kept a shotgun just for this reason. In her stocking feet, she tried to make as little noise as she could on the carpeted floor. Nora could still hear the muffled voices of the men arguing downstairs. She hoped they didn't hear her as she quietly opened the closet door. Nora was shocked to find the shotgun missing! Her heartbeat began to thunder in her chest. Where could it be? She frantically pulled the hanging clothes out of the way to the back corner where it was kept. Still no gun. Why wasn't it there?

"I thought I heard someone moving around up here," said the man with the strange accent. Nora froze in the closet, hearing that voice and the creaking of the stairs. It was an east coast-style accent, but she had only heard people talk like that in movies, and then it seemed almost funny.

It was horrifying to hear these intruders walking around in her house. It made Nora sick, and she was forcing herself to not throw up. Sweat began to pour down her face in the stifling heat inside the closet.

"I thought so, too," said another man, this one with a heavy southern accent.

Nora could hear them move down the hallway, then stop outside the door of her parents' room. She knew that her little brother, John, was sleeping in his room directly across from where

165

she was right now. She winced when she heard his door open loudly, banging against the wall, and his cry in the chaos.

"Who are you?" John cried out, half asleep nestled in his Star Wars sheets.

"I'm your nightmare maker, boy!" the man yelled out, followed by her brother's tortured screams. They were shrill and piercing.

Nora bit down on a shirt hanging in her father's closet to muffle her own cries, hearing the thrashing about in John's room. She feared he was dead. Tears were pouring down her face as she shook with rage. *Where are Mom and Dad? They should have been home by now! Maybe John will survive? Maybe I'm dreaming all of this?*

Just then the door of the closet swung open, and the bedroom was awash with bright overhead recessed lights. Her father always used high wattage bulbs so he could see when he was cleaning his guns. It was something he did once a month with every gun he owned. There were several.

A large, burly young man was standing in the doorway. His dark hair was cut in a very short crew cut. His eyes were intense and glimmering, as blood spatters covered his face and sweat-soaked upper body. In his right hand was a large, ten-inch butcher knife that he likely took off the kitchen counter. The blade was dripping with blood. Nora knew whose blood it was, but fear had her paralyzed. She didn't even take a breath.

"You can run, but you can't hide, darlin'."

The madman brought the knife down between her shoulder blades with tremendous force. He pulled the knife out and continued stabbing her repeatedly in a frenzied blood-lust, grunting and growling like a wild animal. As she lay dying in the closet, amongst a pile of her father's clothes, she could hear the phone ringing in her room down the hall.

Jimmy finally decided to call.

******

Ernest and Dorothy Ledney were pulling into their driveway after a fun night out at the Belleville VFW Friday fish fry. They tried to make it to as many of them as they could, especially now that Nora was old enough to watch John for a few hours. Most of the time, they would sit with Dorothy's parents and Ernest's aunt and uncle, Angie and Art. Ernest made sure his Uncle Art was going to be there so he could check out one of his shotguns that was having problems ejecting shells. He had taken the gun along and told Art to take it with him and let him know what was wrong, since it was just an old shotgun he kept in the house for protection. He didn't want to spend much to fix it and would probably just get another gun to replace it.

"What on earth?" Dorothy said, seeing the front door was standing wide open. The headlights from their Chevy Suburban illuminated the entire front of the house, and that open door looked strange this time of night.

Ernest stepped out of the truck. His boots crunched in the gravel.

"Stay here a minute, Dorie," he told his wife. She argued with him for a few seconds, but he held his hand up to silence her in mid-sentence, realizing something was wrong. She was scared. So was he.

I bet Nora had one of her friends over, and they forgot to lock the door. Telling himself that calmed him down a notch or two. Gingerly, Ernest made his way up to the front door. Stopping at the threshold for a moment, he walked in, switching on the hallway light.

Dorothy couldn't see him any longer. Sitting in the truck was driving her crazy. She also had a bad feeling about that door being left open. Dora wouldn't do that. She was more responsible than that. Against Ernest's wishes, she stepped out of the truck and started walking toward the front door.

Suddenly, the still summer night air was cut with frantic screams coming from inside the house. It was Ernest! Moments later she saw him running to the front door, someone behind him closing the gap. Blood was pouring down his face and all over the white button-up dress shirt he wore.

"Run, Dorie! Run for your life!" Ernest screamed, spitting up blood, and his eyes open wide in terror.

The young man was nearly upon him on the front porch, waving a large metal poker from the fireplace at his head. A dull crunch sounded as the poker dug into his skull, and the two men cascaded down the porch steps.

Dorothy couldn't move, despite only being a few feet away from the spectacle. Ernest tried to cover his head and face from the harsh blows, as the young man pummeled him over and over with the cold steel. He was dead, yet the madman continued to hit him with the poker, screaming and shrieking the entire time.

Dorothy turned to run, but within seconds, the man had her down on the ground, ripping at her dress. She blacked out at the rest of it, which was merciful, as the killer raped her several times, even after she was dead.

******

St. Clair County Sheriff, Tom Coles, pulled into the driveway of the Ledney home in rural Belleville, Illinois the following day. There were three county deputies on the scene already.

"We got the neighbor who called it in sitting on Randy's car, Sheriff," said Deputy Sanders. He was standing outside, securing the scene and chain-smoking, as he waited for the sheriff and detectives to arrive. A half-empty coffee cup filled with his cigarette butts gave him away.

Sheriff Coles saw the bodies of Ernest and Dorothy on the front lawn as they had been found. Ernest's skull was crushed, likely from the large metal fireplace poker lying next to his body. He was face down and soaked in blood. Dorothy was completely naked, lying only a few feet from her husband, covered in bite marks and what appeared to be cigarette burns on the inside of her thighs. Her face was covered in blood, and the obvious signs of her being beaten to death were harsh in the early Saturday morning. Sheriff Cole had seen many dead bodies since his time in law enforcement. But having known the Ledney's for years and attending many holiday dinners at their home, it hit him hard.

"Sheriff, there are more bodies inside. Also, some strange writing on the walls."

The sheriff was hearing about every other word, still trying to grasp the fact that his friends were dead. They had a cook-out for the 4th of July just a couple weeks back. Where they were standing

168

now was where Ernest had set up the horseshoe pits. It didn't feel real.

"What was that? More bodies? Fuck."

"Yeah, it's bad, Tom. Why don't you go home? You shouldn't have to be here to see this."

Sheriff Cole struggled to even speak. "Thanks, Dave. But I need to be here."

More visitors arrived at the scene as investigators began to look closer and collect evidence. The body of young John was found in his bed, multiple stab wounds covering his little body. His Star Wars bed sheets were soaked in blood, as were the St. Louis Cardinal curtains that he was likely reaching for to escape his attacker, or attackers. At a quick assessment, the investigators believed there were multiple assailants, due to the excessive damage inside and the variety of implements used to kill the family. It was almost difficult to walk through the house without stepping on broken glass and furniture. Blood was spattered on almost every wall in a haphazard fashion.

They found Nora face down on her parents' bed, naked except for black and grey striped knee socks, with multiple stab wounds on her back. They also found bite marks on her arms and neck, which appeared to be the same wounds left on Dorothy. She had been raped several times, too. On the large mirror in the bedroom, the killer used blood to write I AM YOUR GOD. Several pictures were taken of the entire scene. More crime scene specialists were called, and two showed up from a nearby Illinois State Police station. This was far beyond what the St. Clair County police were experienced to handle.

Sheriff Cole was leaving the house to meet with his staff outside, in anticipation of the media showing up to the scene any moment. He noticed another message, written on the wall of the living room, over the fireplace. It said NIGHTMARE MAKER in bold capital letters. He noted it looked like a different hand writing as well. The writing upstairs was in lower case letters and appeared to be written by someone with a shaky hand. The NIGHTMARE MAKER above the fireplace was more pronounced and the letters more distinct, its author more confident. While the sheriff knew Belleville was susceptible to random criminal acts, being off a major highway in downstate Illinois, it was still a small town, and murders were rare. Most of the deaths in the county were caused by car wrecks and natural causes from the elderly population. There was the occasional suicide during the long, cold winters.

"Sheriff, one of those state guys just said to let you know they were calling the FBI on this one," said a young deputy. "I guess they just saw something from Missouri. An elderly couple were brutally murdered. They think it's possibly related to this scene."

"That assumes an awful lot this early."

"I guess they found the words NIGHTMARE MAKER written in blood at the scene. The female victim was also found naked with bite marks all over her body."

Sheriff Cole's Saturday morning went from good to hell-in-a-handbasket within a couple of hours.

5

The crime scene at 1212 Lakeview Drive in Wichita, Kansas was completely locked down, much to the anger of the local police department that wanted access. There were four Kansas State Police cars parked on the street and several state police officers guarding the property with orders to allow no one access unless they had FBI credentials. The neighbors were standing in their yards, some talking with each other, giving their opinion on what was going on. Others showed concern and kept to themselves at the obviously serious nature of what had happened at the Edwards' home. The Edwards family typically kept to themselves, but in a residential subdivision in the summer of 1985, everyone knew their neighbors. The stark yellow and black crime scene tape strung up and police lights flashing at dawn spoke volumes and piqued imaginations while feeding the endless appetite for gossip.

A black Suburban with tinted windows pulled up to the property at 7:00 am sharp, and one of the Kansas State police officers approached. An automatic window lowered, revealing a young male driver, a probationary agent a few weeks from going to Quantico, Virginia to become a special agent.

"Welcome to Kansas. Sorry you have to see this," said the police officer, looking at their credentials briefly.

"Thank you, officer. We need to get inside and make an assessment quickly," said a voice from the front passenger seat. It was the senior special agent in the detail from Dallas office, Edward Stella. With more than 25 years at the bureau, Agent Stella had his eyes on retirement in the next two years. "I've got Washington breathing down my back for information on this scene."

"Of course, sir," he replied, bending slightly to attempt to make eye contact. The inside of the vehicle was dark, and with the occupants dressed in black, it was like a bottomless pit.

The driver took the credentials back and parked the Suburban. He stayed in the vehicle as Special Agent Stella exited, wearing a summer-weight black suit, followed by Agent Maria Santiago and a new agent on the job, Glen Evans. Agent Evans had just recently completed the 21-week course at Quantico and was at his first real murder scene. Agent Santiago was tasked to train the young special agent, and she was impressed at how quickly he was catching on. She had heard this scene was especially bad and wanted to see how the young man would react to seeing something like that. Training at Quantico could only go so far. He needed to see the real thing.

Captain Rob Burbage greeted the federal agents at the end of the driveway. He was a hearty, middle-aged Kansas trooper who had gotten his captain bars two years ago. His countenance spoke volumes.

"Greetings," Captain Burbage said, extending his hand to each of the agents. "I've been a cop for 24 years. I've never seen anything like this." He met the gaze of the agents, one at a time. His grave demeanor made it obvious he wasn't kidding.

He led them slowly into the house through the front door, since the garage was an important part of the scene with a lot of blood, potential murder weapons, and the body of a young teenage male that had not yet been identified. He was hanging from the garage door overhead track. There was also a lot of blood on the walls and floor, especially at the threshold of the door that led to the kitchen. FBI field investigators were already there collecting evidence, but they were under direct orders to not move the bodies or disturb the writings found on the walls until Agent Stella told them to.

Captain Burbage paused halfway into the kitchen and pointed to the dining room.

"This is how we found the adult male and female victims. We believe they are the husband and wife who lived here, Phillip and Janice Edwards. This is an extremely graphic scene," the Captain said.

Agent Stella looked over the scene with no expression. He did have a handkerchief up to his nose, as the odor of the entire house was rank with death and human waste. His eyes darted about, scanning the gruesome scene. Agent Santiago did her best to keep a poker face as she looked at the brutalized bodies of Phillip and Janice Edwards. She was a single mother from abject poverty, who rose to be a success story and inspiration to others. The FBI had her speak at high schools in hopes of bringing more qualified young women to the bureau. She didn't want to show emotion, but the horror before her was like nothing she had seen. The amount of blood that painted the walls and ceilings of the dining room was unbelievable. It was like something spawned from a horror film. Knowing that it was real gave her a chill deep down. She knew that Agent Evans was probably looking at her, as was her supervisor, so she buckled down and stood straight – vigilant.

Nothing in his 21 weeks at Quantico could have prepared young Agent Evans for what he was looking at now. The blood on the ceiling seemed to grab his attention as his imagination wondered what would have caused such an atrocity. When his gaze met with the ravaged body of Janice Edwards, he knew why the ceiling was painted red, as were the walls, floor and every surface of the room. Her body was in two bloody halves, and with the ragged cuts in her gaping flesh and the chainsaw laying in a pool of blood, it was obvious what happened here. The victim's face was completely obliterated, but one of her eyes hung down, staring at Agent Evans. It was telling him just what had happened in the dining room with the chainsaw, and despite his best efforts, he was unable to purge it from his thoughts. The whine of the chainsaw and the screams that ensued were consuming Agent Evans.

Then he noted the body of Phillip, lying on his back next to the table. His entire body was covered in his wife's blood, and his own, as multiple stab wounds scattered his body in random, helter-skelter patterns. Looking at the gaping cuts, he thought they appeared to be made by different implements. Some were deep and gashing, while others were staccato in nature. Whatever the cause, it had been a disturbing and violent ending. The only thing that could be seen of the victim through the thick, now coagulating coating of blood, was the death stare of Philip. His eyes were open wide. Agent Evans could not take his eyes from that stare. He could hear the tortured cries even after he was led from the dining room into the living room, in a sickening chorus with Janice as the chainsaw whined, its motor working through her thick bone and dense flesh.

"Come on Evans, let's move," said Agent Santiago, looking back for a moment at the grisly dining room scene while moving him along. Field investigators were taking pictures of the crime scenes as they crept by.

The vicious scene in the living room was even more disturbing. Agent Evans immediately saw the body of Tammy, who was beaten so badly that it was impossible to determine her sex. She was lying face down with savage lacerations and obviously broken bones in her arms and legs in an unnatural position. When he saw the crumpled body of little Todd, headless and bloody, the effect was staggering. He had never seen anything so terrible. Nothing in his training so far could have possibly prepared him for this. The gaping hole in Todd's shoulder was likely made with the bloody tent stake still stuck in the wall above his body. Blood spattered the wall, and when Agent Evans saw his little head a few feet to the left of Todd's corpse, he vomited into his hands and ran from the room, gagging. He would remember the empty stare of the boy, whose head had been so savagely torn from his tiny body.

"Evans! Evans! Get a fucking grip!" yelled Agent Stella, glaring at the young agent, handing him his handkerchief. "Get him the fuck out of here!"

"Yes, sir!" replied Agent Santiago.

"God damn him!" screamed Agent Stella.

Despite his harsh façade, deep down, the tiny head of Todd Edwards bothered Agent Stella a great deal. He couldn't help but think there was a likeness to his own young grandson, and that fact made him want to run out of the room behind the young agent. In his position, Agent Stella could not show his real feelings, and his hardcore reputation meant only outward rage at the situation.

"Agent Stella, we need you in the master bedroom and garage. The killers left behind some writing. Writing in blood," said a young female field agent, in charge of the investigators collecting the evidence. He only heard every other word. The vacant, tiny eyes of the little boy still seared into his brain.

Before his eyes teared up, he changed his focus to the writing. He knew this was a very important part of the scene that would tie it to the rest of the killings.

"Yes, show me the writing."

******

"So where did you drive to after you left Belleville?" asked Brent, his eyes trained on Nolan.

Nolan was getting tired and had almost nodded off twice in the past 30 minutes. A cigarette was barely dangling from his lips. The smoke was going up into the vent.

"We drove to Mexico."

"What? Mexico? I didn't think you left the United States."

Nolan laughed. "No. Mexico, Missouri. It's a small town on the way to Columbia."

Brent felt stupid. "Oh, I understand."

Nolan nodded, a thin smile across his face, but his eyes were tired. He took a deep drag of the cigarette, then let it fall to the concrete floor for Brent to stomp out.

"You said *we* drove. Were the twelve killers still with you?"

"Yeah. They were with me all the time. We drove that bus around, stopping randomly and just killing people. No rhyme or reason to it. Just killing mother fuckers."

"So, are they with you now?" Brent asked.

"Yep."

"Really? Why don't they come out and talk?"

Nolan was looking down, not wanting to make eye contact. His leg chains rattled a bit.

"They don't want to right now. They've been letting me drive the bus since I got locked up."

There was a loud pause in the holding cell. Brent heard one of his crew shift and make a slight noise to break the tension.

"So, what happened in Mexico?"

"Stopped for a piss break. We got into it with the clerk at a gas station. She gave back the wrong change and wouldn't admit it. Fucking thieving bitch," replied Nolan, he became agitated thinking about it. The veins of his neck began to protrude slightly.

Nolan coughed, then continued, "So Lyle killed her. He strangled her behind the counter and took a bunch of cash, cigarettes, lottery tickets, and some snacks. It was one hell of a score."

"Then you left town?"

"No. There was a family of four in a van pumping gas. They heard the screams, and the father confronted us leaving the gas station. So, we had to take care of it."

Brent knew what he meant, but asked, "Took care of it?"

"We beat the mother and father up bad. Lots of blood. Rasmus raped the mother, stupid mother fucker. One of them strangled the kids with the mother's pantyhose. I think one of them wrote some shit in blood on the back window of the minivan they were driving."

"I read somewhere that those messages you were leaving really had the police baffled."

"Yeah, they figured out the messages were written by different people right away. They just didn't know the people were all living inside me," Nolan said, his voice becoming increasingly listless.

Suddenly the loud buzzer sounded, and the holding cell door opened. Sergeant Whitlock and a different corrections officer stepped inside.

"OK, gentlemen. This session is over. Time to go back to your cell, Weeks," said the barrel-chested Sergeant Whitlock, while the young officer began to unlock Nolan's leg and arm restraints.

About ten minutes later, Brent and crew were signing themselves out at the sally port where they had to enter and exit the prison each time. Sergeant Whitlock approached them, a concerned look on his face.

"I'm glad I caught you," the Sergeant began, "I heard that they have an execution date for Weeks, but you didn't hear that from me."

Brent was surprised it had happened so soon, but remembered he was in Texas, where more inmates were executed than anywhere else in the United States.

"Oh, wow. That was quick."

"Yes, it is, but I'm not surprised. Between you and me, the warden has had a hard on to execute Weeks since he got here. He's sick of the press hounding him about Weeks, with requests for interviews and all that."

"So, when is it?"

"Two weeks from today. That's not much time. They'll be moving him back to the death watch cell where he'll be by himself and closely monitored. The staff will also be making the arrangements for the execution. Witnesses, media, and all that. A lot of shit goes into killing an inmate."

"So how is that going to affect the rest of the interviews, Sergeant? We have a lot yet to cover with him."

Just then, the sally port gate was opened, and an armed correctional officer nodded and gave the crew a "thumbs up" to signify they were cleared to leave the prison.

"I can't say, sir. I'll see you the day after tomorrow, and we'll just have to play it by ear."

Brent couldn't help but wonder if he would ever see Nolan Weeks again, and if he did, he had serious doubts they would finish the interviews before he was to be executed in two weeks.

******

Agent Glen Evans was put on medical leave from the FBI so he could get some rest after his bad experience at the Wichita crime scene. He went to stay with his parents at their Seattle home on Buzzard Lake. At first his parents were happy to see him, since it wasn't often enough that they got to see him since joining the FBI. Tom and Joan Evans were very proud of their son. He was their only child. Glen was a model student in school, lettered in track and baseball, and never got in any real trouble.

Two weeks passed, and Glen was barely leaving his bedroom. His parents were very concerned about him. He barely took showers or changed his clothes, and his bedroom was filthy and horrid-smelling. They tried to give him some space and hoped he would snap out of it. On his bed were piles of newspapers where Glen had been clipping out articles about the murders in Wichita. There were a lot of them, since many were speculating that the cross-country murders were all connected to a Satanic cult. Various experts on the subject seemed to pop out of nowhere, spouting on about how cults worked and how they could suck normal kids into doing their bidding. Glen was obsessed and spent countless hours clipping out the articles, reading them, and logging various information about the murders into notebooks. If he was of sound mind, it may have been a way to help the investigation, but he was not in shape for any such thing. His notes were useless ramblings. The piles of newspapers grew, and his parents were at their wits end with worry about their beloved only son.

It was during the small hours one night when Tom Evans heard the gunshot. It sounded like a pistol. He woke up his wife,

Joan, and together they ran down the hallway toward Glen's bedroom. Tom was the first one to see Glen's brains and blood splattered all over the wall, and his lifeless corpse slumped over into one of the piles of newspapers on the bed. Tom's .38 revolver was on the bed next to his son. On the other walls, he wrote with his own blood that he had been getting from pricking his fingers with a sharp hunting knife. The words made no sense to Tom or Joan, and both were on their knees and sobbing with grief at the horrible sight.

The one message that was bold and easy to read was NIGHTMARE MAKER in capital letters. It made no sense to Tom or Joan, but the FBI would be very interested to know what had become of their new agent and why things ended up the way they did at the beautiful house by the lake.

6

Brent sat at the edge of the bed, craving a drink more than ever. The feeling was choking him; he couldn't shake its savage grip. His mind had been playing tricks ever since he got to his hotel room after dinner with the crew. The network had gotten Brent his own room, while Danny and Sal shared a room down the hall. On the dresser, where the television was mounted, was a bottle of Jim Beam. Brent could see as plain as day the honey brown color of the bourbon and the classic white label with black lettering, but he knew deep down that it was not really there. He wished it was, though. Brent could see an old-fashioned rocks glass there, with one ice cube and filled halfway with whiskey. That's how he saw his grandfather drink whiskey as far back as he could remember. He could taste the coolness as it went down followed by its wonderful warm embrace. Brent missed the intimacy he felt when he was drinking. It was like curling up in bed with a dangerous woman you knew you should stay away from, but the yearning for forbidden fruit won out.

Admitting he was an alcoholic during several stints of rehab, he realized that he loved every part of drinking. He would admire the bottle, bask in breaking the seal and opening it for the first time. The smell of the whiskey as it permeated his senses and the selection of the glass to drink it in was all part of the courtship. Right now, he was feeling a bit nostalgic, and so the old rocks glass sounded good. Sometimes a shot glass was all he needed to get the job done – the equivalent of a quickie in the bedroom. Brent closed his eyes to try and get the images out of his mind, but as soon as he opened them, the Jim Beam was there again - inviting.

Now he found himself staring at the phone on the end table by the bed. He thought about calling Cindy, his ex-wife, and trying to get Brandon on the phone. He missed his son terribly. They were living in Memphis now, after Cindy got her masters and became a nurse practitioner. She was making great money and skyrocketing in her field. It was the opposite of Brent's trajectory. Since their divorce two years ago, he was making less than her for the first time since they had met 22 years before. Brent hated the thought of making less than Cindy, but it was good for reducing his alimony to almost nothing, despite the fact he still had to pay substantial child support. The damage it did to his old-school manhood was tough to handle. Brandon was 17 now, and that meant that in only a few months, he wouldn't have to pay child support either.

His addictions to alcohol and prescription drugs was a major strain on their marriage, but his multiple affairs poured gas on the fire. It was these illicit affairs that had done the marriage in. When Cindy found out about the tryst with Brent's co-host at CNN, Carly Dayton, she reached her limit. Carly was half his age and struggling to make it into the dog-eat-dog news business, where blondes with attractive figures who could read from a teleprompter were standing in line to take her job. Carly was a strawberry blonde, buxom young woman who was naïve enough to think sleeping with Brent Dowling could help her career. Little did she know, the rest of the crew laughed about the affair and joked that she would have made better connections if she had been caught with the night janitor in a broom closet at the studio. Cindy found out about their affair when she called a hotel room where Brent was staying on assignment. Carly had answered by mistake while Brent was in the shower. She wasn't the first woman that Cindy found out about, and she knew that there were probably others. She filed for divorce the following week.

After an hour of debate within himself, Brent finally broke down to call. He stared at the bottle of Jim Beam as he dialed the digits.

"Hello?" Cindy answered, sounding tired. Brent forgot she was an hour ahead of him.

"Hey, how's things? You sound tired."

"Yeah, I am. You do too. Things are fine though, just busy at work. They've got me working 60 hours a week, so the money is great." Brent could hear a door slam in the background. The comment about the great money stung a bit.

"Is that Brandon? Can I talk to him for a minute?"

Cindy paused. "I'll check."

He could barely hear voices in the background but couldn't make out what they were saying. The 30 seconds Brent waited on the other end seemed like a lot longer. He could see in his head the last argument he had with Brandon, face-to-face, more than a year before. It was when they put Brandon in rehab, at his intervention. Brent was quite the hypocrite there that day, and Brandon made him feel every bit of that. Having gone through rehab himself two times, Brent sat in judgement of his son and said some things he wished he could take back. He wasn't the only one, but Brandon didn't seem as hurt by things he heard from his mother, or from his older sister, Barbara. He heard what his dad was saying, and those words stuck into his skin like tiny arrows. Some were more like a railroad spike in the heart. Brandon was very much aware of the problems his dad had with alcohol and pills, hearing his parents fight about it all the time.

"Hey, Dad," Brandon said, in a reserved tone. He was nearly 6-2, just like his father, and had a booming voice. He had considered going into television himself, until things fell apart with their relationship. Now he was talking about going to law school after college. It was hard to imagine that only last year he had been planning to graduate high school early, but due to his drinking, he had to take a year off and get well, using a private tutor to keep his schoolwork up. He had come to grips with the concept of graduating with the rest of his class due to the lost time, even with the tutor.

Brent felt the butterflies in his stomach fly away.

"Hey, Brandon. How are you? You sound fantastic!"

"Good. Been working a lot. Going to school. Usual stuff. I'll be graduating in two months."

"That's great," Brent said, trying to keep the conversation from stalling out. He could tell Brandon didn't want to talk, but Cindy probably asked him to. "I'm still down here in Texas on assignment. But I'll be back for graduation. You know I will. I'm really proud of you, son."

"Thanks. Yeah, Mom told me about Texas. You're really interviewing that guy? Everyone at school has been talking about him." Brandon sounded more interested in the conversation.

"Yes. It's very interesting."

"Aren't you afraid," Brandon asked, "that he's going to kill you, too?"

Brent laughed, then replied, "No, there are guards there with us. He's in chains."

There was a pregnant pause. "I've been sober now six months."

Brent looked at the dresser. Jim Beam was still sitting there. He could see a little condensation on the glass, dripping down in streaks toward the dresser.

"That's awesome, Brandon. I'm proud of you." He wished his son took after another trait and not the one that had been his Achille's heel all his adult life.

"Thanks, Dad."

Brent fought back tears, hearing his son say "thank you". He knew it was a start at mending their shaky relationship. Before he could reply, Brandon hung up the phone, but the euphoria continued until he went to sleep, and visions of Nolan Weeks paid him a visit, to remind Brent of exactly what he was dealing with.

He woke up screaming at exactly midnight.

******

"So, what do you think, Jerry? I mean, cut to the chase."

Jerry Hall looked through his notes, searching for something. He was brilliant, but very disorganized both in his private and working life. Agent Stella was at the front of the room and losing patience with Jerry with each rustle of paper. A cigarette burned itself nearly to the filter in Stella's right hand. The small room that they were working out of was filled with smoke, due to poor ventilation and the fact that most of the agents chain-smoked. The yellowed ceiling tile in the room was a testament to that fact, as well as the heaping ash trays that lined the large rectangular table where they sat. Littered among the ashtrays and piles of papers were pizza boxes and empty Chinese take-out food containers. An old coffee maker was being stressed beyond its limits as the agents drank their weight in strong black coffee. There was a dry erase board at the front of the room that Stella had been using for various lists they had been compiling since they started this meeting at 7:00 am. Pictures of victims covered the bulletin board next to the dry erase board. A piece of paper was taped to the center of the wall, just above the dry erase board that read: TASK FORCE NIGHTMARE.

Stella had not been sleeping well since taking charge of the task force. The relentless heat he was taking from his boss, John Carroll, who was the agent in charge of the Dallas-Fort Worth office, was enough to make him want to put in his retirement papers. He knew John wouldn't accept his resignation, especially with the Midwest murder spree going on. Calls at all hours of the day and night were taking their toll on Edward, who barely slept as it was. Stella knew that the shit rolls downhill and that John was catching heat from his boss in DC.

Normally a Midwest case would be handled by Chicago or St. Louis, but both offices had interim directors, and the DC office wanted John Carroll to handle it – despite being in Texas. John was tough, and everyone knew he had the best supporting cast around him to catch the killers. The media attention to the manhunt was like nothing anyone at the bureau had ever seen before. That was why they put together Task Force Nightmare, aptly named after the writing left behind by the killers at almost every murder scene.

"I agree with Billy. It's most likely a gang or a cult of some sort. How many people? I'd say at least 10," said Jerry, still shuffling papers. "Devil worship is on the rise. Our California offices have been saying it for years. It's spreading everywhere, and I think that's what we've got going on here, based on the writing left behind and the gruesome nature of the murders."

Billy McHugh was the senior profiler in the Dallas office. He had recently helped solve a case involving a Satanic cult in Davenport, Iowa, that had caught a lot of attention with the FBI. He agreed with Jerry about the spread of devil worshipping.

"We've had the best handwriting analysts look at the pictures from the murder scenes. One told me he believes at least seven different people are involved," Billy added. "Some of the writing is almost childlike, while others are much more educated and mature."

Sitting next to Billy was a young agent on the rise that Edward recruited for the task force. Agent Louzar Ellis was raised a military brat with a father in the Army, last stationed at Fort Sill, Oklahoma, where Ellis went to high school, before leaving to go to college in Texas and then working for the FBI. Born to a mixed-race family of eight, with a mother who was white and a father who was black, he learned to get along with most people, and his outgoing personality made him a strong asset. Ellis scored the highest on the intelligence tests the FBI gave him, and he was in the top 1% in his physical fitness scores as well.

"Strangely, though," began Ellis, "We still have only one set of positive fingerprints."

Stella nodded. "Yeah, if there were that many people involved, why only one person's prints? I can't figure it out. They must be very disciplined about leaving prints behind."

"Agreed, it doesn't make sense," Billy chimed in, grabbing the last piece of pizza, much to the dismay of Agent Santiago, who had been eyeing it up herself. "Usually a gang doesn't clean up after themselves. That's why I have my reservations about saying it's a Satanic gang."

"I would like to try and use that new DNA fingerprint technology they're using in England, boss," said Ellis, looking at Stella. "I think it might help here." Santiago rolled her eyes. She was doubtful of this new cutting-edge technology.

Stella found himself staring at the faces of the victims, while Louzar's voice seemed to fade into the background. Some of them he had seen at the various murder scenes in Iowa, Missouri, Illinois, Kentucky, Indiana, Kansas, and Wisconsin. The path the killers took was unorthodox, winding around almost in circles and giving law enforcement virtually no chance to catch up. Their collective voices were almost deafening in his head now, almost pleading to the senior agent to catch their killers. He hoped that the gang would be stopped soon. Once this was over, Stella was planning to put in for retirement and an end to his 24-year career. He thought he would spend an entire year doing nothing but fishing. Maybe then he would find peace? Maybe then the victims would stop filling his head with their pleas for justice?

Just then, the door opened. One of the young secretaries at the office poked her head in.

"Sorry to interrupt, sir. I've got Director Carroll on line two for you. He said it's urgent."

Stella walked over to the secure phone and picked up line two. The rest of the group didn't pay much attention to the call, as they poured through their notes, trying to brainstorm on what they could do to help bring the killing to an end. The look on Stella's faced showed intense concern as he listened, saying no more than "Yes, sir," several times into the receiver.

Just then he hung up the phone. "Fuck!"

Santiago asked, "What is it, Edward?"

"The son-of-a-bitches just struck again. This time in Ardmore, Oklahoma. Same writing on the walls. State police are saying there are six victims. Hacked up real bad."

Ellis looked at the map on the wall where colored push pins tracked the killers. "My God, it's like they're coming straight at us."

The cacophony of victims was growing louder in Stella's head. Ellis was right. This was the first anyone knew of them killing outside of the Midwest. Now they were moving south on interstate 35 and right for Dallas. Stella's fishing pole wasn't going to be needed any time soon.

******

Deputy Brian Scott was sitting in his Cooke County patrol car, enjoying a cup of coffee from his favorite diner on highway 82 in Gainesville, Texas. It wasn't the coffee or the food that made Tiny's Diner his favorite, it was the cute red-headed waitress, Ramona, that made the law man visit at least twice during his overnight shift. The other officers made fun of him about it, saying that Ramona was a woman with a bad reputation, and that he was wasting his time caring about someone who most men over 18 in Gainesville knew in a carnal sort of way. There may have been a bit of truth in that statement, since she had three kids with three different fathers, and none of them were still in the picture. Two of the three were locked up and doing time somewhere in the Texas penal system, and the third was on the run. Rumors were swirling that he was in Florida, shacked up with some trailer park queen in a single-wide with three screaming kids.

Even Tiny himself admitted that Ramona was a bad girl, but she was willing to work the shift that his other waitresses wouldn't. Since they were located near the intersection of interstate 35 and highway 82, they had seen their share of robberies over the years. Tiny kept a shotgun in his office for that reason. What he didn't tell Deputy Scott was that she also gave him a toe-curling blowjob every now and then for some extra money when something unexpected came up or when there were Christmas presents to buy for the kids. Tiny quite liked the arrangement and was willing to put up with Ramona being late. He also knew his customers liked to stare at her ass, and that was good for business. She wore her skirt a bit shorter than the other waitresses and had the long legs to do it justice.

Deputy Scott was watching the sun come up in an empty commuter parking lot on highway 82, just west of the diner, when an urgent call came in over the radio.

"Brian, we got a code 36 and a 37 reported at Tiny's!" crackled Marla, the dispatcher. Her thick Southern drawl was unmistakable.

Deputy Scott knew that meant a robbery and shooting. He almost knocked his coffee off the dashboard and all over his lap. He had only been a deputy with Cooke County for a year, and during that time, he had not been on a murder scene. Most of his shifts were filled with routine traffic stops, domestic disputes, lot lizards at the truck stop, and drunk and disorderly patrons from Miss Thing's Strip Club.

"Holy shit!" he replied into the handset. He turned on the siren, and as its wail cut the pre-dawn silence, "I'm on my way." He was only two miles from Tiny's place. Marla went on to tell him there was another car about five miles away and she was sending him there, too.

"Proceed with caution, Brian. Tommy McFalls called it in. He must have got there just after they left. Said the place is a bloody mess."

Deputy Scott couldn't help but wonder if Ramona was OK. When he had just left the diner 30 minutes before, she was the only waitress, and Pedro was cooking. Tiny wasn't there yet, but he usually arrived at 6:00 am every day. It was Sunday, so that meant the usual breakfast crowd wouldn't be there that early.

"Marla, I'm at Tiny's. It looks quiet. I see Tommy standing out by his truck, and I see Ramona's car and two others I don't recognize," Deputy Scott said into the radio handset, calling in the plate numbers. One was a Texas plate, and the other was Oklahoma. He knew Pedro walked to work from one of the nearby trailer parks.

"Roger that," Marla answered, "Donny should be there any minute."

As Deputy Scott approached the front door, he walked past Tommy McFalls, a local who owned a trucking company. He was distraught and obviously shaken.

"Christ. It's bad in there, Brian. Really bad." His right hand held a cigarette, and it was shaking slightly.

"Just stay put, Tommy."

Deputy Scott heard the other car arrive with Deputy Donny Somers as gravel crunched under his tires. His siren was off, but the lights were going. Donny had been with the county for three years.

"Hang on, Brian. Let's go in there together."

Deputy Scott wasn't thinking clearly. He wondered if Ramona had survived whatever had Tommy McFalls so freaked out. He knew Tommy was an Army veteran who did two tours in Vietnam, and so if he said it was bad in there, it had to be awful. As he approached the front door, it swung open in the breeze, and music could be heard from inside. Ramona liked to play the radio that Tiny kept on the counter when it was quiet in there. It made her feel less alone on that dark, two-lane highway about a mile from the interstate.

"I'll go around back," said Donny, his gun drawn.

Brian nodded, still thinking about Ramona. As he crossed the threshold, he could smell the metallic odor of blood. To his left were two tables and four booths. A puddle of blood was widening under the tables, coming from a slumped over patron in one of the booths. Brian didn't recognize the man. His throat was torn open, as if a wild animal had claimed it. He had never seen such savagery. The unknown victim's eyes were wide open, likely frozen in place upon realizing he was to meet his end in such a brutal way.

I walked the floor, the whole night through. You're cheating heart, will tell on you. The small radio on the counter played on.

Brian saw two more bodies on the other side of the diner. One was a local, Ron Childers, who he knew from high school. He was slumped over the counter, his neck obviously broken. His biscuits and gravy were still steaming, and his coffee mug was knocked over and spilled on the floor. The other body was in one of the booths, slash marks on his arms and a gaping wound across his face. He appeared to be breathing, but barely. He looked up at Brian, his lips moving as if to try and tell him something. Brian was worried about Ramona and didn't stop to try and find out what the dying man had to say.

As Brian made his way behind the counter and into the kitchen, he was heartbroken to find Pedro on the tile floor, a pool of blood gathering beneath him. He had known Pedro and his family for many years, and he admired the hard-working group of immigrants a great deal. Pedro was also a deacon at St. Mary's church in Gainesville. His skull was crushed on the left side and his face was indistinguishable. A large butcher knife was in Pedro's hand, that he likely had used to try and defend himself. Unfortunately for Pedro, he was not able to fight off the attacker. A pile of hash brown potatoes was sizzling on the grill, and four pieces of toast were popped up in the commercial toaster.

On the other end of the kitchen was the door that led to Tiny's office, where the shotgun was kept. Brian had not yet seen Ramona, so he hoped that maybe she did get away. Just then he saw Donny, who entered the diner from the side door that led to the dumpsters out back. Donny pointed to the office door, and silently the two deputies crept closer to it, not knowing if they would discover the killer or killers in the office, looking for money.

Donny kicked the flimsy door in, hoping to surprise the killers inside. What the two deputies found was gruesome, and it caused Brian's knees to become weak. The small, thin naked body of Ramona was lying on the desk. Her legs were spread open, and there appeared to be obvious trauma to her privates, with blood pouring down her legs and the front of the metal desk. Stab wounds were scattered across her chest, nearly cutting her left breast off. Her flowing red hair was matted with blood and covering her face. The same face that Brian had fantasized about in his dreams was now dead and growing cold. Tears began to well up in his eyes as Donny tried to get him to leave the office.

The phone and other items that were on the desk had been pushed violently to the floor. Blood was all over the walls and still dripping down the old wood paneling. The Dallas Cowboys' Cheerleader calendar on the wall behind the desk was drenched in her blood, as were the other papers Tiny had tacked up on the walls. Tiny's favorite Farrah Fawcett poster was half torn down, and what was left of it was also blood-spattered. Farrah's beautiful smile was flecked with red spots.

Just then the diesel engine of Tiny's Dodge truck rumbled to a stop just outside the side door. Both deputies knew that was where he parked each morning, by the sign that read, Cowboy Fan Parking

Only. Donny ran outside to greet the portly owner, while Brian stood agape in the middle of the office. His eyes now fell upon the strange wounds on Ramona's bare stomach. They appeared to be made with a small knife or maybe even a razor blade. He couldn't be sure, but it looked like it spelled out something. The blood made it hard to distinguish, but his first thought was that it looked like it said NIGHTMARE MAKER.

It wouldn't be until later that morning when the FBI showed up at Tiny's Diner that the early edition of the Texas Observer newspaper was found sitting on the chair behind the desk. It showed the front-page headline, above the fold, DALLAS FBI OFFICE ESTABLISHES TASK FORCE NIGHTMARE TO CATCH CROSS-COUNTRY KILLERS. Beneath the headline was a picture of Director John Carroll with a smiling Agent Stella and a caption that read: *Veteran agents John Carroll (left) and Edward Stella (right) vow to stop the killers.* A knife was thrust through the newspaper and into the chair.

7

"Warden Greene," the warden barked into the phone like a drill sergeant on the parade field. The wall behind his desk was an array of degrees and certifications that only a career government employee, with 30 years under his belt, would be able to display.

"Sir, you've had seven calls this morning about inmate Weeks," said Selma, his secretary. She was the only one at Huntsville State Prison who was able to stand up to the warden and wasn't afraid to strut her stuff when necessary.

"Oh, for Christ's sake," he continued barking, "I don't want to hear from them. What the hell do they want now?"

"Well, ABC and NBC are requesting interviews with you about the new execution date. CBS asked for the same and a tour of the execution chamber." She already knew what he would say, but she expected he was going to deal with the media surrounding such an explosive case such as this.

The warden replied, "No. I'm not doing any of that. We've got the guy here from CNN talking to Weeks, and that's enough."

Selma sighed, then said, "I know. They're all upset because you're allowing CNN in here. You can't blame them."

"Well, you know as well as I do, that's only a favor for the governor. That's all."

"Yes, sir."

"He's probably running around with some cute CNN reporter and he owes her a favor. Who the hell knows?" Warden Greene let out a gruff laugh.

Selma laughed too. "You're probably right, sir."

The warden added, "That reminds me, would you please be sure to call that reporter at his hotel and let him know we're moving Weeks to his death watch cell later today? Have Sergeant Whitlock talk with him about any security issues and what sally port he wants them to check in with tomorrow morning."

"Oh, and Eliza called at 8. She said to remind you about the dinner tonight. She'll meet you there at 6," Selma said, "and don't be late." She smiled at the last part. He hated to hear anyone accuse him of being late. He was always ten minutes early.

The warden laughed and thought *I got people jumping when I raise my voice, and the power of life and death in my hands, but my damn wife bosses me around just like that. Selma too. Ain't that just some bullshit?*

******

"You look like shit, Nolan."

Nolan looked at him. His bloodshot eyes spoke volumes, yet oddly at the same time, they said nothing at all. They were in a small windowless room in the death row section of Huntsville State Prison. The floor was concrete and painted battleship grey, while the walls were concrete and eggshell white. Nolan was in a hospital-style bed, but made of much sturdier galvanized steel, so he could still be shackled securely. The fluorescent lighting was waging war with the cameras, and there seemed to be some sort of humming sound in the audio that Sal was saying was due to a bad ground or dirty power – both of which made no sense to Brent. He just smiled and told them both to just do their best, knowing that every interview they did with Nolan could be their last. Sergeant Whitlock made it sound like this was a major security issue at the prison, having them inside death row, and so he could not guarantee another session. For that reason, Sergeant Whitlock got them another hour with Nolan, but only if he was able to speak despite his illness.

"You don't say." His voice was raspy from cottonmouth. "Can you get me that water?"

Nolan was lying at a 45-degree angle so he could see Brent better. He looked bad. Nolan took a sip of water through a straw, as Brent held the cup up to him. Despite his muscular build, Nolan did not look like he had the energy to do much of anything but lay in his bed.

"So, when did they move you in here?" Brent asked, making some small talk to see how Nolan was going to be today. Plus, Sal was getting some sound levels and still waging war with the power.

"Yesterday sometime. My cell is down the hall. It's a lot nicer than where I've been staying. Too bad I won't be there very long." Nolan laughed under his breath, giving Brent and the crew a chill with his bluntness.

Brent tried to smile, but couldn't. "Sergeant Whitlock said they had you away from the others, since we were doing this interview," Brent said, "and the other inmates might raise hell."

"Yeah, I know. He says that it's all about my safety, but they're the ones trying to kill me. So, you figure that shit out." Nolan coughed up some phlegm. "Fucking hypocrites!"

Brent didn't know what to say to that. Nolan had a point. He also knew that Sergeant Whitlock was really going out of his way to help keep these interviews going. The warden was hell-bent on carrying out the execution in a week, and Nolan was very ill. It did seem odd that the warden would be pushing it so hard, but he knew that having Nolan at the prison was a major hassle with all the media attention his case got. Brent had requested an interview with Warden Greene, but he was avoiding his messages. The prison staff set them up in this holding cell in the death watch block so they didn't have to move Nolan far. It did require Brent and his crew a much farther walk in each day with the gear, but he wanted to do whatever he could to finish up the interviews with Nolan since time was short.

"So, we left off with you talking about being caught near Fort Hood, Texas."

"Yeah, in the little town of Nolanville, about a dozen miles from the base. What's the odds of me being caught in a town with name like that? Not much there but a couple trailer courts and a small Mexican take-out joint. Damn good chorizo at that place," Nolan muttered, his voice weak. He was looking off into the distance, possibly tasting the chorizo from El Jefe's Mexican Restaurant. "But those damn refried beans got me sicker than a dog. Never puked like that since. Even eating this shitty prison food."

Brent didn't know what to say to that. He knew from following Nolan's case that it was the food poisoning he got from eating those refried beans that had led to his capture. A Bell County deputy found him on the side of the road puking his guts out and noticed a bloody towel in the backseat of the Chevy Impala he was driving. He also had some blood on his shirt and pants. The deputy called in the plate, one thing led to another, and two squad cars were called in for back-up. In five minutes, they had him handcuffed and headed to Bell County jail. They didn't know what they had at first, but things began to unravel once his fingerprints were taken. A hit came through right away, and the FBI was contacted - the number one most wanted man in America was sitting in cell 13 in A-block, doing a crossword puzzle and drinking black jail coffee. The guards couldn't believe they had the same guy who was part of a gang that had been terrorizing the US for two years. Despite being told to keep things quiet, it didn't take long for phone calls to be made, telling their family and friends about the VIP killer.

"I've had food poisoning myself, and it's horrible." Brent watched to see if Nolan had any reaction to recounting his capture into police custody. But he did not seem to react at all. Nolan was listless, due to lack of sleep and probably some of the medication they had been giving him. Brent noticed he looked quite a bit worse than the last time he had seen him.

"Yeah, I was a rock star at Bell County, but the FBI was there the next morning to take me to Dallas," Nolan said, "and they had a convoy of government vehicles with at least ten armed agents to drive me up there. You'd of thought I was the devil or something!" He laughed out loud at that.

Brent shifted in his chair, then looked back at Danny and Sal to be sure they were filming. Both nodded to him in the affirmative.

"So, once you were in police custody, which of the others were in charge? Were you still feeling like you were on a bus with them, like you said the other day?"

Nolan thought for a moment before answering. His lips were dry and parched, and Brent gave him another sip of water.

"Yeah, it's funny. Until you asked me that, I didn't really think about when it happened that I became the driver. But when they put me in the Bell County police car, handcuffed and all, that's when I became the driver. The rest of them have been pretty quiet ever since," Nolan said. "I don't know if that's a good thing or not."

"Really? That's strange."

Nolan laughed. "The whole fucking thing is strange. Since I got to my parents' house in Heyworth, everything has been real fucking whacked."

Brent didn't say anything.

"They've been quiet, but I know they're just waiting. They know what's going on, and they're watching me," Nolan said, "and when they need to step up and take the wheel, then that's just what they'll do. Right now, they're just sitting in the seats behind me, and they got me on a short fucking leash."

Brent asked, "You think so?"

"Yeah. I think they're trying to kill me right now. As I lay here, I'm getting weaker and weaker," Nolan said, coughing twice. "It's like behind in a giant vice, just crushing me slow."

"Killing you?"

"Yeah, killing me slowly."

"Why?" asked Brent.

"Because I'm telling you about them. They don't like that. Not one fucking bit." Nolan winced in obvious pain.

Brent replied, "So why do you do it, then?"

"I want someone to know about this. They're going to kill me in a week, and then no one will ever know what happened. You're telling my story for me." He winced again, grabbing at his abdomen.

"So, is that what you meant by me having to do something for you? Me telling your story?" asked Brent.

"No. What I need you to do is much bigger than that."

"You still having me wondering what that could possibly be, Nolan," said Brent.

"I know. When it's time, I'll tell you all you need to know."

That was the first-time Brent realized that he felt a bit sorry for Nolan and his situation. He also felt more apprehension about what this was that Nolan wanted him to do. His imagination would run wild for the next week just thinking about it.

******

"Mr. Weeks, we would like to discuss some details of your case."

"Don't fucking call me that."

"What is it you'd like us to call you, then?"

"Nolan. Just Nolan is all."

Nolan shifted in his seat. He was at the FBI office in Dallas, somewhere in the basement level. Everything around him was concrete, with uncomfortable chairs and bright lights that forced him to squint slightly. He could see the three doctors before him, sitting behind a large wooden table – papers, pictures, and other items laid out before them. The doctor in charge was middle-aged, with a thin build and grey curly hair. His glasses slid down his nose as he looked over them to talk. Next to him was an attractive woman in her early 30's, also wearing glasses, but in a sexy librarian sort of way. He found it hard to not stare at her. On the other end was a large black man, well over six-feet tall and muscular like a football player. He was probably also in his 30's, with a slight graying in his goatee. Nolan did his best to contain himself in their presence, but he noted each one of them was afraid of him to some degree. He could smell the fear, like a rotten odor coming from a garbage can on the other side of the room.

"Ok, Nolan. I'm Dr. David Eckstein. I'm the psychiatrist in charge here at this office," he said, smiling in a clinical sort of way. He was wearing a white coat, looking all doctorly and official. "To my left are staff psychiatrists here, Dr. Alana White and Dr. T.C Crampton."

Immediately, Nolan zeroed in on the beautiful Dr. White. He thought she looked like what an Alana should look like. Her long blonde hair that cascaded down beyond her shoulders drew him in like a moth to a flame. She shifted uncomfortably in her seat as she noticed the killer leering and clearly thinking of something perverted. Nolan also noted her curves and long legs that were peering out beneath the desk. He was entranced by her thin legs encased in barely black nylons and the white high-heeled pump that she dangled precariously from her right foot, without realizing she was doing it. He noticed every detail about the sexy Dr. White. Nolan's fantasies ran wild, while Dr. Eckstein continued to speak on deaf ears.

Dr. White felt the temperature in the conference room rise as Nolan persisted in gawking at her. When she realized that he was staring at her legs, the doctor knew dangling her shoe to expose her stocking foot was not a good idea in the presence of a sexual deviant such as Nolan Weeks. She had read the case file that the Dallas office had compiled. The results of his initial psychiatric exams showed his perversions were off the charts, and the number of fetishes that he possessed were disturbing. Dr. White had some experience dealing with sexual sadists, but he was different. His cruelty and inability to feel emotion was inhuman. Suddenly her vision was altered, and she felt dizzy. The room began to spin, and she was now sitting on the couch in her own Fort Worth apartment, while Nolan was standing over her, a wide grin on his face and saliva dribbling down his chin. He reached down to pull on her blouse, and the buttons popped off and scattered. Dr. White did her best to cover her ample breasts, but Nolan was shoving her down and pulling her bra off at the same time. She couldn't hear anything in this disturbing vision, but she felt his rough, calloused hands over her body, and despite the sheer terror that overcame her, there was an odd sense of sexual excitement. She was unable to break away from his entrancing stare. Now he was ripping and pulling off her pantyhose and throwing them to the floor, as he began to unzip his pants and rape her savagely – her knees shoved violently into her face as Nolan growled like a wild animal. As much as his thrusts hurt, Dr. White felt an insatiable need for him to be inside her. Her entire body was overcome with euphoria in his violent grasp. She shook with a white flash that filled her field of vision, and it felt like her head was about to explode.

"Nolan, we understand that you told Agent Stella that there are several people living inside of your body. Is that true?" asked Dr. Eckstein, staring directly at Nolan. Dr. White was still experiencing Nolan in an intimate way and was not part of the present conversation. Her teeth were biting down on her pen cap, nearly severing it half, and her eyes were closed.

Let me introduce myself, Alana, while I'm fucking you on this couch! Raymond Dalripple at your service, bitch! Chicago is my town, and I'm the best salesman at Homestead Appliances. No woman can resist me. They let me in every time. Every fucking time!

Dr. White snapped out of the dreamlike state she was in, the maniacal Raymond Dalripple sweating and grunting over her. She looked at Nolan, and he smiled back at her. She felt a wave of nausea overcome her, and she leaned over to the left to vomit.

Was it as good for you as it was for me, Alana?

"Alana, are you OK, dear?" asked Dr. Eckstein, reaching over to help her.

Dr. White merely held up a hand as if to signal she would be fine.

"Yeah. I told him that. I told a hundred fucking people that when I got here." The veins in Nolan's neck began to protrude.

"Relax, Nolan. We are just trying to understand what's going on here. A true multiple personality disorder, or multiple as we call it, is extremely rare," said Dr. Eckstein. He looked down his nose at Nolan, in what the killer perceived as very condescending.

Nolan stared back at Dr. Eckstein, chilling him to the core, as something odd began to occur. Nolan began to fidget nervously and rub the palms of his hands across his lap toward his knees, making a loud noise. Then he began to crack his knuckles and look around, like he was trying to find someone who wasn't there. He appeared to begin to perspire under the harsh lighting.

"What's going on, Nolan? Are you OK?" Dr. Crampton asked, also noticing the strange, jittery movements and beads of sweat begin to trail down his face.

"Nolan isn't here right now," he replied in a distinct New York City accent. "He's not driving the bus now. I'm driving now, Doc. He's in the back and can't hear us now."

Dr. Eckstein asked, "Who are you? Where are you from?"

"Paul Rosati. Yonkers, New York."

Dr. Eckstein felt a strange warm sensation rush over him. He was from the Bronx, not far from Yonkers. The voice of Paul was swirling around him as if coming from every possible direction. He tried to look at Dr. White and Dr. Crampton, but things were fuzzy and he couldn't see much detail at all, aside from shapes. Then a tingling feeling swept over him and his vision came into focus, like he was climbing a staircase. The stairs were steep, and he was doing his best to ascend them quickly, a sense of dread coursing through him. At the top of the stairs was a door to an apartment. It was apartment number 319. The same one he lived in when he and his wife, Susan, were first married and he was still in medical school. She was teaching first grade at PS 78, only a block from their apartment on Fish Avenue. Dr. Eckstein continued to climb the stairs while the screaming of a woman was prominent in the distance. It sounded like Susan. He did his best to reach the apartment door.

It seemed like an eternity before Dr. Eckstein made it into their apartment. The door was slightly open, and Susan's screams were louder now. He continued, fearing what he would find. His body felt as if it were ten times heavier than it really was; each step more difficult than the one before. He was now standing in his old kitchen. Susan was tied up securely with a brown nylon stocking to one of the kitchen chairs. Her face was flush, and tears poured down her face as she screamed and pulled at her restraints, ignoring the fact her husband was now standing there. Nolan sat across from her at the table, a checkered cloth napkin tucked into his shirt, a serving fork in his right hand and a large carving knife in the left. He looked at Dr. Eckstein and laughed, and that's when the blood was visible across his face and down the front of the checkered napkin. He grinned in a manic sort of way. The bright red blood made the entire scene like something from a terrible nightmare.

Dr. Eckstein realized the true hideous nature of what was unfolding before him. Their infant daughter, Elizabeth, was on a large platter in front of Nolan as he calmly carved her up like a holiday turkey, humming to himself with frivolity. The only thing distinguishable about the baby was her severed head that Nolan had placed in the middle of the table like an ornament. He carved off slices of her still-warm carcass and chewed with delight at the tender flesh, sampling it with fervor.

Would you like some, good doctor? The flesh is so tender. Maybe you'd like to try a bite?

Dr. Eckstein was abruptly awakened from the nightmarish vision. His clothes were soaked in sweat, his heart was racing and his breathing ragged. The other doctors didn't notice him, as each of them appeared to be locked into their own strange reality at the whim of the sadistic madman seated before them.

"Are you still with us, Paul?" asked Dr. White, trying her best to keep her composure at the display of a true multiple moving seamlessly from one to the other. Something she had never seen herself in person. She had read about the well documented case of the Ohio mental patient, Billy Milligan, who was found to have more than twenty distinct personalities and was on trial for brutally raping a co-ed. Dr. White did her best to not think about the strange sensations she felt, but the demented gaze of Nolan was still locked in on her. She vomited once again.

Nolan smiled big. "No, he's not driving the bus anymore. He's given me the wheel."

"Who am I talking to?" asked Dr. Eckstein.

"I'm Edward, the butcher. I bought my own delicatessen. The best in New Haven."

Dr. Eckstein was surprised at how seamlessly Nolan was shifting from personality to personality. He was furiously taking notes to keep track of the various "people" they had met here this afternoon. In his experience with multiples, Dr. Eckstein did not believe this was an act. He was trying his best to focus on Nolan, but he was rattled from the horrific vision he had only moments before.

Nolan continued, "I fed my wife and kids as hamburger to my customers." He laughed out loud.

Now Dr. Crampton was taken from the meeting into some alternate universe. He was standing in Edward O'Rourke's delicatessen as Nolan stood before him in a blood-soaked white apron and with a menacing cleaver dripping with blood in his grasp. Dr. Crampton tried to run, but his body was moving in slow motion. Soon Nolan was upon him, the cleaver raised high, and the blade gleaming in the bright overhead lights. Dr. Crampton tried to raise his arms to protect himself, but they would not budge. No matter how hard he tried, the doctor was not able to move them. He was helpless as the cleaver came down with a shattering intensity into his left shoulder. The pain was unbelievable. Blood sprayed in every direction.

Looks like I've got some fresh hamburger coming right up! Don't mind if I do, Dr. Crampton. We all bleed red, don't we?

The conference room came back into focus as Dr. Crampton re-joined the meeting. He instinctively reached up to his left shoulder, thankful it was still in one piece. His heart was racing, nearly jumping from his chest. He blinked his eyes three or four times as he questioned where he was at that moment.

Next time you won't be so lucky!

Nolan stared at each of them as if they were the only two in the room. It was as if Nolan was multitasking with various evil entities that lived inside of him, clutching each of the psychiatrists in a personal embrace of death.

Dr. Eckstein continued, "Some psychiatrists don't believe in multiples."

"I don't have a multiple personality disorder, doctor. I'm sick and fucking tired of you all saying that." Nolan's voice rose in volume. His veins continued to protrude in his neck, and the muscles in his face tightened up.

"Well, then what do you think is going on, Nolan?" asked Dr. White, smirking.

Nolan sat there expressionless for a moment. None of the doctors knew what personality they were dealing with now. He showed no emotion.

"I've got twelve evil entities inside of me. I don't know why they're in there, but that's what they tell me," Nolan said.

"It sounds more like demonic possession," replied Dr. Crampton, looking at Nolan with an air of disbelief.

"Yeah, I think so."

"Should I call for a priest, then?" asked Dr. Crampton mockingly.

Nolan laughed again. "He won't fucking help." He spit on the floor.

Dr. Eckstein laughed. "You expect us to believe in some Hollywood hocus pocus like demonic possession?"

"I don't give a fuck what you believe," Nolan sneered. Now the temperature in the room began to descend rapidly.

As Nolan looked at the three doctors before him, scoffing and laughing amongst themselves, he felt an incredible sensation throughout his body. He closed his eyes and could see himself on the school bus with the others. They were driving around in the country somewhere. Cornfields were on one side of the road, and beans on the other. One of the killers in the back of the bus stood up and snapped his fingers. *I'm your nightmare maker!*

"My God! I can't see!" screamed Dr. White, her hands rubbing frantically at her eye sockets. She tried to stand and staggered backward, falling to the concrete, the glasses falling from her face and sliding across the floor.

"I can't see either!" cried out Dr. Eckstein. "I'm blind!" His hand knocked several of the papers from the table to float helter-skelter in the air.

Dr. Crampton fell to his knees, weeping. His hands were held up in front of him, aimlessly looking for something to hold on to. "I'm blind, too!"

As the three doctors cried out and wept before him, all Nolan could do was laugh. Maybe now they would take him seriously? Now the three of them would have a lifetime in darkness to wonder if Nolan was coming for them next. His maniacal laugh echoed in the room, as Dr. Eckstein furiously pounded on the security alarm near his chair, to signal the guard outside that something went wrong.

8

"You wanted to see me, John?" Agent Stella asked, lightly rapping on his boss's open office door.

"Yeah, have a seat, Ed," replied John, putting a cigarette out in the heaping ashtray on his desk. He looked haggard. It was times like this John wished he was a field agent again and didn't have to play political games.

Stella sat down gingerly, looking at his boss, who was unable to make eye contact with him for more than a second. He noted that John's office smelled like bad coffee, stale cigarettes and body odor. Not a pleasant combination.

"What's going on?"

John Carroll lit another cigarette and inhaled deeply before exhaling it straight up into the cloud that permanently hung above his desk.

"I just heard that Dr. Eckstein and Dr. White won't be coming back here anytime soon. They're not leaving St. Luke's for a while. Dr. Crampton was just discharged, and he already put in his retirement papers."

"That's what you called me in here for? After what I heard went on in there, they're all lucky to be alive," said Stella. He was skeptical about the real reason his boss called him into his office. He rarely did that. From the look on his face, he knew there was more going on here than a medical update on three psychiatrists.

"No. There's more." John looked up, and his eyes were bloodshot and tired.

"I fucking knew it. What?" Stella leaned forward slightly, while John lit another cigarette.

"The fucking Governor's office called. They're coming to pick him up today."

Stella stared straight ahead. He could feel his blood pressure mount, pounding in his temples as one whopper of a headache was soon to follow.

John added, "Weeks. They're coming to get him today."

"What? Are you fucking kidding me, John?"

"I wish I was. Believe me. I'm fucking sick over it."

Stella shifted in his seat while a rush of heartburn tore through him. "That's bullshit, and you know it. How can they do that? We're the fucking FBI, dammit!"

John rubbed his eyes with the heels of his hands. He worked with Stella long enough to know what his reaction would be, and he couldn't blame him. If the roles were reversed, he'd be pissed too. Probably more enraged than what Stella was exhibiting.

Stella slammed his hand on John's desk, shaking his name plate a few inches back. Several cigarette butts were jogged loose from the overflowing ashtray.

"Goddamn it! I've been working on this case for two years," said Agent Stella, "I got two fucking ulcers to prove it. Not to mention a divorce that cost me a fortune, and three adult kids I barely talk to anymore. Fuck!" Stella stared at his boss, who wasn't making eye contact.

"I know, Ed. I'm sorry. DC called me earlier. They said their hands are tied. Something about the Governor in Austin raising hell with someone way up the food chain in Washington. They wouldn't tell me who, but I guess it doesn't matter. Typical big brass bullshit."

Stella closed his eyes. The emotions flooding in were bringing him to the breaking point. He couldn't believe what he was hearing from his boss. He knew it was out of John's hands, but he couldn't help but be upset at him – the messenger. It was like a big arrest they had made together, before John became the boss, when they were working in Oakland as field agents. The two of them had spent months working the case, with many sleepless nights on stakeouts. When it came time to bring the bad guys down, DC had stepped in and let one of the big brass take all the credit. Stella and John had been fuming mad over it. Stella knew John understood how he was feeling right now. It still sucked more than 20 years later. In some ways, it stung even worse. At least in Oakland the two could say "there will be many more cases". Now, this was likely the last rodeo. There would be no more cases. Definitely not one like this.

"Then I am going to turn in my retirement papers first thing tomorrow. I'm done."

John exhaled. "I understand, Ed. I hate to see you go. We go way fucking back."

Stella didn't say another word. He stood up, nodded, and with a lump in his throat, he left John's office.

"Fuck!" John muttered under his breath, then leaned over and vomited into a small garbage can under his desk, bile stinging the back of his throat. He opened his bottom desk drawer where he kept a bottle of vodka. With a shaky hand, he poured himself some in a stained coffee mug and tried to dull the pain his own way. He grimaced as the drink went down, feeling like he might have to vomit again.

******

Nolan would be dead in one week. He knew the execution date wasn't going to change this time. Warden Greene had a hard-on for killing him, even though Nolan was slowly dying on his own. Nolan knew it was the fact he was telling Brent about the twelve entities living inside of him. Each day that went by, a small piece of his life would die. Now that it was the final week, Nolan felt it was coming on quicker.

He was fitfully sleeping in the death watch cell that the staff had moved him to, as was customary a week prior to execution at the Huntsville State Prison. There was a process on how to kill the condemned, and in some ways, the clinical nature of the process made it seem more like prepping a patient for surgery, than strapping them down and giving them a lethal injection. Since the condemned were usually on death row for years, while the appeal process crept like a glacier through the legal system, they didn't think it would ever happen. Yet when the time would come for the guards to march the inmate to the execution chamber, that was when reality reared its ugly head, and the prisoner knew time had run out. In Texas, they had no reservations when it came to executing prisoners, and most of the condemned were dead in less than ten years. Some cried, and others remained stoic, so as not to give the prison staff the satisfaction of seeing them break down. Each one met their execution in a unique way.

Nolan was dreaming about being on the bus again, the school bus with the twelve killers sitting in front of him and one of them behind the wheel. Usually it was Vic driving. That's what they all called him. He was in his 40's and was from some shit town of 200 people in rural Arkansas. Nolan could tell with his strong accent and the way he would carry on about the food and women in Arkansas. Vic was louder than the rest and very much the leader of the group. He was always rambling on about things, to the point that Nolan doubted he was telling the truth. When they left the bus to satisfy their lust for murder, Vic was usually the one raping the women and yelling about being their nightmare maker. He would write it on the walls in blood, saying it was their calling card. When the newspapers reported the murders, Vic loved to see them reference his writing on the walls. The others started doing it, too. When the FBI announced the name of the task force as "nightmare maker", Vic had a hard-on for a week. He was the one who put the knife through the copy of the newspaper in Tiny's restaurant. The cat-and-mouse game with law enforcement made Vic want to raise hell even more.

Nolan was having dreams like this ever since he was sent to Huntsville, but the past week it had gotten much more intense. He would awaken many times through the night, soaked in sweat and screaming. There appeared to be a sense of dread amongst the passengers on the bus which Nolan could feel. In most of the dreams, it was noisy with conversations between some of them, while others kept to themselves and didn't say a word. Yet this dream found each one of them completely silent, and tension was hanging in the air like the smell of greasy fried fish.

Suddenly the bus began to slow down. Nolan looked out the windows to see what they were stopping for. He couldn't see anything but endless fields of corn, tassels listlessly blowing in a soft summer breeze. The hiss from the air brakes brought the bus to a stop. Heat shimmer was rising from the sunbaked asphalt on the country road that lay before and after them. There were no signs of life in any direction, only a group of rusting grain silos on the western horizon. The swaying corn stalks were the only movement for what seemed like eternity.

"What are we stopping for?" asked Nolan, nervously looking around.

"You haven't heard?" asked Doc, who was sitting directly in front of Nolan. He was one who rarely spoke. When he did, you could tell he was one of the most educated of the bunch. Nolan had heard he was a real doctor from Boston, which would explain the funny accent.

"No," replied Nolan.

Doc continued, "We're picking up a new member of the group."

"Yeah, a real bad ass," said Paul, a creepy looking skinny guy with an obnoxious New York City accent. He had a hook nose and beady eyes.

"Just shut up, Paul. Doc is handling it," snapped Raymond, who was sitting across the aisle from Doc.

Someone from the front of the bus let out a loud "ssshhhh!" Everyone became silent. Vic reached over and pulled at the controls to open the door. Nolan could feel his heart beat quicken as the rest of the passengers sat silently, waiting for this new person. *A real bad ass* Paul had said. Nolan was confused. Whoever this new person was, the rest of them seemed to know who he was and were extremely afraid.

A tall, lanky man climbed the stairs into the bus. He wore a black suit and tie with a Fedora, which he removed from his head as he nodded to Vic in the driver's seat. The door shut behind him. Nolan had never seen him before, but the elderly man met his gaze with icy blue eyes. He was unable to look away. The man continued down the aisle, and the bus remained parked on the side of the desolate country road. The men in the seats in front of Nolan sat motionless, staring straight ahead. The air inside the bus went from hot and stifling to chilly as the man with the piercing eyes made his way slowly toward the rear of the bus. His eyes were still locked in on Nolan. His hair was in a buzz cut and peppered with some grey. He was probably in his early 60's and very fit, yet his gate was slow and deliberate as he made his way closer to Nolan, before sitting down in the very back seat on the other side of the aisle. Nolan stared straight ahead, clearly shaken by the mysterious passenger.

"Driver, please continue," the man said, setting his hat down on the seat next to him and turning toward Nolan. Vic slowly pulled the bus back on the road.

"Hello, Nolan. It's nice to finally meet you." The man reached a hand out.

Nolan took the invitation to shake the man's hand. His touch was cool, almost icy. Nolan met the man's gaze once again, and those piercing blue eyes almost seemed to swirl when he looked at them. His facial features were chiseled, and his jaw was strong. Nolan felt incredibly intimidated. He did notice a small gold cross lapel pin on his suit jacket.

"Have you come up with a plan yet on what you're going to do about all of us?"

Nolan was speechless. He only stared at the man.

"You'll be dead in a week, Nolan. You know that. What will happen to all of us if you die with us inside you?" The man shifted slightly in his seat, yet he maintained constant eye contact. Nolan stared at the cross pin on his jacket; it appeared to be inverted!

"I have a plan. But there are too many variables." Nolan looked him in the eye. "It needs some work."

The man's voice became stern. "Well, you better work it out. Because you don't want to know what an afterlife of torment will be like if we all die along with you, strapped to a gurney with pancuronium bromide in your veins to cause respiratory arrest, followed by potassium chloride to stop your heart. Then it's over. No, you don't want to know what that kind of hell is all about. A very private hell indeed."

Nolan didn't know what to say. When the man spoke, a fine mist of frost came from his mouth and swirled around him like a wreath. It was intoxicating to watch. Nolan shivered as the bus continued to get colder.

"How rude of me, Nolan. I didn't introduce myself. I'm the 13th one. My name is Patrick. Father Patrick Reilly, but you can just call me Abbot," he said with a wry smile and an intense stare that held Nolan like a rope being twisted around his throat.

The 13th one . . . 13th one . . . suddenly Nolan was overcome with those words echoing in his mind and an icy mist of frost circling around him. He was awake in his prison bunk - soaked with sweat once again and screaming. Nolan's heart was thumping, and his chest felt like it might explode. Thoughts were rushing into his mind in rapid succession. He was seeing images from his two-year killing spree flashing before him as he was walking down a long, dark hallway. There was a red hue to the floor below him. As he walked by each room, Nolan looked side to side and saw the grisly carnage left behind. Random body parts on the floor with ragged ends like they were torn off by a wild animal. Lifeless eyes on the faces of his victims. Their cries for mercy were distant but many. Men, women, children and even household pets were savagely beaten, stabbed, slashed, raped, and desecrated in the most violent ways. Buckets of blood adorned the walls, ceilings and floors as he saw, one by one, the horrific piles of dead in his wake. In his head, he could hear his own heart pumping and the blood coursing through his veins. His temples were pounding at the fury, like ball-peen hammers striking the sides of his head.

Nolan tried desperately to remain in control, yet in the darkness, he saw movement near the door. He sat on the edge of the bunk, debating whether to see what it was, when more movement caught his eye only a foot in front of him, and Nolan was thrown back to his mattress by invisible hands that were incredibly strong. He bounced nearly a foot off the bunk before falling back down, and a mass of darkness swirled around his entire floor like a storm-ravaged sea.

Once again, he heard the words from the mysterious man on the bus. *The 13th one . . . the 13th one.*

******

1987

Warden Vernon Greene was in his office when the call came from the governor. He had been unable to sleep the night before, knowing there was a lot of political fighting going on when it came to prisoner Nolan Weeks. Just hearing that name made his blood pressure rise. He stared at the family picture on his desk of his son Earl with his young wife, Gloria, and twin six-year-old boys Earl Junior and Virgil. Earl was in his Army dress uniform, adorned with the First Cavalry Division patch, sergeant stripes, and impressive "fruit salad" of ribbons and pins. They had family pictures taken last Christmas. Seeing it now brought tears to his eyes.

He knew staring at the phone wasn't going to make it ring, but Warden Greene couldn't help it. Staring at the picture, the warden was haunted by visions of their violent demise. They were all slain at the hands of Nolan Weeks, in their double-wide trailer on the outskirts of Harker Heights, Texas. They were the last victims before the killer stopped for some Mexican food in the neighboring small town, ironically named Nolanville. It was an odd twist of fate that a two-year cross-country rampage involving the FBI and several state police departments would end with some bad refried beans in a town bearing the killer's own name. The irony was rich and thick like good cream, yet at the same time rancid in his stomach.

Earl was stationed at Fort Hood with the First Cavalry Division, about a dozen miles to the east. He had been home for only two days after a month-long trip to the field with his tank platoon. The family had gone out for pizza to celebrate in nearby Killeen and were random victims at the hand of Nolan Weeks hours later while they slept. The warden was distraught, along with his wife and the rest of the family, that there were no survivors. His dreams were infiltrated every night with the cries of his twin grandsons and visions his mind conjured, since the police didn't allow anyone access inside with the brutality of the crime scene. Earl's unit paid for a cleaning company to come in and get the place ready to sell, so the family didn't have to see the mess. No matter how hard he tried, the warden was not able to think of much else. That was when he had made the call to the governor. He knew the man owed him big time for helping him win the last close election, and now was the time to call that favor in.

The shrill ring of his desk phone made him nearly jump from his chair.

"Warden Greene." he barked into the phone.

"Warden, it's Tom Stewart. I wanted to call you myself with the news," said the governor.

The warden let out a sigh of relief.

"He's on his way to Austin for processing. We picked him up an hour ago. He is ours, Vernon. He'll be in Austin under our charge through the trial."

"Thank God!" exclaimed the warden. "I really appreciate it, Tom."

"I'm glad I could make this happen. I had to call in a favor or two myself with some people I know in Washington, but in politics, you always have dirt on someone. These two had a little too much fun last time they came to Houston, and I had to help cover their asses."

"So, he'll be coming here to Huntsville?" asked the warden, glancing again at the family portrait. Earl Junior and Virgil smiled at him in their Cub Scout uniforms. The warden's eyes welled up, remembering helping the boys with their pinewood derby cars.

"Yes. After he's found guilty and sentenced to death. Then he's all yours, Vern. Until then, play it cool. No saying anything in the media. Or to anyone for that matter. The damn media is going to go crazy with this one."

"Yes, of course."

The governor replied, "We did the same thing with Henry Lucas. The feds wanted him, but since he was caught in Texas, we got first dibs. Plus, they know Texas doesn't fool around when it comes to executions."

"You got that right," said the warden.

Warden Greene closed his eyes and thought of being a witness to the execution of this scum of the earth. He wanted to kill him more than anything he had ever wanted before in his life. He owed it to his son Earl and his beautiful family. They were all god-fearing people and took "an eye for an eye" literally.

******

The words continued to echo through Nolan's mind as the swirling evil began to take shape, his eyes adjusting to the pitch black of his cell. From the darkness, arms reached out to him as he remained pinned down on the mattress with tremendous pressure from all sides. He was completely immobile, only his eyes could glance down at the things grabbing him. Nolan screamed, but no sound came out. Bony fingers with claws as sharp as talons began to dig into his flesh, and pain seared through him like electric current. No matter how hard he tried, Nolan was unable to make it stop. Closing his eyes didn't help, as several hands were upon him, ripping his prison jumpsuit to ribbons, chunks of his flesh plucked from his body. While he endured his own very private hell, blood began to spatter on the walls of the cell, looking like some sort of morbid modern art masterpiece.

"Have we made ourselves clear as to what will happen if you die before we can get out?" asked a familiar voice at the foot of Nolan's bunk. Unable to move his head, Nolan's eyes peered in that direction, amidst the slithering hands that continued their busy work. Nolan wanted to speak but could not. The intense pain was consuming him.

The man laughed. It was Father Patrick, the stranger on the bus from his vivid nightmare. He was wearing the same black suit, a small cross pin on his lapel, and the Fedora perched on his head. *I'm the 13th one.*

"No use in trying to talk, son. It's best you keep quiet. We don't want to bother those guards anyway. They couldn't save you even if they wanted to. My guess is, they wouldn't want to meddle anyway."

Nolan stared at the elderly priest. The man seemed to enjoy watching his tremendous suffering, while the hands ripped and tore at his flesh, and the pain escalated to madness. He began to doubt whether he was dreaming, but the intense agony felt all too real, as he began to fade from consciousness.

"An eternity of this agony, night after night, day after day. Just remember that, Nolan."

Just then the sound of keys jingled outside of his cell. Nolan opened his eyes, and suddenly the cell was filled with bright overhead lights. The dark, swirling chaos on the floor was replaced with the battleship grey painted concrete. There was no elderly priest at the foot of his bed, taunting him while he was strangled by incredible pain and torment. Nolan looked at his body as he sat upright, noting that his prison jumpsuit was not shredded and that his blood was not splattered all over the walls.

"God damn, Weeks. You look like shit. You all right?" asked the guard who opened his cell door. "I got breakfast."

Nolan stared at the tray. Powdered eggs, dry toast, and something that resembled hash browns. There was a cup of coffee there, too, and as he peered into it, he could see his reflection in the liquid. He froze in place. The spoon he had fell to the floor. Looking back at him was the reflection of Father Patrick. He was laughing, while Nolan looked on in horror.

An eternity of this agony, night after night, day after day.

Nolan knew what he had to do. He had known it all along. He just hoped he would have the strength to do it when the time came. So many variables and so much on the line.

9

"This is probably the last time I'll see you."

Nolan smiled, his two crooked teeth visible between dry, cracked lips. His eyes were distant. He was reclined back in the same hospital bed as before. He looked markedly worse than the last time Brent saw him only two days before.

"I'll be dead in five days."

Brent moved his chair a bit closer and said, "I know, five days will be here before we know it. I wish there was something I could do to stop this."

"I don't see the warden or governor getting a change of heart." Nolan's breathing had a mild wheeze to it.

"I've tried to talk with the warden. He ignores me. Our producers tried to get a sit down with the governor. No deal. Everyone is acting strange over this."

Nolan cleared his throat. Brent noticed the circles around his eyes were more pronounced, darker, and more telling about his condition than anything else.

"He's got good reason to want me dead," Nolan said, his eyes drifting away, like he was remembering something.

"Really? I'm not getting you," Brent replied, frustrated at the situation and further confused at what Nolan said.

"No, with him it's personal, man." Nolan lowered his voice to barely over a whisper. Sal, the sound engineer, raised the volume on the microphones and tweaked some knobs on his mixer to capture the quiet audio.

Brent was intrigued. "Personal?"

"Yeah, the last victims were his family. His son . . . " Nolan was now locked in and looking directly at Brent. His eyes got darker and swirled with evil. The camera operator, Danny, brought the shot into better focus, trying to capture the moment.

Brent was feverishly going through his notes. Nolan watched quietly.

"Here," Brent said, holding up a laminated newspaper article. "The last victims in Harker Heights were Earl Mayfield, an Army soldier, his wife Gloria, and their twin boys, Earl Junior and Virgil. That was his son?"

"Yes. 30 years ago, the warden was fucking one of the female guards here at Huntsville. Her name was Helen. She was white, and back then, that wasn't tolerated, especially in Texas. He was her supervisor but 20 years from becoming warden."

Brent was floored! "Wow. I had no idea."

"No one did. They kept it quiet, and as careful as they were, they failed in a major way. She ended up pregnant. He was married and was not going to ruin his career in corrections over it," said Nolan, his voice getting weaker. "So, he helped with money for bills and expenses to raise Earl Junior. Being a mixed-race kid, it wasn't easy on him, either."

"Holy shit! The warden is pushing for the execution of a man convicted of killing his own son, daughter-in-law and grandkids? Talk about a damn conflict of interest," replied Brent, desperately writing notes to not forget the details later. "The media would have a field day with that story! How has this been kept quiet?"

Nolan shrugged and took a sip of water as Brent held the straw up close. The chains restraining his arms and legs to the bed clinked and reminded Brent that he was talking to a condemned murderer. Sometimes he forgot, as strange as that seemed. Whether he wanted to admit it or not, Brent was feeling sympathy for Nolan and how he had ended up on death row at Huntsville State Prison. Brent had a different vision of what death row looked like. This was an almost sterile environment, like they were waiting for cataract surgery or fishing for kidney stones. He heard no screaming and yelling like in general population. Death row was eerily quiet. The condemned knew they were going to die, and most had come to grips with that long before they were moved here. Some of the inmates looked forward to dying, to take them far away from Huntsville, even if many of the prisoners were unclaimed by family and buried in the cemetery on the south end of the grounds. They were, for the most part, very docile and kept to themselves as they tried to reconcile things with God. For Nolan, he had no use for God, and he made it well known when asked if he wanted to see the prison chaplain.

"How the hell do you know all this? Who is your source?" Brent asked.

"I have my sources. It's all true. Check it out if you want," Nolan said, his voice barely above a whisper. His breathing was more wheezing now. Brent couldn't help but consider that Nolan was slowly dying, bit by bit.

Brent looked down at his notes, then jotted a few things down. He knew they only had a few minutes left before the guards were coming in to move Nolan back to his cell. His mind was reeling with this new bombshell of information about the warden. The press would eat Warden Greene alive if they knew he was actually related to the last victims and was now the one pulling the proverbial trigger to kill their murderer. The anti-death penalty crowd was already starting to picket out in front of the prison, and the news cameras and satellite dishes were plenty. Hearing news like this would make it explode into a frenzy. The emergence of 24-hour news meant the stations were in a bar fight with each other to gain the viewers' attention. The old news room motto, "if it bleeds, it leads", was alive and well. This story had all the components for an ongoing lead story on every news network: sex, money, influence, race, and power. There would be experts in a variety of fields speaking in panels and jumping from one network to the next, like lot lizards at a sleazy truck stop.

So many things were swimming around in his head. Where to go first? The story was taking on more angles, and Brent was desperately trying to follow the right ones to make his mark and maybe stage one final comeback to network news. Brent felt degraded on cable news and wanted nothing more than to rise from the ashes. He knew his peers were laughing at his demise, because it meant one more of the competition had fallen into the meatgrinder. No one thought cable news would ever really take off like many had hoped.

"One more thing. Don't forget our deal," Nolan said in low tones, barely more than a whisper. His eyelids were fluttering.

"I keep asking you about that. What is it?" Brent gave him another drink of water.

"I want you to be one of my witnesses at the execution. No family is coming. I want nothing to do with the fucking preacher. So, you're all I got, man," Nolan's eyes welled up slightly.

Brent was surprised. The favor Nolan had asked for had been gnawing at him ever since it came up at their first meeting. He figured the inmate wanted him to help him escape, or to pay for a high-powered attorney to help him get off death row. Brent knew he couldn't do those things.

"Is that all you want me to do?"

"Yeah, that's all." Nolan's eyes were now closed.

"Of course, I'll be there."

Nolan nodded his head, too weak to speak. Just then, the lock disengaged, and the cell door opened. In walked Sergeant Whitlock with two young corrections officers.

"OK, that's it. He's going back to his cell. You guys have ten minutes to pack up and be ready for one of us to escort you to the sally port," said Sergeant Whitlock. The two young officers began to unlock Nolan's restraints.

Brent was zipping up his bag when Sergeant Whitlock came over to him. Nolan was already taken out to his cell. He hunched over slightly and spoke in a quiet tone.

"Can I talk to you for a minute?"

"Of course, Sergeant." Brent looked at him quizzingly.

"I see you're on the list to witness the execution. Warden showed me."

"Yes, that's what Weeks just told me."

"That gives you five days to do some homework."

"Homework?"

Sergeant Whitlock looked around briefly. Danny and Sal were busy wrapping up cables and putting the equipment in hard road cases with casters in the hallway. He handed Brent a folded piece of paper.

"Take this. I found the source of how Weeks is getting money added to his books. It's on that piece of paper I just gave you. Been bugging me ever since he got here."

Brent looked at the paper, but kept it folded.

"It's also the place he was sending out pages he wrote on. I started banging this secretary in the admin office," Sergeant

Whitlock said, "and it's amazing what eating pussy will get you these days." He smiled thinly.

"Yes, I remember he told me he was writing things down. As for eating pussy, I wouldn't know much about that these days," Brent replied, laughing briefly through his nose.

"Don't open it in here. But you might want to check that out. Something isn't right about this whole thing," said Sergeant Whitlock. "It fucking stinks."

"I know. Something is up. I can't figure it out."

"I'll see you in five days. I'll be part of the execution team. Unless you complete a hail Mary pass in the eleventh hour." Brent only nodded at him.

The execution was now real. It seemed like at first, Nolan would never see his executioner. But now it was coming in five days. Brent stared at the folded piece of paper and wondered what was on it. He stuck it into his back pocket, but the natural curiosity of a reporter made it impossible to not think about it.

"OK guys. We ready to go?" he asked Sal and Danny, as he picked up his own bag and made his way to the door.

"You got it, boss," replied Sal.

After getting through the sally port one last time, the crew climbed into the Chevy van that they had rented when first arriving in Texas. Danny got behind the wheel, while Sal loaded the last of the cases into the back of the van. Brent was in the back seat by himself. He quietly pulled the folded piece of paper from his back pocket and read it under the dome light of the van that was still on with the passenger door open. The printing was all in capital letters and neatly written.

ST. MICHAEL'S ACADEMY, MCHENRY IL. ASK FOR ENOCH STRANGE.

Brent put the piece of paper back in his pocket. Enoch Strange? That seemed like a very odd name. He had no idea where McHenry, Illinois was, but once he got back to the hotel, he would look it up in the travel atlas he kept in his suitcase. Maybe it was worth a plane ride to see who Enoch Strange was and why he was sending money to Nolan Weeks in prison. Better yet, why was Nolan sending him pages from the journal he had been keeping?

Once Sal was inside the van, they pulled away from Huntsville State Prison. Nolan would be dead in five days.

******

Nolan tossed and turned in a fitful fever dream just before midnight. The nightmares that plagued him were like a newsreel of the cross-country murder spree that came to an abrupt end on that highway in Central Texas, puking from a belly full of tainted refried beans. He wasn't the only one that night who got touched by food poisoning from El Jefe's. There were seven other reported cases, according to the Bell County Health Department. One of them was the chief of the Nolanville Police Department, Eldon Floyd, and when he had recovered, he was driven to see the demise of the small family-run restaurant for good. It was the second time he had gotten sick from eating there. Two months later, the health department pulled their food handling license, and Nolanville lost their only restaurant. It was a shame, too, since the food was very good authentic Mexican and employed a number of locals.

The visions in his dreams were graphic yet choppy clips from the dozens of murders that Nolan had perpetrated on an unsuspecting public. The ghastly images of his horrific handiwork were shown in faces being strangled as their eyes bulged from their heads, turning blue and slipping away. Or gaping wounds in bodies that poured blood, the death rattle of people slipping away to the other side. Piles of the dead were everywhere, oozing on the floor in disgusting pools of blood, bile, and urine. Then the various writings on the walls, made by the hands of the various killers, in the blood of the deceased. It was what had driven the FBI and the various state police agencies crazy, as they thought they were on the trail of a Satanic gang, but instead only one host with a demonic entity inside him, spawned from the souls of twelve despicable murderers. Each had their own signature, and while some were more prolific than others, they all had blood-soaked hands. Nolan was the lone bystander, sitting in the back of the bus, watching the carnage unfold as they drove on. Since he had been at Huntsville, Nolan had not heard much from the twelve, but once they moved him into death row, they had come alive once again. Soon after the 13th one, as they called him, had joined the group, things began to spiral down even faster.

"Having a hard time sleeping, Mr. Weeks?" asked a familiar voice. Nolan's heartbeat thumped in his chest at the sound of it. He knew who it was, and he was beginning to understand why the rest of the killers on the bus were frightened of him. It was the Abbot, Father Patrick.

Soaked in a feverish sweat, Nolan looked at the foot of his bed, where the Abbot's voice originated. He was not there. *Where the hell was he?*

The Abbot laughed. "Over here."

Nolan looked across the cell to the small metal chair that was anchored to the concrete floor and found the Abbot sitting there, his frosty breath evident in the air as the temperature dropped several degrees in his deathly presence. His pallor was grey, and his skin didn't look well. Nolan knew he was dead. The Abbot took the Fedora from his head and glared at Nolan, those intense blue eyes still blazing like beacons in the dim light of the cell.

"Where did you come from?" Nolan asked, his breath ragged and his heart racing. The fever had his face flushed and sweat beading down in large droplets. The thin mattress was soaked from sweat.

The Abbot laughed. "From Hell." The frost from his mouth came down like a waterfall, rolling to the floor and slithering across the cell, encircling Nolan's feet, hanging off the side of his bunk. He jumped back. The Abbot laughed once again. The frosty breath crept up Nolan's body and across his face; the smell of death was heavy in its wake, and the chill gave him goosebumps.

"You need to be more worried about what's going to happen to all of us when you die in four days," the Abbot began, "because your plan with lots of variables isn't making any of us feel good about the situation." The Abbot sneered at him, and added, "And yes, it's just after midnight. So yes – you're dead in four days."

Nolan noticed the floor begin to swirl as it had the night before. He stared into the center of the mass, which was filled with the tormented faces of their many victims. In the distance, Nolan could hear a cacophony of screams and tortured cries as the faces kept moving, becoming engulfed in what appeared to be blood, frothing and bubbling as if it were boiling over from a huge kettle. Now the cell began to heat up as the blood began to slosh around, splashing up on the walls and onto Nolan's bunk. He could feel the sharp sting as the crimson droplets touched his skin, each one hotter than the one before it, and leaving red welts behind. The room felt as if it were on fire from the intense heat. The blood hissed as it got hotter.

The Abbot was now squatting in the metal chair, hysterically laughing at Nolan's misery. As Nolan was writhing in agony on the bed, the boiling blood slowly rose and began to cover him. The pain was excruciating. Nolan could feel his skin being eaten away and peeling from his flesh. He glanced at the Abbot, his insane laughing now reverberating the cell walls, floor, and ceiling. As he squatted on the chair, his arms began to twitch and change. Nolan was witness to the hellish display, as the Abbot's arms morphed within moments into two huge, black wings. They were like giant, leathery bat wings, with black hair and bulging veins that pulsated before him. The Abbot stared directly at Nolan, his steel blue eyes now turning red. The frost that had once poured from his laughing mouth now became flames that licked across the boiling blood, making it even hotter.

Nolan was in and out of consciousness, the blood now up to his chin and slowly cooking his body as the maniacal Abbot flapped his demonic black wings, fanning the flames and causing the inferno to rage well into the small hours of the day. Nolan knew he must carry out the plan to get rid of the twelve killers, now being led by the diabolical Abbot, who appeared to be straight from the depths of Hell itself.

Nolan would be dead in four days.

10

Maria Santiago was on medical leave from the FBI and staying with her aunt and uncle in Salt Lake City. She had been plagued with terrible nightmares since she had been a part of the Nightmare Maker task force. The fact is, Maria Santiago had been having the *same* nightmare every night. It was always a re-run of horrible evil, and no matter what sort of medication she took to help her sleep, the nightmare would play out every night without mercy. When she told her supervisor, Special Agent Stan Robinson, about the dreams, he told her that the two profilers who were part of the task force were also having similar dreams. Both had them every night, just like her. The final straw was when the young superstar FBI agent, Louzar Ellis, confessed that he, too, was having the same nightmare as the rest of them. So, Stan took them all to mental health to be evaluated.

They were all put on medical leave after the FBI Dallas office psychiatrist, Dr. Allan Ribkin, had met with them in a group as well as one-on-one. Dr. Ribkin was not about to allow any of them to stay on duty, or have access to their service weapons, so he put them on leave immediately. He also made necessary arrangements for them to get follow-up care in the cities where they were going to spend their time away. Dr. Ribkin felt they would be better served to be in a relaxing place of their choice, instead of a hospital, while still getting good outpatient care. He felt very comfortable with the doctors that he made the arrangements with.

Maria was staring at the tall elderly man sitting at the foot of her bed. He wore a black suit with a fedora in his hands. There was a gold cross lapel pin on his jacket, and his eyes were a brilliant blue.

Even in the low lighting, they were like brilliant blue beacons, but when she stared at him, they looked like bottomless pools filled with dread. It sent shivers up her spine just to look at him. It was the same man she had seen in her nightmares. The man with the frosty breath and the gray skin. He was the embodiment of evil, and, without saying a word, Maria was frightened in his presence. Now that he was sitting at the foot of her bed, she was paralyzed in terror.

The recurring nightmare she had took place in the same old farm house. As she walked from room to room, she saw piles of dead bodies, in various stages of decomposition. Like most dreams, she felt as if she were walking in slow motion and unable to change the path she was on. No matter how many times she had the dream, and saw the bodies in the same places, they still frightened her. She always walked through the house the same way and paused at the same places as if she were in a play and finding her mark. The middle-aged woman at the kitchen table, dead in her chair, staring at Maria – made her heart nearly beat out of her chest. Her skin was a blueish color, and it was beginning to fall off in places. When Maria got to the last two rooms of the house, suddenly the elderly man with the frosty breath and gray skin appeared, waving a straight razor and laughing hysterically. In the dream, Maria ran back the way she came in, the mysterious dark stranger chasing behind. She would wake up from the nightmare screaming and gasping for breath. The others in the task force gave the same basic description of the nightmare, including the part where they also woke up screaming and out of breath.

Now she was staring at the same gray-skinned man in the black suit. His bony hand gave her a straight razor with a fine pearl handle and gold trim. Maria didn't know why she took the razor from him, and without hesitation, slit both her wrists. He smiled at her when the blood started to pour from the sliced flesh and pool up on the tile floor of the guest bedroom she was staying in. As she began to fade to black, the only thought in her mind was that she didn't have to go to bed every night, fearing she would see the evil man.

On this same night in three other cities, Tallahassee, San Diego, and Indianapolis, the other agents all met with the same fate, as the mysterious man provided to them all the implement to commit the deed. They all bled out before someone found them.

******

Brent was standing in the lobby of the main building at St. Michael's Academy in McHenry, Illinois. There was only a skeleton crew still working there, since they had closed the school ten years before. The church was still in operation, and the small crew the diocese in Chicago allotted for could keep three of the buildings open, while shutting the rest down and winterizing them to avoid pipes bursting during the cold months. The grounds were kept minimally and not even close to the grandeur of when Father Patrick served as Abbot. Brent didn't realize it, but they had erected a statue of the former Abbot in the main lobby, with a plaque that heralded his accomplishments. Of course, the diocese left out the many terrible deeds that he had dealt upon the staff and others, as well as the Satanic black masses he regularly held in the woods surrounding the campus – including human sacrifice. Another thing that Brent didn't realize at the time was that someone on the staff at St. Michael's kept the lobby immaculate, paying special attention to the statue of Father Patrick. The bronze statue gleamed in the sunshine that came in from the east windows. The terrazzo floors were kept to an incredible shine, showing great love and care had gone into its maintenance.

"Mr. Dowling? Sorry to keep you waiting," said Joe Montgomery, the head of maintenance at St. Michael's. He held a hand out and shook Brent's aggressively. He was a short, portly black man in his mid-40's, with a ring of keys on his belt and a beaming smile on his face.

"Yes, thanks for taking the time to meet with me, Joe."

"Let's take a walk."

Joe led the way to the south side of the property, past several buildings that were closed. Some of the windows were boarded up, in response to local kids coming on the property at night and throwing rocks at them. The lone overnight security guard was in his 70's and could barely see three feet in front of him. The diocese had moved him around many times, due to his penchant for young girls, and once the school closed, they figured St. Michael's was the safest place to stash the old pervert. Arthur Belfour sat in his office most of the night, except when he would walk down the hallway to use the bathroom. He loved to read large print Ellery Queen detective novels while he drank black coffee and ate pickled eggs. So, the vandals had their way with the place when Artie was working.

"You mind me asking you where we're going?" Brent asked, struggling to keep up with the fast pace that Joe was keeping. He was oddly fast for a chubby man.

"Well, on the phone you said you wanted to see Enoch," Joe began, "so I'm taking you to him."

They passed the last building on the south end of the property and were now on a narrow cobblestone path that led them across a wide-open field. Brent didn't realize there was so much property surrounding St. Michael's. In the distance, he saw a row of four small cabins, each with a pitched roof, and a porch with a rocking chair.

Joe spoke as they walked. "Years ago, they raised livestock out here and kept one hell of a large vegetable garden. Most of the food they ate, they raised and grew right here. That was way before my time."

Brent enjoyed the wide-open space now that was tall grass for a few hundred yards before it reached the tree line.

"What's that up there?" Brent asked.

"Those are the hunting cabins. They used them when the monks and priests wanted to do some hunting on the property. Lots of deer in these woods. It was a treat to have some venison on the menu, so they used these quite a bit during hunting season," Joe replied, pausing for a moment to mop his sweaty brow with a handkerchief. "Or when they wanted to get away for the night." He laughed. "I heard some stories that would make a truck driver blush."

"I can imagine," Brent replied.

Brent was grateful for the breather. He didn't realize he was this out of shape, but he hadn't been to a gym in a few years. All the years of drinking and popping pills did his body no favors. He sure as hell wasn't 20 anymore. Time was marching on and stomping him into the ground along the way. Brent made a mental note to get back to a gym when this assignment was over. He was looking forward to seeing his son at the high school graduation in June. He hoped their recent conversation would make for a better visit, instead of a series of uncomfortable moments.

Just then a stiff breeze came from the south, hitting the men in the face. It was oddly cool. Brent noticed that a strange look came over Joe as he shivered slightly.

"This is as far as I'll go, Mr. Dowling." Joe said, staring at the cabins in the distance.

Brent was also looking at the cabins. He noticed the one on the west end appeared to have someone in the rocking chair on the small porch, but he couldn't be sure at this distance.

"Why? Should I be concerned?" Brent looked him in the eye, wondering what the sudden apprehension was about. "Are you OK?"

Joe took a deep breath, then looked down. "I'm fine. I won't go into my reasons. I just don't like going down there," he added, pointing toward the cabins about 100 yards ahead.

Brent could feel the tension. The strange breeze continued blowing at them. He found it unsettling that Joe wouldn't look him in the eye. "OK, well I came all this way. I'm not turning back now."

Joe continued to stare ahead at the cabins.

"He doesn't talk. He can't. You'll see why. I'm not sure why you came, Mr. Dowling. You need to prepare yourself for what you're about to see. When you're done, just ask for me in the main lobby, and I'll see you to your car." Joe turned and walked back toward the main building, his keys rattling against his hip as he hurried along, not looking back.

As Brent continued down the cobblestone path, his eyes began to focus on the cabin on the end. He was right. There was someone rocking slowly in the chair, facing west and wearing some sort of hooded robe that blended into the wood planks which made up the cabin exterior walls and porch. It appeared to be a small person. *Could it be a child out here?*

"Hello. I'm looking for Enoch. Enoch Strange." Brent said as he approached the porch.

The rocking chair stopped moving. Brent noticed a small card table set up in front of the chair, with a chess board set up. The pieces were scattered, as if there was a game going on. They were like chess pieces he had never seen before. They appeared to be chiseled from stone, and while they bore some resemblance to classic chess implements, they each took on a sort of eerie presence, like barely visible demonic faces that seemed to move and shift.

As Brent got closer, the person turned toward him. He was aghast at the face that stared at him from inside the dark hood. It appeared to be a man, but the features were so distorted, that he doubted if it was truly human or not. The skin was a sickly, yellow jaundice color and covered with terrible sores and what appeared to be tumors or bumps throughout. His eyes were barely visible amidst the pocked landscape, beady and filled with a foreboding darkness. Brent could not help but stare at the disfigured creature. His mouth was literally sewn shut, with what appeared to be a thick nylon of some sort, with only tiny gaps between the stitches. It looked painful, and he wondered how it could eat or drink. Because of this, the thing had to breathe mainly through his nose, making a tortured wheezing sound with each effort. The rest of its body was thankfully covered by the dark robe. Only his gnarled hands were visible and covered with oozing sores, making them nearly unusable.

"Excuse me. Are you Enoch Strange?" Brent asked in a hushed tone as he stopped at the bottom of three steps that led to the porch.

The creature nodded. Brent couldn't help but feel pity for the tormented being. He didn't see him as human in such a distorted form. *So, this is Enoch Strange? The name fits the poor thing.* It was hard to tell from a seated position, but Brent would have guessed him to be barely five feet tall.

"Can I sit and talk to you? I've come a long way."

Enoch motioned with his head to a chair on the other side of the porch. Brent went and dragged the chair over to the opposite side of the card table that the chess board was set on.

"I used to love to play chess. My grandfather taught me when I was a kid," Brent said, trying to break the ice in some way. "I won the chess championship in fourth grade."

Enoch wheezed, nodding slightly. His left hand, horribly disfigured, reached for one of the black chess pieces. There was a strange face moving up and down the piece, until he moved it, and then the face disappeared.

"So, you want to play?" Brent began to assess the pieces in mid-play.

Enoch nodded again.

Brent reached out to one of the white pawns. As soon as he did, he felt a strange tingle run up his arm and into his right shoulder.

A faint set of eyes was visible at the base of the piece, then vanished as quickly as it came.

Don't be afraid.   I knew you'd be coming to see me eventually.

Brent was startled. He clearly heard a voice in his head as soon as he touched the pawn.

Yes, you are correct.   That was me.   I'm Enoch Strange, a name I was given as a punishment, a very long time ago.

Enoch moved one of his black knights, capturing Brent's pawn. Brent was still somewhat in disbelief. He continued to stare at the horribly distorted face of Enoch, and then at the knights who appeared to snarl with mouths full of razor sharp teeth, before fading into the obsidian volcanic rock they were carved from. The edges had been sharp originally, but were now dulled from decades of use while Enoch Strange played alone.

"How long have you been here at St. Michael's?"

Since 1928. Seems like forever. I lived in the basement of the monk dorm for fifty years. I barely saw daylight. They treated me terribly for a long time. In the beginning, I was beaten nearly every day, starved for days on end and kept in seclusion in my dark room unless I was working. Even then, they kept me away from the rest as best they could, usually making me work overnights, when few others were awake.

"Why? What happened to you?" Brent asked, staring at the rough nylon stitches that made their way in a zig zag pattern across his lips. They were crusted, and the holes in his lips were oozing with infection in spots. It was like something from a horror movie.

Yes, I'm not easy on the eyes, I know. It's a long story, and at my age I don't have as much energy to tell it all. So, why don't we talk about you and why you're here?

"How old are you? If you don't mind me asking, Enoch."

I don't really know. I've been here 60 years now, but I was old when I got here. My only memory is being here. Nothing before.

Brent moved his rook but quickly regretted it as he lost the piece to Enoch's bishop on the other side of the board. Enoch wheezed loudly as he took Brent's piece off the board. The haunting face of a woman in torment appeared for a few seconds on the rook as he set it down.

"How do you eat with your mouth sewn shut?"

I drink my food through a straw. Soup mostly. I've tried to tear the stitches out. Each time I do, they come back tighter and closer together. But again, enough about me. Tell me why you came here to St. Michael's?

"Someone told me to come see you here. He didn't say why. Only that I should before the execution of a condemned man in Texas this Friday. I only have three days left."

Yes, I know. Nolan Weeks. His time on this earth is short.

Enoch wheezed, then took another one of the white rooks, this time with a knight. Brent watched his tangled hands move the piece off the board. The white pieces were more of an ivory color and carved from rare elephant tusks.

"Was it you sending him money in prison?"

Yes, through a trust fund set up for him. So, if something happened to me, he would get a monthly stipend from the bank. I was tasked with setting that up for him upon his arrest.

"But why? What is your connection with Nolan Weeks?"

There was a long pause. Enoch appeared to be wrestling with demons in his own head.

I'll show you. Stay here, Mr. Dowling.

Enoch got up from his chair slowly; his bones creaked and popped as he tried his best to stand straight. His spine was cruelly twisted, and he was unable to avoid hunching over. Brent found it almost painful to watch the man move in such a manner. Enoch hobbled into the cabin with an inhuman gait, his left foot dragging slightly behind, causing a scraping sound on the wood floor. Brent could hear noises, like Enoch was looking for something. Within a couple minutes, Enoch limped back to his rocking chair, holding an old wooden box approximately the size of a briefcase. It was covered in dust. With strange dexterity, Enoch removed the top and looked inside at the contents. His gnarled hands held on to the box tightly, as if he was guarding his supper from a pack of hungry wild animals.

Brent put his hand on one of his pawns. He could feel the same odd tingling sensation up his arm as Enoch Strange continued. His voice sounded more intense. Enoch did his best to shuffle through the papers at the top. It was full of documents.

These are the papers Nolan sent to me from the road, and then later from prison. Among other things. It explains a lot. A lot of stuff I just don't have time to share with you, Mr. Dowling.

"So, he was sending those to you?" Brent was astonished he might get to see the elusive journal. He had read that Nolan had kept a journal while he was on his two-year cross-country murder spree. No one had ever found it. In his trial, it had come up a few times, but without proof it existed, the prosecutor didn't pay much attention to it when presenting his case.

He sent the journals to me. The last one he sent only the day before he got arrested. The rest of the loose pages are from Huntsville.

Enoch handed the box to Brent, and he took it, his hands trembling slightly in excitement.

Go on and take it, Mr. Dowling. It's yours. I don't need it any longer.

"How did Nolan know to send these to you?" Brent asked, almost in disbelief.

We both work for the same end. We share the same boss, if you will.

Brent peered into the box, looking at the journals and loose pages, dog-eared, stained, and covered in a variety of handwriting styles and ink colors. There were crude drawings on some of the papers. He did notice the words NIGHTMARE MAKER in various forms – all capital letters, cursive, and in what appeared to be done by a finger dipped in blood. He was mesmerized by it all and couldn't believe it was just handed to him. He wondered how Sergeant Whitlock knew about St. Michael's and the bizarre Enoch Strange.

There's a lot of information there. I don't have much time now for that. I need to lay down. But, there is one more important thing I need to give you.

Brent set the wooden box down on the porch. He kept it close.

Nolan is going to try and trick you, Mr. Dowling. A bad trick.

"A trick?"

Yes, an evil one. He needs to get those twelve killers out of his body before he dies. Or he'll be tormented for eternity. It's been his desire since he met you. You'll be the new host. He will die in peace. You, on the other hand, will be host to an even more violent pack of savage killers.

Brent was reeling. He began to hear Nolan's voice in his head, telling him about paying him back for the interview. Brent had done his best to pry out of Nolan what exactly he wanted him to do. He knew it was something, but what is the trick that Enoch was talking about? How would he become the new host for those twelve deranged maniacs? What did Enoch mean about them both working for the same boss? The whole thing was overwhelming and unreal. Brent wondered if he was dreaming. He hadn't had dreams this vivid then when he was abusing prescription drugs and drinking heavily.

Just like his father passed them to Nolan, he will try to pass them on to you, Mr. Dowling. Don't you remember how he told you about that day in Heyworth? When he went to see his parents? How his father passed the entity on to him before he died?

Brent's hand was frozen in place on his king as Enoch began to back the piece into a corner of the board. The white king looked as if it were wrapped in a hissing serpent for a few seconds before disappearing into the ivory. Despite the serious nature of the conversation, Enoch continued to play with the skill of a grand master, while Brent was doing everything possible not to lose his mind. The entirety of the situation was settling in, and Brent thought maybe he should just get on a plane and go somewhere far away. He knew whatever this was, he was in the middle of it, and the evil surrounding him would follow to the ends of the earth.

Every time they pass from host to host, they get stronger. The evil becomes more intense and bloodthirsty. His grandfather was the first host. Then his father, and now of course it's him. If you don't watch it, Mr. Dowling, you'll be next. You'll be trapped on that school bus just like Nolan. I believe the final body count was 86 when he was arrested in Central Texas. How many will you end up killing, Mr. Dowling? Maybe 186? Or 286?

"How is he going to do this? The next time I see him will be as a witness to his execution on Friday," Brent asked, his heart racing. He could feel sweat beginning to build up on his face. He prayed this was a dream he would soon wake from. But it continued.

He's going to ask to see you, a sort of final request, on the night of his execution. That's when he'll likely draw you in close, only to pass them to you. Don't let him grab you, Mr. Dowling. Don't let him pull you in. Do you understand me?

Enoch stared at him, those yellow beady eyes squinting, and the wheezing from his nose even louder. Brent could tell he was deadly serious about what he was saying, and he gingerly nodded in agreement. Just then Enoch reached into his robe and pulled out a long object in an old leather sheath. In the shadows of the porch, Brent couldn't quite make it out. Enoch handed it to him.

You must take this knife, Mr. Dowling. You must plunge it into his heart before he pulls you in close and passes them to you. This is a special knife made for Dr. Wilfred Weeks. He is a distant relative of Nolan's. If we had more time, I'd explain much more. In the box, you'll find some references to Dr. Weeks. Stabbing him through his evil heart is the only thing that will stop the transfer of the killers. If you can do that, the curse will end. You will be spared and can go on with your life. Maybe even a resurgence of your failing career?

"Why me? Why did he choose me for this?" asked Brent, his head swimming with all possibilities. He stared at the sharp knife with the initials WW engraved on the handle, then put it back into the sheath Enoch passed him.

I do not know how you became his target, but all you need to know is you are destined to be the new host unless you listen to me. End it.

"What will come of you?"

I will remain here, like I always have, Mr. Dowling. I always remain.

11

An hour had passed since Brent dropped Danny and Sal off at the airport in Houston. He figured there was no sense having them stick around, since filming was complete. They would be working at the network studios in Atlanta around the clock until the video and audio was edited down to make it work for the five-part series Brent was putting together. Upon Brent's return to Atlanta, he would do the necessary voice-over work to finish it up. There would be a single camera for the press pool at the main gate to Huntsville State Prison, and CNN planned on using that and some one-on-one with Brent, reflecting on the actual execution, since he would be a witness. The prison was not allowing cameras of any kind inside the gate. Protestors had been outside the gates now for two weeks, and with the execution coming in two days, it was beginning to escalate. Small groups gathered, holding signs in the air and chanting for or against the death penalty. Nolan would be dead in two days.

Brent was sitting on the hotel room bed with the contents of the wooden box he got at St. Michael's in piles, as he began to organize things. If ever there was a time for Brent to fall off the wagon and sneak a drink, it was now, with only 48 hours until the execution. Things were coming to an end quickly, and his visit to McHenry made things much more complicated than before. As much as Brent wanted to put a brave face on, it bothered him to think he was going to witness an execution. In his years of reporting news, he had been in some bad places, and he saw his share of death and destruction. As a beat reporter, Brent saw hurricanes, tornadoes, tsunamis, terrorist attacks, gang killings and much more. The worst of it was probably at the very beginning of his news career, when he was reporting in South Vietnam, when Saigon fell, and thousands of innocent people were murdered by the invading communists of North Vietnam. Brent was a veteran in the business who had seen a lot.

This was different. This was the state-ordered murder. Despite the gruesome details heard during the interviews with Nolan and years of reading police and coroner reports of each crime scene, part of him felt pity for the killer. Brent found it difficult to believe that he could feel anything but sheer disgust for a person who had committed such heinous crimes. Yet, he did. Nolan had shown absolutely no mercy on his victims and had not discriminated between men, women, children, the elderly, or even the infirmed. He was a murder machine. In Nolan's own words, he was truly a nightmare maker.

During his rampage, there were reports from leading psychiatry publications that claimed there was a 10% rise in patients diagnosed with a variety mental disorders, stemming from a fear of the random killings. They went on to claim that doctors were prescribing more sleep medication than ever before and that gun dealers were selling a record 50% more hand guns and shotguns for home defense. Even locksmiths and home security system installers were enjoying huge sales with people worried they could be next. The constant coverage in the nightly network news, talk radio, as well as the drip of the 24-hour news on cable television didn't help squash fears. Local newspapers, even in smaller towns, would publish articles about how to protect your home from intruders, and people were genuinely worried about it. School districts were vigilant and often sent home information to parents on how to make sure their children were protected at the bus stop or if they walked to and from school each day. The dealers of all forms of news were reaping the benefits of more viewers, listeners, and most importantly – advertisers.

There were also articles written by psychiatrists who didn't believe Nolan's account that he was a host with twelve killers inside of him. Later, to add a thirteenth member to that murderous club. Several cited well-known cases of "multiples", such as Billy Milligan and Sybil. In the case of Billy Milligan, he was the first person to successfully gain an acquittal based on the fact he was a multiple. In his case, many experts in the field did not agree with the diagnosis and felt he was purely psychopathic and clever enough to fake the disease. Yet a jury found him not guilty, and he was admitted to a mental hospital to continue treatment for his disorder. Years later, Milligan was cured and went on to lead a relatively normal life. Brent scoured through all these articles to try and come up with his own stance on the matter. It seemed the more he read, the muddier the water got, and he found himself flip-flopping.

He thought about the bottle of Jim Beam he saw on the dresser the other night. He did think about how good it would feel to have just one drink. But he knew one drink would lead to ten, and he would hate himself when he sobered up. Brent knew he had to continue to resist and try and bury himself in his work as a distraction. He did consider calling his AA sponsor, a college friend who was now an English professor at Clemson University, but he felt he had it under control. Thinking about seeing Brandon when this was all over, at the high school graduation in June, made not drinking the obvious choice. He also didn't want to face his ex-wife Cindy, knowing he was drinking again. She would know. If anyone else in the world could tell when he was drinking or taking drugs, Cindy could. Even before she became a nurse, she knew all the signs, and those were the precursor to many bad fights between them. Unfortunately, Brandon had a ring-side seat to most of them. Exposing his son to all that fighting was easily at the top of Brent's list of regrets. He worried the boy would take those lessons into his own relationships, especially in light of the fact that Brandon had the same weak self-control that Brent had displayed.

As he looked at the piles of papers in front of him, scattered on the bed, Brent thought about Cindy and how she was always the organized one in their relationship. She balanced the checkbook and paid the bills on time. Cindy kept a very clean and organized house, with written meal plans for two weeks at a time. He could have used that skill set now, sifting through the journals and papers in the box. In total, there were seven journals in spiral notebooks. They were completely full of writing inside and outside on both the front and back covers. Some were stained and dog-eared from a rough life on the road or from the chaos of Huntsville State Prison. Nolan had all kinds of detailed artwork scattered throughout. Some of the art was very good and skilled, while others looked like they were done by grade school children. Even the writing inside the journals, and on the white unlined paper the prison provided inmates to write letters, appeared to be from different hands. Some was neat and well-written, while others were barely legible and from someone of diminished mental capacity.

Brent looked at the clock and noted that it was just after 6:00 pm. He was going to read through all the materials in hopes of finding some other solution to the problem than the one Enoch Strange shared. Brent could hear the words from the mysterious creature, living in the hunting cabin on the south edge of St. Michael's property.

You must take this knife, Mr. Dowling. You must plunge it into his heart before he pulls you in close and passes them to you.

Brent was filled with serious questions about this. How was he supposed to get that knife inside the prison? With the execution coming, security was ramped up beyond the normal procedures, and correctional officers were on the highest alert. Even if he got the knife inside the gate, Brent had mounting doubts that he would be able to bury the knife into Nolan's heart. It wasn't in him to kill someone. Unless maybe in self-defense. Yet, according to Enoch, Nolan was going to do something bad to him. In that case, wasn't it self-defense? So many new questions came to mind. It was overwhelming.

Brent had grown up in a tough neighborhood in Pittsburgh, raised by blue collar parents – Donald and Cheryl. His father was a proud union steel worker. Both grandfathers were also steel workers, and each of his seven uncles. Brent's mother, like most of that era, had stayed home to raise him and his three older brothers. Rick and Eddie had gone on to work at the steel mills like their father, and they had died in their 40's from asbestosis. His oldest brother, Ronnie, was drafted by the Marines and sent to Vietnam. Corporal Ronnie Dowling died two weeks before he was to come home after his first tour. It had crushed both his parents, and it steered Brent to journalism, with pipe dreams of making the world a better place and telling people the truth. He had heard his parents talk all the time about their disdain for the war, and it became part of his fabric as well. These things provided the fuel for his interest in journalism, and it stoked the fire for his interest in politics at a turbulent time in the United States.

His parents were both proponents of the death penalty. Brent was not, and so it bothered him to think he was going to witness the execution. While he wrestled with the idea of Nolan being accountable for his actions, Brent kept drinking black coffee and closely going through everything, in hopes there was a better option to end the misery.

******

Enoch Strange was sitting quietly in his cabin listening to jazz on an old radio the church had given him to help pass the time. He especially liked the stuff of the 1920's and 30's like Cole Porter and Jelly Roll Morton. One dim bulb from a small lamp was casting shadows across the old wood plank floor. There wasn't much to the cabin. It was built in 1912 and hadn't changed much since. It was an open room with one side acting as a kitchen with a small refrigerator, wash basin, and an electric toaster oven on the counter. On the opposite side was a simple bed with an end table, clock, radio and lamp. There were two small windows, one on each side of the door, and there was an outhouse behind the cabins. A well was there for drinking water and to use in the basin for washing dishes. The monks at the time built them sturdy, but practical. They certainly gave the appearance of sparse conditions, which perpetuated the illusion of their vow of poverty.

It was in the 1920's that the cabins were used for more nefarious activities. When Father Patrick was the Abbot of St. Michael's Academy, he would host orgies in the cabins with the nuns that participated in the black masses he led deep in the woods, and far from the watchful eye of anyone who didn't participate. The Abbot made sure there was plenty of wine, whiskey and other illicit spirits during Prohibition, and the very best decadent food his chef could prepare. It was the best-known, well-kept secret in the diocese. Since many of the attendees were esteemed clergy and administrators from Chicago, the cabins provided more anonymity for those who desired it. Some nights they would play poker and hire prostitutes to entertain the group. If the walls of the cabins could talk, they would have some sordid tales to share.

Suddenly the sound of footsteps could be heard on the cobblestone path outside. Enoch felt his heartbeat quicken and a lump rise in his throat, stifling any sound. He rarely had visitors, especially at night, when the staff of St. Michael's were afraid to encounter him. Many of the staff over the years claimed that the cobblestone path and cabins were haunted when the sun went down, and the creepy stories of ghosts, moving shadows, and strange noises sent people running back to the academy. Enoch had never encountered anything that would back up the stories and enjoyed the solitude. He had been treated so horribly by the previous staff that his move from the dank basement of the monk dormitory to the cabins was welcome. He worked third shift and was basically left alone to clean the main building. He paid special attention to the bronze statue of the former Abbot, Father Patrick Reilly, as well as the terrazzo floors that looked like glass when he was done with them. It gave him great pleasure to make the building shine, even though no one ever gave him credit. The many compliments visitors would voice to the staff fell on deaf ears.

The footsteps were getting closer. Now creaking boards were heard on the porch. A rank breeze seemed to slither under the cabin door, and with it, the foul stench of rotting flesh. It was death, and there was no mistaking its sweet, yet rancid, odor. He had smelled it before and knew of its putrid embrace. Enoch was petrified, and his chest tightened, which always seemed to precede a visit from the one he feared more than any other. It was like a tornado warning siren that told him bad times were coming. Enoch reached over to shut off the radio as the cabin door slowly creaked open. Moonlight cast itself on the dimly lit room. The horrid smell was ever present now, and Enoch gagged slightly. The temperature in the room became ice cold in an instant. Enoch didn't even need to look up, because he knew who had come to call.

"Hello, Enoch. I hear you've been entertaining company out here," a raspy, yet powerful voice boomed. It resonated in the room with a guttural manifestation, soaked in malevolence. His rancid breath crept from between black, rotten teeth.

Enoch was still. He knew that voice. It was one that he had only heard a handful of times. It was the one person who didn't need to play chess to hear Enoch's voice. It was Dr. Wilfred Weeks, his creator and jailer all in one. He had been dead for more than 300 years.

Yes, I did, master. Yes, I did.

Dr. Weeks was bathed in shadows and moonlight, standing in the doorway, the epitome of pure evil. He wore a top hat, which he removed as he took a step inside and slammed the door behind him. Enoch quivered, and his beady eyes twitched at the sight of the evil doctor with flaming red hair that cascaded in curls past his shoulders like falling embers. His face appeared chiseled from rock, yet it was a sour grey color that explained the foul stench of death that encircled him like a miasma. The aroma surrounded the tall man and wafted easily to all corners of the small cabin as he made his way into the light.

"You better hope he'll get the job done." He took on a deeper, raspier tone as if he had been chewing on razor blades.

Dr. Weeks took two big steps toward the quivering Enoch, and slapped him with tremendous force across his scarred and putrid face. A loud crack resounded. Enoch fell to the floor with a whimper, but sharp back spasms forced him to cry out in pain. The left side of his face was swelling and throbbed with a sting. He didn't realize it, but tears were welling up in his narrow eyes. The force of the blow felt like a jackhammer. Enoch's mind was reeling at the sudden show of force, and his head was pounding.

"You know what will happen if he fails, right? You know all about agony. You bastard!" he screamed, backhanding Enoch to the right side of his face, as he attempted to get up from the first strike. Now his entire head was stinging, and his vision was erratic. Enoch was hyperventilating in panic. His heart thundered along.

Yes. Yes, I know.

"What was that? Yes, I know? Yes, I know – who?" Dr. Weeks growled, picking Enoch up off the floor by his robe, and with little effort, he tossed the pitiful being up on the small table in the kitchen area. His red hair looked like serpents twisting and turning – hissing in concert. His eyes were a vibrant green and seemed to etch themselves into whatever they gazed upon -hypnotizing. They looked like a stormy sea, punishing a fishing boat against a rocky shore.

Yes, I know . . . sir.

He grabbed Enoch and slammed his head hard against the table with a loud thud. Enoch cried out.

"That's better. You will treat me with respect. I'm the one who allowed you to stay out here. I can put you back in the basement of the dorm if you like. It's crawling with rats since they closed it down. Would you like that? I bet they'd pick your carcass to bones in one night."

No, sir. Thank you for letting me stay out here.

"Do you really believe he's going to be able to drive that knife through his heart? He's got to do it and end this freak show. Your prior hubris is why this abomination ever began. It must end! It must be done by a living person, or I'd do it my damn self."

The man tore the hood down to expose Enoch's misshapen head, as he lay with his back to the table, squirming with apprehension. The demonic doctor reached into the pocket of the black jacket he was wearing.

"Just to make sure you know how much is riding on whether that reporter can do what we need him to do, I've got something for you," he said, pulling from his pocket a ball of crude nylon thread and a filthy, crusted sewing needle.

Please, master. Don't hurt me! I did my best. I did. I gave him the knife and told him what to do. He'll do it. I swear, he'll do it!

Dr. Weeks grabbed the top and bottom eye lids from Enoch's right eye as cried out in pain. While Enoch shook in terror on the table, the man quickly threaded the needle with one hand. He did so with incredible dexterity, like the skilled surgeon he was. Enoch was flailing around; his twisted back was arched in a disturbing posture off the table. The vice-like grip on him would not permit escape. The next thing Enoch felt was a searing pain in his right eye lid as the doctor drove the needle and thread through, pulling it tightly to the knot on the other end, and jerking the skin in the process. Blood was pouring down Enoch's face.

The pain is terrible, master. Please stop. Please! Show mercy!

"Mercy is weakness!" His sour, rotten breath was overwhelming Enoch. "I will not relent!"

He stuck the needle in again, as Enoch cried out for mercy. It only made Dr. Weeks want to stick him harder and slower to amplify the pain. The thick nylon thread dug into Enoch's thin eye lids, and the pain washed over him with a fury as the blood continued to pour. White flashes of pain shot through Enoch's brain like high voltage power. The needle sunk in again, and again once more. Enoch was fading on the table, but the doctor wasn't about to let him fall unconscious. Dr. Weeks shook him awake and slapped him once more across the face.

"Tonight, I only do one eye," he sneered, "but tomorrow I come back for the other. That will give you some time to think about what it will be like to be blind the rest of eternity. We both live forever, and I set the rules." The doctor's intense green eyes were wide open and wild, and the long red hair made him look like a deranged madman. Perhaps he was. To Enoch, he was the Devil himself.

******

It was nearing midnight at Brent's hotel room in Huntsville. He had already drunk two pots of very strong coffee and was reading the journals Nolan kept. It amazed him that Nolan was so meticulous with the dates and places he traveled. Brent found it ironic that a person as tormented as Nolan claimed to be, as a host for twelve terrible killers, would be able to keep a day to day account of everything that happened. As excited as Brent was about this find, and the information he was gleaning from scouring each page, he couldn't help but think about the financial reward of a book deal and a release of the journals. His agent would represent the sale to anxious publishers. This was the sort of thing that true crime and serial killer aficionados would pay any price for. He even thought about having them printed just as they were in full color. The passages were written by the various killers, in their own hand, with bizarre notes from other killers in the margins – arguing about various things and details of the murders. It was madness on paper before his very eyes!

The first journal he looked at was when the murders started in the summer of 1985. It was in a spiral notebook with a red cover. Nolan had written all over it with different words and phrases in a variety of pen colors, pencil, and even some markers. Brent couldn't tell if they were Nolan's own words or song lyrics. There were also crude drawings on both the front and back covers of the notebook. Inside the journal, the first entry was one of the few from Nolan himself. He writes a brief passage about his encounter at his parents' home in Heyworth, Illinois. Brent had heard Nolan tell his account of that day first hand, but seeing it written on paper, in such a cavalier way, gave him chills.

Saturday, July 20, 1985
Waynesville, Illinois
 I'm at my trailer and just packed up all the stuff I could fit in the Ford. I don't have much money. Maybe $200 in cash here I can grab. I wish I could get the money Tommy owes me, but there's no time. I'm still not sure what the hell happened at mom and dad's. I hope I'm dreaming. I know the cops will be here soon, so I gotta get going. I'm sure I'll cry later about seeing Mom like that. Dad too. All those bodies. I can't understand what the fuck happened out there.
 Nolan Weeks

The entries that followed that first one are much different. Brent could feel the change in the personalities as each killer explained things from their own disturbed mind, in their own blood-soaked hands. There was one written after he had been on the road for about two weeks. There were some blood-smeared fingerprints in the margins, like the killer held it in his hands, still wet with blood. There was also a different writing in pencil in the left margin that said, "Billy was here" and another in red pen that said, "Fuck the Pope" in the right margin.

Wednesday, July 31, 1985
Iowa City, Iowa
 Lots of blood tonight. We got lucky with a house filled with women. Good lookin' ones too. I got a hold of a teenager with red hair. She had to be a virgin with all the blood. All the screaming. Edward chopped off three heads. He's sick. He was rolling them down the hallway like bowling balls and laughing his ass off. The other girls freaked out seeing that. Then Doc made him stop and helped me strangle the rest. That one retarded kid, Rasmus, he started messing around with the bodies. Grabbing their tits and stuff. Someone needs to get that boy under control.
 Paul Rosati

Reading entries like that were appalling, but he couldn't resist. Six hours had passed since he started going through everything, and it seemed like ten minutes. As Brent looked up at the clock and saw it was past midnight, he wondered if he should try to get some sleep. He knew with only one day left before the execution, he was going to be busy with work. Larry was already raising hell back in Atlanta with the amount of footage they shot and how long it was taking to sift through it all. He would never be happy, and that's why Larry was a miserable prick. Brent hoped that he could leave CNN and get back to network news. Maybe with a big book deal, he wouldn't even have to do that?

Then his thoughts came back to reality and the decision that needed to be made. He was no closer to deciding what he should do if Nolan were to call him in to his holding cell before the execution. He opened the drawer of his nightstand, where he kept the knife in its leather sheath, and he looked at it for a moment before shutting the drawer again. The thought of plunging that ivory knife into Nolan's heart was sickening. *If he does change from one killer to another, how do I even know who I'm talking to? I could maybe do it if it was Paul Rosati or one of the real sadistic killers. But what about the slow kid, Rasmus? Or what about Nolan? Who is Nolan? Have I ever really spoken to him?* Every question he had fathered three others. It was an endless web ensnaring him tighter and tighter.

Brent decided he would go for one more hour and then get some sleep. He picked up the third journal and started reading. As he read, he was submerged in the trek from state to state, killing people at random. He began to visualize the scenes, as they were described by some of the killers in exquisite detail.

Monday, August 12, 1985
Simmons, Iowa
Me and Jack had a good time tonight. He's a real ladies man, and we come upon this group of college girls trying to buy some beer at this grocery store. Jack went and bought them a case, and somehow worked us into going to drink it with them. It didn't take too many beers before Jack started having sex with one of them in the bathroom. Then she started screaming and ran out of the bathroom naked, with blood all over her tits. Jack bit her damn nipples off! That's when things went off the rails. I grabbed two and started stabbing them with a knife I found in the kitchen. They were screaming and raising a fuss about it. So, I cut both their tongues out. Paul came over and ate both of the damn things, and they passed out. Then we had sex with their dead bodies and left.
Edward O'Rourke

******

Enoch laid in his bed for the rest of the night in total darkness. Dr. Wilfred Weeks had left him bleeding on the table, with his right eye sewn shut, just as he had done many years before when he first sewed his mouth closed. As pathetic as Enoch felt in his present condition, he knew that Dr. Weeks could not take away his intellect. For all the fuss that the doctor made over Enoch's hubris, it was plain to see Dr. Weeks' narcissism was beyond compare. The fact that most people thought Enoch was ignorant, because of his grotesque appearance and inability to communicate, was something he used to his advantage. It was his only real weapon. He learned a lot of things by simply listening, since no one had reservations about saying things in front of him, assuming he was stupid.

Enoch knew more about the ivory knife than he let on. He remembered, in his previous life, having read some things about the knife and the incredible power that it wrought. Apparently, Dr. Weeks had it made while studying the dark arts in Africa. It was given to him by a witch doctor who introduced him to the Devil. What Enoch wasn't sure about was if Dr. Weeks truly didn't realize what was going to happen if Brent summoned up the strength to carry out the deed. Or was he just playing a game, knowing good and well what was going to happen? Enoch really couldn't be sure. It was like a high stakes game of poker with two seasoned card players wielding nerves of steel. It was also 60 years since Enoch had seen the Darkness Visible documents. Sometimes Enoch would question his own memory and if he would be able to recall some minute details buried in those ancient texts. In his previous life, his brain was like a machine that could recall even the most minor facts with amazing skill and speed. But that was a long time ago, and the ravages of time had not been kind to Enoch Strange.

The thought of Dr. Weeks coming back to do the same thing to his other eye the following day was frightening to say the least. It wouldn't matter if Enoch hid, because Dr. Weeks would find him. That would just make things worse. He had learned that over the many years at St. Michael's. Having one eye closed shut was bad enough, but not being able to see, in addition to his many other physical impairments, was a horrible thought. Having the ability to

243

read and pass the time, and of course his love for chess, would be gone. Enoch wouldn't be able to play like the master he was if he couldn't see the board. There was something about scanning the pieces and their alignment on the board that Enoch found delectable. It was chess that seemed to keep his mind sharp, despite everything else crumbling around him. Taking that away meant he would retract and probably die inside for good.

In 24 hours, he would know the answer to the question. Would Brent be able to do it or not? If he did, what would happen once the knife pierced Nolan's heart? He clenched his teeth thinking about how much he hated Dr. Weeks and how sweet it would taste to be right this time.

******

The sun was shining into Brent's hotel room, and he was still wide awake on the bed. Despite his hope to wrap it up and get some sleep, he had found it impossible to stop reading the volumes of pages piled up around him. Going through the passages written by the twelve killers was addicting, yet at the same time, it was horrifying to hear it told with such detail. Some of them rarely wrote in the journals, and there were a few of the more dominant ones that did most of it.

The one that scared Brent the most was Vic Chesterfield. He was from Arizona but had spent most of his adult life in Arkansas. He was a sadist and carried out the most brutal attacks on women of all ages. He was also the killer who liked to write on the walls and leave his mark of NIGHTMARE MAKER in the blood of his victims. The other killers started doing it too, but Vic was the one who led the charge. Vic was the leader of the band of maniacs. Brent figured every group had to have a leader, and in this case, Vic was it. It was the writing of Vic that made Brent realize that Nolan really was nothing more than a vessel. The few entries he read of Nolan's were not about doing any killing, but being a witness to it and riding on the bus, while Vic drove to the next town.

Nolan would be dead in one day. Brent just didn't know if he had the courage to be the one to make him dead, or if it would be the State of Texas that did it.

12

Five years before Nolan Weeks arrived at Huntsville State Prison, Correctional Officer (he was not yet promoted to sergeant) Rollie Whitlock had found himself nearly hysterical with worry at the West Houston Medical Center. He was in one of the private consultation rooms where no one ever wants to be, in the intensive care department of the hospital. His youngest daughter, eleven-year-old Sarah, had been brought in a helicopter life flight from George Bush State Park only ten minutes before. Rollie was barely able to sit on the couch and wait for the doctor who was supposed to brief him on Sarah's condition. She had been on vacation with her mother, Rollie's ex-wife Morgan, and other family, camping and fishing at the park.

Sarah loved to fish, and Rollie enjoyed spending time fishing with her above all else. She was his world, since his other two children were adults and lived in other parts of the country. Sarah was his baby, and he saw her every other weekend and his share of the holidays. Plus, two weeks in the summer, when they always planned a fun trip that involved fishing. It was never enough. Just as Rollie loved her, Sarah was very close with him too. She always had been.

Today, a bad accident on an ATV had critically wounded her when she lost control and hit a tree. She was put on a ventilator by the first responders to stabilize her before taking off in the helicopter. Sarah barely had a pulse and was unresponsive the entire flight. The crew had called ahead, and everyone was ready at the West Houston Medical Center. Things looked very grim.

Suddenly there was a soft knock on the door, and it opened.

"Mr. Whitlock, I'm Dr. Nathan Engell. Nice to meet you, sir," said the young blonde-haired doctor in a white coat, as he shook Rollie's huge hand. He noted how large Rollie was, as he stood up and towered over the physician by several inches.

"Thanks, Doc," replied Rollie, "how is she?" His face was painted with worry.

Dr. Engell smiled. "Please sit down."

Rollie complied, but he didn't like it. He knew the news was going to be bad. He wanted to scream and break things.

Dr. Engell sat down in the chair across from him and looked at Rollie sternly. Despite his age, the young doctor had a lot of experience already with these types of conversations. It was never easy.

"Mr. Whitlock, your daughter is in an extremely fragile state. She is still on the ventilator and unconscious. We have her stabilized, but my concern is that she may not be able to breathe on her own if we take her off it. Plus, we're concerned about possible brain damage. She also has several broken bones, contusions, and other blunt force injuries."

Rollie felt like his entire world was crashing down. He heard some of what the doctor said, while the rest of it was caught up in a whirlwind.

"My God!" Rollie said, his head in his hands.

Dr. Engell continued, "Right now we are doing everything we can and running all the tests we can, sir. I would suggest you speak with our chaplain. He can provide comfort and help you through this."

"You think she's going to die, Doc?" Rollie asked, his eyes bloodshot from crying. His face was wet with tears. "Be straight with me."

"Yes, yes I do. I'm sorry."

Rollie stared straight ahead, looking through the doctor. He could see Sarah. They were fishing at Lewis Pond – her favorite spot. She was pulling in a bass and squealing with delight. The bright sun was sparkling off the water.

"We're doing everything we can, sir. Only God can help her now. I'll send for the chaplain." He quietly closed the door.

Only five minutes later, the chaplain arrived in the consultation room. Rollie had been crying since getting the news, and he barely realized the man was there until he sat down across from him and removed his hat.

"Mr. Whitlock, I'm sorry to hear about young Sarah. She's a beautiful girl," said the chaplain, putting a hand on Rollie's shoulder as he wept, stooped over with his head in his hands. He did not reply, only heavy sobs.

"I'm the hospital chaplain, Father Patrick. Are you Catholic, sir?"

Rollie pulled it together the best he could and looked up at the elderly priest sitting before him. He wore a black suit with a gold cross lapel pin. He was in excellent shape for an older man, with chiseled good looks and deep blue eyes. His face showed concern and true compassion.

"No. Methodist."

Father Patrick smiled. "Close enough. God hears all our prayers. As the hospital chaplain, I can assist in most denominations. What can I do for you, sir?"

"You can let my daughter live. Can you do that, father? Can you call God and tell him he can't have my angel? Can you?" Rollie said, his voice getting louder and more agitated at the hopelessness of the situation.

Father Patrick leaned back slightly in his chair. His right eyebrow raised. His mind was working through something.

"The power of prayer can be strong," said Father Patrick, opening his bible.

"I don't mean any disrespect, father, but I don't think praying is going to do much here. I need a miracle," Rollie said. His eyes were still bloodshot.

Father Patrick smiled. "None taken." This was followed by an uncomfortable silence as the two men looked at each other. The priest was sizing Rollie up.

"I can guarantee Sarah lives." Father Patrick's face was stoic.

"What? What did you just say? The doctor said she was almost guaranteed to die. Or maybe severe brain damage," Rollie said, his eyes welling up again. "I can't deal with this!"

"I said I can get her through this. Sarah will live. She will recover 100%. But I'll need you to do something for me," Father Patrick said, leaning slightly forward. Rollie began to feel elated at this news. Even a slim possibility was something to hope for. Better than what the young doctor was saying.

"What do you mean, I have to do something for you? I'll do whatever you want, father. Anything to save my little girl," Rollie said, drying the tears off his face with his shirt sleeve.

Rollie was wearing his correctional officer uniform. When the call had come, he was only halfway into his ten-hour shift at Huntsville State Prison, and he drove himself south on highway 45 to the West Houston Medical Center. He made the one hour and twenty-minute trip in just under 45 minutes in his new Dodge truck. It was a wonder he didn't get pulled over for speeding.

"I see you work at the prison in Huntsville. A guard, correct?" the priest asked him, already knowing the answer.

"Yes. A corrections officer. Been there 15 years, and I'm stuck walking the mainline in general population every day."

"Very good. Well, if I do that for you, I may have you do me a favor sometime. Something that could help me out," Father Patrick said, as Rollie sat before him on the edge of the couch cushion.

Rollie was desperate, and Father Patrick knew it. That was why he was there. The real hospital chaplain was in the back of the custodial closet in the basement. His throat was slit, and his body was stuffed in a large bin used for dirty rags. It had been quick work, and the old chaplain didn't know what happened.

"Anything you want. Anything."

Father Patrick smiled. "Consider it done, then, Mr. Whitlock. Or can I call you Rollie?"

"You can call me whatever you want if my girl lives. How can you guarantee it? The doctor said . . . "

There was an urgent knock on the door, and it opened quickly. A nurse was standing there, nearly hyperventilating.

"Mr. Whitlock, please come right away. It's Sarah! She's awake! Dr. Engell is dumfounded. She's off the ventilator and asking to see you!" She reached for his hand. "It's a miracle!"

Rollie was completely shocked at the great news. He took her hand, then looked to his left to thank Father Patrick. He was gone!

"Thank God!" Rollie exclaimed, assuming the priest had walked out of the room in the excitement of the moment.

Rollie ran down the hallway toward Sarah's room, the nurse trying to keep up with him. He forgot all about Father Patrick as he entered her room, seeing his daughter sitting up in bed, surrounded by two doctors and several of the intensive care nurses. It would be several years before that favor would be called in. Rollie didn't know it at the time, but he had made a deal with the Devil.

******

Sergeant Rollie Whitlock was eating his typical evening meal at home in Riverside, only 13 miles northeast of the prison on highway 19. It was a plain chicken breast, a plain baked potato, and a large salad with vinaigrette dressing. His diet was more restrictive since he had turned 50 and his 2% body fat had crept up to 6%, and he didn't like it. Rollie always prided himself on being fit, and he wanted to set a good example for his men after being promoted to sergeant a year before. He started paying attention to physical fitness while serving in the US Army as an infantry soldier. He had left the military and took a job in corrections when Uncle Sam started cutting back funding to the armed services. His father had called in a favor to get him on with the Texas Department of Corrections. His military service and clean record, coupled with his father's pull, got Rollie a spot in the next cycle at the corrections officer academy in Austin. He was at the top of his platoon in everything, especially physical fitness.

It was Thursday night, and Rollie was looking forward to watching the Texas Rangers game on TV. He was hoping it would take his mind off the execution scheduled for tomorrow. The prison had been insane with the media and protestors outside the main gate. Warden Greene had been a ball of nerves as well, and since shit rolls downhill, Rollie had been getting a steady dose of attitude for the past two weeks. He would be glad when this was all over with.

Warden Greene had taken Rollie off his usual duty at the main building and put him in charge of Nolan Weeks on death row. Ever since he had been put in charge of inmate Weeks during the CNN interviews, the warden seemed to think Rollie was the only one who could handle him. Rollie didn't mind it, but as the weather was finally getting nice, he wanted to fish more than work. He was counting down his time until he reached the age of 55 when he could retire from corrections and transfer to the Department of Wildlife. A job like that would keep him outdoors more and give him plenty of time to fish, especially with Sarah, who was now 16 and starting to drive. He had bought her a Toyota Corolla with only 50,000 miles from a friend who was retiring and wanted an SUV. Rollie didn't want to lose her like he had his other children, but he knew once kids started driving, they didn't spend much time with their parents. Thankfully, Sarah still liked to do things with him on the weekends they were together. She still loved to fish with him, and he with her.

Sarah still had a few scars from the ATV accident five years before, but they rarely talked about it. There were days when Rollie would have a moment, where a memory of being in that private consultation room, talking with Father Patrick, would flash before him. As quickly as it would come, the vision would subside. There were at least three different occasions since the accident when Rollie could have sworn he saw Father Patrick. Once, driving home from work one night, and he had seen a man on the side of the road changing a tire. It looked a lot like the elderly priest. He had turned around to help the man, but realized it wasn't Father Patrick.

Another time, he was in a grocery store in Huntsville before work, and he could have sworn he saw the priest bagging groceries. The bagger smiled at him, and Rollie felt that it was Father Patrick. When he finished shopping, the bagger was gone. The last time Rollie believed he saw the clergyman was a month before. Rollie was in a movie theater with Sarah and one of her friends, and he thought he saw the priest across the aisle from him. The priest had been alone, wearing that same black suit he had on that day at the hospital, casually eating popcorn and watching the movie. Rollie kept staring at the man, trying to determine in the low lighting if he was the creepy Father Patrick. Near the end of the movie, the old man got up, looked at Rollie, smiled, and walked toward the exit with his empty popcorn and drink. The man never returned.

Rollie remembered the words he had exchanged with Father Patrick at the hospital that day. He had been so wrought with despair that Sarah was likely to die, he would have agreed to anything to save her. Unfortunately, Rollie didn't know what sort of favor the priest would have for him. What could he be expected to do that was on the same level as saving a person's life? The life of his dear, little Sarah. Since seeing the mysterious man at the theater,

Rollie had started to have dreams of Father Patrick. The dreams were violent and frightening, despite the tough disposition of Sergeant Whitlock. He was a hardened individual who had seen violence and hate few could understand during his time at the Huntsville State Prison. He had spent his entire 20 years there. So, if Rollie was frightened by dreams of the priest, then they were truly horrible.

The Rangers game was getting ready to start, and Rollie grabbed the remote to turn it up. They were playing the Yankees tonight, and he hated them. Rollie always loved to see the Rangers win, but if they beat the Yankees, it was even better.

There was a sudden, very loud knock on the front door. Rollie sat upright, his heart pounding. Instinctively, he reached for the Glock 9mm pistol he kept under the chair. He turned around to face the door, gun drawn. Then there was another loud knock. This time there were three of them, each one louder than the last.

"Who's there?" Rollie asked in a commanding voice. Inside he was fluttering. His gun was still drawn – steady and pointing at the center of the door. Center mass of whatever was on the other side. He crept toward it, very slowly, his pulse racing. His adrenalin was on high!

There were three more loud knocks on the door. The last one made it shudder in the frame. It sounded like someone was beating the door with a baseball bat.

"It's Father Patrick, Rollie. Please open the door," said the familiar voice that Rollie instantly remembered like it was yesterday. A very proper, highly-educated person was behind it. It was a deep, resonating tone that reassured and instilled confidence. Rollie thought the priest sounded European, but he couldn't place the accent.

Rollie stopped only three feet from the door with his gun still drawn. He had known who it was when the first knock sounded. He knew that the priest was going to call on him to do something. What that something was, Rollie really didn't know. He feared it would be something illegal. The thought of jeopardizing his career was not an option. So many things hinged on him working five more years at the prison, retiring and then working for the Department of Wildlife. He was also considering doing some fishing guide work to make some extra money. Ruining that plan was not possible. The priest was just outside his door and likely getting angrier by the second.

"Rollie, open this door before I break it down!" Father Patrick boomed. His voice demanded respect.

Rollie opened the door slowly. A foul stench crept into the opening, as Rollie took a step back, lowering his weapon but keeping it at his side. It was the sweet stench of death that rolled in like fog across the floor. In the dim porch light, Father Patrick looked like he did that night Rollie had met him in the consultation room. The only noticeable difference, aside from the odor, was that his skin was grey and his eyes were sunken in and less vibrant than before. They were bottomless pits, glowing blue and bubbling with evil. Even in his deathly state, the priest was oddly charismatic.

"Are you going to invite me in? Or am I to stand out here like some rogue?" asked the priest, staring directly at Rollie, noticing the gun. He sneered.

Rollie put the gun away and stepped inside, letting the priest in. His mind was racing. *Is he dead? If he's dead, can he do anything more than scare me?*

"Let's sit down and talk about squaring up some old debts, Rollie. This looks nice," he said, motioning to the small kitchen table with only two chairs. He had a leather satchel and set it down on the table in front of him.

"Of course," Rollie answered. He debated running out of the house and to his truck. But he knew it wasn't an option. He wondered if shooting the priest would stop this whole thing, but he knew it wouldn't do a thing. The man was already dead from the smell of things. Rollie knew that dead things couldn't die, and as bizarre as that sounded, it made sense.

Father Patrick sat down, setting his hat down on the table next to his satchel and neatly putting his hands together in front of him. He stared intensely at Rollie, smirking.

"Well. I have something I need you to do for me. Are you prepared to do this, or will I need to take necessary steps to foreclose on our deal?" Father Patrick kept his eyes locked in on Rollie's. He began to tap his right forefinger on the table like a metronome.

Rollie swallowed hard, trying desperately to get a grip on the overwhelming dread that swept over him. Even with his countless hours of law enforcement and military training, he could think of nothing. His training didn't teach him a thing about dealing with the undead. For the first time, Rollie had no idea what to do next.

"What if I said no?" Rollie asked, fearful of the reply.

"That would make this interesting, you can believe that. Well, I'll make sure Sarah wraps her Toyota around a tree Saturday when she drives out here. I'll make sure it's one close by, so you can see her bleed out." His blue eyes raged like a storm.

Rollie gritted his teeth at the thought of her in an accident. Especially after the ATV incident five years before.

"So, do you want to play games here, Rollie?" Father Patrick asked, a thin smile across his dead, grey face. "I can play lots of games if that's your thing. Yet, you won't like my games." His finger continued to tap on the kitchen table.

"No, I'll do it." Rollie looked down.

Father Patrick laughed and the tapping ceased. "I thought so. Now, tomorrow night at the execution. I need you to let that reporter inside the gate with something."

Rollie licked his lips nervously. "What kind of something?"

"A knife."

"A fucking knife? Are you crazy?"

"No, I'm not crazy. Not one bit. A knife. A long, ivory knife. A dagger."

Rollie closed his eyes for a minute and sighed. He had no idea how that would make it past the usual security, but with the execution, things had tightened up considerably. Even if he let it in, there were other layers of security that would likely catch it. Then people would look to him and question why he didn't find the weapon. A dagger! That would be difficult to explain, and it could lead to instant termination. Then where would he be?

"He's going to have it strapped to his right leg. Below the knee."

Rollie didn't know what else to say. "OK."

"He'll be there at 6 o'clock. At the sally port like always. Be there waiting. Make sure he gets inside," said the priest, "Are we clear?" He began tapping his finger again. It added to the tension in the kitchen that was already at a fever pitch. The priest was more than aware of this.

"Yes, I'll do it." Rollie closed his eyes and tried to take in deep breaths to calm down.

"Good. Now there's something else I'll need you to do."

Rollie couldn't believe his ears. "You said one thing. Not two."

"I never said such a thing. Believe me, Sarah won't be the prettiest girl in the county when her little car meets that big oak tree a half mile from here. She'll look more like raw hamburger. Terrible stuff, those car accidents. It can be arranged quite easily, Rollie. We can play some games."

"OK. Stop saying that. I'll do it."

"I'll need to explain this in detail, because it's a bit involved. You might want to get some paper and a pen to write this down," the priest said. "This may take a while. You're going to miss the ball game." In the background, the baseball commentators were discussing the designated hitter rule in the American League.

Rollie got the paper and pen, then sat back down. He was focused. Sarah's life depended on it.

"It won't matter that you miss this game. The Yankees will beat them 7-5 anyway," said Father Patrick, laughing like a madman. "A blown save in the ninth. Texas doesn't have a bullpen this year."

******

The phone rang in Brent's hotel room in Huntsville. He had been up all night, and it was 4:00 pm. He had lost track of how many pots of coffee he drank. All day Brent had read through the journals and the pages Nolan wrote in prison that were sent to Enoch Strange for safekeeping. Much of his prison writings were rambling passages that said nothing more than recounting his mundane life in a maximum-security prison. Huntsville had Nolan in protective custody due to the notoriety of his case, and inmates were lining up to take him out. Brent had a hard time discerning which killer was which, since Nolan wasn't signing them by name like he did in the journals. Brent felt the journals were fascinating and were used as a map to plot Nolan's course. It was obvious why the police had no idea where he would strike next, since the path he took zigzagged the Midwest. It took months before the law enforcement in states where the murders took place began to talk to each other and realize they were dealing with the same Satanic gang of killers. At the time, they never would have never figured it was one man doing all that killing. The body count was staggering.

The phone rang a second time, and Brent jumped up from the bed to answer it.

"Hello?" He was slightly out of breath, his neck stiff from stooping over for hours on the bed.

"Mr. Dowling. How are you doing? This is Ann from Warden Greene's office."

"I'm doing fine. What's up?"

"I know you are aware that you are on the witness list for the execution tonight. We originally told you to be here at 8:00 pm to get processed in and seated."

"Yes, that's correct."

"Well, the warden wanted me to call you right away. Apparently, inmate Weeks is asking to see you in his holding cell prior to the execution."

Brent closed his eyes in disbelief. Enoch had told him this would happen. He felt ill.

"Are you sure?" he asked.

"Yes, Mr. Dowling. I'm sure. He denied seeing our chaplain, and that's standard for our condemned to meet with the clergy. There was no family that contacted us to be present at the execution. He only wants to see you. The warden wants to honor his request. So does the governor."

"OK. What time do you want me there?"

"6:00 pm at the sally port. Sergeant Whitlock will be there to meet you, provide escort to see inmate Weeks, and then take you to the execution."

Brent didn't say anything.

"Oh, and you should be aware that he's in bad shape. He's very touch and go, so please brace yourself for that."

"Why in God's name are you going to execute a man who's ready to die on his own? That makes no sense to me."

"I just follow orders, sir. 6:00 pm at the sally port. Thank you, and have a nice day."

Brent stood there, speechless, the dial tone sounding in his ear. He walked over to the end table and opened the drawer. The ivory dagger was still there. He closed the drawer and sat on the edge of the bed, his head in his hands.

Nolan would be dead in eight hours.

******

Nolan was lying in a hospital bed brought in from the infirmary, with two nurses to tend to him around the clock. Ironically, he was in a deathwatch holding cell, only hours before his scheduled execution at 11:59 pm. Machines beeped, hissed, and sounded alarms as the nurses wrote things down and administered pain medication to keep him under control. Nolan watched the clock as it marched closer and closer to his demise.

The entire time Nolan was at Huntsville, it was like a hazy dream. He would go to sleep and find that he had missed entire days. No one would believe him if he told them, so Nolan kept it to himself. He assumed that it was the killers inside of him, taking control of the wheel and forcing him to the back of the bus to watch the freak show. The medicine he was taking through an IV was dulling his senses and causing him to feel as if he were floating on a cloud. Then thoughts would enter his mind, between reality and dream on a balance beam, provoking flashbacks to his childhood in Heyworth. But now, both of his parents were gone, and the house he grew up in was left in ruin. His entire childhood had burned to the ground. Only cinders remained.

Every night for the past three days, the killers had come to him in his sleep, and the frightening Abbot had led the nightmarish visions. They kept telling him over and over, how he was supposed to pass them on to Brent, or else he would endure eternal misery. They showed him visions of Hell that were worse each time. He couldn't imagine it day after day for eternity. He knew what he had to do, he just didn't know if he'd have the strength to get it done.

******

Brent arrived at the sally port with minutes to spare. He could see Sergeant Whitlock pacing back and forth inside the gate, smoking a cigarette. *Funny, I didn't realize he smoked. A guy in that kind of shape, smoking seems weird.*

"Sergeant, thanks for meeting me here."

"Of course, sir. The warden wanted me to make sure you got VIP treatment tonight," Sergeant Whitlock said, stomping out his cigarette. "Nasty habits die hard, I guess."

Brent laughed, "Yeah, I know what you mean." For a quick instant, he thought about that bottle of Jim Beam on the top of the dresser back at the hotel and the rock glass next to it with an ice cube. Just like grandpa.

The gate of the sally port buzzed open, and Brent went in. He was nervous, too. After much thought at the hotel, and going through the journals, he had decided what he should do. In the final moment before he left to come to the prison, Brent opened the drawer of the end table by the bed. He stared at it for several minutes. He guessed the ivory dagger was at least eight inches long with the sheath. The top of the bone-white knife gleamed inside the drawer, and it complimented the light brown leather sheath. The initials WW on the handle stuck in his mind. Brent had read the name Wilfred Weeks in some of the later writings, when Father Patrick Reilly joined the killers on the bus. Something didn't sit well with Brent about those two. Something wasn't right. A pure evil seemed to permeate their existence. Brent found the ivory dagger enchanting. It was what he was being asked to do with it that he reviled.

A young female corrections officer approached Brent from the left. Sergeant Whitlock stepped between them abruptly.

"I've got this, Smithson."

"OK, Sarge," she replied, writing something down on a clipboard.

Brent felt turbulence in his stomach as he thought about the execution. He couldn't believe it was going to happen. The crowds gathering at the front gate could be heard at the sally port, chanting their slogans and arguing with each other. *Maybe he'll get another stay?* Then his mind started to wander to what it would be like seeing him in the cell, after what the warden's secretary described about his advanced illness. Brent had never met with a condemned man only a few hours before his scheduled death. He felt like he needed to throw up.

"Step over here, sir," Sergeant Whitlock said, a bit jittery.

Brent moved to the right, following directions. He felt like his head was going to explode with the thoughts running through like a pack of coyotes on a wounded fawn.

Sergeant Whitlock began to pat him down. He started at his upper body, which was different than the bottom to top method that Brent had seen done before. The big sergeant was sweating profusely. Brent looked at his eyes and sensed fear. He didn't know if it was the officer or a reflection of his own very real terror.

"Looks busy here tonight," Brent said nervously to break the tension.

"You got that right, sir." Sergeant Whitlock was now down near Brent's knees, patting his khaki pants from each angle. Brent thought his head would explode.

Sergeant Whitlock started to pat Brent's right calf and stopped for a moment. Brent stopped breathing. He was trembling and doing his best to hide it. The sergeant continued patting down his right calf, but more gingerly than the left, and then stood upright. He stared directly into Brent's eyes. He knew all about it. Brent knew he had to, because the sergeant had felt something strapped to his right leg. Brent knew because he put it there. That's where Enoch told him to put it. Enoch had been right up to this point, and so Brent decided not to question it.

"Let's go. Follow me," Sergeant Whitlock said sternly. He motioned to the officer at the gate that led into the prison.

The inner gate buzzed open. Behind them were two corrections vans bringing others into the sally port. The loud noise made Brent jump. A steady rain began to fall, and Brent heard thunder in the distance.

"Come on, sir. We need to get going before it rains any harder. Stay with me at all times."

"OK. Let's do this."

Brent followed Sergeant Whitlock through the rain, and all he could think about was that others could see the ivory knife in its leather sheath, strapped to his calf. Only a thin layer of khaki separated it from the rest of the world. He hoped the rubber bands he used would hold up and not send the dagger tumbling to the ground.

13

Sergeant Whitlock and Brent entered the small anteroom outside the death watch cell where Nolan Weeks had spent the last week. Both were soaked from being caught in the rain outside at the sally port. There were two corrections officers there, and one stood up as they entered.

"Sergeant Whitlock, I didn't expect to see you here, sir," said Corporal Yates, a lanky young officer who had been at Huntsville for five years, gaining his promotion only a month before. His father had just retired as a corrections officer at another penitentiary in Texas.

"Yes, Corporal. I'm doing something for the warden. So, you'll need to replace me out at the sally port. You better take your rain gear. As you can see, it's fucking pouring out there," Sergeant Whitlock replied, dripping on the tile floor.

"Yes, sir." Corporal Yates grabbed his hat and left the anteroom.

Brent was still in a daze from what had happened out at the sally port with Sergeant Whitlock and from the fact he had a dagger strapped to his leg in the presence of corrections officers at a moment of high security. The execution was in a few hours. A high profile one at that. He noticed several monitors were mounted to the concrete walls in the anteroom. One of them showed Nolan in a hospital bed inside a large cell. Apparently, they had to put him in a larger room due to the size of the bed and essential medical equipment he needed. The secretary was right. Even on the small monitor, Nolan looked like he was literally on his death bed. His face was almost gaunt, showing signs of the toll his body was taking, since he had begun to tell his story. Part of him felt bad for the condemned inmate, knowing it was because of the interviews that Nolan had started his rapid descent. Yet even Nolan would say it felt good to let it out, and he was afraid that if he died without telling anyone, his story would never come out. The real story. The real story according to Nolan, that is.

"Go on and open up the cell. Mr. Dowling is going in, by order of Warden Greene," said Sergeant Whitlock. He was doing his best to keep it all together, but an overwhelming sense of dread was swimming inside of him. He wished he was at his house watching this whole fiasco on TV.

"Yes, sir, they called down here earlier and talked to the corporal" said a young corrections officer, Arthur Williams, who was only three months on the job. Like many of the other officers, he had two brothers and an uncle working for the department of corrections. Arthur had wanted to work in corrections ever since he could remember.

There was a soft buzzing sound as the metal cell door unlocked. There was a small window, approximately one foot wide by two feet tall, with special security glass so they could see inside. It was several inches thick and woven with security wire inside, which made it slightly blurry when looking through it. Brent felt a lump in his throat and a burning in his chest. His mind was racing with thoughts.

Sergeant Whitlock held the door open. "We'll be out here. As always, be careful. Remember who he is and why he's in that cell. You've got one hour, and then I'm coming in." Sergeant Whitlock looked directly in his eyes. Brent didn't know what he knew, but whatever it was, it was obvious that he realized something bad was about to happen. His eyes spoke volumes.

"Get it done," the sergeant whispered to him. Brent felt a chill, the dagger cool to his skin.

Once the door closed behind Brent, he flinched slightly as he heard the lock engage. No matter how many times he heard that noise since arriving at Huntsville, it still made him jump. There was a sort of finality in it.

Sergeant Whitlock quietly made his way to the security monitors and unplugged the cable from the wall that connected them to the rest of the network. The 1975 security system was sadly out of date, but the State of Texas was in no hurry to update things like video monitors on death row, where they had so few problems. If it wasn't for the high-profile nature of Nolan's case, the prison would have almost appeared like nothing special was happening. Executions were common at Huntsville, and the local news would typically mention it the night or two before, and then after it was done. There were seldom protestors.

Officer Williams didn't notice the monitors went to static. He was reading a Sports Illustrated magazine at the desk and drinking coffee. Seconds later, Sergeant Whitlock reached his massive right arm around the young man's neck, tightening like a vice with incredible force. Officer Williams grabbed for the sergeant's muscle-bound arm, thrashing around and knocking his cup of coffee and magazine off the desk in the process. His eyes were bulging in place, his thin legs kicked violently, and his face was turning blue as the grip got tighter. Williams was gasping for breath, but none came, and he began to black out. Then Sergeant Whitlock twisted the officer's head abruptly to the right, snapping his neck with a resounding crunch. Williams fell limp to the floor. Sergeant Whitlock moved the body out of the sight of the camera eye. He also made sure that there were no other officers in this wing of death row, to avoid anyone interrupting the plan. It was one of the privileges of setting up the schedule and where the officers would be stationed this evening. As long as things went smoothly, there would be no problems.

The phone on the security desk rang shrilly. Sergeant Whitlock expected it.

"Whitlock here."

"This is Sergeant Lopez. Looks like there's something wrong with the security monitors there. Everything OK?"

"Yes. Looks like the cable came out of the wall. I'll fix it now."

Sergeant Whitlock plugged the cable back in.

"OK. I see, we're back up. Thanks."

"No problem, Gabriel."

Rollie took a deep breath, paused for a moment, then exhaled thinking about the situation. He was well past the point of no return. He thought about the disturbing dead priest who had control over him like a marionette. Rollie didn't like it one bit. He liked being in control as an alpha male who was always the leader of the pack. Rollie knew that no matter what the priest wanted him to do, he had to do it. He couldn't allow anything to happen to Sarah. The more he thought about the vile preacher, the more he wanted to exact revenge. But Rollie had no idea what to do to a person who was already dead. He also knew if he was going to have any hope of making it to sunrise, he had to remain calm as possible and take each thing as it came. He couldn't help but think of Sarah, as well as his other children. He didn't want to think about them too much, because any rational person would not have put himself in such a precarious position with a dead officer only a few feet from him and a murder about to happen inside the deathwatch cell.

He stared at the monitor that showed the inside of the cell, and then the one that gave them a look at the hallway that connected this cell to the main corridor. Since this was a larger cell to accommodate the medical equipment, it was in a more desolate part of death row, which worked even better for Rollie's plan. They were also close to an outside door that he could open with his keys. He knew Williams was already one casualty, and by the looks of Nolan Weeks, he may not even make it to 11:59 pm for his date with the executioner. Rollie knew this would be the longest hour of his life.

******

Nolan was drifting in and out of consciousness as Brent slowly walked toward him. With all the beeps and noises from the machines around him, Nolan was doing his best to be as alert as possible. He didn't know how this night would end, and if he would make it to 11:59 pm, when the State of Texas would pull the plug. Terrible dreams played over and over again from his cross-country rampage. Since that fateful day in Heyworth, where they first entered him, he had large gaps in time missing from his life. He was not even sure when he was there and when he was shoved in the back of the bus, while they took over and killed over and over again. As they moved from state to state, there were times that Nolan would be missing several days or even weeks at a time. It was probably better that way, because having to watch the horrible things they did would have been almost too much to bear.

At some point, Nolan experienced a clear memory from his childhood, growing up in the country in rural Heyworth. It seemed strange in comparison to the hazy memories of the school bus and the two-year killing rampage. His memory was on the last day of 5th grade. It was early June of 1974. The bus dropped him off at the end of the driveway, and he noticed the stifling heat and humidity that was no stranger to the Midwest in the summer. Nolan heard noises coming from one of the many outbuildings on the property. His father's truck was in the driveway, so he must have had the day off work for some reason. Nolan was drawn to the noises. As he got closer, it was the sound of a chainsaw. He assumed his father was chopping up wood for the next fall and winter, when most the home's heat was generated by several wood-burning stoves.

Nolan opened the sliding door of the barn where he heard the sounds. He must have startled his father, who was standing there with a bloody chainsaw, it's motor idling, and half a dead body on a wooden table. His father yelled to him to go in the house and to forget what he saw out in the barn. Nolan was so scared, he turned and ran, leaving the door of the barn wide open. The dream was so clear, and a flood of emotions rushed over little Nolan. In his young mind, shutting the memory off and locking it safely away was the only way he knew how to deal with it. If he thought about it much more, other visions would come to him, showing his father's true reasons for staying up late at night in the barn. He was a cold-blooded killer, who disposed of his victims by chopping the bodies into bite-sized pieces and feeding them to the hogs. As soon as the dream came to Nolan, it vanished into a black hole.

As Brent approached his bed, Nolan could tell that something was wrong. Nolan wasn't sure what that was, but Brent was acting strange. Nolan knew what needed to be done, in order to die without those evil beings tormenting him for eternity. He felt bad, since Brent seemed like a decent enough person. Yet at the same time, it was a dog-eat-dog world, and Nolan knew he had no choice but to do what needed to be done.

Thinking about his dreams brought back memories of talking to his father's brother, his Uncle Donny. Donny was a raging alcoholic and usually spent most Friday and Saturday nights at their house in Heyworth, drinking cheap beer, smoking unfiltered Camels, and telling stories about all the crazy things he did. One of those stories was usually told much later, after any of the young ones were in bed. Donny had done two tours in Vietnam in 1970 and 71 as a grunt with the Big Red One from Fort Reilly, Kansas. Fading in and out of consciousness, Nolan could hear his scratchy voice like he was sitting right there.

"I remember those nips were sneaking up on us every fuckin' night while we was sleepin'. We got in some awful fire fights with those bastards. Lost two or three good buddies over that shit."

If he concentrated, Nolan could see his dad and a few of their friends gathered on the front porch, listening to Donny tell his stories. None of them served, so hearing it from Donny was captivating, especially when he was on a roll with a twelve-pack in him.

"So, we set up some claymore mines. You know, the ones that are curved and get stuck in the ground. They got hundreds of little bb's inside, and they cut those fuckers in half when they get up on it."

Nolan could hear Donny crack open another beer, and light another cigarette to continue.

"On one side it says – this side toward enemy. This a ways, you don't blow your damn self up," Donny said in a serious tone, "and when you push that plunger, those bb's spray out far and kill most of them that are close."

That always stuck with Nolan, as he grew up as a loner. He had friends and a few girlfriends over the years, but he just never felt like he fit in anywhere. He did like hanging out with Uncle Donny, though. Donny did more stuff with him than his dad, who always seemed to be working or sleeping. The claymore mine with the side that said "this side toward enemy" was sort of like how he acted with other people. He showed his tough side, the side he would point at his enemies or people he didn't know well. It was a self-defense mechanism for him, and like a turtle's shell, he felt safe behind the claymore mine. If he needed to protect himself, Nolan would "push the plunger" and let loose those bb's inside. He had a few run-ins with the local police, but it was typically mischievous vandalism like throwing rocks through windows, or getting in fights at school.

Uncle Donny died five years ago. It was liver failure, which didn't surprise anyone. He was drinking a case of beer and smoking two packs a day up until the day he died. Doctors told him for years to stop drinking and smoking, but Donny just laughed and said he didn't want to live past 65, and amazingly, he died at 64 and a half.

So, now with only a few measly hours left to live, Nolan was crouched behind his claymore mine and hoped his enemies would see "this side toward enemy" and know he would fight to the death.

******

Brent stopped about five feet from the foot of Nolan's bed. He stared at the condemned, not knowing what to say. He found himself not wanting to think of him by name, but rather as the inmate or the condemned. Nolan wanted to see him, and if Enoch Strange was right, he was going to try and pass the evil to him. Brent wasn't about to let that happen. After reading the journals for hours in his hotel room, he did realize that Nolan had been telling the truth. The entries in different handwriting, obviously written by different people, were proof enough for him. Reading it was captivating, as the various identities argued with each other and touted the bloodshed they dealt. He had felt bad for Nolan. Brent couldn't imagine what that would be like, to be a host for twelve deranged maniacs, killing at will, without a way to stop it. What concerned him, in the back of his mind, was which one of the killers was he talking to during the interviews? Was he talking to Nolan himself? That's what he claimed. But Brent couldn't help but wonder if Nolan was stashed away, like he was on the bus, and one of the entities was playing games with him. It was all too possible, and that made his decision even more difficult. There was too much on the line, and it was overwhelming him. Could he drive the ivory dagger into his heart, not knowing who he was killing? Even if he was sure of his guilt, Brent questioned his resolve to kill the man. It was against everything he believed in. His hardscrabble upbringing aside, Brent wasn't a killer, and he knew it.

"I'm glad you were able to come, Brent," said Nolan, slightly out of breath. His voice was strained and distorted from all the medication he was on to lessen the pain. It sounded tinny, like he was speaking through an old transistor radio.

"Of course, I made you a promise, and I'm living up to my end." Brent stared at Nolan, desperately trying to see inside his soul. Was this really Nolan?

"I'll be dead soon. You have been the only person who has been decent to me since this whole thing started," Nolan said, coughing at the end. One of the machines beeped loudly, then stopped. Brent could hear Nolan's erratic breathing. Things seemed to stabilize after a few moments.

"I just wish I had the chance to . . . " Nolan began, then drifted off into a whisper.

Brent took a step closer. "I can't hear you very well."

Nolan stared at him. "Come closer, please." He wheezed sharply.

Brent froze in his tracks. He thought about the dagger strapped to his leg. As sick as Nolan looked, Brent doubted he would be able to do anything but cough or whisper. The machines continued to beep. Brent glanced at his watch. It was almost 7:00 pm. Nolan would be dead in less than five hours. That is, if he didn't die in this cell on his own. He looked terrible laying in the hospital bed. The lights above were bright, and it was large for a prison cell at nearly fifteen feet by fifteen feet. The floor was the staple battleship grey painted concrete, as were the walls and ceiling. The entire corridor that led to the cell was dreary and oddly quiet, even for death row. Some of the officers referred to this hallway as the highway to hell. Sometimes on nights of an execution, some of the inmates would sing AC/DC's song "Highway to Hell" when the condemned prisoners were being led to the execution chamber. The officers didn't mind at all, and some even found it a good send off.

"Come closer."

"What is it you want from me, Nolan? What was it you wanted me to do? I'm confused. I know that's what this is all about."

Nolan said something that Brent couldn't make out. Then Nolan closed his eyes. Brent took one step closer. If he reached his left arm out as far as he could, Brent could touch the edge of the bed.

"Have you ever heard of low twelve, Brent?"

"Low twelve? No, I never have."

Nolan coughed and shifted slightly in his bed to get comfortable. Brent kept his eyes fixed on him. He was looking for any sign of aggression and thought about the dagger.

"It comes from the teachings of Freemasons during their third-degree ritual. It's what members must go through to become a Master Mason. Masonic scholars use the term low twelve to mean the very end of the day, just before midnight. Others say it has a deeper meaning and believe it to be the moments right before your death. The end of your life. I find it a fascinating concept," Nolan said, barely above a whisper.

Brent didn't say anything. Nolan's breathing became erratic again.

"Who will be there when I draw my last breath?" Nolan began, still at a ragged whisper, "Whose eyes will mine be the last to see?"

"I don't understand you. What are you saying?"

"A brief pause, as I pass on from this world," Nolan said, drifting off again, "will be my low twelve as darkness comes to call."

Brent was trying to figure out what he was saying. It sounded like some sort of poem. It was very strange. Without realizing it, Brent took one step closer to try and make out what Nolan was saying. He watched Nolan's chest rise and fall, and the machines that monitored him continued to buzz and purr along. A lump settled in his throat as he got closer to Nolan. He bent over and reached for his right calf. He took hold of the dagger and jerked it free from the rubber bands holding it in place. He only took his eyes off the dying man for an instant.

Brent never saw Nolan's left hand move, and before he realized what was happening, he had Brent firmly in his grasp, pulling him on top of him in the bed. Brent couldn't believe how quickly it had happened!

"Don't look surprised, Mr. Dowling," Nolan sneered, "after all, you knew this was coming, didn't you?" Nolan's voice was stronger, his strength was beyond compare, and Brent was unable to move as he stared face-to-face with the condemned man. His grip on him was inhuman.

"Who am I speaking to?" Brent stammered. He had the dagger firmly in his right hand, but he was not able to move his arm at all, with the firm hold Nolan had on him.

"All things will be revealed here tonight, in time," Nolan hissed.

Brent began to wiggle his right arm slightly from the grasp, feeling the cool handle of the ivory dagger. He knew it was now or never and that he had to summon the strength to do what Enoch told him had to be done. He remembered asking Enoch how he would know if the dagger worked, ending the curse. Enoch had said, *you will know when the dagger shows the true color of the beast's heart.* Brent wasn't sure what that meant. Those words were now present, as he was moments away from changing things forever.

In a quick movement, Brent was able to pull his arm free and held the dagger high for only a moment to build up the power. Nolan screamed out, a primal cry that nearly shook the walls and floor of the cell. Brent drove the knife down with all his force directly into Nolan's heart. He screamed out again, as Brent drove it as deep as he could. Blood gushed from the wound as Brent held on for dear life while Nolan began to thrash back and forth and up and down – nearly coming off the bed.

Brent stared into Nolan's face as he twitched, trying to get him to let up on the dagger. The facial expressions began to slowly change as Nolan's head moved back and forth, screaming out like an animal fighting for its life. Brent was horrified to see his face change from one of the killers to another, each with telltale features and a variety of scars and tattoos that made them stand out. It was like something out of a nightmare, but Brent had awakened something buried deep inside, a sort of bravado that even he didn't know he had. His father and brothers all loved to hunt, but Brent never did. They messed with him a lot about it, especially when he went to college to become a journalist.

Then the entire cell began to change. The concrete floor was cracking slowly, working its way across the cell and under Nolan's bed. It made a strange crunching sound, like something from deep below the ground was starting to work its way up to daylight.

The blankets and sheets flew off the bed, one of them ending up on the cell door, covering the window. Another wrapped itself around the lone video camera in the corner of the cell. The bed began to shake as Nolan was writhing in agony, the dagger firmly in place. He began to yell at Brent as the various entities made their rage known.

"You fucking bastard! Let go of that knife!" a voice he had never heard, with a British accent. It was Lyle Miller, a despicable necrophiliac who liked to kill prostitutes.

Brent was paralyzed, as Nolan's face changed to yet another madman.

"You heard him, Dowling! Let go of it. I'll kill you myself!" screamed Denny Gutierrez, the arsonist who killed children and held a nun at knifepoint. His manic shrill tone sounded like a siren at a distorted volume.

This back and forth mayhem continued on as a wind howled through the room, nearly tossing Brent off Nolan. He held on with all he had to the knife. Enoch warned that Nolan would put up a fight. It was like he was fighting twelve people, and in essence – he was.

Brent couldn't believe his eyes as the ivory white dagger began to turn black! It was the darkest black he had ever seen, and gazing into it was like looking down a bottomless pit. Was that what Enoch was saying? The dagger turned black because that's what Nolan's heart was? Black and pure evil? Flames began to flicker behind Brent where the crack began in the concrete floor. It was now a gaping crevice, steam hissing from the void. The wind began to take hold, making everything in the cell fly around, banging into the walls. The medical equipment was breaking apart in pieces. Shards of glass and twisted metal were going in all directions, as was the bed Nolan lying down in. Brent remained on top of Nolan, the black dagger still in his heart, as a storm raged inside the deathwatch cell. He hung on for dear life, afraid to let go of the blackened knife that was the only thing keeping him from being swept up in the storm and hurled into the raging fire behind him. He could feel a tremendous pull.

"Die you son-of-a-bitch!" screamed one of the maniacs as the wind nearly drowned it completely out. Brent was bracing for certain death.

******

Rollie was glued to the monitor that showed what was happening inside the cell. He was going out of his mind with worry and guilt about what he had done with Officer Williams. Oddly, he was more concerned with losing his job than being questioned about the discovery of a dead body. He was so wrapped up in what could happen to Sarah if the priest followed through with his threat the night before, that Rollie wasn't thinking straight. It took him back to that day five years ago, when she was in the ATV accident and he thought he was going to lose his little girl. He had never felt so helpless in his life, and when Father Patrick showed up and threw him a life preserver, without question or hesitation, Rollie had taken. If he had to do it again, he would do the same thing. He couldn't bear to lose Sarah then or now. He planned to move Williams into the cell when the hour was up and blame it on Weeks. He didn't know if it would be believable, but Rollie figured no one would think that he had broken the young officer's neck.

Rollie could see Brent standing several feet from the bed and that the two men were talking. In his discussion with the priest, he knew there were a few possibilities that could happen here, and hoped he was ready when the time came to get Brent out of the cell and to safety. That was the deal he made with the dead priest in order to save Sarah. As it got closer to 10:00 pm, there would be more corrections officers in the execution chamber and adjoining witness rooms, to handle the guests and staff. They were supposed to move Nolan into the execution chamber at 10:30 pm, so he could begin the protocol for the execution. There were several things the state medical staff needed to do to prepare him for the procedure of lethal injection. The prison staff practiced the routine often, since Huntsville was the only institution in Texas where male inmates were executed. Warden Greene prided himself on having a smooth process, and training on it regularly was paramount in making that happen. If ever there was a time to shine, it was tonight, as the media circus was in full force covering the execution. Some of the national news shows searched for family members of victims, or the rare person who escaped the clutches of Nolan Weeks. There weren't many, but the networks found them, and exploiting the weeping survivors to the fullest.

Rollie stood up for a moment to stretch when he saw Brent take a step closer to the bed. Suddenly the monitor image shook and then went to white noise. *What the hell is going on?* He ran to the cell door just as a blanket or bed sheet flew across the room and covered the window! Rollie hit the switch to open the door, but the door only buzzed. It did not open, despite repeated attempts. Instinctively, he banged on the door, as if that would do anything. It was more an act of desperation. Rollie grabbed the keys in the desk drawer, which were a manual means of entry in case the system was down or the prison lost power and the generators failed. He tried several times, but the key would not turn the lock. His hands were shaking to the point where he gave up trying the keys. Rollie put his ear up to the door but could hear nothing on the other side. Out of sheer frustration, he banged on the cell door repeatedly.

"Fuck!" he yelled in disgust.

Just then the phone rang on the security desk. Rollie wasn't sure how to handle this sudden change in plans. He closed his eyes and took a deep breath.

"Whitlock here," he said. His eyes were locked in on the cell door, the blanket still blocking the window. *Damn it. What the hell is going on in there?*

"Hey Rollie. What's going on? I see the monitor is out again."

"I'm working on it, Gabriel. I think it's a bad cable. Let me see what I can do."

"OK. Let me know. I can send someone in maintenance to replace it if we need to."

"No, that won't be necessary. I can see into the cell from where I'm standing. Everything is fine. Mr. Dowling will only be in there for another twenty minutes, then I'm supposed to escort him to the execution witness room," Rollie said, sweat beginning to stream down his face. The blanket was still firmly against the window.

"OK. Makes sense. Let us know if you need anything. The warden was just here. He's out of his mind about all this."

"I'm sure. I'll let you know if I need anything."

Rollie hung up the phone, his hand still shaking slightly as he set the receiver down. He thought about smoking a cigarette for the second time tonight, despite the fact he had given up the habit when he discharged from the Army. He did find himself craving a cigarette during times of extreme stress, and this was about as stressed out as he had been in his life, with so many variables that could bite him in the ass. Or worse, make him an inmate at Huntsville instead of a corrections officer. That was any corrections officer's worst nightmare.

He looked at his watch and noted Brent had only 18 minutes before coming out of the cell. Rollie wondered what he would do if the door would still not open. He tried not to think of it, but that was impossible. He put his hands in his pants pockets to stop them from shaking.

******

"Very good, Mr. Dowling. I didn't think you had it in you," said Nolan, as Brent held the dagger tight. There was something in his eyes that seemed different than they were when he first approached the bed.

Brent didn't know what to say, and he was confused. How could Nolan still be alive and talking to him with the dagger through his heart, blood still spewing from the opening?

"You haven't been speaking to Nolan at all, Mr. Dowling. He's been tucked away, so to speak, while the rest of us have been using his mortal body as a shell to do our bidding," Nolan said, his voice sounding different. He sounded more educated and didn't have a bland Midwestern accent any longer.

The cell continued to shudder and shake, and the flames behind him raged like an inferno. Searing steam and hot gasses were spewing up from the crack in the floor, which had widened to more than a foot across. The fissure was red hot, and flames leapt out nearly two feet in the air. He was amazed that he hadn't caught fire. It was incredibly hot in the room. Sweat poured down Brent's face to sizzle as it fell on Nolan's.

"Then who are you?" he screamed out, as the scorching wind continued to howl through the cell. Brent looked at the door briefly, hoping Sergeant Whitlock would come in and stop the madness. The blanket was still covering the window. He wondered what the sergeant was thinking on the other side.

"I'm Father Patrick Reilly, but those who know me well call me Abbot," he said, laughing. With each breath the priest took, the blood poured out faster. Now it was turning from red to dark black, just like the dagger. It was spewing like magma from an active volcano.

Brent thought about that name and quickly recalled where he had heard it before. It was the name on the statue in the lobby of St. Michael's in McHenry, Illinois. He was the former Abbot of the academy! Pieces of the puzzle were beginning to fall into place.

"I'm in charge here. I'm the 13th one. I'm the one in charge of these deranged maniacs, as despicable as that may be for a man of my stature. A man of my piousness. Ha, how hypocritical I am!" He laughed maniacally over the howling wind.

Suddenly the dagger began to crumble in Brent's hand, and small black pieces of the knife scattered in the wind like dust in a hurricane. The Abbot pushed him off, and Brent landed several feet away, feeling the incredible heat from the flames that were shooting up from the chasm only a few feet away. He tried not to look at the fire, something deep down inside told him not to. Instead, he kept his gaze upon the Abbot, who was now thrashing on the floor and clawing at his own chest. Despite the fact that the body looked like Nolan Weeks, Brent no longer looked at him that way, thinking about all the conversations they had. Was it possible that he never had spoken with Nolan, but instead the former Abbot, Father Patrick Reilly? He began to doubt the advice Enoch gave him about ending the curse. Did Enoch trick him? Had he made a terrible mistake? Would he make it out of this insanity alive?

One hand reached out of the Abbot's chest, and then another. Brent was horrified at the sight, as a steamy black liquid oozed from the chest cavity and a person very slowly crawled out of it. The figure was a man, large in stature with a white apron, covered in blood and the disgusting black ooze. The man glared at Brent as he walked by and directly into the fire! Behind him were others, also clawing their way from the quivering body of Nolan Weeks, which was now only a mass of flesh on the floor. Just like the first man, they all walked directly into the fire. One of the men was older, with a white lab coat, and Brent assumed it was Doc, as Nolan had referred to him. According to the journal, Doc was Dr. Rollin Arbuckle, a man who killed his own patients and sold the bodies on the black market in Boston. He stared at Brent with empty eyes as he shuffled by and into the flames. The smell of burnt flesh began to permeate the cell, making it nearly unbearable.

The hot wind continued to whip, and Brent couldn't believe his eyes with the spectacle taking place before him. He hoped Enoch was right, and stabbing Nolan with the ivory knife was putting an end to the curse for once and for all. In the back of his mind, he wondered if maybe something had gone wrong, since Enoch never mentioned any of this. Things continued to get stranger by the minute, and he had serious doubts.

One by one, the rest of the twelve killers left the carcass that was Nolan Weeks and walked to the fire, never looking back for a moment, acting as if on direct orders to do so. They were good soldiers of Hell. Maybe it was the Abbot commanding them? The twelfth one to leave was headless, yet he still staggered to the fire like the rest. It was a terrifying sight to behold.

Finally, one last person climbed from the steaming body. He wore a black suit with a gold cross lapel pin. Brent had read enough about him to know it was none other than the infernal Abbot. He was an emissary from Hell itself. He had taken various forms in life and death and had a seemingly infinite amount of charisma about him. In his hands, he held a severed head, and he rolled it into the fire.

"Take that, Victor, you rogue," said the Abbot, now facing Brent from only a few feet away. "I couldn't stand him yelling and carrying on about all that Nightmare Maker business, so I removed his head."

Brent remained silent, watching everything unfold, as the scorching hot winds, flames, and gasses began to turn his skin a bright pink.

"Remember this, I always remain," said the Abbot, with his hands held up in defiance. His skin was still a sickly gray pallor. His bright blue eyes, still piercing. Still evil. His voice was powerful.

Brent heard those words and knew where he had heard them before. Enoch had said them! *I always remain. I always remain . . .*

******

Rollie looked at his watch again. Brent had exactly seven minutes. No matter how hard he tried, he was unable to stop looking at the cell door, with the blanket still pressed firmly against the security window.

The phone on the security desk rang and nearly knocked Rollie off the chair he was sitting in. He grabbed for it, knocking the receiver down to the floor. Cursing, he picked it up.

"Whitlock here."

"Sergeant Whitlock. Are you OK there? You sound like something's wrong," said Warden Greene. He was calling from his office, where he too had been watching the clock, but for different reasons.

"I'm fine, sir." Sweat was pouring down his face, and his uniform shirt was soaked.

"Good. Is Dowling still in there with Weeks?

"Yeah." Rollie still stared at the door. The blanket was still firmly in place.

"They'll be coming for Weeks at 10:30 pm. So, make sure Dowling is at the execution witness room before then. I don't want any problems." The warden was on his second glass of malt scotch - neat. He was doing his best to keep from exploding. He stared at the picture of his son and family on his desk. He wanted to see Weeks die more than ever. He lit up a cigar in his office to celebrate the occasion.

"OK."

Rollie looked at his watch again. Five minutes.

******

Suddenly a rumble from deep below shook the cell. Brent felt the floor move and watched the crevice open wider as steam and hot magma spewed to the surface through fissures in the concrete. The Abbot was standing near the door, smirking like he expected it. In his supreme arrogance, the Abbot sneered and let out a maniacal laugh, his head thrown back in a cackle. A tall dark figure rose from the flames, one that Brent had only read about in the journals. It had to be him! As he came into view, it was the flowing locks of flaming red hair and top hat that gave him away. It was the famed Satanist, Dr. Wilfred Weeks, author of the Darkness Visible ritual. Brent had read some things about the ritual in some of the later journals, where the Abbot was the author. Most of it was stuff Brent didn't understand. He gathered that it was the source of the twelve killers and how they ended up possessing Nolan. He didn't quite get the link between Darkness Visible and what was going on now. It was obvious that the Abbot and Dr. Weeks were enemies. The hatred between the two was palpable.

"Dr. Weeks. How nice of you to join us here!" the Abbot said with a hearty laugh.

"Father Patrick, I thought you would have learned a lesson the last time," added Dr. Weeks, his green eyes piercing, despite the haze. "Did you enjoy your stay in that hideous beast?" A low rumble of a laugh emanated from deep within.

The Abbot began to walk to his right as Dr. Weeks moved to his right too, like two prize fighters moving in a circle, sizing each other up before a bout. Dr. Weeks had the same deathly pallor about him as the Abbot. These were evil beings, not of the mortal world. Brent was cowering in the shadows, hoping the two would kill off each other and spare him. He glanced over at the bloody pulp that was Nolan and couldn't believe what was happening.

"You talk a big game, Dr. Weeks. You never finished Darkness Visible. But I did. Yes, I completed the work you were unable to," the Abbot spouted, his perfect teeth gleaming, against the grey backdrop of his skin, lips and gums. Something began to move behind him, but Brent was unable to tell what it was. It looked like a fluttering.

Dr. Weeks continued to move in a circle with the Abbot. The two seemed unaffected by the tremendous heat and flames lapping at their legs from the gaping crack in the floor that was now two feet wide.

"Remember what happened the last time you tried to do that? Do you? You created this damn mess that I had to come back and put a stop to," Dr. Weeks cried out, tossing his top hat to the floor and shaking his head in rage. His eyes were alive with hate.

The Abbot laughed, his hubris unbridled. "That was then. This is now!" he screamed, as suddenly two massive black wings appeared on his back. He flapped them, fanning the flames around him. Large veins protruded from the wings that were covered with a fine fuzz of black hair. They were hideous – an abomination. His blue eyes appeared red in the hot steam rising all around him.

Brent was open mouthed at the display. Of course, if Nolan were there, he would have remembered seeing the Abbot and his demonic black wings, like an infernal monarch from Hell. Dr. Weeks seemed shocked at the display, as the Abbot flapped his thick, leathery wings again.

"You are now going to feel the tremendous loss that I did all those years ago, my dear doctor. You will become the antithesis of what you are. Where you are strong, you will become the weakest among us. Where you were vibrant and strong, now you will be feeble. The whole time, you will have your mental faculties, which makes the agony so much richer. So much more delectable. As you will soon find out, to know what's going on mentally makes the torment so much worse." The Abbot was now flapping his black wings in rhythm as Dr. Weeks began to show fear. His face quivered as thoughts of what had gone wrong plagued him.

"You have no such power," cried out Dr. Weeks, slowly backing into a corner of the cell.

"You are wrong! You will see what it is like to become something so horrid, that no living thing wants anything to do with you! Even your manhood will be reduced to the size of a child's thumb." The Abbot laughed hideously.

Dr. Weeks staggered as his hand felt the wall of the cell, realizing that he could not move any longer. The Abbot was inching closer to him, and now the doctor was on one knee, shuddering in his presence.

"You will now become what I was all these years. You underestimated my intellect. I was trapped in the body of Enoch Strange. You remember, don't you? The poor son-of-a-bitch who you cruelly beat up and abused. You subjected my mouth to be sewn shut, and then my eyes. But I remembered the power of that ivory dagger, and it released me from that gnarled body. When that dagger pierced the heart of our host, and the ivory turned black, I was no longer that cretin in the cabin at St. Michael's. I became that Abbot once again!"

Dr. Weeks was sputtering on his knees. He didn't know what to do, and begged for his life. Tears were now streaming down his twisted face as the realization of what was happening to him set in. Another low rumble shuddered from down below, and the cell shook with fury. It was as if it were about to crumble within itself. The crack in the floor widened. Now fissures were evident in the walls and ceiling, as small pieces of concrete began to fall and then whip around in the fetid hot wind. It was sheer mayhem.

"Sniveling does not become you, dear Doctor. No, it does not!" the Abbot cried, his blue eyes a raging storm at sea. He raised his hands up again, as if summoning something from beyond. The rumble sounded again, and the concrete floor began to shift and move, and the magma rose up like a sea of boiling lava, hissing and spouting upward.

"Please, no!" screamed Dr. Weeks as his body was suddenly engulfed in fire. A sickening black smoke poured from his burning flesh as he became consumed by the flames shooting up from the chasm.

Suddenly something rose up from the blackness. At first it was indistinguishable, causing another rumble from below. Then another. As it rose higher and higher, long sharp teeth were visible. It was a giant mouth, with a greenish black tongue that slithered within it like a demonic snake. It hissed and showed its razor-sharp teeth, and then it grabbed on to Dr. Weeks' leg, pulling him in. The infernal doctor thrashed and screamed, silently, as the sound the giant mouth made as it rose was ungodly. It was a low, demonic furor that caused more cracks in the concrete and more dust to fall. Then the tongue pulled the broken body of Dr. Weeks into the throat, grinding him to pulp until he was no longer.

Now the Abbot turned to Brent, who had soiled himself watching the Abbot turn Dr. Weeks to flame and the giant mouth swallowing the remains, as he screamed in agony the entire way. Brent shuddered in the presence of the embodiment of evil. The Abbot's voice was like thunder, and the wind and mayhem died down for a moment to allow their master a moment to concentrate his power to the true task at hand. This was the entire reason for what had transpired this evening, and the deranged priest was center stage and completely in the moment. Brent was powerless in his shadow.

"And now to complete the process! Are you ready to receive, Mr. Dowling? Are you prepared for your big adventure?" the Abbot cried out, his bestial wings fanning the flames. Then everything went black.

******

"Mr. Dowling! Wake up! Mr. Dowling!"

Brent slowly began to gain consciousness. His eyes fluttered and attempted to focus. Everything was hazy, and his head was pounding, like he had gone ten rounds in a boxing ring.

"Hurry up. We don't have much time." Brent realized it was the voice of Sergeant Whitlock.

"What's going on?" His head was spinning, still throbbing.

"Here, put this on and fast. We need to put your clothes on him," the sergeant said, handing him a corrections officer uniform and pointing to the dead body of the young officer who was outside the cell when Brent went inside.

Brent had seen so much in the past hour, he was numb. He looked around in disbelief at the death watch cell. The floor was the same battleship gray and intact, as were the walls and ceilings. There were no cracks or fissures; the concrete was pristine. There was no sign that raging fire, liquid magma, and blazing hot winds had ravaged the 15 by 15 room for an hour. It was as if nothing had happened at all. Brent also heard the beeps and noises from the life support that Nolan was connected to and the prisoner's ragged breathing. Brent turned his head to see in disbelief that Nolan was still alive! His eyes were closed, but his chest was rising and falling.

"How is that possible?" Brent asked, putting on the corrections officer's uniform. Sergeant Whitlock said something to him, but it was white noise. Brent was trying to grasp the situation and could not believe that Nolan was with the living again. At least for a short time until his execution. Brent looked at his watch and realized that was just over 90 minutes from now.

"Brent," Nolan called out above the beeping noises. There was an urgency to the weak cry.

Brent walked over to the bed and immediately saw a different Nolan lying there. He was barely hanging on, but at peace, like a man who had come to grip with the certainty of his death with a clear conscience. There was a general sense of calm about him, despite his dire situation. Brent had seen him at his worst, tormented by the twelve killers, and later by the Abbot himself. The 13th one. The Abbot has broken the cycle and tainted Darkness Visible by changing the recipe. There were only supposed to be twelve according to the ancient ritual, but the Abbot had not made an error. It was a calculated decision to change it, to finish writing what Dr. Weeks had not been able to do before his public hanging. The Abbot knew exactly what he was doing. He wanted to be the manifestation of Satan on Earth. He wanted to be the light-bearer himself, and so by finishing what Dr. Weeks had started, the Abbot was becoming what he always wanted to be. He wanted endless power and wished to have mankind quake in his presence with a cadre of demons at his disposal.

"Nolan, is that you?" Brent inched even closer, no longer worried about becoming the host. He knew that it was over.

"Yes, it is," he said at barely a whisper. His eyes fluttered open. "This is my low twelve. I'm leaving this world on my own." The machines around him flatlined, and a prolonged alarm rang out. Brent shed a tear. Nolan died with his eyes wide open, but clear and free of anguish.

Suddenly Sergeant Whitlock grabbed Brent by the arm and snapped him into reality.

"Let's go!" he screamed out, as Brent turned away from Nolan, who finally had passed on, cheating his executioner and dying at peace without the entities inside him. "Stay with me, and act like you're one of us."

The two men casually walked away from the death watch cell and out the exit door that they had entered a little more than an hour before. The rain had subsided, but the crowds outside the main gate could be heard in the distance. The rain deterred some, but the hardcore among them were still in a frenzy. They screamed and chanted as the execution neared. They waved signs and banners, and the media was there filming it, while reporters spoke live about what was going on and providing viewers a countdown to 11:59, when Nolan was supposed to die.

What none of the masses at the gate realized, was that the condemned was already dead.

******

Sergeant Ricardo Espinoza picked up the phone and dialed a four-digit number he knew from memory. It was a call he dreaded having to make.

"Warden Greene," barked the fiery head of the institution. He was getting ready to make his way to the execution chamber, but he heard the phone ring. He decided to pick up, as he was the only person in the office at this hour. He feared it was the governor, wanting to give a stay of execution.

"Sir, I have some bad news."

"What is it?" The warden sat back down.

"Weeks is dead. We got here to take him, and his machine is flatlined, and he's got no pulse. No heartbeat. Nothing, sir." Espinoza winced at the response.

The warden was raging. He stared at the picture of his son and his slain family on the desk before him. He felt dizzy for a moment, unable to process what he had just heard. In his entire time at Huntsville, no one had escaped their date with the executioner. He had done his best to keep the condition of Weeks from the press, but he feared now the whole thing would unravel, as well as the major conflict of interest. Would his affair so many years ago finally come out? What would Eliza say?

"Where's Whitlock? God, damn it!" He pounded his fist on his desk, nearly knocking his pictures to the floor.

"I don't know, sir. He's gone. Mr. Dowling is too, and Officer Williams is dead on the floor inside the cell. For some reason, he's not in his uniform, but in civilian clothes."

While he spoke with Sergeant Espinoza, Warden Greene could hear the alarm on Nolan's machine in the background, and the mounting chaos in the death watch cell as more security and corrections officers gathered to assess the situation. It was only a matter of time before the media would get word of this. He let the phone drop to the floor and put his head in both hands. In moments, he was sobbing uncontrollably.

"Sir? Are you there? Warden?"

******

The Dodge extended cab pick-up truck rumbled down county road 11 with a sense of extreme urgency. Driving the truck was Sergeant Whitlock, and next to him, donning the same uniform was Brent Dowling. He had the window cracked open, enjoying the cool air across his face. The two barely said anything as they drove away from the Huntsville State Prison. They both knew there would be a lot of unanswered questions from what they left behind. Neither had given it much more thought than that. Tomorrow seemed like a million miles away as the Dodge got as far away from Huntsville as it could.

Suddenly, something caught the attention of Rollie. A movement from the passenger's seat in his peripheral vision.

"You better keep it at the speed limit, my good sergeant. We don't want some young, go-getter of a policeman pulling us over.

Do we?" a voice in docile tone said. Rollie's heart skipped a beat. Maybe two. He knew who it was. He had heard that voice before. Rollie had been face-to-face with the vile creature. Where did Brent go?

The Abbot laughed as Rollie's face became ashen white.

"Didn't expect to see me again, did you Rollie?" he sneered, "I didn't think so. It was nice of Mr. Dowling to be a good host and get me out of that disgusting institution. The whole place stinks. I've got him tucked neatly away. I know you wondered about him."

Rollie stared straight ahead, trying desperately to figure out what to do. His gun was in the glovebox, directly in front of the priest. He didn't think he could get it out fast enough, without losing an arm. Rollie didn't even know if a gun would do anything to the monster. He did notice that the man didn't have the same foul smell that he did when he showed up the night before at his house.

"You can look now, Rollie. I'm human again. Well, kind of." He laughed again, a giddy type of howl.

Just then, Rollie grabbed on to a large flat-head screwdriver he had on the floor board next to him. He drove it into the priest's chest all the way to the handle. He looked at the Abbot, who was pulling the screwdriver from his body, with little effort. It didn't do anything at all but annoy the priest. Rollie wondered if the priest would turn back into Brent. Then with lightning speed, he stabbed Rollie in his right thigh, all the way and pinning him to the driver's seat. The sergeant let out a horrible scream as pain shot through his body like electric current.

The truck veered sharply to the left, crossing the median. Luckily no one was coming the other way. Rollie had no control over it, and then the wheel turned the other way, swaying the truck to the right, causing it to nearly tip over. The accelerator was pushing down, by control of someone else. They were moving at a dangerous speed while Rollie fought to keep the truck on the road as the speedometer approached 80 miles-an-hour!

"Isn't this the way Sarah usually takes to get to your house? I thought so. I hope she didn't decide to leave after work and come to your house tonight instead of tomorrow morning," said the Abbot, drenched in sarcasm. "Maybe she planned on surprising you?"

Rollie could feel an anger swell inside him that he was unable to control any longer.

"I did what you asked me, priest. I did it, you son-of-a-bitch!" He glanced at the Abbot, then back to the road.

"Well, now. That's not very nice, Rollie. Yes, you did do what I asked."

The truck was moving into the other lane again, the speed increasing. They were at 85 and climbing.

"Then you're a liar! A fucking liar!" Rollie screamed out, desperately trying to control the steering wheel. At the speed they were driving, he feared he couldn't keep the Dodge on the road.

"Well, that's not the first time someone has called the Devil a liar."

As the truck swayed back and forth, the Abbot lowered his window. Rollie didn't notice.

"I must be going now, but you make sure you say hi to Sarah for me!"

Just then Rollie's truck crossed the median again and smashed head-on with a small Toyota Corolla. It was Sarah, and she had no idea what hit her. Rollie did see her face as they collided. Both were killed on impact, and a fire ball rose up in a last act of defiance as the two burned to ash on the desolate country road. Sarah had her fishing gear on the back seat, in anticipation of a fun weekend. It was almost midnight, when Nolan was supposed to have been executed.

The Abbot said he had Brent tucked away somewhere. The tormented news man shed his mortal coil and vanished into the flames like the others. As the smoke rose into the sky, the angry cries of the dead could be heard faintly in the distance, voicing their rage at the terrible situation they each found themselves in on that quiet Texas road.

Split seconds before impact, the Abbot let loose his leathery black wings and jumped out of the window. He flew away quickly, rising above the trees like a phoenix from the ashes. In the distance, a choir of the damned cheered for their fearless leader, extinguishing the waning cries of the dead. Below, the fire raged as the Abbot smiled, enjoying the cool breeze whipping across his face.

Epilogue

One Year Later

The Abbot sat behind the large desk in his opulent office at St. Peter's Academy in Jerome, Arizona. At one time dubbed the "wickedest city in America", Jerome was a former mining town (with more than a fair share of bars and brothels) that resembled a small European city with narrow streets and an eclectic collection of shops and eateries. St. Peter's sat at the top of the town, overlooking the Arizona landscape and nearby Cottonwood, more conservative than its geographical neighbor. There was a monastery on the small 10-acre campus, a church, and a school for gifted high school students. The nuns at St. Peter's were from a convent in Prescott.

Sitting across from him was his servant, who spent most of his time in a small, cramped basement storeroom in darkness. The only time he was granted permission to leave his quarters was when he was working on third shift, when almost no other staff, students, or visitors would see him. The only exception was when the Abbot summoned him for a special task, such as now at nearly 10:00 pm on a Saturday.

He was rather horrible to look at, covered in sores, tumors and pock marks. He sat hunched over in the dim light of the Abbot's office. His mouth was sewn shut with what appeared to be a heavy nylon fishing line, with only enough space between the stitches for him to use a straw to drink. When he took a breath, it made a wet sucking sound through the grotesque aberration he called a mouth. His eyes were a deep green, though barely visible with the deformed face he wore, covering a rather sad and depressed thing beneath. His mind was intact, for the most part, aside from the damage done by the ravages of time and the torment of his peculiar situation. Knowing what he was once, and how much power and esteem he had wielded, made his condition and outer shell that much more deplorable.

"I summoned you for a reason tonight, Enoch," said the Abbot, his fingers together, forming a steeple at his chin. A thin smile spreads across his face.

Enoch could not speak, but his mind was moving at all times. For obvious reasons, he despised the hypocrite priest before him. At night, he dreamed of choking him to death.

"I noticed you looking at the young novitiate from the convent, who has been coming up here the last month," the Abbot began, "What's her name again? Oh yes, Sister Ada." He smirked at Enoch, seeing a reaction from him, even if subtle.

Enoch stared at him. He did love to see the young nun. She was beautiful and was kind to him, in contrast to how the rest of the nuns treated him. Sister Ada had beautiful golden blonde hair and the biggest blue eyes he had ever seen. Enoch knew he looked like a monster, but at night when he closed his eyes, he dreamed of being alone with her in his former life. He had bedded so many lovely women during his life, that an eternity in the twisted and disgusting figure he occupied was unbearable. Even worse, the tiny appendage that hung where his manhood once was, was only functioning for the bathroom and not for making love.

"You like her, I can tell."

Enoch wheezed through his deformed mouth.

"Well, I'm going to give you a special treat here tonight. I think I'm feeling a bit in the holiday spirit with Christmas coming next month and all," said the Abbot, a twinkle in his deep blue eyes. He was in a much younger body than before, because he had the ability to transform himself into various forms. Now, he had chosen to be 30 years old and in his prime once again.

Enoch knew that the Abbot never did anything kind towards him, but he thought that maybe, just maybe, he was in a good mood. Maybe he would let Enoch see the beautiful novitiate for a little while before sending him back to the utter blackness of the basement? Could it be possible, a year later, the Abbot might reconsider his condemnation and life sentence of being Enoch Strange?

The Abbot rose as a soft knock sounded on his office door. He opened it to reveal the angelic face of Sister Ada. Enoch's heart skipped a beat. He took a deep breath through his deformed nose, trying desperately to take in her scent.

"Please come in, my dear," the priest said as he took her hand.

"You've met Enoch Strange before, I presume?" He motioned her to sit down.

She smiled. "Yes, Abbott. Hello, Enoch." The young nun looked at him briefly.

"That's very nice," the Abbot said. "Please follow me, Enoch."

The Abbot opened the door of a small storage closet next to his desk.

"Get in here." The Abbot stared at him. The young nun stared ahead, not looking at either of them.

Enoch paused, then realized the Abbot was serious. He had no idea what the man had in store, but he was beginning to worry. His hope was fleeting that the despicable Abbot would have had a change of heart. Enoch stood in the closet and turned to face the Abbot.

"Now get on your knees. I don't want to hear a peep out of you." He shut the door abruptly, leaving Enoch in darkness. "Enjoy the show. I'd have you here in the office with us, but I don't think I could bear to see your horrid self while in the act."

Sister Ada giggled. The Abbot laughed out loud. Enoch hung his head, fearing what was going to happen.

For the next hour, the Abbot and his young, beautiful novitiate had mad passionate sex in his office. On the desk, on the floor, on one of his chairs, and even up against the closet door. It was loud, boisterous and frantic as the young woman squealed with delight as the virile Abbot gave her orgasm after orgasm without pause.

Tears streamed down the face of Enoch Strange. Because of his gnarled hands, he was even unable to cover his ears to muffle the noise.

Afterward & Acknowledgements

I'm glad you made your way through to the end of the book. Take this Afterward and Acknowledgements as the proverbial cigarette after the encounter. Don't worry, your secret is safe with me. I wanted to explain why I decided to write The Dreadful Lives of Enoch Strange and how the story evolved into what you just read. I read a lot of books myself, and I often wonder what the author's motivation might have been to write it. Or how long did it take, and were there lots of obstacles to overcome? Some of these things you might find if they do an interview after the book is published. But why wait for that? I want to strike while the iron is hot. The first draft took me six months to write, and with the subsequent drafts and re-writes, the whole process took about two years. Keep in mind I was also working a full-time job at the time and did take some time off between part one and two to work on some other short-term projects. I also had a tremendous personal tragedy when my wife of 27 years, Sheilie, died in May of 2017. This knocked me down for two months, until I was able to dust myself off and get back to writing.

After I completed my first novel, Six, I was considering my options for the next novel. I had a few ideas, but nothing was really grabbing me. When an idea hits me, it's got to be like a 2 x 4 to the side of the head. If I was going to spend the incredible amount of time it takes to write a novel, I knew it had to be something that I found interesting and worthy of such an investment and blood, sweat and tears.

In 2006 I wrote a story set to music and lyrics for my band, Low Twelve. Song by song, we told the story of what was at the time entitled, This Side Toward Enemy. I explained the significance of that term in the novel you just read. Being an Army veteran myself, I had to set up the Claymore mines that bear those words so the soldier arming the mine doesn't blow himself up. That original story was about Nolan Weeks and his rampage of death across the country, his capture, the stay of execution, interviews with Brent, and of course, his eventual death. I always liked the story and felt there was tremendous potential. I decided to write a graphic novel, with an artist who agreed to do the project. Unfortunately, the artist was not able to do it and the novel part of it was about 40,000 words and more like a novella without the illustrations. I decided to just leave it alone, and it was never published. I even wrote a screenplay for the story, thinking maybe someone would want to make a movie about the exploits of Nolan. At the time, I didn't have the knowledge I do now about how some of that works and who to even send it to. It's still a huge mountain to overcome, but at the time, I had no idea what to do with it. So, I moved on to the next project.

Fast forward to 2016 at the completion of Six. I was talking with my beta reader and good friend, Chris Kovacs, and he wanted to read This Side Toward Enemy. I sent it to him, raw and exactly how it was written back then, and he really loved it. He urged me to do something with it. After several conversations, I agreed that the next project would have to be about Nolan and the evil entities raging inside him. Yet at 40,000 words, there wasn't enough there. As a novella, there wasn't much I could do with it as is. Some say that 80,000 to 100,000 is a good length for a first-time novelist. While it was not my first book, I felt it was a good mark to shoot for. The Six novel was just over 90,000 words.

I thought about adding to the story and beefing it up that way. I also thought about an idea I had years before in the band. I suggested to the guys to do a prequel to This Side Toward Enemy. I thought a story of how the entities inside Nolan came into existence would make for an interesting tale. I only had very sketchy ideas on what I was going to do, but I knew there was something there to work with. The more I thought about it, I decided the best way to do it was to write the prequel of the story as part one and the story of

Nolan would be part two. I also realized that I would have to be able to tie the two stories together so as not to confuse the reader when the time jumped from the 1920's to the 1980's.

I wrote the first chapter of part one as a stand-alone short story that appeared in my collection, Creation of Chaos: Volume I, that I published in October of 2017. The story was called Thirteen Nuns. I really loved the character of the Abbot and the way he is introduced in the first chapter. To me, he's the perfect antagonist for this story. Playing with these characters and setting the table for what was to follow gave me the feeling I was onto something. I ran with it from there and wrote the additional chapters to make up the rest of part one. I was very pleased with the wild ending of part one, getting things all set up for the rest of the story in part two. Yet I felt that something was missing. It needed something to stitch the two parts together, and that's when it hit me in the side of the head with a resounding thud!

Enoch Strange was the answer. It is an odd name and that's why I decided to use it. The mysterious thing about this character, as you have just experienced, is that he can't really be explained in a simple way. He's complicated. As you know, "he" is really more of an "it". It's as if Enoch has the ultimate dilemma of an identity crisis. But it was Enoch that gave me something to tie the two parts together, just as his eyelids were sewn shut by Dr. Weeks. He is introduced during the apocalyptic ending of part one and then brought back into the story as part two begins its white-knuckle ride to its own wild conclusion.

I couldn't resist bringing back the Abbot into part two. I know a "parent" isn't supposed to have a favorite child, but in this case, I will admit it. The Abbot is my favorite character to work with. He's so horrible and evil. He's the worst of the worst. That's what makes him interesting to put in the middle of situations. I even think I may use him in a cameo appearance in something else in the future. I really like him that much. Dr. Wilfred Weeks also is in both parts, and he is also a pivotal antagonist in the book. I liked making his appearance very intense and crazy, as it seemed to fit his charismatic personality. In death, as you know, Dr. Weeks was a bit of a grouch; as an alpha male he had little patience for anyone trying to own center stage. His feud with the Abbot made for interesting scenes at the concluding chapters of part two. Even though part two was written first as the original novella, I completely re-wrote it and added lots of content, such as the FBI task force and the other elements of part one that reared their heads as needed in the second part.

Even the title of the novel went through changes as the novella became what it is today, at just over 112,000 words as The Dreadful Lives of Enoch Strange. Originally, I was going to call the whole thing This Side Toward Enemy. Then I changed my mind to calling it Nightmare Maker, which was the title of a short story I wrote years before, where I introduced the character of William Weeks, Nolan's grandfather, and the scene at the Bartonville Insane Asylum. The more I thought about it, I didn't like the title. I thought it made the book sound cheesy. The story was anything but cheesy, so I wound up naming after the character that crudely sewed together the two parts. The character that really defines the essence of what the story is about.

As Enoch is a living thing, his penance is to act as a living prison. As the Abbot and Dr. Weeks are painfully aware, being inside the prison of Enoch Strange is a dreadful place to take up residence. I thought the concept was unique and compelling. I've always had an interest in stories about the toughest prisons in the world and find it horrifying to even consider what it would be like to be in such terrible places. My father was a parole officer in several maximum-security prisons in New York during the 1980's and 90's. I heard many frightening stories at the dinner table. I wanted to capture that raw fear and curiosity. My invention became a living prison, with an appearance of sheer disgust and horror, where the captive soul would have to endure misery beyond compare. This feature to me is one of the terrible things about Enoch. The person residing inside committed their horrible deeds with the aid of their dashing good looks, yet now they must bear the gnarled appearance of Enoch Strange. How humbling that would be! How truly terrifying! The Abbot and Dr. Weeks are characters who did horrible things, and their time inside Enoch was very appropriate.

I would like to thank the people who helped make this project a reality. First and foremost, my good friend and beta reader supreme, Chris Kovacs. His patience reading the book, chapter by blood-soaked chapter, was unwavering. We talked every week, usually on Sundays, about the chapter he had read the week before. He kept me accountable and made me want to freak him out as the story twisted and turned. I never told Chris what was coming next, so he read each chapter as you did, but in its raw form as the first draft. His belief in the story was vital and gave me added incentive to see the novel to its conclusion!

I would like to also thank my proofreader, who wishes to go only by JBS, as a very big part of my team. She is also a friend and a person I've known for a long time. Horror and suspense is not her choice of reading material, but as she made her way through the chapters, she became intrigued by the story of Enoch Strange. It was an interesting change of heart, and it also gave me added incentive to forge on and get her reaction to events that transpire, just as I had with Chris Kovacs. We did have an issue on the first chapter of part two due to the extreme, graphic violence that ensues. But thankfully we got through it, and JBS was able to make it across the finish line.

My good friend and artist, Brian Uziel, was also very important to bring to life my creation of Enoch Strange. We discussed ideas several times over the phone. I sent him chapters where Enoch appeared, so Brian could get the full descriptions of what he looked like and what his actions were. He has done other art for me before and so our working relationship is excellent. Brian has a great way of nailing what I have in my mind and making it come to life. He got it so right with this project.

I have several other people that were instrumental in helping me with information or details about things they know about. As a writer, it's a great way to do research and think about those you know who have various areas of expertise. I have a friend who works in the Texas Department of Corrections, and his help with the scenes I had to write at the Huntsville Prison was incredibly helpful. He wished to be anonymous.

Another friend of mine works at a Catholic high school and was great at explaining to me the chain-of-command in that type of institution, and of course that's where the Abbot was first conceived in my mind. He also wished to remain anonymous. Another friend of mine in law enforcement was helpful when I had questions about the FBI task force and some things concerning police procedure. He also needed to talk off the record.

There are probably more people that I have not mentioned here, and to those, I apologize. You know who you are and what you did – so thank you!

Now I've explained how all this came to be and the evolution of what ended up as The Dreadful Lives of Enoch Strange, so why wouldn't an obvious question be how did Enoch Strange end up as such a tragic, horrible being? That would be a good question. The answer is, you never know what might come next, and as they say, never say never. But don't be surprised if you see Enoch Strange rise and show up somewhere in something I'm working on. I mean, if the Abbot can do that, why not the grotesque Enoch Strange?

Pete Altieri, August 2018
Heyworth, Illinois

www.ingramcontent.com/pod-product-compliance
Lightning Source LLC
Chambersburg PA
CBHW070307260626
47160CB00003B/747